The Victim

By

Joe B. Parr

First Edition

http://joebparr.com

My Girls Publishing Fort Worth, TX

Print ISBN: 978-0-9913947-0-8

eBook ISBN: 978-0-9913947-1-5

For my girls - Greta, Caitlin and Aubrey
Thank you for allowing me this indulgence

JOE B.PARR

Chapter 1

The Victim walked down the dark street watching his shadow shift from in front of him to behind him as he passed under the few dim street lights that still worked in this part of town. It was late, almost two in the morning and this was definitely not his neighborhood. A white man dressed for the office in a long, wool overcoat had little business walking down South Calhoun Street in broad daylight much less at this time of night. He knew this but would not be deterred. This was for her. As he moved south toward East Daggett, he passed the dirty walls of the Supreme Golf warehouse and a handful of abandoned buildings. Off to his left, the slow creak of a northbound BNSF car carrier echoed as it skirted the east side of downtown.

In the distance he heard the muffled sounds of Blues music coming from one of the late night clubs. The air was cool for early November, but not really cold enough to warrant the heavy overcoat he wore. Between the coat, the walking and the pounding of his heart, he had begun to sweat, wiping his brow every so often.

He stalked down the street. Passing by a darkened alley, a movement and a voice jarred him. "Hey man. Where you goin?" The wino shuffled as he tried unsuccessfully to sit up. The Victim's heart nearly jumped through his chest. His breath caught. He almost hyperventilated, choking on the wino's body odor. He stepped down the street, just far enough to be away from the wino and leaned his back against the grimy brick as the wino broke into a rendition of 'Stormy Monday.' He tried to catch his breath, calm his nerves. *Maybe this wasn't such a good idea after all. Maybe I should just get back to my car and get out of here.*

His beat up rust bucket 1985 Chevy Impala was parked on East Vickery in front of the Builder's Equipment and Supply warehouse. The car fit in perfectly with the neighborhood. It reeked of urban decay with at least three different paint colors, all tinged with an undertone of rust. The exterior appearance of the car was deceiving. Underneath the rust, the engine, transmission and suspension were pristine. He'd bought it for reliability, not style.

After a few minutes he slowed his breathing and his heartbeat was at least at jogging level. He sweat more heavily now and wiped his forearm across his face. He pushed off the wall and continued slowly south away from the wino's serenade and further into the night. He reached both his hands into his coat pockets, searching, gripping, feeling comforted.

His walk tonight wasn't so much about a destination as it was the journey itself. He didn't want to get more than a few blocks from his car. No matter what happened tonight, he wanted to be able to get away quickly if needed. After all, he would either find what he was looking for or he'd make his way back and move on to another location, another journey.

He continued across East Daggett. The wind was out of the north to his back. It wasn't strong but seemed to push him along as it shoved his hair into his face. There was an empty parking lot to his right with a large clump of trees on the backend. A car was parked up under the trees, doors opened, thumping music blasted out. A couple of young thugs, hard looking, leaned against it with beers in their hands and bandanas on their heads. He picked up his pace as they just stared and swigged more beer.

Once he crossed Daggett, the crumpled remnants of the sidewalk were used as parking for a few cars. He stepped around them, out into the street and moved closer to East Broadway. He could hear sounds behind him, shuffling feet, beer bottles dropping to the ground. His heart raced again. *What have I gotten myself into? Have I lost my mind?*

He picked up the pace again, almost to the corner. The sounds continued behind him. He didn't dare turn around. Not yet. When he reached the corner, the Victim stopped momentarily. The sounds had faded. The streetlight on the corner was broken, prey to a well-placed rock. The only light came from a block away casting his faint shadow long to the east.

THE VICTIM

He stole a look over his left shoulder. He couldn't hear anything but swore he saw a shadow move behind one of the cars he'd just passed. The sound of his heart thudding pounded in his ears. His eyes flitted back and forth, searching the urban landscape. *Are they following me? Was it just my imagination?* He felt like breaking into a sprint but where would he go? If they followed him, he'd have to run past them to get back to his car. To run away from his car would be suicide.

It took a moment for him to get his legs working, but then he started toward South Jones. He moved slower, more cautiously hoping to make the block, and loop back to his car. He walked with the building on his left, more crumpled sidewalk under his feet. Coming up on the corner of the building, he heard something ahead, stopped in his tracks. His breathing was so heavy now it was audible. *Oh shit. What now? Should I turn back? Should I run?*

Before his mind could process the situation, someone stepped out from behind the building and stood, facing him, maybe ten feet away. The Victim froze, looking at a black guy, late teens, maybe twenty. He wore baggy jeans, hung low, an oversized jacket, blue bandana. There wasn't much light but the Victim could see a scar along his jaw line, hard features. With his eyes hidden by wrap-around sunglasses, he had a menacing appearance.

The Victim felt his knees quiver, his stomach knotted and his throat constricted. His mind raced trying to figure out his next move. Even in the middle of all his synapses firing, the oddest thought crossed his mind. *He's wearing sunglasses at night.* Now, on top of his near panic, that crappy song started playing in his head. '*I wear my sunglasses at night so I can, so I can...*' It was oddly calming and after a quick moment he was able to regain his composure.

The Victim looked at the man standing in front of him. The guy's right hand was down by his side holding something, a club maybe. It was almost hidden behind his leg. He brought it forward, tapped it on his leg, his hand twitching.

"Say dawg. Where you goin'?" There was almost a laugh in his voice but it sent a cold chill through the Victim.

The Victim didn't say anything but started to take a step toward the street. The man moved quickly to his left holding up his hand.

"Whoa, whoa, whoa, dawg. No need to be runnin' off now. We got business to do tonight." His jaw continued to move, chewing gum at a rapid pace.

The Victim finally found his voice, weak as it was. "Leave me alone. I'm not bothering anyone."

The Victim once again tried to take a step. This time the man moved a little closer, clearly revealing the club. "Well now, that's where you wrong honky. You see, just you bein' on this street is botherin' me."

Now the Victim turned, started to run. His eyes went wide. Reality crashed down on him. There was a second guy behind him. He moved back to the sidewalk and turned where he could see both men, his back to the building. To his right was a carbon copy of the first man, same baggy pants, similar jacket, same blue bandana. No sunglasses but eyes that in the shadows of the street looked like black holes. It was as if his pupils were the size of dimes.

The Victim literally had his back to the wall. His hands were still deep in his pockets, the front of his coat was unbuttoned and opened slightly. He managed to squeak out, "What do you want?"

This time the second guy answered. "We here to collect the honky tax." This brought a snicker from the man with the sunglasses. He added, "Yeah, that's right. The honky tax." Directing his comment to his partner, he added, "How much is that these days?"

"Oh that's easy. The honky tax is everything you got on you." His black eyes were now joined by a wide smile, gold capped teeth. This brought a chuckle from the man with sunglasses.

They both took a step closer to the Victim, his back now pressing against the wall. He could feel the outline of the bricks across the back of his shoulders. It seemed like his feet were involuntarily trying to push him through the wall.

The Victim summoned everything in him to sound brave and said, "Leave me alone."

Now the man with the sunglasses barked, "Look muthafucka, you in no spot to be spoutin' orders." They both took another step forward, each now standing barely more than arm's length from the Victim. He tapped the club on his open palm. "Now give me your wallet and your watch right now and we might let you live."

THE VICTIM

The Victim didn't move. His mind was racing. *Oh my God. Is this really happening? Am I going to die? Can I do this?* He took a deep breath, thought about her. *I won't let it end like this.* A calm washed over him. He fixed his stare at a point between the two. In a voice he'd never heard before, he quietly, calmly said, "You don't want to do this." As he said it, his posture straightened, no longer cowering.

"All right, I warned you." The man with the sunglasses took a step forward raising the club from his palm.

In a single move, the front of the Victim's coat flew open, both hands came out from inside holding identical Beretta 92SB 9mm pistols, one pointing in the direction of the each assailant. There was no warning, no talk. The guns exploded almost in unison, each two times. All four bullets hit their marks and the Victim stood alone, his back still against the wall, his deep breaths sucking in the smell of burnt gunpowder.

Death echoed off the buildings. The night went quiet, nothing but a ringing in his ears and the beating of his heart.

He looked down at the two bodies sprawled on the jagged concrete, one convulsed. Dark circles expanded on their chests, blood pooled beneath them. The momentary rush left him, his knees buckled. He caught himself before he fell. *Oh God. Oh God. I did it. Oh shit. Oh shit.* Sweat drenched his forehead, spit dribbled from the corner of his mouth. He swiped his forearm across his face, leaned forward and rested the warm guns on his knees and caught his breath.

Focus damn it, focus. Sucking in several quick deep breaths, he fought for his bearings. *Get out of here.* He stepped out to the street between the two bodies, turned to his left and passed the man with the sunglasses. As he stumbled away, he holstered one of the guns. He stopped and pulled both hands out of the coat pockets. He had cut away the pocket linings so his hands could grip the guns up without taking them out of the pockets. This night had most definitely been planned.

He ran to the corner, turned left and took off in a full sprint heading north back to East Vickery. As he ran behind the storage yard of the Builder's Equipment and Supply, his mind raced, his heart pounded and he was so out of breath it felt like he'd run miles not yards. *Get to the car.*

Jones Street was only two blocks long. *Why is it taking so long?*

He came flying up to where Jones Street spilled on to East Vickery. He stopped, leaned against the wall behind a dumpster, his chest heaved with each breath, every muscle burned. He held the 9mm down at his side and listened. Silence. No sirens. No feet. No voices. He stepped around the dumpster to the street corner, poked his head around to see if anyone was on Vickery. Empty.

He was twenty feet from his car. He reached into his pants pocket. He'd rigged his car with remote locks and a remote starter. He pushed the button, heard the doors click and the engine crank. In a few quick strides, he was in the car. He dropped the gun on the passenger seat, slammed it into gear and headed east in seconds. *Get out of here.*

He had mapped out his route ahead of time. His head still spun, his pulse continued to pound. It was hard to focus, to see. He had just killed two people. Thugs sure, but still people. He was on autopilot, took a left on the South Freeway feeder road. He swerved, driving too fast. *What have I done? Oh my God.*

He stopped for the light at Lancaster. The emotion overwhelmed him. He opened the door and puked onto the street. Heaving, taking deep breaths, wrenching until there was nothing left in him. He sat back in his seat, closed the door, closed his eyes, and regained his composure. He started again, two quick turns and he was on I-30 and gone.

Chapter 2

Detective Jake Hunter reached up and cracked the blinds to see if there was any sign of an early morning sunrise. His efforts were futile. This time of year, the sun wouldn't be up for at least another hour. He sensed movement behind him but didn't react. As his hand let go of the blinds, he felt a bump on the back of his leg. He looked down and grinned. "Good morning, Panther. How the hell are you today?"

The large, pitch black cat responded by performing a tight figure eight around his shins. "Yeah. Don't blame you. I'm not much in the mood to talk either until I get my breakfast... Or at least my coffee. Let's fix that."

Hunter moved from the back window into the kitchen absorbing the quiet of the house, filled Panther's bowl with the flavor of the week cat food and poured himself his second cup of coffee. Even though it was still dark outside and barely six o'clock, he'd been up for a while pounding on his laptop at the kitchen table. He couldn't remember the last time he hadn't seen the sun rise. Would he ever get used to sleeping in an empty house?

He sat back down, took a long sip, breathed in the aroma and reached for the laptop again. After he'd returned from his two month leave of absence, his boss, Lieutenant Jeff Sprabary, had assigned him a special internal project, reviewing the backlog of cold cases to find new angles on any evidence to get them moving again. New leads were illusive even for a guy with his experience. His expectations hadn't been too far off, although he had surprised himself with a handful of revelations passed on to the guys working the cases. Those revelations had resulted in just enough arrests to continue to justify his efforts, at least in the eyes of the Lieutenant.

As satisfying as it was to figure out possibilities that your fellow detectives had missed, he'd been working the project for almost three months now and he was ready for it to end. Besides, he knew it was just a stepping stone, something to keep him focused until they got him back on the streets.

He was deep in thought when his cell phone vibrated on the table. He stared at it for a moment, processed why his phone would ring at 6:10 in the morning. Of course, he knew.

He grabbed his earpiece. "Hunter here."

"Hey Cowboy. Harrison here. Got a one-eighty-seven off Vickery. Lieutenant says you're the man." Harrison was the night shift Desk Sergeant, a crusty old timer just marking time until his retirement. Hunter had known him since he joined the force fifteen years ago.

Hunter didn't respond immediately, frozen as his mind went through a checklist he hadn't accessed in a while. Harrison prompted. "You there Cowboy?"

"Yeah, I'm here, just getting my notepad." His free hand reached for his pad.

"You up for this?" Harrison's gruff voice had a tinge of concern on the edges.

"Yeah, yeah. No problem. Give me the highlights."

"Well, it seems that a couple of Fort Worth's finest citizens decided to get themselves popped on East Broadway between Calhoun and Jones."

Hunter let out a small sarcastic chuckle. "Anyone roaming that area in the middle of the night is anything but a fine citizen. What else you know?"

Harrison gave him what few details he had while Hunter scribbled notes throwing out the occasional 'uh huh'. After hanging up, Hunter let out a breath and swigged what remained in his cup. He set the cup in the sink, leaned with both hands on the counter and looked out into the family room. He felt his heart beat and butterflies in his stomach. He closed his eyes and shook his head chasing away the memories of his last active case. Six months seemed like yesterday.

"Well Panther. I guess my vacation is over." The cat just glanced up at him with a disinterested look, blinked and set his head down on his paws getting comfortable for his early morning nap.

THE VICTIM

Hunter filled the small breakfast nook as he stretched, trying to get awake. At six foot two, he was lean from life, not the gym. He rubbed his face and ran his hands through his hair. Not too many years ago, his hair was longer and with considerably less gray. Now the close cropped salt and pepper look mixed with the slightly noticeable laugh lines, aged his rugged features just enough to give him some gravitas. When he looked over at Panther, his easy smile somehow still came off sad, maybe it was his eyes. Years of pondering crime scenes were etched on his forehead. Even so, he knew he didn't look as old as he felt.

He slid his notepad and laptop into his computer bag, reached over and took his dark blue sport jacket off the back of the chair. He slipped it on over a white, buttoned down Polo and faded blue Gap jeans. He sometimes caught grief from his fellow detectives for dressing too preppy, but he was comfortable.

He picked up his cell phone and blue tooth, checked the battery level and slid the phone into his jacket pocket.

He turned to yell goodbye but caught himself, embarrassed. What was he thinking? She wasn't there. He shook his head, grabbed his bag then rubbed Panther's head eliciting an immediate purring sound. "Hold the fort down buddy. I'll be back in a bit."

Once in the garage, he crawled up into his Ford Explorer, punched the button for the garage door and started the SUV. While he was waiting for the door to clear, he unclipped his holstered Glock 17 gen4 9mm, checked the magazine and chambered a round. He had learned long ago that even a cordoned off crime scene is not necessarily safe.

Hunter lived in a mid-level residential area in Northeast Tarrant County, a subdivision called Summerfields. It was hundreds of acres of neighborhoods spread over three or four little cities full of young families and first time home owners. Developers had started building in the area in the late seventies and were still churning out cookie cutter fifteen hundred square foot homes just as fast as the illegal construction workers could build them.

He made his way out of his neighborhood down Western Center and turned south on I-35W towards downtown Fort Worth, TX and a date with a couple of stiff gang bangers.

Twenty minutes later, Hunter guided his Explorer onto Calhoun from Vickery. The darkness of the industrial area was shattered by vehicles with flashing red and blue lights. The headlights from the traffic behind him on I-30 also added an ambient glow to downtown. After a block, he noticed a parking lot to his right, decided he'd park there instead of adding to the crowd a block down. When he came to a stop, out of habit, he scanned the general area. His eyes registered a car parked in the back only because it seemed out of place. The mid-nineties Caprice was tricked up with dark blue metallic paint and twenty inch chrome spinners. There was a blue bandana tied low on the antennae. It didn't look like it had been there long but no one was near it. In this neighborhood, once the cops vacated, it wouldn't last long.

Hunter braced against the morning chill, stepped out, slid his holster onto his belt and headed toward the crime scene. His gaze moved rhythmically, absorbing the area as he walked down the crumpled sidewalk.

Coming to the corner, Hunter had to weave between two police cruisers. The crime scene team had taped off essentially all of Broadway between Calhoun and Jones. That wasn't a huge inconvenience to anyone in this neighborhood at this time of morning. The visual barriers obstructed the view of the bodies to onlookers, not that there were many, just a few early shift workers at the Morrison Plumbing Supply warehouse around the corner.

The crime scene wasn't crowded, but busy enough with four patrol units, a crime scene van and the ME's truck. Hunter stopped before going under the crime scene tape, took in the scene noting where everyone was and what they were doing. Four patrol officers, there ostensibly for crowd control which so far wasn't necessary, were gathered in pairs on each end of the perimeter, drinking coffee and talking. There was one CSI roaming the area just outside the sight barriers searching the ground with a flashlight. Someone was behind the barriers, maybe the ME.

One of the patrol officers noticed him walking up and started his way. Hunter pulled out his credentials, flashed them. The officer waved him through. Hunter nodded, attached a neck lanyard to his ID and looped it over his head. After he ducked under the tape, he moved slowly toward the barriers and reviewed the scene as he walked.

He stopped and was looking down at a footprint the CSI had marked when he heard a woman's voice coming from the direction of the barriers. "Now there's a sight for sore eyes." There was a lilt to her words that implied a Scottish heritage. "When's the last time you and I got to work a scene together Cowboy?" Stacy Morgan was petite and fit nicely into her form fitting slacks. Her CSI Supervisor's vest accentuated her curves. She had shoulder length auburn hair and a faint scar underneath her left eye that was oddly attractive. Her vibrant green eyes seemed to reflect the warmth of her smile.

Hunter looked up with a smirk. "Hey Stace. How ya been? I haven't seen you since…" The smirk dimmed. "Well, it's been too long. Glad to see you."

"Glad to see you too." She paused. "You doing okay these days?"

"Yeah." He smiled sadly. He appreciated her concern but not the attention. "I'm doing fine. What do we have this morning?"

Stacy gestured dramatically. "Well, step into my office." She directed him around the barriers and he looked down at two dead bodies. The ME had stepped away for a moment while he was looking at the footprint. Only a mild odor lingered, mostly the smell of dried blood. Thank God. The corpses hadn't been there long; it was outside with a slight breeze, no sun and cool temperatures. "We've got two vics, both males, black, early twenties, potentially gang bangers." Hunter looked down at the body closest to him. The young man was on his back, eyes open, dull, dry. The mouth was open as if he was in the middle of trying to say something. His skin, once dark brown, was now a pale gray. His lips were blue.

Pointing to the corpse, Stacy continued, "This one took two in the chest. We found four 9mm casings on the ground. The other two are deposited in his buddy over here." They both turned to look at the man with sunglasses, still wearing them. He looked like a video game zombie.

"Time of death?"

"Doc says sometime between 1:30 A.M. and 3:00 A.M. based on body temp."

Hunter made a hrumph sound. "Three in the morning and this

guy dies with his shades on?"

"Yeah. Gotta love it. Cool to the bitter end."

Hunter squatted down, looked at the left hand of the man with sunglasses. "See the tats?"

"His buddy has one just like it."

"I think your 'potential gang bangers' description is confirmed. That tat is the sign of the Eastcide Kings." Hunter continued to peruse the bodies. "The Kings are usually the ones doing the killing, not being the targets."

"Yeah the world has lost some real top notch citizens. Who knows? Maybe they were poaching in the wrong territory." She kneeled down beside the second victim and started taking his prints.

Slowly shaking his head, "Nah, it may be on the edge but this is definitely in their zone." Hunter stood up, looked at the wall and scanned the immediate area. Stepping toward the wall in between the two bodies, he stopped and turned back to face them. "I don't know. Something's not right about this... Think about it. What's the typical MO on a gang hit? Either drive by or execution, right?" Stacy nodded. He continued. "If it was an execution, they'd have been on their knees, probably with hands tied and shot in the back of the head." He paused, looked at the bodies as if confirming that wasn't the case. "As for a drive by, that doesn't fit either. You said the casings were found on the sidewalk. Also, there're no bullet holes in the wall. Well, at least not new ones. The shooter was standing here with them."

Stacy held up a finger. "Ah! You might mean shooters." Hunter raised an eyebrow. She signaled him over to her evidence box and pulled out a couple of baggies. "Not positive yet. We'll need it confirmed by ballistics, but it looks like two different guns. On two of the casings, the firing pin hit dead center. On the other two, it was slightly off."

"Really?"

"Yeah. Another interesting thing about the casings. They were pristine. No prints. Not even a smudge. Whoever loaded the guns was very careful to wipe them down as he loaded."

"Two shooters?" Hunter was clearly confused by this prospect.

"Well. Either two shooters or one shooter with two guns. How often do you see that? Seriously? Most people can't hit the broad side of a barn shooting with one hand, much less both, at the same time."

"No kidding." He started pacing slowly. It had been several months but he was starting to feel the buzz again. Stacy had seen this before. She just smiled, waiting for him to continue. "Let's think about it for a second. These guys were shot at close range. What? Three to four feet?" She nodded. "And look how the bodies landed. These two guys were almost facing each other and they're angled as if they were looking toward the wall so the shooter... or shooters, had to be positioned between them, probably with their back to the wall." He continued to pace slowly, rubbing his chin.

"So Cowboy, add this to the mix while you're pondering scenarios." He stopped and looked intently at her. She continued. "Both of our vics were packing but neither had pulled their weapon."

He smiled. "So what does that tell us?"

"I'm guessing they knew their shooter or at the very least, weren't a bit scared or concerned. Last night was just another walk in the park for them."

"One that came to a surprise ending. They never saw this coming." He was back to pacing now. A few minutes later. "What about DNA?"

That brought a chuckle from Stacy. "Well, we haven't gotten to that just yet but I wouldn't get my hopes up. Look around. What do we have? A thousand cigarette butts? Thirty or forty beer bottles, soda cans and fast food cups? Another twenty or thirty pieces of chewed gum?" She shook her head and smiled. "Oh, we've got DNA alright... From half the population."

"You know I had to ask... So, let's see. No signs of struggle. One minute these guys are just standing here chatting with one or two of their closest friends and the next minute, they're blown away."

He started to continue, but she cut him off. "Well, maybe not quite 'chatting'." This piqued his interest. She continued. "It looks like our friend with the sunglasses had a short club in his hand. They could have been threatening someone."

"Threatening someone, or someones, who just happened to be packing two 9mms? This same someone, or someones, was then able to draw weapons and fire before either of our boys was able to react?"

Stacy smiled wide, her eyes glowed in the early morning sunrise. "You see Cowboy. That's what I love about you. You can take the most 'who gives a shit crime scene' and turn it into a Sherlock Holmes whodunit."

"I'm a little out of practice… But I try."

"Well, look what the cat dragged in." A man's voice boomed from behind them. "Detective Jake Hunter, my favorite cowboy. I haven't seen you since Frank's… Well, since…" There was an awkward moment of silence, the cheery tone of his voice dissipated. "Anyway, it's great to see you Cowboy. You've been missed."

"Thanks Doc. It's good to be back… Even if it does mean having to bump into you standing on a nasty street looking down at two stiff hoodlums."

"Yes, well. There is that. Our friends here have certainly seen better days."

Doctor Benjamin Grimes was a large man, mostly around the middle. He spoke as if he'd spent his formative years in European boarding schools. He never advertised the fact that he grew up in Waco, TX. What was left of his hair was gray and disheveled. His charcoal gray suit was wrinkled and his yellow paisley tie, circa 1995, was loosened and hanging midway down his chest.

"Speaking of our friends…" Doc turned toward Stacy. "Miss Morgan, when will you be ready for me to chauffer them down to the morgue?"

"You can take them anytime you'd like. I've got another couple of hours tying up loose ends and then I'll meet you there to help process them."

Hunter snapped his fingers. "Damn. I knew I forgot something. I told you I was out of practice." Doc and Stacy looked his way and waited for him to continue. "Stace, you may be here a little longer than you'd planned. There may be a second scene to process." Her eyebrows arched. He continued. "I parked around the corner at Daggett and Calhoun. When I got out, I noticed a car in that lot up under some trees. Didn't look like it had been there all that long. There was no one around that seemed to claim it but considering the bandana tied around the antennae matches the ones our boys are wearing. I'm guessing it's their ride. We'll need to at least check it for weapons and run the plates."

Stacy threw her hands up in fake exasperation. "There you go again, being thorough. Just my luck. Why couldn't I have gotten a half assed Dilbert to work this case? It's not like you don't have a few in the department."

"Ah, come on now. You didn't have anything else to do." Hunter smiled. "I'll walk you over there and show you. I've got a few more thoughts to bounce off you along the way." He turned to Grimes. "Doc, I'll stop by your office next time I feel the need to hang out with dead people."

Doc nodded. "I'll have these young lads gone by the time you get back."

The morning sun was now high in the eastern sky and the city had come to life all around them. The breeze pushed her hair back from her face and now that they were away from the bodies, Hunter caught a hint of her perfume, lilac maybe. He subtly breathed it in. It had been too long.

As they weaved through the parked cruisers, Hunter started up again. "Now, were you able to find ID's?"

"Yeah. Both had wallets. We bagged them. Once we get them back to the station, we'll compare them with the prints."

"Great. After you cross check them, I'll get those from you. We'll need to get histories on both of them." They stepped into the parking lot and started toward the car. He glanced in her direction. It had been a while but she was still just as beautiful. *All right, get your head back in the game.* "You know. I had a thought earlier. What's the number one rule in homicides?"

"Let me see..." Stacy acted as if she were thinking hard. "Oh yeah. What? Ninety percent are committed by friends or family."

"Exactly. Now I'm pretty sure in this case, Mom and Dad are clean, but... We do need to consider this might have been an internal thing within the gang, especially when you think about the fact that they were obviously close to the shooter but were completely surprised. Fellow gangster?"

"Sounds reasonable. I'll let you chase that one down. Looks like I've got another scene to process." They were standing by the car looking at unopened beer bottles in the seat.

Hunter nodded. "Does look that way."

The two of them continued to scour both scenes while Hunter took dozens of pictures with his phone. They bantered and swapped theories as the morning transitioned into lunchtime. It was November but the sun was out, the air was clear and Jake Hunter was back on the street where he belonged.

Chapter 3

After grabbing a quick lunch with Stacy at Mexican Inn on Commerce Street, Hunter took her back to the crime scene. He looked over, caught Stacy smiling at him and looked down to avoid her eyes. After a short hesitation, she leaned across the console and gave him a quick hug. Hunter was slow to react, not knowing what to do with his hands.

"It really is good to have you back. I'm glad things are better." There was an awkward pause before Stacy quickly got out.

They had caught up on how he'd been since his return. Her normally playful flirtation had a tinge of concern to it. There had always been an attraction between them, and maybe he imagined it, but her stares seemed to linger a bit longer than before. Hunter contemplated this as he purposely took his time driving the few short blocks back to the station.

Located on an island of land bordered by freeway on ramps and North Jones Street, the FWPD Central Division HQ is on the eastern edge of downtown. A squat two story yellowish brown brick building, it's modern, heavily tinted windows contrasted with the 1950's architecture. Even in its heyday, it was not an architectural prize. Now, in the shadow of modern glass towers, it seemed caught in a time warp.

After making the rounds with the usual suspects, Hunter had settled in at his desk. Defying his 'Cowboy' nickname, Hunter was actually one of the more tech savvy guys on the force. He was rarely without his laptop or smart phone and used the internet extensively for his cases. When it came to tracking case notes, he had built his own custom database to cross reference all kinds of data elements on victims, suspects and crime scenes.

He was busy typing notes into his laptop when a female voice broke him out of his zone. "Hey Cowboy. Boss wants to see you." In her role as Lieutenant Sprabary's Admin, Paige McClaren often got to deliver that bad news. She seemed to enjoy it a little too much. The one saving grace was that, with her wavy brunette hair, chocolate brown eyes and knockout figure, she looked so good delivering the news, most of the guys didn't care. Well, at least until they got into the Lieutenant's office.

Hunter wasn't fazed by her looks or concerned about the Lieutenant's reputation for chewing ass. He'd seen dozens like her come and go, and had known Jeff Sprabary for almost a decade. For whatever reason, he was one of the few detectives Sprabary liked.

"And what would our fine Lieutenant want with me today?"

Looking coy, Paige replied, "Hmm… Don't know, but he looked a little agitated."

Hunter smiled to himself. "OK, I'm on my way. Just need to save my work."

"Tata…" Paige sashayed back through the department as heads swiveled, tongues wagged and a variety of office supplies were fumbled on desks. Her departure brought several politically incorrect comments and almost unanimous head shakes from the crew of detectives.

Hunter finished up his notes, headed down the hall, knocked on the open door and poked his head in. "You wanted to see me, boss?"

Lieutenant Sprabary hung up the phone and motioned him to a chair. Sprabary was a spit and polish guy who always wore a suit and tie and rarely took either off. Hunter noticed that the Lieutenant did seem a little on edge, shrugged it off as fairly normal and sat down as directed.

"How was the scene this morning?"

"Nothing bizarre, just a couple of dead gang bangers. Working a scene felt good."

"Well, I know I've been holding you back a bit, but it was time. Got to get back on that horse eventually." Sprabary tried to stifle his smile when he realized his pun. He was one of the few people in the department who didn't refer to Hunter as 'Cowboy'.

"Agreed."

"Look Jake, I wanted you on this case for a couple of reasons." This got Hunter's attention. "It was time to get you back in the game and considering it was a couple of gang bangers, it probably won't end up being too high profile."

Hunter shifted uncomfortably in his seat, focused a hard look toward Sprabary. "Lieutenant, are you worried I'm not going to be able to step up? Because if that's a concern, let me assure…"

Sprabary cut him off with a raised hand. "Hold on. Hold on. That's not the case at all Jake. In fact, it's just the opposite." Hunter relaxed, but kept an eyebrow raised. "Look, I know we haven't really talked about this too much, but I've purposely not assigned you a new partner since Frank's death."

This made Hunter sit up straight. "Lieutenant, I'm really doing just fine without a partner so if this is about assigning me a new one, that's not necessary."

Calming him with his hands again, Sprabary continued. "Damnit, Jake, stop jumping the gun. No, this isn't about assigning you a new partner, at least not permanently." Hunter started to say something but Sprabary gave him a look that suggested it might not be prudent. "We got a new detective assigned to the team last week. A guy named Billy Sanders. I need someone to break him in, teach him the ropes and evaluate if he's got what it takes to stick."

"Aw, come on boss, a newbie? I'm really not…"

"Jake, you're one of the best detectives on the team. You're thorough. You work a crime scene better than most CSI's. You're meticulous with your notes and your paperwork is always right. Trust me. If it was up to me, I wouldn't have taken a newbie at all, but I didn't have a choice. Look, this isn't permanent, just long enough to run the cycle on this case. Like I said, this isn't a high profile case so he really can't screw it up."

"Well, Lieutenant I'm not so sure it's that clear cut. Based on what Stacy and I saw this morning, it really doesn't look like your typical gang on gang type of thing."

"Really? Why?"

Hunter spent the next several minutes reviewing the details of the scene. Sprabary bounced questions off Hunter and listened to his theories.

Finally, Sprabary pushed back his chair, stood up, walked to the window. "Hmm. All right. I'll hand it to you that it might not be quite cut and dried, but at the end of the day it was a couple of gang bangers. Anyway, I still need someone to check this newbie out and I've got no one else open to do it."

Hunter just shook his head in resigned disgust. "Hell. I guess if it's just temporary..."

Sprabary smiled as he reached for his phone. He punched the intercom button. Paige's voice crackled. "Yes?"

"Tell the new guy, Sanders, to get his butt in here."

"With pleasure." She signed off. Hunter swore he could hear glee in her voice. He just shook his head.

Sanders, after five years of working his ass off on patrol trying to make Detective, had arrived in Homicide a week ago and spent the entire time sitting at a desk reading procedural manuals and twiddling his thumbs. Paige's bubble was popped once again when he reacted to her summons with excitement instead of dread.

A moment later, Paige opened the door and ushered Sanders in. He was severely overdressed in chocolate brown dress slacks and a light brown plaid suit jacket worn over a form fitting crew neck T-shirt. In his late twenties and a few inches shorter than Hunter, he outweighed him by a full thirty pounds, all of it solid muscle. His eyes were wide with anticipation, his jaw set with determination. There was a barely noticeable sheen of sweat on his forehead.

"Yes sir. You needed me?"

"Sit down Sanders," Sprabary barked. As he sat, he looked at Hunter and acknowledged him with a quick nod. Hunter absorbed every move Sanders made, but didn't return the gesture. Sprabary didn't wait until Sanders was fully seated. "Sanders, this is Jake Hunter. He's one of my Senior Detectives and he has agreed to let you run second on a case he pulled this morning. Your job is very simple. Do everything he tells you to do, how he tells you to do it and when he tells you to do it. Do you understand?"

"Yes sir." Turning to Hunter, he started to extend his hand. "Nice to mee..."

"This isn't a goddamned social society. I don't have all day to sit around and watch you two bond," Sprabary bellowed. "Hunter, can you get Mr. Sanders the hell out of my office before I get agitated?"

Hunter looked down hiding his smile. "Yes sir."

They were out of the office in seconds and heading down the hall, Hunter leading, Sanders quickly trailing. After a few steps, Sanders asked, "Is he always like that?"

Hunter kept walking. "Nope. Usually he's an ass." He turned into an empty conference room, waited for Sanders to follow him in, motioned for him to sit down. Sanders sat as he ran his hand over his shaved scalp and let out a long breath. It looked to Hunter as though Sanders might be reconsidering his move to Homicide. "I'll be right back. I need to get my notes. When I get back I'll get you up to speed." He was gone before Sanders had a chance to respond.

Hunter returned with his laptop, connected it to the overhead projector and without preamble, started talking about the case. He spent an hour going over every detail of the crime scene, showing Sanders pictures he'd already downloaded from his phone. He explained why each detail mattered and the questions each raised. Sanders took furious notes. When he finished, Hunter asked, "What do you think?"

Sanders sat for a moment, flipped back through his notes, grinned and in a smart assed tone, said, "Well, it's a hell of a lot of information for a couple of dead gang bangers."

Without cracking a smile, Hunter replied, "A vic is a vic, doesn't matter who they are, our job is to figure out who killed them. Now, what was missing from all that information I threw at you?"

Sufficiently reprimanded, Billy looked back through his notes, finally smiled and said, "You never mentioned the victim's names."

A big grin spread over Hunter's face. "You just might have some potential. Exactly! So that's your assignment for the day. You need to get with CSI Stacy Morgan. She's probably at the ME's. If not, you can get her cell number from the lovely and talented Paige. Morgan pulled wallets off both vics. You need to find out who they were and pull a complete history. I want to know everything about them. Check with the gang unit to see if these guys are players or just soldiers. Check with CPS to see if they were in the system growing up. If they have a criminal record..." With that, he stopped and smiled. "Well, that's pretty much a given, but... Pull their record and since they are now deceased, see if we can get their juvenile records."

Hunter got up, started pacing, pondering. "In the absence of an obvious suspect, we need to start with the victims to see if we can figure out a motive. Motive leads to a suspect. With these guys, our problem will likely be having too many people that had reasons to kill them."

"So, what if it was just random?"

"If that's the case, then we're hosed. Quite honestly though, a truly random murder is pretty rare. Look, it's four o'clock. Get moving. I want those histories by in the morning. Anything else?"

"What do we do after we have identities?"

"Well, we won't get the lab results, autopsy reports and ballistics until late tomorrow at the earliest, probably more like Wednesday morning. So we've gone about as far as we can with the crime scene until then. Assuming they're Eastcide Kings, we'll probably need to pay Shadow AK a visit."

Before Hunter could continue, Sanders started laughing. "Who?"

Hunter never cracked a smile, just looked him in the eyes. "Shadow AK is the leader of the Eastcide Kings. He started off as a runner when he was a teenager, worked his way up to assassin and now is their undisputed leader. He likes to think of himself as a businessman now, but down deep he's just your everyday stone cold killer."

"How did he get that name?"

"When he was an assassin, he was known for blending in with the shadows, never being seen. His weapon of choice was an AK-47." Hunter paused to let that sink in a bit. The smile had left Sanders's face.

Hunter continued. "We do have one lead we can follow. There's some wino that might have seen something last night. One of the uniforms canvassing the area found him. We'll need to talk with him. Other than that, we'll have to just go where the ID's lead us."

Sanders nodded. "Sounds like a plan." He grinned and added, "So, how did you get stuck with the newbie as a partner? Is it the 'crusty old veteran gets to break in the rookie' thing?"

A tight smile came across Hunter's face. "Your powers of observation are stunning." He started heading for the door. "One correction though..." With a cold stare, he added, "We're not partners. See you in the morning." He was gone before Sanders could speak.

Chapter 4

The gavel slammed down, echoing through the courtroom. There was a rumble from the crowd. A woman let out a sound, a cross between a cry and a gasp. A man muttered loudly under his breath. The judge bellowed, "Order in the court. Ladies and gentlemen, quiet down please or we'll have to clear the room." Judge Robert Feldman wagged his gavel at the spectators in the gallery and glared over his large, black rimmed glasses that leaned slightly to the left. His comb-over was ragged around the edges after a long day on the bench.

Assistant District Attorney Timothy Daris ran his hand through his perfectly layered blond hair and shook his head in disbelief. "Your Honor, the people strongly object. The confession was filmed, recorded on tape, written and signed by the defendant. How is it possible that it can't be admissible as evidence?"

"Objection overruled. Mr. Daris, the defendant says no one read him his rights."

Daris' frustration was clear. Though only in his thirties, Daris was an experienced veteran of the Tarrant County courts and had argued numerous cases in front of Judge Feldman and was more pissed off than intimidated. "Your Honor, this is unconscionable. The detective did read him his rights. He testified to that fact earlier today."

"That was not on the video or recordings, there was no signed waiver and you have no other witness to corroborate the detective's testimony. In my courtroom even defendants have rights, Mr. Daris." Judge Feldman was in his late fifties, mostly bald on top with a droopy face. He was probably the only liberal judge in Texas, outside of Austin, but he made up for it with zeal. He made even full-fledged 'bleeding hearts' look like Judge Roy Bean and believed there was no one who wasn't redeemable.

He had an especially tolerant view when it came to gang members and believed that the Police were out to frame every one of them. Today was no exception. The All American looking young man sitting at the defendant's table wearing slacks, a white shirt, tie and a smirk had confessed to aggravated sexual assault and murder of a local college student. Once his defense attorney showed up, he'd recanted and claimed the detectives had coerced him.

"Counselors, it's almost four thirty. This is a good place to stop for the day. We will reconvene at nine tomorrow morning. This court is in recess." With a quick slam of the gavel, he was up and out of the courtroom.

As the bailiff cuffed the defendant and led him away, the assistant counsel to the defense clapped the lead defense attorney on his back and smiled. It was a good day to be a defense attorney. In Judge Feldman's courtroom, it usually was.

Tim Daris stood for several minutes in a state of complete disbelief. *How could he possibly throw out the confession?* As the courtroom emptied, he packed his papers and notes. He slammed his briefcase shut then sat with his elbows on the table and his head in his hands. He was an experienced prosecutor, one of the best in the office. This was not his first time in Feldman's court. He knew what he was in for and had prepared. Obviously not well enough. He shook his head. *I had a signed confession for God's sake. How can I possibly lose a case with a signed confession?*

He finally turned to leave the courtroom and stopped in his tracks, his breath caught in his throat. The woman was standing, in her late fifties, face hollow, her eyes swollen with tears. The man, close cropped thinning gray hair, sat, jaw set, rage in his eyes. His mind raced. How could he face them? It was obvious he was failing them and their daughter. He stepped through the wooden gate and approached them. "Mr. and Mrs. Bennett... Jim, Rose... I, uh... I'm..."

The voice was almost a growl, his jaw barely moving. "How could he do that? How can he let this animal get away with what he did? My daughter..." The man's voice broke, his face contorted. "My baby... was raped... beaten...and..." His voice started to fade.

"Mr. Bennett, we're doing every..."

28

The man exploded, stood up and shouted. "What? What are you doing? That lunatic judge is going to let him off to roam the streets and claim more victims because someone didn't videotape his rights being read? That's insanity! And what are you going to do about it Mr. Daris?" His wife reached over and touched his shoulder. When she did, he stopped for a moment. He stood, body trembling. "I'm sorry Mr. Daris. I'm not blaming you. I just don't understand... This isn't justice. Justice won't be served until that animal and everyone like him are dead in the gutter!"

"Mr. Bennett..." Daris stopped, not knowing what to say. Finally he reached over, held the man's shoulder and rasped, "I'm sorry." What else could he say?

As he left the courthouse and walked down the pink granite steps, he stopped and looked straight down Main Street. The Tarrant County Courthouse faces southeast on East Weatherford Street with its back to the Trinity River. It was built almost completely out of pink granite in 1893; its Renaissance Revival style closely resembles the Texas State Capital. Even over one hundred years later, the classic look holds up well.

He could see all nine blocks down to where Main Street dead ended into the Fort Worth Convention Center. The weather was nice for November but there were signs of clouds off to the southwest. A cold front loomed, probably a day or two away.

He reached into his jacket pocket, grabbed his phone and stabbed at the keyboard with his free hand. "Kenny. It's Tim. Got time to grab a brew?" He started moving again, down the steps and toward the crosswalk. "Yeah, that son of a bitch Feldman threw out my confession." He made his way across East Weatherford and down the sidewalk on Main. "Yes way. I couldn't believe it. How the hell do you throw out a confession that's filmed, recorded, written and signed? How the hell is that even possible? This guy's a goddamned menace to society. Look, get the guys and meet me at The Flying Saucer. I'm so pissed, I may try to make their Hall of Fame tonight."

The Flying Saucer beer emporium's specialty was having nearly two hundred beers from all over the world on tap. Regular customers kept track of all the different beers they've drank over time. Their Hall of

Fame was reserved for the select few who successfully ordered and drank every one.

Daris slid his phone back into his jacket and continued down Main Street. It was five o'clock when he reached the heart of Sundance Square. The twenty-somethings were pouring out of the various downtown high rises, texting and cell phoning their way to hotspots like Billy Miners, Piranha's Sushi and Cabo Grande. He barely noticed Fort Worth's up and comers. His mind was still reeling over Judge Feldman's latest round of 'catch and release'.

He crossed in front of Billy Miners and across the parking lot. When he entered the Saucer, the place was already packed. He grabbed one of the few empty tables in the back patio and started perusing the long list of beers.

"Hey hot stuff. Where's the rest of your crew tonight?"

Hearing the familiar voice made him smile. "Hey Cindy. Don't fret. The boys will be here soon. I'm going to get a head start on them and try something new. How about an Affligem Dubbel?"

"You got it. I'll be right back. If I see the rest of your posse, I'll send them back."

Daris started checking his email and voicemail on his phone while he waited. He was listening to a message when Kenny, Robert and Edmond filed in, found him and sat down. The group of ADA's looked like they could be cast for a prime time courtroom drama; young, good looking, perfect hair, big teeth, gray suits, white shirts, subtle ties. Future right wing politicians doing their time in the DA's office, so that in campaign speeches they could claim to be hard on crime.

When Daris hung up, Kenny started in, "Dude, give it up. How on earth did that left wing nut justify tossing your confession?"

Tim launched into a detailed recap of the afternoon's proceedings. By the time the story was finished, the group had whipped themselves into a frenzy, each adding to the stream of profanity laced rants against liberals, gangs, the ACLU, sloppy police work and anything else that stood in the way of a conviction. They finally wore themselves out and started focusing on the exotic beers and young talent all around them.

Sounding dejected and philosophical, Daris mused, "I'll tell you.

You should have seen the Bennetts. They were destroyed." He shook his head, starred at his beer. "A waste of time. You've got these gangbangers out there raping, robbing and beating people at will and there doesn't seem to be any way to nail them. Even when you get a conviction, the sentences are ridiculously light and they're back at it before you can even get the paperwork finished." The group was quiet for a moment. He sipped his latest brew; something called Lime N'Lager, and continued. "Makes you want to take the law into your own hands."

At that, Edmond's eyes lit up. "Yeah well, speaking of that, last night somebody popped a couple of gangbangers over off Vickery." That got everyone's attention. Tim leaned back in his chair listening. "I heard it from a buddy of mine over at Central. Doubt it was someone getting justice, but anyway it goes, the city is less two scumbags. Whoever did it had balls. Shot them both at close range. Each had two 9mm slugs in his chest."

"About time," Robert clanked glasses with Edmond.

Kenny nodded. "No shit. They finally got a taste of their own medicine."

Daris looked at Edmond. "Do the cops have any idea who did it?"

"Don't think so. It's early. Don't even have the evidence processed yet. They'll figure it out though."

Daris smiled. "You seem to have an unduly high level of confidence in our brothers in blue. Why's that?"

"Sprabary assigned Hunter to the case."

"Hunter? I thought he was still riding a desk."

"Not anymore. They paired him up with some newbie."

At that, Daris frowned and leaned in. "Well, while you girls fantasize about blowing away gangbangers, I've got to get home to prep for tomorrow. Without that confession, this is going to be a bitch to win. Besides, there's no telling what that whack job will throw out next."

Tim tossed a twenty on the table to cover his tab, gave the appropriate fist bumps and handshakes to his boys and made his way through the crowd. Once outside, he scowled and headed back toward the courthouse parking lot.

Chapter 5

Deep in thought, his footsteps falling in quick cadence, Hunter moved southwest on Fourth Street. With his laptop bag slung over his shoulder, he was heading for his favorite late morning refuge, the Barnes and Noble Starbucks across from Bass Performance Hall.

He had spent the early morning hours keeping Panther company and working from home on the cold case assignment. It was a just a hair after ten on Tuesday morning when he strolled in to join the line of caffeine addicts and early morning bookworms.

This time in the morning was usually a great time to get in, grab the cushy gray chair in the corner and work in relative calm. After all, crunching data and reviewing notes while listening to Jack Johnson or Neko Case, and enjoying good coffee always beat the hell out of the sounds and smells of the station. Today he wouldn't be able to stay but he did want his late morning caffeine hit.

The overly pale, black haired guy behind the counter saw him, nodded and gave him a sly grin. When Hunter got to the front of the line, the guy greeted him in a haughty tone. "Well, if it isn't Jake Hunter, my favorite Cowboy Cop? Missed you yesterday. Were you out making the world a better place for humanity?"

Hunter returned the sly grin. "Seems humanity needs a little help in that regard, Bernard."

"You got that right. Your usual today?"

"As always."

Bernard turned to his counterpart and said, "Need a Grande Orange Mocha Frappucinno minus the orange, the chocolate and everything else except the coffee." His coworker's confused look made him continue in a droll tone. "He wants a large black coffee." He turned back to Hunter. "I'll bring it out to you in a moment."

"I'm taking it to go today."

Bernard raised his eyebrows. "Hmm, crime must be up in the city."

Hunter made his way back toward the station, the aroma from his cup teasing him as it came and went in the breeze. He found an empty conference room on the second floor, set up his laptop and called for Sanders.

Sanders came in carrying a note pad and two overstuffed manila folders. He mumbled "Good morning", grabbed a chair and started arranging documents in neat piles.

Hunter looked at the piles. "Looks like you've been busy Newbie."

"Yeah, well, our dearly departed had serious histories. Not sure anything I found will get us closer to the killer."

"Run it down for me and we'll see."

Sanders pulled out his notes and cleared his throat. "Okay. Let's kick it off with Darrel Jackson, A.K.A. D-Jack, sometimes known as Wheels. He'd be the one without the sunglasses. Nineteen years old, born at John Peter Smith on February 12, 1990. He was your average bad boy, nothing special, dropped out of Trimble Tech High in tenth grade after his third arrest for auto theft." Sanders stopped, grinned. "Gotta love the fact that his forte seemed to be stealing cars and the guy never even bothered to get his license." He continued. "According to our boys in Gangs, he was strictly a foot soldier, name only comes up occasionally, activity started around the time he started boosting cars. Childhood looks fairly normal. He grew up over off Rosedale, lower income neighborhood but with an intact family, Mom, Dad, two older sisters. Everything was going well, good grades, no trouble, until he got to high school. Things went downhill in a hurry then. Within months of arriving at Trimble Tech, he was skipping school, landing in detention, sleeping in class. His grades nosedived. His first arrest was that fall. Next one was after the first of the year, got off with a slap on the wrist for both. His third was that summer, spent a couple of months at the state school and came home a seasoned thug."

He paused shuffled through some papers and continue. "By his eighteenth birthday, he was a full time member of the Eastcide Kings.

He's got a laundry list of run-ins with law enforcement, mostly low end stuff; public drunkenness, disorderly conduct, etc. He did get busted for assault and attempted rape once. In both cases, the charges were eventually dropped due to lack of witness cooperation."

Hunter was up pacing, rubbing his chin. "Anything in the school or court records give an indication of what sent him south in the first place? Family trauma? Anything like that?"

Sanders smiled broadly. "There appears to be a direct initiating event." Hunter stopped, looked at Sanders, motioned for him to continue. "That event would be named Jarvis Wright, A.K.A. Shank. We know him as Mr. Sunglasses. This dude was bad to the core. Talk about pure evil." He picked up his notes. "All right, let's start with the basics. Wright was twenty years old, born in Compton, CA on August 8, 1989. His dad was a 'fence jumper', mom an addict. The California CPS reports started piling up almost before he got home from the hospital. Somewhere around six years old, after repeated reports of neglect and abuse and threats from the state to take him away, his mom somehow ended up in Fort Worth with relatives. She continued to spiral out of control and by the time Jarvis was ten, she had just evaporated." He paused, looked over at Hunter and said, "I can't find anything on her. She's either dead or so far off the grid that she might as well be." Hunter nodded, his face a stone but his eyes absorbing the pain of the story.

Sanders went back to his notes. "Jarvis was supposedly raised by an aunt and uncle but spent more time on the streets than in school. His first run in with the law was at eight for vandalism. Progressed from there… Shoplifting and Breaking and Entering at ten… Drug running by twelve. He made several visits to the Crocket State School along the way and was finally there for an extended stay after being convicted of assault at fourteen. He got his nickname 'Shank' based on an incident that happened shortly after his arrival."

"Bet I can guess where this story's going."

Sanders nodded. "Yep. He managed to scam materials from his shop class and make a homemade shank. He put a kid in the hospital, but as you can guess, there were no witnesses. So other than being disciplined at the school, he got off clean. His conditional release at seventeen required him to go back to school. By that time, he was a couple of years behind his age group." With a deep sigh in his voice and a roll of his eyes, he added, "He was 'mainstreamed' at Trimble Tech High School. " He paused for emphasis. "So at seventeen, a convicted felon and a known attempted murderer was a sophomore alongside a bunch of fifteen year old kids, one of those was Darrel Jackson."

Hunter reached up, pinched the bridge of his nose, and shook his head. "How many times have we heard this story before? You mix the good apples with the bad ones and they all end up spoiled. Damn. I'm sure I can guess the rest of the story, but you did the research so you get the honors... Continue."

"Well, as you said, same old story. Jackson and Wright connected and Jackson went straight off the rails. He was the follower, Wright the leader. He was the car thief, Wright the killer."

"Killer?"

"Well, suspected killer. Four years ago, shortly after he started at Trimble Tech, there was a wino beaten to death over on the east side near Beach Street. It appeared to be a gang initiation that went too far. Wright was the suspect but there wasn't enough evidence to make it stick. From there, he rose through the ranks and became heavy muscle, internal enforcer."

Hunter was lost in thought when he realized Sanders had stopped. "Nice work. That's a lot of information. We'll see if it takes us somewhere."

Sanders shook his head. "Yeah, that's what I thought too so I went and talked with his aunt this morning. Even she thinks he's..."

The words blew out of Hunter before he could stop. He bellowed, "You did what? What the hell do you mean you went and talked to his aunt?"

"Well, I..."

"You don't ever go anywhere without me knowing. Understand? I decide when and where you go and who you talk to. And you sure as hell won't do it without me."

Hunter's tirade continued for several minutes, Sanders not managing to get a word in edgewise in his defense. It was so loud that even with the conference room door closed, most of the detectives had stopped what they were doing to listen to the muffled yelling.

Hunter punctuated his point by almost ripping the door off the hinges as he tore out of the conference room and down the hall. His last words were, "Don't even breathe until I get back!"

The office stood in stunned silence for a moment. Sanders stumbled out of the conference room, dazed and confused, his face drained and his mouth agape. He almost bumped into Jimmy Reyes, a veteran homicide detective as he stepped into the hall.

Reyes gave him a concerned look. "You okay? You must've really hit a hot button. I've known Cowboy for almost a decade and I'm not sure I've ever heard him raise his voice. What exactly did you do?"

Sanders stood, thought for a moment and told Reyes what had happened.

Reyes's face went solemn. He nodded toward the conference room and gently guided Sanders back inside. Once they were seated, Reyes chewed on the inside of cheek as he contemplated what to say. After a moment, he started. "Look Billy... You need to know some history. I guess I would have assumed that someone would have filled you in... Were you aware of what happened to Cowboy's partner, Frank Riley?"

"Just that he was killed in the line of duty."

Exhaling loudly, Reyes continued. "Let me fill in some details. Frank and Cowboy had been partners ever since Frank made detective almost eight years ago. They grew up as detectives together. Last spring, they were working the early stages of a shooting investigation, just checking with witnesses, kind of where you're at in this case. They decided to divide and conquer on some of the legwork, both were going to check some leads. So Hunter's talking with his witness and realizes based on what this guy's saying that the 'witness' Frank is talking to may actually be the suspect. He blows out of there heading for Frank's location. He tries him on his cell, no answer. Found out later Frank's cell battery had died. He gets backup dispatched to the location." Reyes paused, blinked several times, struggled to continue. "Hunter... Hunter rounds the corner as the 'officer down' call is going out. Frank died on the front porch. He never drew his gun, never saw it coming. He thought he was going to interview a witness. Turned out to be the shooter."

They both sat in silence for a moment. Sanders's face was even more drained than after the tirade. After a moment, Reyes tapped his fingers on the table and got up and moved toward the door. "I know he shouldn't have gone off on you like that, but... Under the circumstances... Well, I guess... Look, just don't take it personally. Cowboy's a good guy. You just stepped in the wrong hole."

Chapter 6

Shortly after lunch Hunter returned to the station. It had taken him a while to regain his composure. When he came into the detective's work area, a few conversations quieted and a couple of heads turned his way. Although uncomfortable with the attention, he did his best to disregard the looks. The sudden quiet made Billy look up. Hunter got his attention and motioned for him to come into the conference room.

Sanders entered the conference eyeing Hunter with a wary look. He started to say something but Hunter cut him off with an upheld hand and motioned for him to sit down. Sanders complied. Hunter shuffled his feet and looked around the room, obviously not wanting to look at Sanders.

"Billy, uh… I owe you an apology. I shouldn't have gone off on you like that. I know you don't know me but I'm really not like that."

"Look, Jake, it's okay. I really didn't know about… Well, about what happened. Reyes filled me in. If I'd known man…" His voice trailed off. "Anyway… I shouldn't have gone without telling you."

Hunter stood nodding his head for a few uncomfortable moments. "Let's just chalk it up to a learning curve for both of us… But just to be clear, its department policy that anytime you leave the building on police business, you are required to check out through Dispatch. That includes interviewing witnesses, serving warrants, visiting crime scenes, whatever. Okay?"

"Works for me."

Hunter smirked. "So now that we've had this special little bonding moment, you think we can get back to the case?" Sanders smiled and nodded. Hunter continued. "All right then. Tell me about the aunt."

"Well, it's a little anticlimactic. All I was really going to say was that she didn't exactly seem surprised or heartbroken about her nephew's demise. She just rattled on about him being ungrateful and a waste of time and money."

Hunter was leaning against the wall with his hands folded, his forefingers pressed together in front of his lips. "Okay. I know it's a long shot but you mentioned an assault and an attempted rape. We'll need to get the names of the victims for any serious arrests for either of these guys. I want to at least track down their whereabouts, check them off the list of possibilities. We can do that later. Who knows? I've seen crazier things." Hunter pushed off the wall and paced for a moment, lost in thought. "Damn, beyond that it kind of sounds like we've got a great big bag of nothing." He stopped in front of the table, started collecting his laptop, notebook and phone. Sanders looked at him with a look of anticipation. Hunter stopped, looked over at him, said, "Pack up. We've got a couple of folks to visit. We'll check out with Dispatch on our way to my truck."

"Okay, who're we going to see?"

Hunter smiled. "A wino and a shadow."

The two exited the back of the station, climbed in Hunter's Explorer and pulled out onto Fourth Street heading southwest. Three blocks over, they made a left on Houston. After weaving through the maze of one way streets in downtown, they hit Jennings Avenue. That took them under the railroad tracks and I-30 and dumped them on Vickery, heading straight back toward the crime scene.

From the passenger seat, Sanders surveyed the buildings and people as they move west on Vickery. "So, what's the story on the wino?"

"One of the patrol guys, Smith, said he was rambling on about seeing someone that night."

"How do we find him?"

"According to Smith, he lives in a cardboard condo tucked back in the dead end of East Daggett right behind the Builders Supply and the Supreme Golf warehouse."

As Hunter took a right off of Vickery onto Calhoun, Sanders asked, "How will we know it's him?"

Hunter let out a sad chuckle. "Smith said to look for the crazy drunk guy wearing purple sweat pants and red converse."

Sanders smiled. "Nothing like a man with good taste in clothes."

Once they turned left into the dead end of East Daggett, it took only seconds to spot their witness. Both detectives smiled and shook their heads.

Hunter reached for the door handle and as he got out, mumbled, "Let's get this over with."

The man was sitting on one of several upturned five gallon plastic buckets scattered around. He was leaning with his back against the back wall of the Supreme Golf warehouse, nursing a bottle of wine. His cardboard condo was actually a semi-permanent looking structure made out of a combination of old wooden pallets, large sheets of cardboard and a much worn blue vinyl tarp. He was singing to himself and hadn't seemed to notice Hunter and Sanders until they were standing a few feet in front on him.

Hunter had seen this too many times. "Excuse me sir."

The man jumped to his feet, eyes wide, black curly hair going in every direction. "What? Leave me alone! I didn't do nothing!" He backed against the wall, his chest heaving as he gulped air. His eyes darted around in a panicked state, looking for an escape route.

Both detectives took a step back. As calmly as he could, in a soothing voice, Hunter said, "Sir, we're not here to harm you. Please... Just relax... We only want to ask you a few questions."

Hunter nodded to Sanders and both detectives took a few more steps back. As they did, the man's breathing slowly normalized. "Who are you? What do you want?"

"I'm Detective Jake Hunter. This is Detective Billy Sanders. We just want to ask you a few questions about what you saw the night before last when those two men were shot around the corner."

Visibly relaxing, smiling. "Oh... Yeah... When Donald Trump came by."

Sanders looked at Hunter, smirked and shrugged. Hunter didn't return the smile, his eye's saddened. After all that time with Gina, he'd become adept at talking to drunks. He turned to the man. "Sir, why don't we sit down and you can tell us about it." The man nodded and staggered cautiously back to his bucket and sat down. Hunter took out his notepad. He and Sanders stepped forward, found buckets and sat as well. "Can you tell us your name?"

Throwing his head back in a formal fashion, he declared in a booming, almost elegant, though slurred tone, "I am Sir Elliott Winston... A direct descen... dant... of the North Caro... lina Winstons." He raised his wine bottle in salute, almost falling backwards. As described, he wore red converse and faded purple sweat pants. On top of that, he had a worn army fatigue jacket and what at one time might have been a white T-shirt.

Hunter continued, "Mr. Winston..."

"Sir" Winston said absent mindedly as he appeared to watch a fly buzz around his head. Hunter couldn't see anything.

"Excuse me?"

"Sir Winston... My name... is Sir Winston." He starred at Hunter, wavering on the bucket, trying to focus his eyes. He motioned to Hunter to continue as if granting permission.

Sanders snickered. Hunter, looked down for a moment, blinked several times and nodded. "Sir Winston... Can you tell us what you saw the other night?"

Winston sat for a moment, deep in thought. He pointed with a wandering hand toward the street corner. "Was sitting by the corner... Dark... Cold." He stared at the ground for a moment as his arms wrapped around himself. "Them boys..." He glanced at Billy. "Playing that damn noise... Too loud... That crap's not music... Now Jazz, Jazz is music..."

Hunter cut him off gently. "So what else did you see?"

Refocusing, squinting as he processed the question. "Donald walked by." Winston thought for a moment, kind of shook his head. "Snuck up on me... Real quiet."

Hunter probed further. "Could you see what he looked like?"

Winston pulled his head back, wrinkled his brow. "You seen his picture... Trump." He shook his head and continued. "Oh, he was dressed nice... Fancy long coat... Nice pants."

Hunter tried again. "Did you see his face?"

Shaking his head dismissively. "Too dark. Donald was in a hurry. I hollered. He kept walking."

Hunter encouraged him to continue. "What happened then?"

Winston shrugged. "Went to bed."

Hunter stopped writing. "Did you see anything else?"

Winston shook his head. "Just heard bangs..." Dropping his head, he looked around. "I got real quiet, stayed inside. Didn't hear nothing else until all the lights showed up."

Confused, Hunter asked, "Lights?"

Winston nodded, his eyes wandered, back to chasing flies. "Red... Blue... Lights..."

Hunter continued asking questions for another twenty minutes but the man's momentary coherence seemed to disappear and nothing more was learned. Finally, he swallowed hard, thanked the man, shook his hand and in the process slid him a ten dollar bill. The man just nodded, saluted Hunter with his bottle and started singing again.

Back in the Explorer, as Hunter guided it onto Calhoun, Sanders chuckled and shook his head. "Wow, that dude was out there. What a waste of time."

Hunter looked away from Sanders, shrugged as he turned right, heading east on Vickery. "Being drunk doesn't make you crazy. Who knows? There's no doubt he'd be useless in court... But he saw someone that night."

Sanders snickered. "Yeah, Donald Trump."

Hunter tried to smile. "Well, maybe after we stop by and see Shadow, we'll call Donald up and see if he has an alibi."

When they crossed over I-35, the landscape changed. They were no longer in downtown, but they were a far cry from the suburbs. To their north as they moved along Vickery was a stretch of empty space that separated Vickery from the Union Pacific rail lines which ran parallel. It was useless rock, dirt and brush scattered with the occasional old semi-trailer used for storage. The desolate view to the north was only slightly better than the urban blight to the south. A series of near abandoned warehouses fronted Vickery with forgotten residential areas hidden behind them. If you looked on a map of Fort Worth, this area was referred to as the Historic Southside.

Their conversation died as they drove the next few blocks. The combination of what they were seeing and where they were going seemed to make small talk even more pointless than usual. When they came to New York Street, they took a right behind the Gospel Outreach warehouse and then a left on East Daggett. He slowed his Explorer but continued moving for another half block where he turned right into a crushed rock parking lot. There were a half dozen tricked out cars parked randomly around the lot with a shiny black Escalade parked near a small building which sat about one hundred feet off the street. The building was plain, about the size of a double wide trailer set parallel to the street. It had off white aluminum siding, one door in the middle and several exterior flood lights.

Beyond the tricked out cars in the lot, there was nothing particularly noticeable about the building or it's setting, with the exception of the two large, angry looking men, one sitting on each side of the door.

As they came to a stop in the parking lot, both men looked serious and Sanders was visibly getting his game face on. Hunter looked at him. "I would strongly suggest you quit bowing up and lose the attitude. Those guys really don't care if you're black or if you're a cop. In fact, that combination might actually piss them off more than just us being here. We're on their turf now and given the right motivation, they'd kill us both without thinking twice."

Sanders looked at Hunter, realized the wisdom in the advice and tried to relax. Hunter pulled his holster and gun off his belt, unlocked his console, opened it and dropped them in. "Put your gun in here."

"What? You're kidding, right? We're going in there unarmed?"

Hunter nodded toward the building where the two large, angry looking men had stood up and were glaring at them. "Do you want one of those two cream puffs over there to disarm you or would you rather do it yourself? They're not about to let us in that building packing."

Sanders shook his head and follow Hunter's lead. "Damn, you got balls."

"Not really. I'm just not very bright. Besides, I know Shadow. He rarely kills someone without a reason."

"Yeah, well. I'm just a little concerned that he might consider two cops intruding on his turf, reason."

"Well, there is that." Hunter got out and started toward the door with Billy on his heels. The two men by the door now moved toward them slowly, one with his hand conspicuously tucked under his jacket.

"That's far enough white boy. Who the hell are you and what do you want?"

Hunter and Sanders stopped. The four were facing each other about twenty feet from the door. Hunter put both of his hands up slightly. "I'm Detective Jake Hunter, Fort Worth Homicide. This is Detective Sanders. We're investigating the murders of a couple of your associates and we needed to speak with Shadow."

"Cops huh? You know I can't let you in with weapons."

Hunter opened up his jacket, Sanders followed suit. "We're not armed."

The one who'd been doing the talking nodded for the other one to do a more thorough check while he kept his hand in his jacket. The other one stepped over, patted both detectives down and nodded the all clear.

"Clack, why don't you let Shadow know he's got visitors? I'll keep these gentlemen company while we wait."

Clack disappeared leaving the three of them uncomfortably staring at each other in the parking lot. There was a light, cool breeze coming out of the north but the sun was high in the cloudless sky so the wait was comfortable. A moment later, he was back waving them in. They stepped in from bright sunlight into bar room darkness. Both men stopped for a moment letting their eyes adjust.

As his eyes came into focus, Hunter absorbed the scene. The main room was split in two. The right half looked like a typical bar and pool hall. A long bar against the back wall, a couple of pool tables and an assortment of tall, round tables with barstools around them. The left half of the room, separated by a half wall, looked more like a home theater and game room on steroids. A big screen TV, at least sixty inches, dominated the far wall surrounded by plush couches and chairs. Along the front wall were a series of video games and pinball machines. There were three doors along the back wall. Hunter assumed those were offices, bathrooms or storage areas.

There were several obvious gang members scattered about the two rooms wearing various versions of the same clothing theme, all had stopped whatever they had been doing and now glared at the two detectives. Hunter saw Shadow in one of the plush chairs. A scantily clad woman sat on his lap but when Hunter caught his eye, Shadow dismissed her with a wave of his hand. She disappeared into one of the back rooms.

Shadow was young, in his mid-twenties, dressed like someone trying to imitate P Diddy, but on a smaller budget. He was neat, clean, with his short cropped hair, oversized gold earrings, tailored black suit, cufflinks, gold bracelet and gold rings on all but his index fingers. He remained seated, showing no respect and motioned for them to enter his kingdom. They were clearly on his turf.

As they moved into the game room area, Shadow eyed both men without motioning for them to sit. "Well, look who's come to call. It's Cowboy and he's brought his own step and fetch it boy. How do you like that?"

Sanders started to bow up and Shadow responded by standing quickly and moving toward him. Hunter stepped in between Sanders and Shadow. Shadow looked to Sanders and started to smile. As he did, his eyes widened for a split second and he cocked his head. He returned his focus to Hunter. His voice dripping with sarcasm, he asked, "What can I do for the man today?"

"Shadow, we're following up on the shootings of a couple of your associates. One named Darrel Jackson, the other named Jarvis Wright. You might know them as Wheels and Shank."

"Well it's nice to see that the FWPD cares enough about a couple of bruthas that they'd assign someone of your caliber Cowboy, but, as you know... We take care of our own."

As he spoke, Sanders watched him closely as if sensing something familiar but not being able to place it. Shadow caught his stare. "What you looking at nigga?"

Sanders was caught off guard, stuttered for a moment. "Uh nothing, you just look familiar is all."

"What's that? You trying to pick me up or something?" Turning to Hunter. "Damn Cowboy, you not only got you a black one, you got you a gay one too. Who'd you piss off?"

Before Hunter could get the conversation back on track, Sanders blurted out, "Jones! Darien Jones!" He started to smile but it faded to confused sadness.

Shadow snapped his head around, stepped toward Sanders, got up close to his face and glared. "What the hell did you just say? I'm Shadow AK. That name don't mean shit to me anymore. Nobody calls me that"

"Hey, no problem. It's just... I knew your brother Jimmy." Sanders glanced around the room as if to look for him. "So how is he anyway?"

Shadow's entire being seemed to shudder. His eyes darkened and any hint of humanity left his face. He gritted his teeth and spoke slowly. "My... brother... is... dead... He was killed by Varrio Central, the same muthafuckas who probably took out Wheels and Shank and the same muthafuckas who are gonna pay the price."

The room went silent. Sanders' eyes had glossed over and his face was contorted. Hunter could see heads nodding in his peripheral vision. He had watched this exchange in stunned silence. Needing to regain control, he stepped close to the other two, almost wedging himself between them. "Shadow, that's one of the reasons I'm here today. I don't think Varrio Central did this."

This seemed to snap Shadow out of his death stare on Sanders. "Yeah? Then who did? Those spics are the only ones crazy enough to fuck with the Kings."

Hunter shook his head. "I know it may seem that way, but let me lay out what we know." He continued, explained the situation and why he didn't think it was a gang hit, doing his best to convince Shadow not to start a gang war with Varrio Central. Shadow listened intently giving away nothing with his expression.

When Hunter finished, Shadow shrugged. "Sounds to me like you got it all figured out 'cept for one thing... If it weren't those fucking spics, then who popped Wheels and Shank?"

"That's what we're trying to figure out Shadow but you've got to give us some time before you do something crazy."

Shadow folded his arms across his chest, his vacant eyes glared at Hunter. "Oh I'm not doin' nothin' crazy Cowboy, but you can bet your ass my boys and me are gonna look into this. And if we find who done it before you do, we gonna save the taxpayers the expense of a trial."

"I'm sure the taxpayers appreciate your concern." Hunter turned to leave.

In the Explorer, the two detectives were silent until they were safely back on the road. After a moment, Hunter audibly exhaled, shook his head and turned to Sanders. "Now that was fun, wasn't it?" Sanders didn't respond, just rubbed his head with both hands. Hunter continued. "What the hell was that stuff about Darien Jones and his brother?"

Sanders took a deep breath, slowly shook his head and turned to look out the window. "Oh man, it's a long story."

"Humor me. I'm young. I've got nothing but time."

"Well… I guess this is my childhood coming back to haunt me… I grew up over near Trimble Tech High School, lived in a house just off Cannon Street. I ran with Jimmy Jones, Darien's older brother. He was a good kid, not a gangbanger." Sanders had a sad look on his face, shook his head.

"Based on their records, both Darien and Jimmy were gangbangers from high school on. How did you miss that?"

"My Dad got a new job when I was fourteen. The summer before my ninth grade year, we moved to Euless so I ended up going to Trinity High School. Darien would have been about eleven then. I never saw either one of them again. I had no idea they'd gotten into gangs." With a strain in his voice, he whispered, "I didn't know Jimmy was dead."

Hunter processed this new information. "Wait a minute… You went to Trinity? You're *the* Billy Sanders from Trinity High School? The running back? Man, I watched you shred Odessa Permian one year in the playoffs at Texas Stadium. Holy crap. What did you get, a hundred and fifty yards that game?"

"A hundred and ninety-three, but who's counting?"

"Man, no one told me I was in the presence of a celebrity. You were a blue chipper. I figured I'd be seeing you competing for the Heisman someday. What happened? I mean… Not to make it sound…"

Sanders chuckled. "Not to worry. I get it all the time… Well, I guess you might say I found out my head wasn't quite as hard as my Momma always claimed." Hunter raised an eyebrow. Sanders continued. "I got a full ride to Texas Tech, played a couple of years. I got a severe concussion my freshman year, followed by three more my sophomore year. The doctors strongly suggested that unless I wanted to be drooling and mumbling by age forty, I'd best hang it up."

Hunter grinned. "So your choice of careers can be traced back to a head injury? Explains a lot."

"Yeah, they honored my scholarship and I got my degree in Criminology. Next thing you know... I'm here hanging out with high class people like you and Shadow. What more could I ask for?"

"Damn right!"

*   *   *   *

The minute the door closed with Hunter and Sanders leaving, the room jerked to life. The gangbangers all started talking at once. Shadow was lost in thought for a moment. He snapped out of it when he heard someone shout, "I say we pop those muthafuckas tonight."

"Chill out Spike." Shadow looked over at a menacing looking man with tattoos running the length of both arms. "We'll pop the muthafuckas when we figure out who done it. Ain't no need to start a war until we know who we fightin'."

Spike shook his head. "Goddamn. Never thought I'd see the day when you went soft Shad..."

Before Spike could finish his sentence, Shadow bolted across the room and had him penned against the wall. "Muthafucka, I show you soft if you want." Shadow choked Spike with his forearm, their faces inches apart. Fear radiated from Spike's eyes. Shadow continued. "Now, like I told that honky cop. We gonna hit the streets, turn this town upside down and find out who done this. When we do, we gonna mess them up so bad, won't nobody ever try this shit again. You understand?"

Spike nodded his head and made a croaking sound. Shadow let go of him, looked around the room. "I want to hit every source we got. Let the world know we on a rampage until we find this muthafucka."

He turned to one of his soldiers standing by the bar. "Copperhead?"

"Yes. Sir."

"Do we still have our contact down at Central PD?"

"Yes. Sir."

"You let her know, I need to see her. Today!"

Chapter 7

The Victim's hand slid across the cold steel of the Beretta lying on the cloth covered table. The metallic feel sent a quick shiver through him. Fingers trembling, he reached over to the leather holster on the chair beside him, unholstered the second pistol and laid it beside the first one in precisely the same orientation. For a moment, he stared at the twin pistols letting his pulse quicken.

Did I really pull it off? Did I really kill two people? People? Hell, more like animals. Those bastards deserved what they got, probably worse.

The events of early Monday morning replayed in his mind, and a distant smile came to his face. It had worked almost exactly as planned. They never saw it coming. They went to their graves smirking, thinking it was just another robbery, that he was just another cracker to intimidate and humiliate. They were wrong and they paid the ultimate price for that mistake. More importantly, for their past sins, for their brother's sins.

He began methodically breaking down the first pistol, piece by piece, laying each out in a perfectly practiced routine. The second pistol followed in the same fashion. He cleaned and oiled each piece, laying each back in its position.

His mind drifted. *What's the right timing for my next mission? Who should it be? A Varrio Central? Would that confuse them or would it lead the cops to realize it's not a gangbanger pulling the trigger? Another King? Hmm, that might be enough to push them to retaliate, start a gang war and do the job for me.* A wicked smile broke across his face.

Before his final step, he slid on a pair of skin tight, latex, surgical gloves. He then carefully picked up each piece, wiped it down thoroughly with a cotton cloth and reassembled the weapons. He loaded the magazines, slammed them into place and holstered them.

JOE B.PARR

He stored the two holstered Berettas in a locked gun case and stashed it in a hidden compartment built into the back of his home office desk. He had already stored the clothes he'd worn Monday morning. The charcoal dress slacks, white button down shirt and wool overcoat with the cutout pockets were neatly folded and stacked in a storage bin hidden in his attic. The Nike running shoes sat on top.

He sat down at his desk, reached for the newspaper. As expected, there had been nothing in the Monday paper. There would have been no way for the story to have made the print deadline. *Let me see. What are they saying about my handiwork?*

He searched through each section, article by article, becoming more agitated as each page went by. *You're kidding me. Two people are shot in the street and it doesn't make the paper? Damn, even PTA meetings make the paper.* He opened the regional section. Skimming through the Police Blotter, he found the story. The words raced across the page in the tiny section. *Is that it?* He shook his head with a look of disbelief. *Hell, even the newspapers don't care when a couple of ghetto gangsters get whacked.*

He neatly refolded the paper and set it down on his desk. He sighed, sat for a moment in thought. Looking to the corner of his desk, he saw her picture. The Victim's eyes moistened and his breath caught like always. *Those fucking animals.* The tears burned as his stare hardened. Involuntarily tearing the page from the newspaper, his hand shook as he crushed it. *She didn't deserve that... They took her from me. They will pay.* When he finally looked down, he realized his hand was still trembling. How long had he been sitting there? He regained his composure, flattened down the newspaper and wiped his eyes.

After a moment, he reached for his computer mouse and the monitor came to life in a pulse of blue light. With a couple of quick clicks, the Google search screen came up. He repeated his search for news on the killings, this time electronically. The result was the same, almost no mention, just the basic facts in the Police logs.

It was obvious that this city didn't care about the scum roaming its streets. *They'll eventually care. I bet when they finally figure out what's happening, the public will cheer. Hell, I'll be toasted as a hero.* He turned back to the computer, pulled up the weather and checked the ten day forecast. *Thursday, lows in the low forties.* Another wicked smile broke across his face as he clicked out of his browser and turned off his computer. *Hmm… Sounds like a nice night to wear a wool coat.*

Chapter 8

Hunter paced slowly, flipping a dry erase marker in his hand. Sanders read through a case file and tapped his pen on the table. They had spent the morning reviewing the details of the case without any new revelations. Hunter finally broke the silence. "So, where does that leave us?"

Sanders steepled his fingers together, exhaled heavily. "Shit. I'm at a loss. Based on the evidence we've seen so far, a couple of invisible shooters took out a couple of bad guys at point blank range leaving nothing but vapor and spent shell casings. Unless, of course, you consider our star witness who claims he saw Donald Trump."

Hunter started to comment on the star witness but was interrupted by a knock on the conference room door. Hunter glanced at his watch as he answered. "Door's open."

When Stacy Morgan walked in carrying a handful of files, her eyes met Hunter's and widen as she smiled. "Hey Cowboy. You look like you could use some coffee."

Hunter returned her smile, locking eyes for a brief second. "That is no doubt the best offer I've had this morning. Unfortunately, my favorite java spot doesn't open for another half hour and I refuse to subject myself to the swill this department claims as coffee."

Stacy set her files on the table, turned toward Hunter. "Well, I guess that means I get to bore you with some findings until you can buy me a cup." She stared a beat too long then turned toward Sanders who watched the exchange with a smirk. "You must be Billy Sanders." She extended her hand. "I'm Stacy Morgan, Crime Lab. We spoke on the phone Monday."

Sanders stood and after he shook her hand, he pulled out a chair for her. "Yeah, thanks for your help."

Stacy smiled. "No need to be so polite on my account, I'm just one of the guys around here."

Hunter chuckled. "Yeah, well. She may be one of the guys but she's the only one that the other guys stare at."

Sanders snorted. "Damn glad to hear that."

Her cheeks flushed as she fumbled with her papers. "All right, let's get down to business so you can buy that coffee." She handed a copy of a report to each detective. "Okay, first the bullets, ballistics and shooting. Each of our vics were shot at close range. The powder residue on their clothing indicates a distance of less than a foot. There were no actual powder burns so it's not likely to have been less than three inches. These shootings were up close and personal. The bullets were hollow points, fragmented on impact and shredded the internal organs. They may not have been dead before they hit the ground but it was a photo finish."

Sanders looked up from his report. "Hollow points? That's a pretty typical load from someone who's carrying for protection, right?"

Morgan continued. "It is. Helps avoid a through and through. Fortunately, we were able to find enough fragments to confirm our earlier suspicion that they were killed by different guns. Nothing in the autopsy or ballistics could answer the one shooter versus two shooters question. At that close of range, it'd be hard to miss either way."

Hunter had been starring off into space. "What about timing?"

"Timing?"

"Yeah. This all happened in a split second and it appears that neither of the vics even reached for his gun. If there were two shooters, how did they coordinate their shots so closely?" He leaned forward looking intently at Stacy. "Think about it. Two shooters would have had to draw their weapons and fire at almost exactly the same second. It would have required a signal." He was getting animated now, talking with his hands. "Any kind of signal... You know, a nod or a shout, would have alerted the vics and they would have reacted in some way. They would have moved back or drawn their weapons or turned away... Something... Right?"

Billy interjected. "That's a good point. Also, the signal would almost have to have been verbal since the two shooters most likely wouldn't have been looking at each other. They'd have been looking at their intended targets... There's no way a shooter could have yelled something without one of those bangers reacting."

Stacy flipped to another page in the report. "Nice segue. That brings me to the tox screen. Both vics had been drinking but not heavily and both had moderately high levels of amphetamines in their systems... These guys were speeding and would have been jumpy. Any kind of shout or quick movement would have sent them through the roof."

Hunter leaned back, opened his laptop. "Well folks, looks like we're looking for a single shooter."

Sanders nodded. "Yeah, a pretty ballsy one." As soon as he said it, he started to apologize to Stacy. She waived it off before he had a chance to say it.

Hunter looked up after typing in some notes. "So what else do we have?"

Morgan pushed back from the table and shrugged. "Unfortunately not much more. Nothing else from the scene seemed to be of much use. No useful DNA or prints. Everything collected appears to just be trash with no connection. As for the autopsies, straight forward – each vic died of two gunshots to the chest. No other recent trauma."

No one spoke for a moment, each wrapped in their own thoughts. Sanders broke the silence. "So a single shooter takes out two victims that no one gives a crap about without any witnesses and leaves no physical evidence behind... Sounds like the perfect crime."

"No such thing." Hunter retorted without looking at him. "There's something. We just haven't found it yet." He paced again. "What about traffic cameras?"

"Thought you might ask." Morgan pulled a sheet from her file. Hunter smiled at her ability to predict him. He had missed working with her. She pointed to a street map with four intersections circled and started pointing to them. "We've got cameras here, here, here and here. As you can see, nothing close enough to catch a car leaving the scene."

"Hmm..." Hunter looked at the map for a moment. "Maybe not, but we should get the recordings from each of them for the timeframe."

After a few moments of silence, Sanders said, "So where do we go from here?"

Hunter smiled. "Well, now that it's almost ten, Stacy and I are going to go have some real coffee. You get the privilege of having another chat with the boys over in Gangs. I want a summary of all gang related activity for the last month with a focus on this past weekend. We'll review it first thing in the morning and then we'll go have a chat with Pinche Loco of Varrio Central."

Sanders raised an eyebrow. "You really think they had something to do with this?"

"No, but we don't have any other leads to run. Besides, if nothing else, we should gauge the Varrio's temperature now that the streets have heated up a bit. While you're doing that, I've got some follow up on the cold case project for Sprabary. I'll see you in the morning around nine." He turned to Stacy and smiled. "Well, are you ready for your caffeine fix?" Her eyes sparkled as she grabbed her purse and stood.

A cold front had crept in that morning so the walk was cool and quick. The Starbucks was warm and the aroma instantly relaxing. Bernard greeted Hunter with his typical banter and after placing the order for Hunter's usual and a Decaf Skinny Latte for Stacy, turned back to Hunter. "Well now. This must be a special occasion. You're in here with something other than that computer." Leaning forward as if telling Hunter a secret but speaking loud enough for Stacy to hear. "Just between you and me Cowboy, this one looks like a keeper."

Hunter turned to Stacy and smirked. "You'll have to excuse Bernard. As you can tell by his skin tone, he doesn't get out much."

Stacy playfully punched Hunter's shoulder and smiled at Bernard. "I don't know, sounds to me like he's got pretty good taste."

After getting comfortably ensconced in a couple of soft chairs, they sipped their coffees and talked shop for a few minutes only to have the lack of progress on the case drag the conversation to a halt. They fell into a surprisingly comfortable silence as each was lost in their own thoughts.

They had known each since Hunter was on patrol. Although she was married at the time, Stacy had been very supportive during the time after his wife's accident. Gina had struggled with drinking for years but he thought she had finally turned a corner. She had started back with

AA and this time it seemed to be working. Hunter had been working a case hard all that week and hadn't been home much, but she had assured him she was going to her meetings. He was devastated when he found her. The months that followed were a hazy blur but one memory that was clear was Stacy's support and encouragement. She helped keep him focused on work and was a major reason he was able to survive, her and Frank.

"Penny for your thoughts." Stacy's voice snapped him out of his stupor.

"Huh? Oh… I was just thinking how good it felt to be back on an active case."

"Well, you've been missed." She paused and added, "I've missed you."

He smiled tentatively. "I've missed you too." Hunter looked at his watch. "Speaking of missing…" He tapped the crystal. "We might be missing our guy while we sit here."

Chapter 9

Multiple gunshots exploded, shattering the silence, echoing off the concrete walls. A trail of smoke rose slowly from the barrel of the semi-automatic 9mm in his left hand. The shooter paused for a moment, looking down the barrel, through the smoke. The bullets had shredded through their intended target in a tight formation leaving nothing but ragged entry points.

A muffled voice came from just behind him. "Nice grouping."

Jim Bennett removed his ear protection headphones. "Huh?"

Henry Lansford repeated. "I said, nice grouping... Damn nice for left handed. How often do you get to the range?"

Jim let the headphones hang around his neck, moved back to the loading table and ejected the magazine. "A couple of times a week I guess, sometimes more. Depends..." His shrug suggested it was just a hobby, his skill suggested anything but. He picked up a second, already loaded magazine and shoved it into the bottom of the pistol grip. He held it out to Henry. "Let's see if you remember anything from basic training. What was that? Forty years ago?" He chuckled.

Henry was short with a protruding belly; his walk was more of a waddle. He moved forward, reached out tentatively and took the weapon. "Well, first of all, it wasn't forty years ago." Looking sheepishly, he added, "More like thirty-five... And secondly, we rarely trained with pistols. That was for the officers. We enlisted guys shot M1's." He stepped into the firing area eyeing the pistol.

Jim chuckled. "Damn, Henry, it's not a snake. Just cock it, aim it and pop a few rounds in the target."

Henry frowned, straightened back his shoulders, aimed and fired. As he squinted at the target just twenty-five feet away, he heard Jim chuckle again. When he realized he hadn't even hit the target, much less come close to the bull's-eye, he had to chuckle a little himself as he returned the gun to the loading table.

Shaking his head, Jim stepped forward and picked it up. "Good Lord Henry. Are you sure those weren't blanks in that gun? I'm not even sure you hit the back wall." He moved into the firing area. "Let me show you how it's done." He proceeded to take five quick shots with his right hand, followed by five quick shots with his left hand. Each of the ten bullets hit the target squarely in the torso of the human silhouette, most hitting within inches of the center chest. He lowered the gun and smiled as he looked through the smoky air.

Henry let out a low whistle. "Are you sure you've only been shooting since... I mean... It's only been six months, right?" The silence hung in the air for a moment. Henry cleared his throat. "Man, I'm sorry... I didn't mean to...."

"It's okay." Jim returned the gun to the loading table. "To answer your question, yeah, I've only been shooting since Nicki's murder."

Henry looked to Jim, his face serious. "Does it help?"

Jim averted Henry's stare, started loading rounds into the magazine. "What do you mean?"

"Knowing that you have the ability to defend yourself... To kill someone if you needed to, or wanted to... Does it make you feel better?"

The weight of the question hit him like a fist, his hands let the magazine and the rounds drop to the table. Looking around for a moment, searching for the words, he bit his lower lip to keep it still. "Nothing helps." His voice was a hoarse whisper. "Nothing will ever help... She's gone Henry... Every night in my dreams I'm protecting her. I'm taking out every gangbanger on the streets. I'm her avenger." He lowered his head slowly shaking it back and forth. "Every morning I wake up to the truth... She's gone. I couldn't protect her... I was useless."

Henry put his hand on Jim's trembling shoulder. "Jim, you know it's not your fault. You weren't there. There was nothing you could have done."

In almost a growl. "I'm her Father, damn it. That's why I'm here. It's my job... To protect my family, especially my girls... I didn't do it."

THE VICTIM

He pounded his fist on the table. "I can assure you. It will never happen again. I will never let anyone hurt my family again."

Henry nodded his head absently. "I hear you man. I know what you're saying... But... Shooting targets is one thing. I'm not sure I could ever fire on another human being."

Jim's head snapped toward Henry, his eyes like lasers. "Oh, I assure you I can... I will." He quickly loaded new rounds into the magazine, slammed it into the grip of the 9mm. He took his position in the firing area. "They're animals Henry. They don't deserve to live. They roam the streets, destroying lives. The Police can't stop them. On the off chance they do catch them, Judges let them go." He aimed and fired several shots into the target. With the smoke hanging in the air and sound of the gun's explosion echoing off the walls, he added quietly. "Someone needs to pay."

Chapter 10

By the time Hunter arrived at the station on Thursday morning, Sanders had left little space on the white board in the conference room. Hunter set his laptop down on a table, took a sip of the drive-thru Starbucks and looked toward the board. "Looks like someone's been hard at work."

Without stopping, Sanders said, "I spent the afternoon making the rounds with the guys in Gangs and met with Myers from Central, Nguyen from Northeast, Sanchez from Northside and Hogan from East. I got a hell of an education on drugs, violence and wasted youth." He wrote a few more notes, then turned to Hunter. "Did you know there are over five hundred identified gangs in the Dallas Fort Worth area? Combined they have close to ten thousand members." He shook his head. "Man, that's a freaking army. Thank God they spend all their time fighting each other. If they ever managed to combine forces..." He let that thought hang as he turned back to the board.

Hunter nodded. "Maybe we should send them all to the Middle East. Let them terrorize the terrorists for a while." He shook his head. "It's been a while since I've paid much attention to the gang scene. The only time I get the call is if someone's dead. We've always been outmanned and outgunned. Good thing we're smarter and better looking," Both men grinned. "So, give me the summary version and we'll see if there's anything that helps us out."

"Well, while there's no doubt about us being better looking, I wouldn't start crowing too loud about outsmarting them. Gangs have become the new organized crime. Most local gangs have national or international affiliations. Our buddy Shadow and the Eastcide Kings, as the name would imply, are associated with the Kings out of LA. Varrio Central has at least loose ties with MS13."

THE VICTIM

Hunter turned from the board and looked at Sanders. "MS13? I thought they were in South America and Mexico."

"They are, but they've gone international. They're now one of the most violent gangs in the world. With the steady increase in illegal immigration, their numbers are growing in the U.S. In cities like Los Angeles they're challenging the Bloods and the Kings in just about every criminal enterprise from drugs to prostitution. Not only does that make for a natural rivalry between our local guys, it amps up the stakes and raises the potential for violence."

Hunter stared at Sanders, eyes focused, forehead crinkled. "Interesting. I was under the impression Fort Worth didn't have a major gang problem. Hogan's always bragging how we compare to other major cities."

"Well, you're partially right. The good news is that Fort Worth has one of the premier Gang Intervention programs in the country. It was started in the mid-nineties and by the turn of the new millennium, gang related violence had become the exception rather than the rule. The bad news is that between the continued influx of illegals, a shift in federal focus to fighting terrorism and recessionary budget cuts, we've seen a significant increase in gang activity. Tensions between all the gangs have started to rise." He turned to the board and pointed to each of the columns of notes. "Keep in mind that the Eastcide Kings and Varrio Central are just two gangs. You've got the Latin Lords and the Tango Blasters near the Stockyards. Northeast is dominated by the Asian Boyz and the Tiny Rascal Gangsters."

Hunter laughed. "Is that really their name?"

Sanders nodded. "Yep. They're home turf is the Beach Street and Belknap area. They're Vietnamese and they apparently make the Viet Cong look like pussies." He turned back to his notes. "On the board, I've listed the six most active gangs, one in each column. Below are bullet points of significant criminal activity in the last few weeks. As you can see, we're not exactly LA, lots of little crap, vandalism, petty theft, drug possession, an assault or two. The only major incident was a shooting at 30th and Ross. Apparently, a couple of cars opened fire near a party, two dead and a couple more in the hospital. From everything our guys have seen, it looks like the work of the Latin Lords and appears to be an internal squabble."

Hunter perused the board for a few moments. "I'm not seeing anything that jumps out at me as being related to our situation. Hell, Varrio Central and the Kings have been fairly quiet."

"Yeah, definitely not anything that would rise to the level of retaliation in the form of a planned hit."

Hunter sat down at his laptop. "I still want to capture this information in my database. That's going to take a bit. I also need to give an update to Sprabary. Why don't you meet me here after lunch and we'll go pay a visit to Pinche."

* * * *

That afternoon, after checking out through Dispatch, Hunter and Sanders weaved through light downtown traffic turning northwest on Commerce Street. The cold front had arrived as predicted and Hunter fiddled with the heater as they passed the Bass Performance Hall, Sundance Square and what used to be the Bass Towers, one was now a bank.

Commerce Street passes beside and then curves behind the courthouse which sits high on a ridge just south of the Trinity River at the bottom of a horseshoe shaped bend. Once Commerce merges with North Main, it crosses the river on a long sloping bridge.

As Hunter crossed the bridge, he thought about the contrast in the city. Behind him was a gleaming downtown with a revitalized tourist district, downtown condominiums and world renowned art museums. A sprawling new glass and chrome college campus sat on the banks of the river west of the courthouse. Less than a decade ago, that very spot was the 'projects'. It seemed that everything in downtown was either new or renovated in the past twenty years.

That revitalization hadn't made its way north of the river yet. Hunter knew that several miles north, the Stockyards were a tourist trap but the twenty-three blocks between the river and NW 23rd Street were a vast wasteland of heavy manufacturing, refining, rundown warehouses and abandoned buildings. This was home to Varrio Central.

Sanders broke the silence. "So, do you know this guy?"

"Our paths have crossed, but I wouldn't exactly classify us as old buddies." Hunter smirked. "I doubt I made much of an impression on him."

"How do you think he'll react?"

"Not sure. Hell, there's a good chance he hasn't even heard about the murders. It's not like he's the type to sit around and peruse the morning paper. Unless he heard it through the grapevine, he won't even know what we're talking about." Hunter slowed as they came off the bridge. "From what I know, unlike his name implies, he's supposed to be a fairly laid back guy. That is, unless you piss him off... And I have no intention of that."

They stopped at the light at NW 4th Street. To their left was a red brick building with boarded up windows and storefronts of businesses long abandoned. On top of the building were two dilapidated billboards advertising restaurants that hadn't been in business for years.

"So what exactly does his name imply?"

"Pinche Loco?" Hunter laughed. "Well, my Spanish isn't great but I'm pretty sure that translates to either crazy fucker or crazy idiot. Note that crazy is in either translation."

Sanders smiled. "Greeeaaaatt"

Hunter pulled through the intersection. A half block further, just past the only building which looked even minimally maintained, a massage parlor, he slowed and took a left into an overgrown lot. It was surrounded by a high wooden fence covered with plant growth and topped with barbed wire. The area inside the fence generally matched the surrounding neighborhood in its state of decay. There were several cars scattered around, some were parked, a couple appeared to be permanent rotting fixtures.

Toward the back of the lot, behind a wall of trees and bushes was a small brick building covered with elaborate graffiti art. The craftsmanship was impressive. Hunter mused as he sat in the Explorer. "Looks like they've got some future Picasso's living here."

"Yeah, remind me to call the Kimbell Museum to schedule an exhibit." Sanders smirked.

As they got out and walked toward the door, Hunter said, "Same drill as last time. Just stay relaxed and follow my lead. We're here to find out if they know anything and to subtly let them know Shadow suspects them."

"No problem Boss."

They stood to the side of the door and knocked announcing themselves as Police. They were met with silence at first and had to repeat the process. Finally, the sound of movement from inside and the door cracked open. A half asleep voice from inside mumbled, "What do you want?"

"We need to speak with Pinche."

After several more questions, the door finally opened wide revealing a short, stocky Hispanic man in his early thirties. He wore gray workpants, a flannel long sleeve shirt, wrap around shades and a green bandana on his head. He glared at them for a moment and said, "I'm Pinche."

Hunter opened his jacket slowly to pull out his ID and to make sure Pinche noticed his holstered 9mm. "I'm Detective Jake Hunter. This is Detective Sanders. We need to talk about a couple of dead Kings."

"Why should I give a fuck about a couple of dead Kings?"

"Because we're trying to make sure that the same thing doesn't happen to you or your boys. Mind if we come in?"

"Yeah I do mind." Pinche stepped forward onto the porch and closed the door behind him. A moment later, a couple of his hombres stepped from around the side of the building and stared through sunglasses at Hunter and Sanders. They both kept their hands conspicuously concealed. Hunter gave Sanders a glance. He responded by moving to face the newcomers.

After surveying the situation, Hunter looked to Pinche and continued. "Look, we don't think you had anything to do with those killings..."

Pinche cut him off. "Then why you here?"

"Because Shadow's pretty convinced that you did."

At this, the glare on Pinche's face softened. "What you talkin' about? That fuckin' Pendejo. We got our own turf. Don't need their fuckin' ghetto. Ain't that right vato's?" He looked over to his boys, both nodded imperceptibly.

"I'm sure that's the case but I still need to ask you some questions."

Pinche shrugged. "Whatever."

THE VICTIM

Hunter and Pinche fell into a tense question and answer session while Sanders and the vatos eyed each other. When he realized the questions weren't getting anywhere and Pinche's crew was getting anxious, Hunter wrapped up the conversation and directed Sanders to the SUV. As they crossed the river going south, Hunter looked ahead at the courthouse silhouetted against the Fort Worth skyline of glass towers and felt like he was returning from a trip into a foreign country.

Sanders broke his train of thought. "So that didn't get us much. Where do we go from here?"

"Well, if nothing else, maybe Pinche and his boys will lay a little low for a while." Hunter stared ahead. "As for where we go, hell if I know."

Chapter 11

The Victim hit the ignition and felt the Impala rumble to life. He smiled. *You may not look like much Betsy, but you do purr.* A moment later, he pulled out of the monthly parking garage. It was across town from his house and leased under an assumed name, one more meticulous precaution. He was driven, not stupid.

A shiver ran up his spine. *Is it that cold? No. Not really.* He turned up the heater anyway. The moon was bright and high in the sky with no clouds. *Great night for a hunt.* He stared ahead, pupils wide, twitching around. His fingers tapping on the steering wheel created the only sound other than the V8's rumble.

The world passed in a blur as he made his way down I-30 and turned south on I-35. He passed over Hattie Street and reflexively looked left, checked his watch. He smiled, took a quick shallow breath. *Right on schedule.* It was earlier in the night than his first excursion. With the colder weather and being Thursday night, he wanted to make sure targets would be out. Who knew, maybe gangbangers didn't stay out as late on school nights.

He exited Rosedale, looped under the freeway and drove north on the access road. He absorbed the low income area surrounding him. *What a hell hole. No wonder the gangs have taken over.* He contemplated that thought for a moment but dismissed it. *Just because a weak immune system allows a virus to spread is no reason to allow that virus to continue to live.* He smiled. *That's it. Just call me the antibiotic.*

As he pulled up to the light at Hattie, he refocused on his task. He turned right, passed the United Rentals lot and began surveying the area. He knew his targets inside and out. As with his first hunt, he had already researched the area on line using Google Earth and Mapquest. Still, criminal records and the internet can only take you so far. Nothing beats old fashioned reconnaissance.

One block down on his left was Van Zandt Guinn Park. As he passed, he looked just beyond the playground area and saw dark figures gathered around a picnic table. He smiled. *As predictable as the sun coming up, or in this case, as the sun going down.* He drove past, circled the block around Van Zandt Guinn Elementary, came back around on Missouri and passed the figures once again. A car was pulling away. One of the figures was walking back to the group stuffing dollars in his pocket. *Four of them. Dealing. Hmm. Definitely Kings. More than expected. Oh well, just means more potential targets. They're clueless anyway.*

Taking a left, he was back to his starting point on Hattie. He turned once again on Kentucky but this time continued on past the elementary school and pulled into the parking lot of the Renfro Foods plant. He breathed deeply as the smell of cooking spices drifted into the car. *Damn, they make good hot sauce. I've got to remember to get a jar of the jalapeño sauce.* He found a secluded corner of the lot, parked and shut off the car.

It was quiet, as expected. He slid a pair of latex gloves on, stepped out of the car and back to the trunk. He'd taken the bulbs out of both the dome light and the trunk light. No need to attract unwanted attention. In the trunk were his tools, the dual shoulder holsters, the 9mm's, his overcoat. There was a duffle bag full of an assortment of items he consider his emergency kit. Hopefully, he wouldn't need that tonight. He meticulously checked each item as he suited up.

When he closed the trunk, his heart rate rose, his breath went shallow. He restarted the car, drove back down Kentucky and parked on the east side of the park. His sight line to the picnic tables was blocked by the school's physical education building. There was an opening in the fence line and he parked the car directly beside it. The music from their boombox blared across the park.

Last time he'd been scared, down deep hoping they wouldn't come after him. This time was different. He could feel it. Nervous, sure, but ready this time. He wanted them to come. He'd make sure of it.

He walked around the school so that he'd come up on their west side. He'd have to walk past them to get back to his car. He moved quickly, staying in the shadows, not wanting to be seen by anyone until it was time. His pulse raced, he started to sweat. He could see each breath as he exhaled. Moving south on the sidewalk on Missouri, he glanced to his right and saw the tan church. *Bless me Father for I have sinned.* He laughed quietly as he realized it was a Baptist church. *Sorry Father, wrong denomination.*

He saw them, his legs stopped involuntarily. His stomach twisted, his lungs froze for a moment and started back with a gulp. *Is this smart? There's too many of them. It's too soon.* Shaking his head, he focused his eyes, took a deep breath and continued.

He was coming up on them now. As he walked past, his peripheral vision caught movement. *They see me.* He cut his eyes sharply in their direction, not moving his head. They were staring. He was on the sidewalk on the outside of the fence. They didn't move, just stared. *Keep watching boys.*

About thirty feet down, there was an opening in the fence that led to the playground area. He turned in, started across the open park area inside the fence. He saw movement from the group. *How will I get all four?* He cut his eyes and turned his head just enough to see. They weren't all coming, just two. *Guess they just sent the soldiers. Good, split them up.* He walked faster. They walked faster, gaining on him at an angle.

His hands in his pockets gripped the pistols. His vision narrowed with each step. He heard their footfalls.

"Hey!" The voice barked. He jumped, kept walking. "Hey muthafucka I'm talking to you."

He stopped, heard the footsteps continue toward him. He looked over his shoulder, caught a flash of light, his heart jumped. The one closest to him was moving fast. *Oh shit. Oh God, a knife.* He reacted, raised his guns as he turned. He saw the knife coming. The gangbanger eyes widened as the first bullet ripped through his chest. The explosion seemed to come long after the hole opened and the tissue sprayed. The knife hung in the air as the banger fell at his feet.

For a split second there was silence. No one moved.

"Muthafucka!" The second man, ten feet away, screamed, moved toward him reaching into his jacket. The Victim opened up with both pistols. The man's body danced jerkily as if being electrocuted.

Flesh ripped and bones shattered. The man fell in a lump. The air was foggy with a mixture of gun powder and human matter.

He sensed movement by the picnic tables. He heard a gun blast. It wasn't his. *Oh God. Gotta move.* He fired once in their direction, turned and ran faster than he dreamed he could. More gunshots, the sound of a nearby ricochet. He was moving fast. They were moving faster. *There's the car. Get the starter.* He holstered one of the guns, dug in his pocket, hit the starter button as he came up on the car. The engine fired. *Thank you Betsy.*

He turned and fired several shots. Both men dove for the ground forty feet away. He was in the car and moving when he heard a barrage of shots. They were unloading on him. He felt one hit the back of the car as he turned left on Hattie.

Not wanting to be on a major street, he took a quick left on Illinois and melted into the neighborhood. He tried to catch his breath at a stop sign. His heart was tearing out of his chest, his lungs ached. He hadn't planned on a foot race. He wheezed, thought he might pass out. *Can't sit still. Oh shit. Witnesses. Will they talk? No, no. Surely not.* He drove slowly through the neighborhood just to keep moving.

His heart rate slowed. He stilled gulped air. *That was close.* He smiled. *Two more down. What a rush!*

He made his way north through the neighborhood, came out on Vickery. As he turned toward the freeway and the downtown skyline, he heard sirens in the distance.

Chapter 12

It was late, almost midnight, as Hunter drove north on I-35. He was heading home after another long day in a very long week. He pinched the bridge of his nose and blinked to keep focused. He slowed when he saw the fire engines and ambulance on the roadside a few hundred yards before the Western Center Boulevard exit. *Damn, that looks bad. I should stop. God, it's late. I'm so close to home. I'll just stop to make sure it's covered.*

He stopped behind the first fire engine, engaged the emergency flashers and got out. He could smell spilled fuel, burnt rubber, and dust in the air. The sounds of commotion drifted from in front of the fire engine. He stepped around the corner and took in the scene. His lungs stopped and he stumbled, nearly falling when he saw the mangled blue Camry. His eyes immediately noticed the 'Keep Austin Weird' bumper sticker and then swept forward to see the figure seated, slumped in the front seat.

Instincts kicked in and he was at her side in an instant. He reached over and gently turned her face to him, his heart pounding, barely able to speak. "Gina! Gina, baby, are you alright?"

She looked up, her hair mangled, blood on her forehead. She smiled. "Yeah. It's just a scr…"

The ring of the phone shattered his sleep and Hunter bolted up in bed. Panther shot out of the bed and down the hall adding to Hunter's confusion. His heart pounded, sweat soaked the sheets. He tried to catch his breath, focus. The phone rang again as his mind raced. He looked at the other side of the bed. Empty… Just as it had been for five years.

The phone rang a third time. He reached over, fumbled in the dark and picked up the earpiece. "Hunter." His voice rough from sleep.

"It's me again Margaret." Deep laughter followed for several seconds. "You remember that song, don't you?"

Hunter shook his head, confused, tried to clear his thoughts. "What?"

"Cowboy, it's me, Harrison. You remember that old song, don't you? You know... I think it was by Ray Stevens. The one about the crank caller who kept calling a woman named Margaret. When he finally got caught and arrested, he got his one phone call at the police station and who does he call? Margaret!" Harrison belly laughed as if that was the funniest thing he'd heard in weeks. Hunter stayed silent, still coming up from his dream. "Well, maybe it's not that funny at one in the morning when you've been sleeping." Harrison chuckled again.

"I'm assuming you didn't wake me up just to remind me of a song I'd hoped would never again enter my mind."

"Ah. You know me Cowboy. I only call with happy news."

"Yeah, right."

"So, you got another couple of stiff gangbangers. Looks like Eastcide Kings. Similar to the last one. Patrol's already on the scene. Crime Scene and ME's on the way."

"Hang on." Hunter got out of bed, shivered when the cool air hit his sweaty skin. He walked to the kitchen, turned on the light and grabbed a notepad. Panther blinked and moved under the kitchen table. "All right. Give me what you know."

Harrison filled him in like last time while Hunter wrote down the pertinent information. He hung up, went straight to the coffee pot. Panther came out of hiding and rubbed against his legs. "Panther, what the hell is going on in this city? We've got gangbangers dropping like flies." He scooped in the coffee, poured in the water and hit brew. "What do you think? Yeah, it's not a major loss for the city, but..." He shook his head, breathed in the aroma of the brewing coffee. "I've got a bad feeling on this one Panther. I think some real bad stuff's gonna hit the fan before it's done." He reached over, poured a cup and walked back to the bedroom. *So much for Sprabary thinking this one was going to be low profile.* After a quick shower, Hunter went through his normal routine; feed the cat, check his gun, check his phone battery, pack his laptop. Twenty minutes flat and he rolled out in his Explorer. As he came up the onramp of southbound I-35, he glanced over, saw the spot of Gina's crash. His dream came back to him and he shared the rest of his drive with memories, both good and bad.

Coming up on the Hattie Street overpass, Hunter saw the glow of lights on his left. He exited and found a spot to park on Missouri Street, west of the playground. Between emergency vehicles and temporary flood lights, two A.M. looked like high noon. He noted that the first responders had secured the crime scene by essentially cordoning off the entire playground area.

Hunter noticed a crowd, maybe forty people, had gathered and lined the park's fences. *Must have been a hell of a disturbance to generate this much attention.* Playing the odds that Stacy would be on scene, Hunter had stopped at a convenience store and bought two coffees to go. Not exactly Starbucks, but it was the best he could do under the circumstances. He grabbed the coffees, flashed his badge and crossed under the tape.

He stopped for a moment and absorbed the scene. Unlike last time, the area was spread out. Patrolmen were positioned around the perimeter for crowd control. Stacy had four techs performing a grid search with high powered flash lights marking evidence as they walked. There were a lot of markers and there were sight barriers set up in two locations. Doc and Stacy conferred near one.

Hunter saw Sanders. "Welcome to Homicide."

"Thanks. Nothing quite like a one A.M. wakeup call. I don't suppose one of those coffees is for me."

"Nope." Before they moved, Hunter motioned out to the area. "Tell me what you see. How does it differ from the first scene?"

Sanders smirked. "At this time in the morning, it's all a blur." He then scanned the scene. "It's bigger, more spread out, more open, a whole lot more public."

"What does that tell you?"

"Assuming it's our same guy, he's getting bolder, maybe a little reckless."

Hunter nodded. "Let's go get a closer look. Stacy's coffee is getting cold." They stepped under the tape and started toward the first sight barrier. Hunter continued. "Walk slowly. Absorb the scene."

Stacy came around the barrier, her smile lit up when she saw

Hunter. *Damn. Even at two in the morning, she looks good.* He held out the cup to her, steam rising from the hole in the lid.

"Aren't you a doll? Thanks."

"We're going to be here a while. I figured you wouldn't take the time to stop on the way."

"You know me too well Cowboy." She put the cup to her lips, took a sip and closed her eyes. "Mmm."

"And where, pray tell, is mine?" Doc's booming voice turned their heads. "I guess I don't rate, do I Cowboy?"

"Sorry Doc, only got two hands. Besides, Sanders will be making a run in a few."

Sanders smiled. "Yeah, Doc, as soon as we get an initial rundown, I'll go take care of you and me."

Doc struck a hoity pose, shot a faux sneer toward Hunter. "Nice to see someone has their priorities in line."

As Doc returned to work on the bodies, Hunter looked at Stacy. "So, what do we know so far?"

"Well, we've still got a long way to go, but… The vics appear to be Kings. Two black males, early twenties, gang tats, doo rags. Both were armed, one with a knife, one with a gun. Both weapons were out but the knife was clean and the gun hadn't been fired."

Hunter stopped her. "The gun wasn't fired?"

"Nope."

Hunter turned to Billy, pointed to all the evidence markers around them. "If this guy's gun wasn't fired but we've got dozens of spent casings all over this crime scene, what does that tell you?"

"One thing's for sure. It was a hell of a gun fight. If it was a single shooter like last time, he couldn't have fired them all. He'd have had to stop and reload. Plus, if these guys weren't firing back, and I think that's pretty clear, he'd have no reason to keep shooting at them. So, there had to be others at the scene, presumably friends of our two stiffs."

Stacy nodded. "Bingo. There were at least four different weapons fired. We've got casings from a 380, a 45 and two 9mm's." Hunter raised an eyebrow. She continued. "Yes. My curiosity got the best of me so I checked some of the 9mm casings. Just like last time, all pristine, two distinct firing pin signatures. Sure looks like the same two guns. Once Doc pulls the lead out of these guys, we'll be able to make a definitive match."

Sanders spoke up. "Any idea how many shells of each caliber?"

"Not yet. We're still finding them. They're everywhere. But we've already counted over twenty for the 9mm's. He almost emptied his weapons. Since only a half dozen hit our vics..." She looked at Sanders. "Your thinking was right on track, he was definitely shooting at something else." She pointed in the direction of Kentucky Street. "There's a whole pile of 380's and 45's all in one spot. Looks like our vic's friends stopped and unloaded, probably trying to hit someone moving away. My guess would be a car. They would've kept chasing if the shooter was on foot."

Sanders nodded. "Any idea on direction? Was the car moving toward Hattie or back north?"

"No idea yet. We just sent a couple of uniforms knocking on doors." She pointed toward some small, rundown frame houses. "If he was moving toward Hattie, all four of those houses would have been in the line of fire. We'll see how many bullets we find in the walls."

Hunter had been pacing, listening to the discussion. "Okay, so we've got a sense of the running gun battle and that there were at least two other Kings here." He turned back to the bodies. "So Doc, what can you tell us so far?"

Doc, who had been kneeling beside one of the vics, stood up and dusted off the knees. "Well, as you can guess, both appear to have died from gunshots, most likely 9mm's. This one..." He pointed down. "Our lad who brought a knife to the gun fight, was shot at extremely close range, a single round straight through the sternum, dead before he hit the ground." He turned back toward the other body. "Our other fellow wasn't quite as lucky. Multiple wounds, at least five, from a little distance. There's a better than good chance he had at least a few moments to contemplate his life before it drained from him. Not long though. Anything else we'll have to get back at the shop."

"Thanks Doc." Hunter nodded as he paced back and forth between the two corpses. After a moment, he looked at Stacy. "I'll let you get back to it. I'm going to check with the guys knocking on doors."

He turned to Billy. "Probably a good time for you to get Doc some coffee. He's starting to look cranky."

Doc looked up. "Incredibly observant, even for a detective."

Hunter and Sanders started back toward the perimeter. Noise and activity made them stop and look up. A car screeched to a stop, the doors flew open and the crowd erupted into chaos. Shadow shoved his way through, one of his bodyguards in tow. People scattered. He was almost under the tape when a patrolman grabbed his shoulder. In an instant, officers and gangbangers were pushing, shoving and yelling. Hunter and Sanders broke into a sprint.

Shadow saw Hunter, rage filled his eyes. "You muthafucka!" Two cops held him back, one was calling for backup. "I listened to you! I listened to you and look what it got me! Never again muthafucka!"

Sanders was at the tape, hand resting on his weapon, his stare intent. Hunter ducked under the tape, went straight to Shadow, his momentum carried him forward as he shoved Shadow. "Don't give me that shit. Where are the others?"

"What you mean?"

"You know what I mean. Where are the other Kings that were here tonight?" Hunter was in his face now, the two men glared at one another.

Shadow gritted his teeth. "I don't know what you talking about, weren't nobody else here, least as far as I know."

Hunter slowly shook his head never breaking eye contact. "Bullshit... Shadow, you can either help this investigation or slow it down. From the looks of things, slowing it down just means more of your boys lying in the streets. Is that what you want?"

Shadow started backing away, moving to his car. Poking his finger in the air as he retreated. "This shit stops here. This shit stops tonight. The Kings will find who done this. We don't need you or your cop buddies." He opened the car door, got in and slammed it behind him, his driver cranked the engine. As they backed out, he yelled, "Someone's gonna pay for this!"

The car turned and accelerated away. A patrolman adjusted his gun belt, looked at Hunter. "Do we need to go after him?"

Hunter's eyes were locked on the disappearing red glow of the tail lights. He shook his head. "No. I know where to find him." He turned back to Sanders who was still keyed up, smiled. "Nothing like an early morning stare-down with a known killer to get the blood going."

"Better you than me." Sanders paused for a moment. "So, why is he wasting his time on this social call? His boys must have seen the shooter. Why not just go hunting?"

Hunter shook his head. "They may have seen the shooter but it wasn't someone they know. That fits with our theory that it's not another gang. They'd have recognized another gang… Shadow's visit was his subtle way of telling us he doesn't know who did it." Concern washed across his face. "Of course, that doesn't mean he won't bust up half the city trying to figure it out."

"It also doesn't help us figure it out." Sanders took a deep breath, his body visibly relaxed. "Looks like we're gonna be here a while, probably a good time for my coffee run."

Hunter smiled and nodded toward Doc. "Yeah, he's looking a little droopy. I'll check with the guys knocking on doors." He turned to survey the scene again. As his eyes moved across, he saw Stacy staring at him, her face stricken with fear, concern. He flashed a reassuring smile. She sighed, shook her head and went back to work.

As the sun broke over the low rooftops east of the park, the scene had started to break up, the bodies had been transported and Stacy directed the last of her team as they packed up. Most of the crowd had ambled back into their houses to sleep through the morning; few in this part of town had early wakeups for jobs.

Hunter sat at a picnic table, rubbed his bloodshot eyes and keyed information into his laptop and downloaded pictures from his phone. Sanders sat across from him, flipped through his notepad with his hand supporting his head.

"Well, don't you two look lively?" Stacy's voice sounded way too chipper considering it was barely sunup and they had been on the scene since before two am.

Both men looked up wearily. Hunter smiled. "At least I have an excuse, I'm older than the rest of you. I don't know what the hell's wrong with Sanders."

Sanders turned quickly to retort but stopped short, shook his head and smiled. "Hard to argue with the truth."

Hunter stretched and stood up. "Why don't we head over to the Paris Coffee Shop for some breakfast and a debrief?"

Chapter 13

The Friday morning rush hour was just building as Hunter headed toward the coffee shop, phone in hand.

"Has the media gotten hold of this yet?" Sprabary's tone was grim.

"No one but the night desk writer so far." Hunter paused as he weaved through traffic. "Won't be long though. My guess is we won't make the end of the day before the calls start."

"That'll be if we're lucky. We need to show some movement on this thing or the loonies will start screaming." There was silence on the line for a moment, Hunter waited knowing Sprabary wasn't finished. "Look, Hunter, this is no reflection on you. I know you're doing what needs to be done. But we need to get more eyes on it. I'm going to reach out to the gang units and see who they can spare, maybe set up a coordinated effort. Check in with me later."

"Will do." Hunter signed off with a sigh as he pulled into the strip center and parked in front of the Paris Coffee Shop. *Coordinated effort? Sounds more like a coordinated headache.* He got out of his Explorer in time to meet Stacy and Sanders as they got to the door.

Hunter followed them into the coffee shop, noted the Texas memorabilia and antique western pictures on the wall. *Not exactly what you'd expect in a place called the Paris Coffee Shop.* A waitress greeted them with a thick twang and said "Sure Hon" when Hunter requested a table in the rear with some privacy.

After ordering full breakfasts, the three sipped coffee and warmed up from the night outside in the cool air. Stacy finally broke the silence. "So Cowboy, what do you think?"

Hunter paused, sipped his coffee and then exhaled heavily. "We all agree that it looks like our boy from Monday, right?" Stacy and

Sanders both nodded as Hunter continued. "Let's run down what we've learned." He looked toward Sanders. "What do we know about our victims?"

Sanders opened his notebook and scanned down the page. "We pulled wallets from both bodies and took prints for confirmation. I'm fairly confident our boys have been in the system before. Our knife fighter was Marcus Stevens, nineteen, and our gun fighter was Terrance Washington, twenty. Both had Eastcide Kings tattoos and wore colors." He grinned at Hunter who had his laptop out and keyed as Sanders spoke. "You ran Shadow off before we got a chance to confirm with him, but it's safe to say these guys were part of his crew. We'll run full histories on them later today."

"Good. I don't expect to find any revelations but we'll review the histories like last time." He shook his head. "Now that we're up to four bodies, the chances of this being personal are slim. Our shooter may have something against the Kings in general but I doubt he hunted down these four individuals." Hunter looked toward Stacy, an involuntary smile crossed his face. "How about you? What else do you have?"

Stacy paused for a moment as the waitress set plates down in front of them. The smell of eggs, sausage and pancakes brought weary smiles. All three dug in. Stacy continued between bites. "So we talked about the assortment of casings. We ended up finding fifteen 380's and twelve 45's. I'm guessing those guys emptied their clips. Several of each caliber had partial prints. Might be enough to identify our other Kings. As for the 9mm, we found ten from one gun and nine from the other. He left the scene with a few shots left."

She took a few bites while she referenced her notes. Hunter interjected. "I'm assuming we never found either the 380 or the 45?"

Stacy shook her head. "No doubt the guns left the scene with our mystery Kings. We did collect the remnants of a tail light at the street corner. I'll have one of my guys research it to see if they can match it to a make and model."

"Another thing we'll want to do is to check for traffic cameras in the area and do a comparison to those from Monday. Who knows? We might get lucky."

Sanders chuckled. "Yeah, right." Hunter shrugged.

Stacy forked her final piece of sausage and raised her eyebrows at Hunter. "How about you Cowboy?"

Hunter had already pushed aside his empty plate and opened his laptop. He scanned down the screen. "Well, I think you're right about the tail light. Based on the number of shots fired and the direction, I've got to believe our gangbangers hit something. I spoke with the homeowners on Kentucky and Hattie. Both houses on Kentucky got hit with slugs and the two houses on Hattie got hit. My guess is that he headed west after he made his turn. That should help narrow down the traffic cameras."

He paused for a moment, continued to scan. "Beyond that and the fact that nobody saw anything, we don't know much more than we did on Monday." He closed his laptop. "All I know is that the shit's about to land on Sprabary's desk and when it does, you know where it's going to roll."

The three finished their coffee in silence. Hunter could feel the weariness of the long night creeping into his bones. It was trumped only by the churning in his stomach as he thought about what was rolling down the hill.

Chapter 14

The Victim sat at his office desk, nervously tapped his fingers on the wood, a sheen of sweat covered his brow as his eyes darted around his desk. The pulse in his temple thumped and he was out of breath even though he had barely moved all morning. *Just act normal. No one knows anything. Those punks bolted as soon as I left.* He smirked for a moment. *Some loyalty. Left their gang brothers dying in the dirt.*

He jumped and dropped his pen when the phone rang. He let it ring twice more while he composed himself. Caught it on the fourth ring and answered. "Yes... Mmm Hmm... Is that today? Are you sure? I'm not showing it on my calendar. Is there any way we can get that pushed back? Yes, yes. Please try. I can't possibly be ready today."

He hung up the phone, reached into his pocket and retrieved a white handkerchief. He wiped his forehead and rested his head on his hand for a moment. *Get it together man. Focus! Get back to work.*

He started reading through some papers but his mind drifted back to the park, the look on the gangbangers face as he realized a bullet had just blown through his chest. He smiled. *Arrogant prick. He thought I was easy pickings. I guess he thought wrong.*

He refocused on the papers and tried again but to no avail. He couldn't work, couldn't focus, couldn't think. Last night kept replaying in his head. *What if those guys talk to the cops? What do they really know? A guy wearing a long coat refused to be a victim? They attacked me. I was just walking across the playground. I had every right to defend myself.*

A knock on the door startled him from thoughts. He looked up as a colleague stuck his head through the door. "Hey man. You've been awfully heads down today. What's up?"

"Just trying to get through these mounds of paper."

The man let himself in and sat down across the desk. "So, did you hear about the shooting over on the east side last night?" The Victim raised his eyebrows in a question. The man continued. "Two more gangbangers were found dead. Just like on Monday... Man, they keep this up, we'll be out of jobs."

The Victim chuckled. "Well I wouldn't start looking for a new job just yet. My guess is there're more than enough gangbangers, pimps and scum to keep us busy well into retirement. I'm not going to get too concerned until that pile of crap in my inbox starts to shrink."

His visitor leaned back. "Yeah, yeah. You're right about that." He looked across the desk. "You sure you're okay? You look a little pale."

"I'm fine, just didn't get enough sleep last night. You know I'm not as young as I used to be."

"You and me both my friend." He got up and moved to the door. "Well, good luck making a dent in that 'pile of crap'."

After his visitor left, the Victim got up and closed the door, leaned against the wall. He wiped his forehead again, looked at his hand. It was shaking. *I can't deal with this today.* He sat back down, turned and looked at the photos on his credenza.

He picked up one of the photos, his eyes glistened as he looked at the family, happy, smiling. He missed her. A part of him was gone. He sat, reveled in his memories. He lost track of time, finally snapping out of his thoughts when a fire engine sped by on the street below his window, siren blaring. *How long have I been sitting here?*

He looked at the clock on his desk. *Only two fifteen. This day's going to last forever. I can't take this. I've got to get out of here.*

He picked up the phone, banged in four numbers, heard a female voice answer. "I'm going to take the rest of the day off... No, nothing's wrong, just need a break. Call me on my cell if anything comes up."

He hung up, wiped his forehead again, packed up his briefcase, and left. The brisk weather outside snapped him out of his fog. *I need to cover my tracks, get the car fixed, find out who those two bangers were. I need to get to them before the police get them to talk.* His mind was focused now, back in the game.

He punched numbers into his cell as he swept through the

lobby. "Hey Trey, how've you been?" He patiently listened to a story about a wife, a car and a garage wall. It sounded like an unfortunate weekend. Once Trey seemed to lose some steam, the Victim interjected, "I was calling to see if you could do me a favor. I know you're not directly involved, but I'm trying to track down some information for a buddy. You know that shooting last night..."

He made his request and moved on to the next number on his list. *Just a couple of discreet inquiries, can't be too obvious but I've got to get those names.* He hung up, slipped his cell into his jacket pocket. A quick change of clothes at home, a drive across town to an out of the way junkyard and his ghetto ride would be as good as, well, a ghetto ride.

Chapter 15

As Hunter left Lieutenant Sprabary's office, he felt the weariness settling into his bones. Long hours were a part of the job and he'd pulled more than his share of all-nighters but for some reason this week and this case had worn him out. He seemed out of practice.

He rolled his head around and stretched his shoulders. As he sat down, his cell phone rang. When he looked at the caller ID, he shook his head and hit the disconnect button. *Andre Kipton. Shit. The sharks are circling now.* His phone rang again, and once more he hit the disconnect button. *Persistent bastard.*

On the third attempt, he gave up, popped in his earpiece and answered. "Hunter."

"Cowboy! I thought you'd never pick up. Are you trying to tell me something?" The voice was overly chipper for the middle of the afternoon.

"Apparently it didn't work. I'd ask you what you want but for some reason, I'm sure you're going to tell me anyway."

"There you go again with that attitude. You know I'm your favorite reporter."

"Isn't that kind of like saying you're the tallest midget?" Hunter smiled at his own joke.

"Sounds like that sensitivity training they put you through is starting to pay off." Kipton paused for a beat and then got to his point. "So I hear you're working the gangbanger murders. What the hell did they do, demote you?"

Hunter shook his head. "Yeah, something like that... Look Kipton, I really can't talk about this thing right now. We're still early in the investigation."

"Early in the investigation? Didn't the first set of murders happen almost a week ago? Sounds to me like the FWPD put it on the back burner cause it's just a couple of black guys that got whacked."

"That's bullshi…" Hunter caught himself before he completely lost it. He took a deep breath. "Like I said, we're early in the investigation. And just for the record, no, it hasn't been a week, it's been four days." He paused for a moment, realized a little publicity might not be a bad thing for this case. "Tell you what Kipton, if you can cool your jets for a few hours, I might be able to get you some information. I'm driving out to my folks' place after work and I'll have some windshield time to fill. I'll call you then."

"Now that's the Cowboy I know and love. Don't stand me up."

Hunter was left with a silent Bluetooth and a growing headache. He spent the afternoon compiling notes on both crime scenes and both sets of victims. It was an exercise in futility. No witnesses. No physical evidence beyond clean shell casings. Victims no one cares about. The only consistencies were that the victims were all gangbangers, specifically Eastcide Kings and done by the same shooter.

Based on his conversation earlier in the day with Sprabary, he knew things were heating up. Race relations in the city had improved over the last few years but not showing enough attention to a set of black victims could torpedo those efforts in a flash. Of course, showing too much attention to the killings of known thugs could get the redneck faction up in arms as well. He knew his best option was to figure this thing out fast.

By 4:30 that afternoon, his eyes hurt as much as his head. He made a final round of calls to Sanders, Stacy and Doc to see what progress had been made. There was little to report. He told Sanders that Sprabary was calling in the reinforcements in the morning and he needed to be ready to provide a full background on both cases.

He checked out with Dispatch, made his way through downtown and headed toward Weatherford on I-30. The day was still chilly as he drove straight into the November sun hanging in the western sky. When he cleared the western edge of town at Loop 820, he recalled his promise to call Andre Kipton. Over the years, he and Kipton, who wrote for the Fort Worth Star Telegram, had managed to maintain a rocky but mutually beneficial relationship. He got help with research, the rare 'planted' story or detail and the occasional delayed article. Kipton got insider information on investigations and the internal department politics. It was a necessary evil.

He made the call and spent twenty minutes bringing Kipton up to speed on the two separate investigations. It was easy to not get too specific with as little as they knew. He kept it to the basics, played down the connection between the cases, left out the theory of the single shooter and played up the thought that this was not 'gang on gang' violence.

By the time he finished with Kipton, he was well outside the city limits, in the open, flat terrain between Fort Worth and Weatherford. It was still a nice country drive between the two cities but not nearly as country as it used to be. As they continued to grow toward each other, it seemed less like a road trip and more like just going across town. There was still enough of a shift from city to country that Hunter could feel the stress of the week begin to peel away as sun dropped toward the horizon.

He looked forward to dinner with his folks. It had been a while, and besides, this new case would interest his father. Charlie Hunter had retired less than a decade ago from the Texas Rangers, the legendary, elite statewide criminal investigation unit. Charlie had spent nearly thirty years with the agency and had worked almost every kind of investigation from murder to narcotics to human trafficking. He even spent two years as the head of security for Governor Ann Richards in the early nineties.

Hunter parked in the driveway, turned off the engine, rolled down the window and sat for a moment. He closed his eyes and breathed deeply. The cold, crisp, fresh country air felt good in his lungs. The only sounds he could hear were the ticking of his engine as it cooled and the myriad of nature noises, the chirping of crickets, the croaking of a frog, the distant rustling of tree branches in the slight breeze. He had never really considered himself a country boy but as he sat and absorbed the moment, it made him feel good to be out of the city.

With a final deep breath of the scent of dried leaves mixed with just a hint of mesquite smoke from the chimney, Hunter rolled the window up and made his way up the rock sidewalk. He rang the doorbell and let himself in the door. It was never a good idea to just walk into a house unannounced, especially if the resident was a former Texas Ranger.

The aroma of grilled onions and spices from the kitchen met him in the foyer and brought a smile to his face. His mother's voice rang out over the sound of a closing oven door. "Is that my long lost son?"

Hunter smiled. "The one and only." He came around the corner into the kitchen. "How are you Mom?"

Tall and lean, like her son, Olivia Hunter was tan, with dark hair and a strong bone structure that came from her distant Texas Comanche heritage. Her striking blues eyes resulted from the slightly more recent German influence. She was a fifth generation native Texan whose roots dated back to The Republic of Texas when her Comanche and German ancestors were often in conflict.

She gave her son a hug, surveyed him up and down. "I'm doing fine, but you look like you haven't eaten or slept in a week. You need to take better care of yourself."

Hunter gently dismissed her comments off with a kiss on her cheek and a wave of his hand. "Where's Dad?"

"Oh, you know your father. He's upstairs in his office. Why don't you grab the two of you some beers and go extract him? Dinner will be ready shortly."

With two cold Shiners in his hand, Hunter stopped in the open doorway to his father's office and rapped lightly on the door. Charlie turned his attention from his computer screen to the door and met his son with a big grin. "Jake!" He stood, reached out his hand to grab his son's hand and was handed a beer instead. His laugh erupted as he set down the beer and embraced his son in a bear hug. Charlie directed him to a chair. "How the hell are you son?"

The two men caught up on small talk, football and the weather. It was clear that Jake was Charlie Hunter's son. They shared the blond hair, although Charlie's was now almost completely gray, and the intense green eyes. Charlie was built thicker and Jake was an inch or so taller but they both had easy smiles and minds that were constantly analyzing.

About the time they emptied their bottles, Olivia called them down for dinner. She had made homemade Chili Rellenos stuffed with grilled onions, spicy chicken and Monterey Jack cheese. Hunter's Mom was a wonderful cook and this was one of his favorites. The three caught up on life as they enjoyed the meal. Hunter silently chastised himself for not visiting more often.

After retirement, his father had purchased forty acres of flat, Texas plains and had spent two years designing and building their retirement home. It wasn't exactly a ranch by Texas standards, but Hunter knew it provided enough room for Charlie to feel like he was away from all the crazies he had dealt with during his career. The house was a sprawling two story ranch style clad in Austin limestone with lots of wrought iron and exposed wood highlights.

One of the unique architectural aspects Charlie had built into the house was a third floor observation room. It was round and accessed by a spiral wrought iron staircase that entered into the center of the room. Because of its height and the floor to ceiling windows, the three hundred and sixty degree views provided were stunning. On a clear night like this one, you could choose to enjoy the starlit night and the dark horizon off to the Southwest or catch the faint city lights of Fort Worth thirty miles to the east.

After dinner, Charlie and Jake were sharing the views and a quiet moment while sipping chilled Patron Anejo Tequila and gently puffing on Arturo Fuente Hemingway Classic cigars. The aroma and taste should have combined as the perfect relaxer but Hunter was fidgeting, visibly anxious. Both had purposely avoided shop talk earlier knowing they would have time after the meal and knowing that Olivia wouldn't have put up with it during dinner.

Finally, Charlie broke the silence. "I hear they've finally got you back on the streets and working homicide again. Is that why you're so twitchy tonight?"

Hunter arched his eyebrow. "Sorry, didn't realize it showed. You've still got a hell of a grapevine Dad. It hasn't even been a full week." There had been a time early in Hunter's career that his Dad keeping tabs on him wasn't welcomed. As time passed, he'd grown to not only understand it, but even appreciate it.

Charlie just shrugged, raised his glass in a mock salute. "Once a cop, always a cop... What do they have you working?"

"Well I think the Lieutenant thought he was giving me an easy, get back in the groove kind of case Monday when we had a couple of gangbangers get popped. It looks like it's turning out a little more interesting."

Charlie puffed on his cigar, motioned Hunter to continue. Over the next thirty minutes, Hunter filled him in on the details. He finished with a question. "So, you ever run across anything similar?"

Charlie stared out into the night view for a few moments before answering. "Well, nothing exactly like what you've described but I do remember a case down in Laredo that might provide some insight." He moved back from the window, sat down and faced Hunter. "We had a case, I guess it was in the late eighties, maybe eighty-six. Out of the blue, we saw an uptick in the number of illegals found murdered. As you know, immigrants dying while trying to get across the border is a fairly regular occurrence and you'll even have the occasional situation where an entire truckload end up dead because some Coyote abandons them. But illegals actually getting murdered is pretty rare. "

Charlie was animated now, his hands moved and his eyes were wide. "At first, because they were spread over a large geographic area and crossed a few jurisdictions, we didn't actually connect the murders for a while. Eventually, when the connection was made by a couple of neighboring Sheriffs, the Rangers were called in to assist. Our first step was to figure out what we were dealing with so we spread a wide net to look for similar situations, ended up with seven."

Hunter looked over at Charlie with interest. "That's a lot of bodies."

"Well, by the time we finally got him, he was up to twelve that we could confirm. Who knows how many more there were." Charlie leaned back, puffed his cigar and seemed to drift into a memory.

"So don't keep me in suspense, how'd you finally catch him?"

Charlie shrugged. "Hell, it was like many of the best solved cases, pretty much a combination of hard work and dumb luck. We kept collecting bits and pieces of evidence from the scenes and finally caught a break when we were able to match a print found at one of the scenes to a hunting license registration."

Hunter sat and stared at his Dad for a few quiet moments as

they both contemplated the story. Finally, he spoke. "I don't get it. How is getting lucky with a print match supposed to help on my case?"

Charlie started to chuckle. "Well, hell, that won't. But what we found out once we were able to question our guy might... Turns out this wasn't just completely random. I mean, sure the individual victims were random but he was targeting illegals for a reason. You see, his house had been broken into and his family had been terrorized by a couple of illegals. In essence, since he had no way to strike back at the specific criminals who hurt his family, he was striking back at all illegals."

Hunter thought for a moment, mumbled, almost to himself, "A vigilante." He stood up, went to the window and stared out at the thin line of light on the horizon to the east. "You know Dad, we went to the point of checking the victims criminal backgrounds to see if there might be someone they'd hurt who would be out to get them. But we hadn't taken it the next step to see if we could identify people who might have been hurt by the Kings or gangs in general." He leaned his hand against the window and shook his head. "Damn, that could be a pretty big list depending on your parameters."

Charlie nodded, got up and walked over to Hunter. "Sure could... But when you finally catch this bastard, I'll bet you a six pack, he was a victim at some point." Charlie put his hand on Hunters shoulder. "Maybe he was a victim of the Kings, some other gang or even just a black guy. Who knows? But he's targeting these guys for a reason."

They both stared out into the night, lost in their separate thoughts.

On the drive back home, Hunter was torn between being excited about possibly having a new logical path to follow and the daunting reality of how wide that path might be. *It's a good thing the Lieutenant's bringing in reinforcements tomorrow. We're gonna need the manpower.*

Chapter 16

Since leaving the crime scene earlier that morning, Shadow had been agitated, stewing. Four of his soldiers had fallen. He'd had to send two more underground knowing they'd eventually be identified and possibly arrested. After Shank and Wheels were popped on Monday, he'd sent his boys out to shake the trees. His informants throughout the city, even in the police department, had come back empty. Whoever had done it was a ghost.

He sat in the backroom, waiting, thinking. *What the hell is going on? Who's doing this? Why?* Business would be impacted. Suppliers were already calling him wanting to know if he had things under control. Now with this second situation, customers would get nervous. Something had to be done. Sitting back doing nothing was making him look weak. He'd ordered Clack to bring in the troops, all of them. They'd assembled over the last hour. Most were there, drinking, talking, getting ready. It was clear what was coming.

A knock shook him from his trance. "Come in." His response was more growl than word.

As the door cracked open, Clack stuck his head in. "They all here."

"I'll be out in a minute."

The door closed. Shadow stood in the center of the room, took a deep breath. He had no problem declaring war, he'd done so before. His concern was not knowing the enemy. He narrowed his focus, his eyes became black voids. He set his jaw in full game face. *Sometimes the shotgun approach is the only option.*

Shadow exploded through the door, all eyes immediately met him, all conversation stopped. He glared at the crowd not making eye contact with anyone yet connecting instantly with everyone. The adrenaline in the room was palpable, the smell of anticipation hung in the air.

He marched to the front of the room grabbing a baseball bat along the way. Once there, without missing a beat, he turned and swung the bat obliterating a half dozen beer bottles on a table. Bottle remnants and beer splatter sprayed into the crowd. He had their attention now.

"This is bullshit!" His voice rocked the building. "We have been attacked and that is un-fucking-acceptable!"

There were several mumbled responses of "Hell yeah", "No shit" and "Damn right."

Now he stared at the group of hard men standing in front of him, this time making eye contact seemingly with each man at once. They were a lethal force that he controlled through shear intimidation and brutality. He maintained his control simply by being the most lethal of them all. There would be no weakness tonight.

He spoke now with a low intensity. "When Shank and Wheels got iced, we tried to be patient, let the system work." He shook his head, raised a pointed finger. "What did that get us? Huh? What?" Heads nodded in silent concurrence. He joined by nodding his head vehemently. "That's right. That's right. All we got was getting Dizzy and TW shot."

Now he raised his head and searched the crowd. A hundred eyes stared back at him, each as void of humanity as his. When he found Spike, he stopped. "Spike, you wanted to pay Varrio Central a visit... Well, tonight... Tonight we not only gonna pay those spics a visit, we gonna rock this entire fucking city."

Spike's face hardened. "Hell yeah Shadow, we gonna take those fuckers out tonight!"

The room erupted. Shadow's eyes glowed. "My bruthas... My bruthas..." He held his hand up to quiet them. "We don't know who did this, but... what do they say? We know 'the usual suspects'." The room was vibrating now, bodies bouncing off each other, moving up and down. "We gonna strike at all of 'em, put the fear of God into this city." And we gonna leave our colors so they know who done it. This is war goddamnit!"

Still gripping the bat with his left hand, Shadow reached behind his back to his waistband, pulled out his Smith and Wesson 45. He stared at the crowd as he slowly caressed his cheek with the weapon. Suddenly, violently, he slammed the bat on the table, racked the slide, raised the pistol over his head and fired two rounds into the ceiling. Small pieces of the sheetrock ceiling filtered down and mixed with the smoke drifting from the gun barrel. Continuing to hold his gun high, he let out a primal scream. The crowd responded with raised fists and returned the scream.

As the room continued to roar, Shadow grabbed Clack by the arm. "Get my lieutenants, bring them to my office. We need to plan."

Clack nodded, moved through the amped up crowd while Shadow headed to his office. His handpicked lieutenants trickled in one by one, each grabbing his hand and bumping shoulders.

Once they were assembled, he leaned back and surveyed his team. "Listen up bruthas. As my chosen leaders, you need to know something." That got their attention. "We know more than the cops do and it wasn't Varrio Central." That brought confused looks from many in the room. "That's right. Before Psycho and Scorpion went on... vacation, they told me that it was some crazy white muthafucker that took out Dizzy and TW." Murmurs filled the room as his eyes glazed with anger. "Problem is this town is full of white muthafuckers, ain't it?"

Shadow surveyed the room, looked into the faces, understood that beneath the trumped up anger, there was also fear. The hunters had become the hunted. He raised his hands to quiet them. "We're gonna strike to let the world know we're pissed off and to let them know we're still the most lethal gang in this city."

After Shadow laid out the plan, he reached into his pocket, pulled out a blue bandana and dramatically wrapped it around his head. After each lieutenant followed suit, he growled, "Let's remind this city who da Kings are!"

Chapter 17

Before driving downtown, Hunter had spent Saturday morning plugging information into his laptop and reviewing digital photographs to prepare for briefing the mini taskforce. Lieutenant Sprabary had scheduled a meeting for later that morning. He also had to tend to an attention starved cat.

Knowing his taskforce counterparts would be grumpy about giving up their Saturday, he decided he'd bring a peace offering of Starbucks with him. A wry smile crossed Bernard's face when Hunter hurried in from the cold.

"Well, well, look who we have gracing our presence, on a Saturday no less." Bernard arched his eyebrows. "How are you today Cowboy?"

"I'd be better if I wasn't downtown on a Saturday." Hunter ordered two gallons of black coffee.

As he rang up the order, Bernard continued his banter. "I do hope you're planning to share. That's a lot of coffee even for java junkie like you."

"Let's just say some of my friends and I are spending our Saturday morning getting a little more focused on a couple of cases and we're going to need some fuel."

Bernard's usually droopy eyes lit up. "Wait a minute. Are you working that series of gangbanger shootings I heard about on the news?" Before Hunter could answer, he continued. "You know, I'll tell ya, as a taxpayer in this city, I'd just as soon you and your friends stay at home on a Saturday. Not that I don't like seeing you, but whoever popped those guys did us all a favor. When you find him, you should give him a medal."

Hunter smirked and shook his head. "Bernard, you know we

can't do that. A murder is a murder and nobody has the right to take the law into their own hands. After all, this week it's gangbangers he doesn't like, next week it might be overly pale latte boys, then what would you think?"

Bernard slid the cardboard jugs of coffee over the counter. "Yeah, well, last time I checked, about the only thing us overly pale latte boys terrorize are little old blue haired coffee drinkers."

Hunter grabbed the jugs, grinned and shrugged. "See you next time."

Several men were already congregating in the second floor conference room by the time Hunter entered. "Boys, since I've interrupted your weekend, I thought getting you some real coffee was the least I could do."

Carter Hogan, a forty something detective who, at nearly six foot five, looked like he might have once been a defensive linemen, smirked. "Yeah, Cowboy, that's the very damn least." A round of half-hearted laughs emanated from the room.

Hunter set the jugs on the table and made his way around shaking hands and making small talk. He eventually landed and sat at the front of the room. He booted up his laptop and connected it to a projector. He looked at his watch, noted it was 10:58am, absently tapped his index finger on the table and surveyed the room for attendees.

The players around the table included Carter Hogan and Pete Nguyen from Gangs, Jimmy Reyes and Blaine Parker from Homicide and Andy Lowe from Patrol. Conspicuously missing was Billy Sanders. He looked at his watch again. It was straight up eleven.

As he stood to kick off the meeting, the door whipped open and Billy hurried in, shot Hunter an apologetic look and sat down. Hunter cleared his throat to get the group's attention. "Now that Sanders has decided to grace us with his presence, we can get started." Sanders seemed to slide down slightly in his chair. Hunter continued. "On behalf of Lieutenant Sprabary, who unfortunately couldn't be here this morning..."

There was a round of laughter and fake coughing. Reyes, who looked a bit like Cheech Marin and was known for his smart remarks, grinned. "Yeah, I bet he's heartbroken about that."

Hunter motioned them to quiet down. "Anyway, as I was saying, welcome to the…" He paused for a moment. "Well, hell, I'm not sure exactly what we're going to call this group." He smiled as a thought crossed his mind. "While 'The Dead Gangbangers Mini-Taskforce' might be accurate, it probably wouldn't play well in the press." The room laughed. "Guys, look, you know why you're here. I want to start off with Sanders giving the basic background. From there, we'll get some insights from the group and talk about where we go from here."

Billy went to the front of the room and spent the next thirty minutes providing detailed background on the two incidents, the four victims and the investigation to date.

Once completed, Hunter stood again. "Folks, don't fool yourselves. There may be some who will contend that these killings don't matter because they were just gangbangers. We cannot take that attitude. The media storm is already brewing and you know they're going to spin it so that these guys look like choir boys. Besides, based on the reports this morning, it sounds like the Kings have decided to let the world know they're pissed." This comment brought some raised eyebrows. "Carter, can you provide us with some insight?"

Carter Hogan had been a detective in Fort Worth for over twenty years and had been integral in creating the gang intervention initiatives that had kept the city off the gang radar for so long. With his size and skin so dark it seemed to absorb light, he could intimidate a room. Those who knew him understood that his passion for gang intervention was very personal and came from a fatherly perspective. His mission was to save kids, not bust them.

Hogan stood and stared at the room, his serious expression transferred immediately to the other faces. "Gentlemen, it seems our shooter's actions have stirred up a hornet's nest. Last night was the most gang related violence this city has seen on one night in almost a decade. This son of a bitch may have destroyed in one week what Pete's team, my team, and the rest of the Gang Units have been busting our asses for years to achieve."

As Hunter and the rest of the team took notes, Hogan laid out the details of the night's rampage. "The Kings went a little crazy last night. We know it was them based on witness reports, locations of the crimes and we did manage to catch a few of them in the act. From what we can piece together, we've got four drive-by shootings, three liquor store robberies, five armed robberies of pedestrians and several assaults or near assaults." He handed out reports as he spoke. "In addition, there were a large number of vandalism incidents reported." He stopped to let them review the pages.

Carter continued. "The human toll included six people hospitalized, three for gunshot wounds and three for assault related injuries. Fortunately, there were no visits to the morgue. In a nutshell, it looks like the Kings have decided to respond to these attacks with a wave of indiscriminant violence. My concern is that this round will trigger retaliations and we will get locked into an escalating cycle that may take years to stop." He nodded to Hunter.

Hunter stood. "Alright, so there you have it. This team has two areas of focus. First, we've got to keep the city from blowing up into a full-fledged gang war. Carter, you and Pete will obviously take the lead in that area. Second, we've got to catch this guy before he increases his body count. We're all going to be active on that task."

He started to pace. "As you heard from Billy, we've got a lot of evidence that will help us in court, but very little that has provided leads. We also have no witnesses." He smirked. "Well, no real witnesses anyway… In the absence of leads, we need to get inside this guy's head and figure out why he's doing this." As his pacing quickened, his hands became more animated. "I was talking with a veteran investigator last night…"

Blaine Parker, a tall, dark haired detective who had clearly grown up on a farm, interrupted. "So Cowboy, how is your Dad anyway?" The group laughed. Most of the guys who'd been around a while knew Charlie Hunter, either in person or by reputation and they knew that Hunter often consulted him on cases.

Hunter grinned. "He's just as ornery as ever… Anyway, he told me a story that might be relevant." Hunter relayed the story to his team. "So, bottom line is that we might be dealing with a vigilante of some sort."

Andy Lowe, the youngest, only non-detective on the team hesitantly piped up for the first time. "You mean like Bernhard Goetz?"

While Hunter started to nod, Blaine interjected, "Well, technically, Goetz wasn't really a vigilante because he didn't go hunting for bad guys. He just happened to be a former victim who was well armed and ready for the next attack."

Carter cleared his throat causing Hunter to look his way. "Not to get in a pissing contest with you Cowboy, but I've researched the Goetz case and based on the trial transcripts, he wasn't exactly an innocent."

Hunter nodded. "Duly noted Carter. Can't say I'm an expert on the case."

Lowe looked a little dejected. "Well, call him what you want, he managed to get four bad guys off the streets in a pretty permanent fashion."

Reyes chimed in at this point. "Yeah and his reward for his community service was jail time and being labeled a nut bag by certain segments of the population."

Carter started to respond but shook his head and sat back.

While the rest of the team nodded, Blaine spoke up again. "Now if you want to talk about real vigilantes, you gotta talk about Sombra Negra."

Everyone around the table looked quizzically at him. "Oh come on guys, don't you read anything other than the Sports Illustrated Swimsuit Edition? Sombra Negra, which in English means Black Shadow, is a notorious vigilante gang who allegedly still exists but was very active back in the late nineties. They're supposedly made up of police and military and they target the outlaw gang MS13. You gotta be pretty ballsy to take on those hombres. Anyway, they're known for executing their blindfolded with headshots."

Reyes smiled. "Are they taking applications?" High fives and fist bumps were traded around the table with a few "Hell Yeah's" thrown in for fun.

Hunter once again quieted the group. "Focus here boys. Those are great stories, but my point with bringing it up is that we need to start looking into citizens who have been past victims of the Kings or of gangs in general."

Reyes let out a long slow whistle. "Damn Cowboy, that could be a hell of a long list."

"Yep. That's why we need the help. I've got the IT department compiling a list of all gang related crimes in the city in the last six months. They should be here momentarily. I've asked them to cull out property crimes. I just can't imagine anyone going on a killing spree because someone stole their car."

"Guess that depends on the car". Blaine was laughing at his own joke before he finished the sentence.

"Good point, but… Once we get that list, we are going to have to look at every case to determine if the victim or a close relative of the victim might be a person of interest." He stopped and looked at the team. "Guys, I know this seems futile but we've got to do something and right now, we've got four bodies and no real leads. I'm open for suggestions on how to make this process easier or for other avenues to take."

After a moment of quiet, Carter Hogan spoke up. "We might want to ask the computer geeks to run a cross reference to see if someone's been a victim multiple times or is a relative of multiple victims." He shrugged. "I mean, we are looking for someone who's been pushed over the edge, right?"

"Good call. I'll get that requested so that we can float those names to the top of the list." He stopped and made himself a note. "Anything else?"

Blaine shifted in his seat and got Hunter's attention. "This is a good direction, but these lists are going to be fairly cold. You know, from just looking at the paper, all the cases are going to look the same. Another thing we ought to do is talk with our boys over at the DA's office to see if they can direct us to recent cases where there have been particularly 'over the top' relatives."

"Damn good idea. We'll hit them first thing on Monday. In the meantime…" He was interrupted by a door opening, followed by a guy pushing a cart with a huge stack of computer paper on it.

Another long, slow whistle came from Reyes. "Holy crap."

"Yeah, holy crap. Let's get moving on the list."

Chapter 18

Sunday morning was cold and gloomy even by November standards but The Victim barely noticed as he trotted barefoot down his front walk to get the morning paper. He'd caught enough news coverage since Thursday to know that he was now the talk of the town. *I bet there'll be plenty of coverage today.*

It'd been less than a week since his first excursion into the darkness but in the world of a vigilante serial killer, that's a long time. He had started to feel like a veteran. After surviving Friday without a visit from the police, he had relaxed in the knowledge that the other two Kings weren't talking. That was good news since his buddy Trey had not been able to come up with any information on who they were. His relaxation evolved into excitement as the news coverage started to build.

Back inside at his kitchen table, he sipped coffee and sorted through the paper separating out all the useless sections of car ads and coupons. He even chunked the sports section. After all, the Mavericks season had barely started and the Cowboys, under their latest retread head coach, had been mediocre all year and were surely headed for another December meltdown.

There wasn't any coverage in the news sections. The coverage of the actual shootings had been in the Saturday paper. It wasn't a lot but it was much more than earlier in the week. He found what he was looking for when he hit the Editorial section. *I knew Phillips would write something. No way he could resist, that bleeding heart lefty. He'll turn it into a race issue. He always does.*

The Victim scanned down the article and wasn't disappointed. *Just what I thought, those poor oppressed gangbangers are being hunted by some mean boogeyman. What a load of crap. They're killers. All I'm doing is fighting back for those who can't.*

THE VICTIM

He finished the article but continued to scan the page for any other coverage when his eye caught an ad. *Hmm, what's this?* A smile came across his face as he read an advertisement for a Sunday morning news program. It was promoting a live panel discussion on the gang killings featuring Star Telegram Columnists John Ray Phillips and J.R. Lambert.

He checked his watch and then confirmed the time by looking over at the microwave. *It's just starting. Gotta hurry.* He bolted into the family room, scanned until he found the remote and jabbed it with his finger until he found the station. *There we go. Perfect timing.*

"Welcome to our Sunday show. This is Good Morning Fort Worth. I'm Scott Martin. Let's start with the overnight news…"

The Victim took a deep breath, sat back on the couch and listened as the talking head droned through the dullness that was Sunday morning news. The commentator finally drove the monologue to the topic of the gangbangers. "Now to our feature story. In the last six days, in two separate shootings, four apparent gang members have been murdered in Fort Worth…"

Murdered! What? Are you kidding me? They weren't murdered. I was defending myself. And what's that 'apparent' gang member shit? Come on. These were hardcore dirt bags.

"Today we have two featured Columnists from the Fort Worth Star Telegram to discuss and debate this issue. John Ray Phillips and JR Lambert, welcome to the show." Both responded with polite thank-you's.

Martin continued. "John Ray, I'll start with you. We ran a poll on the attitudes regarding these killings and found the following: 5% didn't even know they'd happened, 25% said we should be pulling out all stops to solve them but a full 70% said that because of the history of the victims, we were wasting tax payer dollars chasing the killer, essentially good riddance. What are your thoughts?"

"Well Scott, that just shows the inherent racist undertone of this city. Four young inner city black men are gunned down in the streets and no one cares. If this had been white boys from the suburbs, CNN, Fox and every other news organization on the planet would be screaming to solve these murders."

JR Lambert jump right in, "Come on now John Ray, seriously, you think the phone book is racist because the yellow pages are in the back. The bottom line is that these guys were scumbag thugs. To paraphrase, this isn't about the color of their skin, it's about the content of their character."

Amen! You see, the people are on my side. The Victim leaned forward on his couch and hung on every word being said. He was at the center of a social debate. *Amazing.*

John Ray retorted, "These young men may have had a checkered past but not everyone is born with a silver, or should I say, a white spoon in their mouths."

"Oh give me a break..."

Before JR could continue the debate, Scott Martin jumped in. "JR, let me get your thoughts. As a result of these killings, it appears that gang related violence has skyrocketed across the city. There were a number of apparently gang related drive-by shootings, assaults and armed robberies over the last forty-eight hours that police believe are related. How do you address that?"

"Typical. These people are violent felons. How do you expect them to react? When the bully gets bullied, he goes out to find someone else to attack. As far as I'm concerned, they can shoot each other all they want. That's just a few more bad guys off the streets."

"Of course, how do you expect them to react?" John Ray was in full tent revival fervor now. "These people have been oppressed their entire lives. Now they're getting gunned down in the streets and the police are doing nothing to solve the crimes. The authorities can't protect them so they have to protect themselves."

"Protect themselves? John Ray, these guys started this whole mess when they decided to go into a life of crime in the first place." JR gave an exasperated look to the camera.

"So I guess we're back to 'it's okay *not* to solve these crimes because the victim's weren't nice people'." John Ray looked indignant.

"I'm not saying we shouldn't solve the crimes. A murder is a murder... If that's what really happened. All I'm saying is that we shouldn't go to extreme measures such as task forces and heavy manpower. Hey, 'you live by the sword, you die by the sword'."

The debate continued to rage on somehow touching on every topic from unemployment to education to gun control. The lines were clearly drawn, the gangbangers were either victims of society and whoever was killing them was a madman or they were animals preying on society and the shooter was a modern day Batman.

The Victim reveled in every moment and every word. His original plan had been pretty simple – to get payback for his pain by taking out some of the thugs that had inflicted it. The added benefits of having the gangs shooting at each other and having the topic of gang violence being debated in public forums were unforeseen positives. *I'm on the right path. She'd be proud.*

He refocused on the debate as they were concluding. John Ray was rambling. "...And the police should be doing whatever it takes to find this murderer and get him off the streets. The oppression must stop now."

JR rolled her eyes. "Oh, please..."

Scott Martin jumped in, "Folks, we're going to have to stop there. One additional note, the FWPD declined to be interviewed for this story; however, did issue a press release indicating they were fully intent on solving these crimes and had formed a mini-taskforce whose sole focus will be bringing this killer to justice. That wraps it up for another Sunday edition of Good Morning Fort Worth. Have a great day."

As the credits rolled, The Victim leaned back. *Mini-taskforce huh? Well, good luck. I haven't left a shred of evidence yet and don't plan to start. Now, who's next?*

Chapter 19

On Monday morning, Hunter parked in the garage at Taylor and Belknap, a couple of blocks west of the courthouse. The team was working their assignments; Hogan and Nguyen were following up with various gangs trying to get information as well as defuse possible retaliations from Friday night's rampage. Sanders, Parker and Lowe were combing through the lists and building profiles on anyone who looked promising.

He had called earlier that morning and arranged a ten o'clock meeting with Assistant District Attorney Tim Daris. The north wind whipped up from the river through the community college campus and bit enough to make him question his wardrobe. He pulled his light sport coat tight to fight the damp cold. With the weather in Fort Worth leaning to warm or hot most of the year, he had never seen the need to buy a heavy dress coat. Even today, cold meant in the forties, not exactly Wisconsin. Still, the cloud cover and the dampness in the air made him stride faster down the sidewalk.

The Tarrant County District Attorney's office sits on the south side of West Belknap just across from the campus and very conveniently next to the city jail. Hunter had made this walk many times working cases over the years, usually not this early in the investigation. Although he had met Tim Daris, he had never worked any cases with him. Through the grapevine, he'd heard good things.

He took the elevator and exited into the fourth floor reception area. As he stepped off, the receptionist greeted him in a chipper voice. "Well hello Detective Hunter, it's been a long time."

Looking over, he saw a butterball of a woman with a seventies hairstyle. *Oh crap, what's her name? Susan? Sharon?* He put on his best car salesman smile. "Well how are you? It has been a while, hasn't it?"

"Oh, you know me, always the same." She waved him off and smiled flirtatiously. "I understand you have an appointment with Mr. Daris. Let me give him a call."

As she reached for the phone, the thought of a woman that age flirting with him curdled in his stomach. His thoughts were interrupted when she said, "Mr. Daris is ready for you, just go on back, Hon."

Tim Daris was on the phone but signaled Hunter to come in when he knocked. As was his habit, Hunter stepped in and immediately surveyed the office. On the north side of the building, it wasn't large, but functional. The floor to ceiling window looked out over West Belknap and the college. *I bet this is nice for watching coeds.* The fourth floor wasn't quite high enough to have a view of the river but he could see the desolate Varrio Central turf off in the distance.

Daris was seated behind a cherry wood desk with a collection of very neatly stacked manila folders and legal documents. The matching book case held a mixture of legal books, awards and framed photos of Daris with city leaders including District Attorney Tim Curry and Mayor Michael Moncrief. As Daris finished up his call, Hunter's eyes wandered to the credenza which held a laser printer, more folders and a small collection of what looked like family photos. In spite of the fact that there seemed to be a large number of items distributed on the various work surfaces, the office was organized and clean.

Hunter fixated momentarily on a picture of Daris and a woman. She was blond, maybe a couple of years younger than Daris and very attractive. They appeared to be at a high end social function, maybe an office party. *Hmm, maybe a girlfriend or fiancé? Don't see a wedding ring.* For some reason, the family photos kept his attention until he realized that Daris had gone silent. He looked over at Daris who seemed irritated.

Hunter stuck his hand out. "Mr. Daris, Detective Jake Hunter, I think we've met somewhere along the way but I'm not sure we've ever had the pleasure of working together."

"No, I don't believe we have." Daris shook his hand firmly but drove right past small talk. "How can I help you today, Detective?" Daris looked at his watch as he motioned with his hand and both men sat.

"Well, I was hoping to get your insight on a case we're working.

I'm sure you've heard about the gang member homicides?"

Daris seemed to stiffen, nodded slowly. "It's been hard to miss, seems our dead gangbangers have become a cause celeb in the local media." He paused, shifted in his seat. "So, how exactly can I help you? Other than trying to put them behind bars, I'm not much of an expert on gangbangers."

"Actually, what I need has more to do with their victims. You see, we have reason to believe that our shooter is acting as a vigilante and…"

Daris let out a nervous laugh. "You mean some lone white guy is out hunting down and shooting gang members?"

Hunter cocked his head. "I didn't say it was a white guy."

Daris put up his hands in mock surrender. "Sorry. You got me, guilty of stereotyping." He leaned back in his chair. "Still, you really think one guy is doing this and it's not just another gangbanger?"

Hunter nodded. "Based on what we've seen at the two crime scenes, we know that both incidents were carried out by the same shooter and we're fairly certain it's just one person. Now, exactly how he's pulling it off, we don't know."

"Really. Hmm."

"Also, based on the crime scene and talking with both the Kings and Varrio Central, we don't see this as gang on gang violence. As I mentioned, we think he's acting as a vigilante and may have been a victim of gang violence at some point or is maybe the relative of a victim."

Daris smiled, his shoulders visibly relaxing. "So, what you need from me is insight into possible suspects based on recent victims of gang crime."

"Bingo."

"Hmm. You know what." Daris leaned forward, now obviously interested in the conversation. "We ought to tap a couple of my colleagues as well. If you've got the time, let me see if Kenny and Edmond are around."

Hunter nodded and as Daris made the two quick phone calls, he resumed his perusal of Daris' office.

"They're on their way." He stood, interrupting Hunter's

surveying. "I'm sorry. I never even offered you some coffee. The break room is right around the corner. Shall we?" He motioned to the door and ushered Hunter out.

After getting coffee, they reassembled in Daris' office with Kenneth Harper and Edmond Curtis. Introductions were made and Hunter went back through the reason for his visit. "So what we need is for each of you to think about any of your cases where the defendant was a gang member and where either the victim or any relative of the victim seemed overly distraught or unstable."

Kenny blew out a long breath. "That could be a pretty big list. I mean, I can think of three or four off the top of my head. There's probably a dozen if I dig deep and I've only been trying felonies for two years. You know, just about every brother or father has that angry glare."

"Same here." Edmond interjected. "But I'm happy to walk you through them. How far back do you want us to go?"

All eyes turned to Hunter. "That's a good question. We don't know if this is a recent thing or if it's old and some recent event triggered the reaction. Our best bet is to just work through the possibilities you have and see where it leads."

The group spent the next hour going through the names and circumstances of potential victim-vigilante suspects. Almost every situation was unique yet equally compelling. Hunter could see how they all had reasons to want to kill gang members. *God knows I would.* He felt the weight of the futility as he realized there was an even longer list being worked by the team.

As the discussion unfolded, Daris had commented throughout on the cases being discussed but had not offered up any specific suspects of his own. When it appeared that Kenny and Edmond had exhausted their lists, Hunter looked to Daris. "I know I've taken up more of your time than expected. I appreciate your cooperation, but did you have any possibilities to add to the list?"

"Well, I've certainly tried a few gang related cases over the years..."

"A few?" Kenny interjected. "You go after them with a vengeance." The three attorneys laughed at the inside joke while Hunter turned his attention back to Daris.

"Yeah, well. Historically, I guess I don't have that many psycho victims that jump out at me."

"That's because your win rate on gang cases is out there. All your victims get to see those pricks go to jail." Edmond and Kenny both grinned. They were obviously impressed with their slightly more senior counterpart.

Daris tried to seem embarrassed by the attention. Hunter didn't buy it.

"I do have one current case that has been particularly frustrating for the victim's parents and for me. We've had to deal with that nutbag Judge Feldman..." Daris ran down some of the details of the crime for Hunter and explained how distraught the Bennetts had been when the judge had thrown out the confession. Daris' anger over the situation became apparent as he talked.

"You seem fairly pissed off about the case?"

"I don't like to lose Detective. I especially don't like to lose when I know the bastard is guilty."

Hunter nodded. "Well that's a sentiment we share... So, can you tell me about the victim's father?"

Daris shook off his anger, stood up and stepped to the window. "Interesting guy... Jim Bennett is a retired Prosecutor for the city of Arlington. As you can imagine, he's interested in the case details. To his credit, he hasn't tried to run the case for me."

"A former Prosecutor for Arlington, huh? So, he'd have plenty of contacts within the Fort Worth legal system and he'd probably have at least some level of knowledge and experience with the local gangs." As Hunter said the words, the realization hit him, if the shooter had this kind of knowledge, it would be easier to target his victims. *Crap. I may be looking for a cop, lawyer, prosecutor or judge...* His eyes involuntarily glanced at the pictures on the credenza. *Everyone has family members.*

He looked up to see the faces of the three attorneys. It was apparent the same thought had occurred to them. There was an uncomfortable silence for a moment. No one in law enforcement ever liked to think that a 'good guy' could go bad.

Without acknowledging the elephant in the room, Daris cleared his throat and continued. "Bennett's in his late fifties, in good shape, tough as nails. He's no longer a Prosecutor but he's still in practice as an independent lobbyist." He stopped for a moment as if something had just entered his mind. "Interestingly enough, I remember him telling me that his two major clients were a gun manufacturer and a victim's rights group. At the time I thought that was a really strange combination."

"It's not such a strange combination if you're secretly a psycho vigilante killer." Kenny's eyes were wide with the thought. Edmond nodded in agreement.

A pained look crossed Daris' face. "I don't know guys. He seems really straight laced to me. There's no doubt he's pissed off about the possibility of this guy getting off, but I just can't quite imagine him out hunting gangbangers at night. Besides, the case isn't even over yet. In spite of Judge Feldman, we still have a shot at a conviction."

"How long has the trial been going?"

"About a week and a half."

"When did the judge throw out the confession?"

Daris' face went grim. "About a week ago."

"Hmm." Hunter nodded and jotted down a note. *Interesting timing.*

"Guys, I know how this looks." Daris was animated now. "I just don't think this guy's the type."

"We'll obviously do our homework before we have any conversations with these folks but our friend Mr. Bennett just floated to the top of the list." Hunter made a few more notes. "Well guys, I really appreciate your time today. Any other suggestions before I get out of your hair?"

The attorneys were quiet for a moment before Kenny responded. "You know, there's someone else you ought to talk with. He's a defense attorney who specializes in gangbangers..." He looked a question at Daris and Edmond. "What's that guy's name? You know the one that seems to defend just about every gangbanger in town?"

Daris nodded. "You mean Steve Gentry?"

"Yeah, that's the guy." Turning back to Hunter, Kenny continued. "You should definitely talk to him. He could give your insight into the gangbangers and could also provide a second opinion on the list of victims that we provided."

Hunter wrote the name down, stood, collected his notepad and started the handshake procession to the door. When he turned toward the door, he noticed the long wool overcoat hanging on the coat rack. His mind raced back to the conversation with Sir Elliott Winston and he stopped. Trying to sound casual, he asked Daris, "So, how often do guilty gangbangers walk?"

Daris toyed with a pen on his desk. "It happens. Between plea bargains, lack of evidence, lenient judges and stupid juries, it happens way more than it should."

Hunter nodded in agreement, then looked up and met Daris' eye. "You ever have a close friend or relative who was the victim of gang violence?"

Daris' face went hard. He answered slowly, "Hasn't everyone? Exactly why do you want to know?"

"Just curious. You know how detectives are." He nodded and gave a mock salute. "Thanks again for your help. I'll let you know if we get any hits." By the time he hit the lobby, he was so deep in thought he didn't even notice the receptionist smile and wave to him.

Chapter 20

After a quick lunch, Hunter charged into the conference room and boomed, "How're you doing, boys?"

Three sets of dead eyes looked up at him. Parker, Sanders and Lowe were clearly tired. Reyes wasn't there, having left a message for Hunter earlier. It seemed as if the gloomy weather had moved indoors. The frustration level was painted on their faces. The conference room was stale, the smell of cold coffee, leftover food and three men having been cooped up in a small space permeated the air. Sanders set down a folder. "Obviously not as good as you… If your lunch was that good, maybe you should have brought us the leftovers."

Hunter smiled, eyed the empty food containers strewn about the table. "Doesn't really look like you need anymore. No, my mood has nothing to do with food, just finally seeing some movement on this thing."

Blaine arched an eyebrow. "Glad to see someone is… So fill us in Cowboy."

Hunter started to say something but was interrupted by the door opening. Jimmy Reyes walked in and nodded as all eyes turned his way. "Don't let me stop the party." He moved on it and took a seat.

"Are you done with the Lieutenant's little errand?" Hunter grinned just enough to let Reyes suspect he was kidding but not enough for him to know.

"Hey, you gotta do what you gotta do, you know." Reyes shrugged his shoulders and smiled.

"Yeah, well, I'd accuse you of brown nosing, but then how would you know?" The room erupted.

Reyes stopped laughing long enough to retort in his heaviest Hispanic accent, "Hey, you better watch yourself, I'll bring you up on sexual harassment charges man." That brought more laughter from the entertainment starved team.

Hunter motioned with his hands for them to calm down. "All right girls, that's enough playing around. Believe it or not, we may actually have a lead worth chasing." He paused and thought for a moment, his mind flashed back to the credenza in Daris' office. "Maybe more than one."

The group calmed, all eyes turned to Hunter. He continued. "Well, I've had an interesting morning but I don't want to get the cart before the horse. So let's get caught up on what everyone's been doing." He waved his hand at Jimmy. "Reyes, I know you've got nothing." He then turned to Sanders. "Billy, why don't you give us a summary of what the team's culled from the printouts?"

"Sure. We've had Lowe processing the raw list to identify male relatives. He's managed to get through about a fourth of the list. That's about a hundred and fifty cases. Out of that, he's compiled a list of two hundred and fifty male relatives who were mentioned in the on line case notes. I've been running those names for arrest records and have sorted them into three categories – No arrest record, Nonviolent crimes and Violent crimes. As it stands, I've made it through seventy-eight with forty having no record, twenty-two with nonviolent crimes and sixteen with violent crimes."

"So, are we thinking that our guy has a record?" Hunter was up and pacing now.

"Not necessarily, but we wanted to get a profile of the male relatives and see what kind of guys we're dealing with." Hunter nodded and Sanders continued. "So Parker took a different angle and looked at the case files to see if the detectives had made any comments related to the relatives. As it stands, he's gotten through twenty-five and has four cases where relatives made public threats and three more where relatives were unstable enough for the detective to note it in the file. Each of us has been updating a master spreadsheet so that we can cross reference and generate a final list of names."

Hunter pinched the bridge of his nose and squeezed shut his eyes. "All right, I like your process and how you're tracking, but what does it all mean? Do we have four suspects, the guys who made threats?

Do we have seven suspects by adding guys who seemed unstable? Do we have sixteen suspects because they have violent records? All of the above? None of the above?" He shrugged with his hands out as if to say 'who knows'.

"Well, interestingly enough, when you look at the master spreadsheet, you'll see there wasn't any crossover in those groups. The guys who seemed unstable or made threats all fell into the 'no criminal record' group."

Hunter stopped pacing, turned and peered at Sanders as his thoughts churned. "Interesting... Hmm... You know, that might make sense. After all, guys who are actually inclined toward violence don't really waste their time with threats and most people who blow up in public never act on their threats. It's usually just hot air." He went back to pacing.

The room was quiet for a moment. Everyone seemed to be lost in thought or just at a loss for what to do next. Hunter finally spoke. "So I guess in the spirit of casting a wide net, let's keep plugging through with the assumption that we need to look deeper into anyone who falls in the violent criminal, unstable or public threat categories. Right now, that leaves us with what, twenty-three possibles?"

Sanders tapped his pen on his page of notes as he added the numbers together, nodded. "Yeah... But you realize we've barely made a dent in this pile. At the pace we're moving, we could end up with a couple of hundred guys to look at before we're done."

Hunter stared off and seemed to calculate the possibilities. He shook his head as if to clear his thoughts. "It is what it is, but it's only one avenue. We'll keep moving through it but I think we may have at least one road to take that's a little higher percentage play."

He sat down at the table, picked up his notepad and spent the next fifteen minutes recapping his morning activities at the DA's office. When he finished with his summary of Edmond and Kenny's cases, he set his notepad down, stood up and started pacing. "So, in a nutshell, from talking to those two guys, I've got about twenty-five names to add to your spreadsheet. Hopefully, some on them will be duplicates."

Blaine's eyebrow arched again. "Uh, no offense there Cowboy, but umm... did I miss something?" Hunter turned to him with a big grin on his face. The realization spread onto Blaine's face. "You dog. You've been holding out on us. All right, so now that you've made us wait, what do you really have?"

"Well, I did save the best for last, if that's what you mean." He smiled, picked up a marker and started writing on the whiteboard as he talked. "Tim Daris is in the middle of a case against a gangbanger, a brutal rape and murder of a college girl. Daris says the guy confessed and there's no doubt that he's guilty, but about a week ago..." He paused to let the timeframe sink in. "The judge threw out the confession on some technicality and now the guy may walk. Daris said the victim's father, an ex-Prosecutor for the city of Arlington, was absolutely enraged. He says the guy's real straight laced but tough as nails. I say he floats to the top of our list."

"Ex Prosecutor, huh?" Blaine had an uncomfortable look on his face.

"Yeah, an ex-Prosecutor... And yeah, the very same thought struck me as well. We may be looking for someone in law enforcement or around law enforcement. Think about it, both incidents happened in locations that were known King distribution points. The average citizen wouldn't know that but someone... Someone in law enforcement, or a former prosecutor, would."

Reyes let out a long, slow whistle, shook his head. "Damn."

Hunter nodded. "Exactly. Anyway, I think this guy moves to the top of our list." He returned to writing on the whiteboard. "His name's Jim Bennett. He's now a lobbyist and has an office over in Arlington. From what Daris said, he usually works out of his house in Southlake. Lowe, I want you to keep working the list. Sanders, Reyes, I want you to divide and conquer. We need to know everything there is about Jim Bennett. Let's get telephone records, credit card records, criminal history, work history, everything down to whether he wears boxers or briefs." He grinned at his own joke. "I especially want to know where he was and what he was doing on Monday and Thursday nights."

Hunter gathered up his papers while he continued to talk. "I've got to update our lieutenant. I want an update by end of day." He nodded, ending the conversation.

Lowe went back to the printouts while Sanders and Reyes

huddled discussing who would do what.

Blaine stood and walked over to Hunter. "So, where do you want me Cowboy?"

Hunter gestured toward the door. "Walk with me to Sprabary's office."

When they were in the hall, Hunter surveyed the area to ensure they were alone. He leaned in to Parker and spoke quietly. "I need you to very discreetly do some checking for me." Blaine's eyes widened, his face grew serious. "I want to know everything you can tell me on Tim Daris."

Blaine scrunched his face up. "Tim Daris, as in the Fort Worth Prosecutor? Are you serious?"

"Yeah. It's a long shot, but there was just something about the way he acted today, the intensity in his pursuit of gangbangers... I don't know, just a hunch."

"Man, that's one of those hunches where you'd better be right or you may be writing parking tickets for the rest of your career."

"Exactly. That's why I want you to do this under the radar. It's probably nothing, but..."

Parker leaned against the wall, a puzzled look on his face. "So, exactly what do you want to know? He obviously doesn't have a criminal record. He's not married, doesn't have kids so being a family member of a victim is a bit of a long shot. Besides, anything involving him in the last few years would've drawn some media attention."

Hunter nodded. "Good points. Still, he fits the basic serial killer vigilante profile – white, thirty to forty, etc. Plus, he has access to gang information and seems to have a hard on for gangbangers."

Parker laughed. "Hell, based on that Cowboy, we're both on the list."

Hunter met his eyes. "Unfortunately, you're right."

Chapter 21

Two hours in Sprabary's office and Hunter ears ached from listening to the Lieutenant rant. Sprabary had been chewed out by Calvin Jackson and had let the shit roll downhill. Jackson was the outspoken City Councilman who represented the part of town where the shootings had occurred.

Councilman Jackson had more than implied that the Police weren't working hard enough to solve the crimes. The reason, he claimed, was pure and simple racism. He had threatened to 'bring the power of the black community down on the department' if he didn't see some action immediately.

Sprabary's mood was near homicidal by the time Hunter had gotten there. It improved only slightly with the news that the team had a potential suspect.

It was almost six by the time Hunter made it back to the task force's war room. The team was still hard at work. The staleness in the room had only gotten worse and the remnants of afternoon snacks had been added to those from breakfast and lunch. The mood in the room, however, was distinctly different. There was an undercurrent of tension, almost excitement in the air.

As Hunter walked into the room, Reyes looked up from his computer and smiled. "Hey Cowboy, it's about time you got back. I think you're gonna like what we've dug up."

Parker nodded as Sanders chimed in, "No kidding. This guy has vigilante written all over him."

Hunter walked to the front of the room, sat down and opened his laptop. "Well, don't keep me in suspense."

Reyes and Sanders looked at each other. Sanders motioned for Reyes to take the lead. "All right, so let's start with the basics. We were able to confirm Daris' thoughts about Bennett's professional ties. He and his firm definitely lobby on behalf of victim's rights groups as well as gun manufacturers and owners groups. They lobby at both the state and federal level with Bennett as their point man."

Hunter arched an eyebrow as if to ask how they figured that out. Reyes smiled. "I've got a buddy who works at the statehouse down in Austin. He checked the visitor's log for me. Says the guy's there at least a couple of days every week when legislature's in session. Says he's even got enough juice to manage a couple of visits with Governor Perry."

Hunter nodded. "Impressive."

Reyes continued, "So that's not all. It seems his personal interest in these two lobby efforts only cranked up about six months ago... About the same time his daughter was murdered. Coincidence? I think not." Reyes shot a grin over to Sanders and the two shared a quick fist bump.

Hunter looked up over his laptop. "How do you know?"

"He's become a writing machine. He's written everything from letters to the editors, petitions to the legislature and city councils, courtroom briefs and blogs. Google this guy's name and you'll be reading all day. Every article we found has been done in the last six months."

"What kind of topics?"

"Everything from Capital Punishment, Domestic Violence, Morality in Public Policy and Campus Safety to the Second Amendment and Gun Ownership. Hell, this guy's even contributed edits to Wikipedia."

Hunter leaned back in this chair, stretched with his fingers interlocking behind his head. "Okay, so he's got some passionate views. Last time I checked, we have a thing called the First Amendment. He can chatter all he wants. I guess if something like that had happened to my daughter..." He paused as the thought ripped through his chest. "Assuming I managed to somehow maintain my sanity, I might become fairly vocal in my opinions on related topics."

"Fair enough, but... wait 'til you hear the rest." He nodded to Sanders.

Sanders picked up his notepad, his gaze scrolling down the page for a moment. "Looks like our Mr. Bennett has taken his defense of the second amendment to the next logical step. He has a license to carry concealed, which, by the way, he got just weeks after his daughter's attack. We tracked his registered gun purchases and, are you ready for this? He owns not one, but two Beretta 9mm's, purchased, once again, just weeks after his daughter's attack."

Hunter sat up a little straighter. "Now you've got my attention. What else?"

Sanders continued. "It looks like our guy's become quite the gun enthusiast. Membership at DFW Gun Club and Training Center. Based on the amount of ammo he's purchased over the last six months, this guy's either stocking up for Armageddon or he's been spending a hell of a lot of time at the range, certainly enough to become pretty proficient."

Hunter shot out of his chair and paced, staring at the ceiling tiles as he absorbed the information being laid out. "Okay, but let's think about this for a minute. You said he spends a lot of time in Austin for his lobbying efforts. Do we even know if he was even in town the nights of the shootings?"

Reyes jumped in now. "Better than that. We've got a receipt where he bought gas right off I-35 about a mile from the last shooting only an hour before the shooting."

"What about the first shooting?"

"Well, we can't confirm he was in town, but we don't show any credit card purchases out of town that day. Besides, the first shootings were on a Sunday night so he wouldn't have been working that day."

Hunter reached into his jacket pocket for his earpiece, popped it in and before anyone could interrupt, gave a voice command to dial. He paced while it rang and connected.

"Well, it's about time. A girl could get a complex."

Stacy's voice brought an involuntary smile to his face, which he quickly replaced with a look that was all business. "Yeah, sorry about that, been a little involved with our dead gangbangers."

"Yeah, well, I might let you off the hook if you promise to buy me lunch soon."

Hunter's eyes cut to the room, embarrassed, as if the guys could hear his conversation. "Count on it... In the meantime, I need you to check something for me."

"Sure, what've you got?"

"Is there any way to determine the specific model or manufacturer of a gun based on those shell casings?"

"Well, I can narrow it down to a list. Depending on the pin markings, it might not be a short list and it's going to be a whole lot easier if you have a specific gun model or manufacturer as opposed to me going through and trying to create a full list."

Hunter hit the mute button, turned to Sanders. "You said Bennett's guns were Berettas, right?" Sanders nodded. Hunter punched mute off. "I need to know if those shells could have been fired from Berettas."

"I think I can manage that." She paused for a moment. "In fact, if you want to change that lunch to a dinner, you could pick me up in about an hour and I'll have your answer."

Hunter smiled and blushed slightly, turned away from the team. He cleared his throat and forced a professional voice. "Yeah, that sounds good. See you then."

When Hunter turned around, the whole team stared at him in anticipation. He slid his earpiece in his pocket as he shrugged. "What?" The room burst into laughter. He shook his head, waved them off. "Whatever... We've got things to finish so we can wrap up for the night."

"Yeah, okay." Sanders chuckled. "So, what do you think about Bennett?"

"Well, he certainly looks good enough to interview, maybe even good enough for a search warrant." Hunter looked over at Reyes. "Jimmy, I want you to write up the request for a warrant. Go as broad as you can. We want to see his house, cars and office. Write it up assuming the bullets could have been fired from Berettas. I'll have that confirmed by then. I want it ready for signature first thing in the morning." More snickers came from the room. This time Hunter glared at them and silence ensued.

He continued. "Blaine, in the meantime, I don't want this guy roaming the city tonight. We need to verify he's at home, have someone call him or something. Maybe get Daris to pretend he needs something for the case, whatever. Once you know he's home, get a patrol unit to sit on him for the night."

Looking at Sanders, Hunter nodded. "So, while Jimmy's working the paper, you and I need to continue down other paths. Daris and his team suggested we meet with a public defender. We can do that in the morning. By lunch, we'll have the warrant signed and we can move on Bennett."

Sanders nodded. "Sounds good to me."

Hunter was lost in thought. He paced slowly. The others had gone back to their notes or computers. After a moment, he looked over to Reyes. "Jimmy, when you get the paper ready, go to Feldman for the signature. He's always looking to nail a gun freak. Plus, according to Daris, Bennett was fairly obvious in his displeasure with Feldman's ruling last week. Feldman's just petty enough to want to get back at him."

Hunter packed up his laptop, headed for the door. "Good work today guys. We can't assume we've got him yet, but this is promising. Get some rest tonight. Tomorrow will be interesting."

Chapter 22

It was just shy of six o'clock when Stacy crawled up into the passenger seat of Hunter's Explorer. He had picked her up outside the Criminal Investigations Division of the FWPD just west of the downtown courthouse. What little sun had shown itself that day had sunk behind the Pier One headquarters building on the western skyline. The temperature fell with it and Hunter noticed Stacy shiver as he watched her adjust the heater controls on the dashboard.

As he pulled away from the curb, Hunter checked traffic in his side mirror. "So, what'd you find out?"

Stacy shot him a sideways glance. "Now isn't that just like a guy? No foreplay, not even so much as a 'how ya doin'. Just cut straight to it."

Hunter grinned sheepishly. "Sorry about that, just a bit focused... Let me try that again." He cleared his throat and through a not well hidden smirk. "So Stacy, how are you? You look lovely tonight."

She flicked her hand at him as if dismissing him. "Too little, too late to redeem yourself now Buster, but you've got to at least tell me where we're eating before I give it up."

"I was thinking of Los Vaqueros."

"Mmm, now we're talking. I could use a margarita... or two." She laughed and tossed her hair back. Hunter caught a hint of her perfume, enough to make him turn and stare. He caught the silhouette of face noticing her slim nose and angular cheekbones. He quickly turned back to the road before she noticed, but her smile stuck in his thoughts.

She settled into her seat and pulled a small notebook from her purse. "All right, so here you have it. In a nutshell, yes, these shells could have been fired from a Beretta 9mm. That's the good news. The bad news is that they could have also been fired by guns from at least four other manufacturers so it's not exactly conclusive."

"Yeah, but it's probably enough to get a warrant."

She thought for a moment. "Maybe."

"When you add everything else we've got, as circumstantial as it is, we'll get one."

"You sound awfully confident. What else do you have?"

Hunter spent the rest of the drive to the Stockyards area filling her in on everything from his conversation with Daris to the additional research his team had done. As they pulled into the parking lot, she nodded but still looked skeptical. "Well, I hope you're right. If this guy was a well-known sleaze ball, it'd be a slam dunk. A high end Southlake lawyer is going to have a lot of friends and even if the Judge doesn't know him, he's going to see him as a peer."

Hunter nodded and killed the engine. "Good point. We'll see." He got out and came around to open her door but she was out before he got there. The cold pushed them close to each other as they hurried across the parking lot, the north wind pushing them toward the door.

Darkness had settled over the north side of Fort Worth and even though it was a Monday night and cold, the Stockyards area around Main and Exchange was still lit up. The bars and restaurants lining the red brick streets catered to the small mixture of tourists and locals catching Texas food and live music.

Los Vaqueros was a long time standard for Fort Worth style Tex-Mex cuisine. It occupies the bottom floor of what was once an old abandoned warehouse. The top floor is still abandoned with just the external brick skeleton still in place. It makes for an interesting visual when you can see open blue sky through the open outlines where the second story windows used to be.

After settling into a booth in the back, Stacy ordered her margarita. When Hunter ordered only a coffee, an uncomfortable look crossed her face. "Oh, Jake, I'm sorry. I wasn't thinking."

She turned to the waitress to say something but Hunter stopped her and nodded for the waitress to go on and get the drinks. "Stacy, it's fine. Just because I don't want one doesn't mean you can't."

She cringed. "I just didn't know... I mean... It's been a while but... I'm sorry." She paused, looked down embarrassed. "Oh look at me. I'm just stumbling all over the place."

Hunter instinctively reached across the table and took her hand. "Stacy, relax. We've known each other a long time... Gina's struggles shouldn't prevent you from enjoying yourself." He searched for his words. "Look, I may be a little more aware of the effects of alcohol than most, but I'm not some whacko militant. I'll have a cold one every once in a while. I'm just still somewhat in work mode tonight. Besides I'm beat, I'm cold and I've got to drive."

Stacy smiled and seemed to relax. The waitress returned with their drinks and Hunter pulled his hand back across the table. They both blushed slightly as they realized they'd been holding hands.

The waitress looked to Stacy. "What can I get you tonight?"

Stacy looked at Hunter who hadn't even bothered opening his menu. "If you know what you want, go ahead. I'll be ready is a second."

Hunter nodded and quickly ordered the Pescado Vera Cruz. When Stacy gave him a look like he didn't take long enough, he just shrugged. "What can I say? Creature of habit."

She smiled and shook her head. "Well, I like to be unpredictable, so... Hmm... I guess I'll have what I always have too." Hunter laughed as Stacy closed her menu and looked to the waitress. "Fajita Chicken Chimichanga, please, with Queso instead of red sauce."

The waitress disappeared and silence fell between them, both seemingly absorbed in the surrounding white noise of muffled conversations, clinking dishes and Mexican Bolero background music. Both sipped their drinks sorting through their thoughts, Hunter absently played with a sugar packet.

Stacy finally broke the silence. "So, you really think this Southlake attorney is your guy?"

Hunter shrugged. "There's definitely enough to warrant a closer look. I've seen crazier scenarios." He flicked the sugar packet onto the table. "Can't hurt to have a conversation with the guy."

"I hope it leads somewhere."

"We'll see." He returned to playing with the sugar packet. "I just want it to end. As much as I'm a firm believer in the legal process, there's a part of me that just wants it all to go away whether he's our guy or not. I can certainly see the view that society hasn't exactly been devastated by the loss of these four scumbags. Unfortunately, Councilman Jackson doesn't see it that way and if we don't end this thing soon, there could be some major ramifications. It's got to stop."

"True." With a wry smile, she added, "It's just when I think of all the vigilante serial killers I've known, very few were high end lobbyists living in posh suburbs."

Hunter laughed, absorbed her smile and felt the weight of the day begin to lift. The waitress returned with their meals and they fell into small talk as they ate.

As they finished their meal, Stacy looked over to Hunter. "It's been nice having you back in the field."

"Yeah, it feels good. Of course, it's different without Frank." He looked off toward the windows. "Guess it'll never be the same."

"Things never stay the same Cowboy. You know that."

He nodded. "Speaking of things changing, how are you doing with your new situation?"

"My new situation? Oh, you mean Paul and me? Well, it's not exactly new. It's been almost a year since we split."

Hunter blanched. "Really? That long?"

"Yeah, he moved out before then, so for me it seems like ancient history. I guess between me not exactly making it public and you kind of dropping off the grid for a while, well..." She let the thought trail off, leaned forward to him. "You know I tried to reach out to you after the shooting. I left you messages."

"I know you did and I appreciate that. It was just something I had to work through on my own." Hunter pushed back from the table and tried to change topics. "So, at least you got to stay in the house."

"Yeah, that didn't last long. It was too big, too expensive and too empty for me to stay. I moved into a smaller place about six months ago. How about you? Are you still out in Summerfields?"

Hunter nodded. "Easier to stay put."

"Is it tough being all alone out there in the great married suburbs?"

Hunter watched her stare at her finger as she swirled it around the rim of her margarita glass. He waited while the busboy cleared the dishes from the table, pulled his chair back closer to the table. "Well, I'm not exactly alone."

Stacy tried to hide the shocked look on her face. She fumbled with her glass and drained the last remnants of her margarita. She set her glass down and cleared her throat. "Well that's good. I guess I didn't know that you had found someone."

Hunter hid his smirk, shrugged. "Maybe I should have called and let you know I got a cat."

Stacy nodded automatically, eyes down before the words sank in. Eventually, her head snapped up and she stared at him. "What? A cat?" She smiled, picked up her napkin and threw it at him. "You shit... I can't believe..."

Hunter couldn't contain his laughter.

"What's his name?" Stacy asked.

"Panther."

"Panther? Your cat's name is Panther?" She rolled her eyes. "You men and your testosterone."

Hunter smiled. "He's big and black. Besides, considering he's an inside cat and I had to get him fixed, I thought the name might be a boost for his self-esteem."

Stacy shook her head. "Don't think you can smooth talk your way out of this one. I'll get you back when you least expect it."

They were both smiling and laughing as Hunter paid the bill and escorted her back across the cold parking lot to the SUV. He opened the door for her and helped her into her seat.

After a quick drive back down Main Street to downtown, he drove her to the employee parking lot and stopped behind her car.

Stacy smiled, reached over and touched his sleeve. "Thanks for dinner. I enjoyed it. Let me know if you get the warrant. If you need extra hands, I'll help with the search."

She started to move to the door but Hunter caught her arm, pulled her back and gently kissed her on the cheek. "I had a good time too. Thanks for joining me. I'll call you tomorrow."

Her smile radiated as she stepped out of the SUV and walked around her car. She gave him a quick wave and got in. Hunter pulled away, inhaled deeply, caught the last of her perfume and grinned all the way home.

Chapter 23

The Victim turned left onto Main Street off of 28ᵗʰ Street. He'd gone to see her, as he often did. He hadn't stayed long. It was cold and dark and he didn't like the neighborhood.

He drove south, not in the Impala, but his white BMW 300 Series sedan. It was a few years old but still a nice ride. He may not be at the top end of his profession but he got by. As with most things in his life, he kept it pristine.

Coming into the Stockyards area, he slowed as a Ford Explorer pulled out of the Los Vaqueros parking lot and moved south, cutting him off. He shook his head and sighed. *Idiot. Learn to drive.*

The incident was quickly forgotten as his mind processed the past week. *Has it really been just a week? I feel so different. Four down. The cops don't know anything. This could go on forever.*

His smug smile stared back at him in the mirror. He was now almost to the river, the city's lighted skyline directly ahead of him. As he passed through Varrio Central territory, he scouted the neighborhood, noticed the lights of LaGrave Field where the Fort Worth Cats played. The minor league baseball team was the only bright spot in this otherwise bleak part of town. *Who would live in this shithole?*

As he crossed the Main Street Bridge into downtown, he looked in his rearview mirror where Varrio Central's turf sat like a desolate refugee camp. *I'll get to you eventually.* His eyes went cold. *Assuming I live long enough.*

His thoughts shifted from Varrio Central to the Kings and his real mission as he rounded the courthouse. He had planned to just go home but now his mind wouldn't slow down. *What next? How many more? I'm not done yet.*

His mind circled and before he realized it, he was exiting at

THE VICTIM

Rosedale on South I-35. He made the U-turn under the bridge and was northbound on the access road before he was really conscious of where he was driving.

It was a little after eight o'clock, dark enough but way too early to hunt. Besides beyond being in the wrong car, he never made a move without planning. That wouldn't stop him from doing a little spontaneous reconnoitering.

He turned right on Hattie and slowed as he passed Van Zandt - Guinn Park where just a few nights ago he'd taken down two Kings but barely escaped with his life. The park was empty. A slow smiled crossed his face. *Yeah, that's right. I ran you off your own turf, like rats.*

The smile faded as he looked around and realized it was way too early in the evening for much real gang traffic and to look at the place, nothing had changed. The police presence was gone and the empty beer bottles were back. No signs of extra security or of people moving more freely in the area.

As he continued past the houses that had taken the brunt of the Kings bullet shower meant for him, a hopped up SUV thumped by in the opposite lane. The windows were so dark it was impossible to see inside, but on the antennae a blue bandana fluttered in the cold breeze. *The Kings. Bastards.*

His car and heart rate both accelerated slightly out of shear reflex even as he reassured himself that it was silly. *They have no idea who I am. They probably wouldn't even if I was in the Impala*

He took a left on New York and weaved his way through the neighborhood, retracing his path from the other night. Tonight though, in this car, at this time of night, he stood out like a sore thumb. It was too cold for much foot traffic but he still made sure he kept moving, only slowing for stop signs and keeping his eyes moving.

The car seemed to be on autopilot, almost driving itself while he lost in thought. He was directly in the heart of the beast and found himself driving right past the King's headquarters.

He slowed, looked toward the building, not much more than a metal barn really. It looked the same as the last time he'd seen it, same cars, same bulky, menacing figures lurking around the front door, business as usual. His heart sank. *I obviously haven't done enough. They're just like cockroaches. They hide from the light but not even the dark slows them down.*

As he crept past and came to the intersection just west of their building, he could feel the anger build inside him. *Nothing has changed, nothing at all.* He sat for a moment, hands grinding at the steering wheel, face heating up with rage. The headlights of a car reflected in the rearview mirror. He'd sat at the stop sign for several minutes. In this neighborhood, a BMW could be stripped and gone in less than ten, the owner only beaten to a pulp if they were lucky.

He gunned the car across the intersection and down the short block to Tennessee Avenue. He took a quick left, his headlights splashed against the concrete embankment under the Union Pacific Railroad tracks. On it he noticed the words painted – *Don't Try It. Don't Buy It. Deny It.* It was an anti-drug message. He smiled. *In this part of town, they could be talking about society in general.*

He dipped under the tracks moving north past the Fort Worth bus depot on his right. He looked to his left and saw the ever present gathering of lost souls outside the Union Gospel Mission, forgotten people in a forgotten part of town.

He realized as he continued north and crossed over I-30 that he was going from bad to worse and his stomach tightened. If he'd been equipped for hunting, maybe he wouldn't be nervous but entering the projects in this car and unprepared was really pushing it.

He didn't know if there was an actual name for this part of town. Growing up, he'd heard it called the Ghetto, the Projects or his favorite, the Jungle. Whatever you called it, if you weren't black, you didn't go there. In fact, the way it's situated, you had to go out of your way to even get there.

The area is cut off from the rest of society by freeways on three sides, I-30 to the south, I-35 to the west and 121 to the north and the Trinity River to the east. It's almost like an island or perhaps a prison camp. The three roads that lead into the area all come from tough neighborhoods, none can compare.

The Jungle basically consists of two things, I.M. Terrell High School and the Fort Worth Housing Authority's government subsidized housing. These ugly red brick buildings resembled run down army barracks and had been there as long as he could remember. No matter how bad off you thought you were as a kid, your parents could always point to the Jungle as they drove by and let you know life could be worse.

The first thing he passed was I.M. Terrell High School. Built in the 1920's as the Fort Worth School of Colored People, it was and still remains an all-black school. It was later named after the first black teacher in Fort Worth and in its early history was considered quite good, for a black school.

He turned left onto I.M. Terrell Circle and drove past the school's south side, the old unlevel cinder track, the weed covered high school courtyard and into the projects. The area and buildings were originally designed and built with basic subsistence in mind, square buildings with small square concrete entryways. When they renovated the buildings to add air conditioning, they just plopped the compressor units directly on top of the front entryways. This was done to discourage people from stealing the units but it took ugly and made it worse.

The Victim looked around in disgust. *How do people live like this? Most animals live better.* What pissed him off more than the thought that people had to live in some place like the Jungle, was that their own offspring preyed on them just as soon as they were old enough to put down their pacifiers and blankies and pick up a gun or knife. He nodded to himself as he considered that to be one more justification for his actions.

The cold weather had most of the inhabitants huddled behind closed doors, the few that were out stared as he went by. He assumed they thought he was either very lost or very crazy. Maybe he was a little of both.

The streets were lined with an odd mix of cars. There were the barely functioning beaters of the prey parked right next to the hopped up rides of the predators.

As he came around the circle to the north side of the high school, he found what he'd expected to find based on his research. Between the school and the track and football field was a small children's playground area. Just like his last target area, the area where innocent children played during the day became a distribution center for the Kings at night.

Tonight was no different. There were three bangers hanging around the picnic tables with one more apparently making a sale to someone in a car that had pulled to the curb. *What is it with you freaks and hanging out in playgrounds? Some kind of lost childhood bullshit?*

He felt their eyes move to his car and his pulse quickened. He wasn't about to stop. In fact, he'd seen what he needed and it was time for him to move on. As he drove past, he noticed two of the bangers quickly move toward their car. He pressed down on the accelerator. He was around in front of the high school and had turned left onto Cypress Street heading east out of the Jungle in a blink.

The road crested a hill and curved to the north along the river and the empty soccer fields. As he drove under a small bridge and came to Fourth Street he saw the headlights coming up behind him from in front of the school. They followed fast but were too far back. He took a quick left on Fourth Street, passed the Purina plant on the right, through a tangle of roadside trees and brush and under two more railroad bridges up into a recently renovated neighborhood. He was out of the Jungle, back into civilization and on the edge of downtown.

He formulated his next strike plan as he ambled his way through the downtown streets and headed toward home. *I'll see you soon, boys. You better be ready.*

Chapter 24

Hunter pulled to the curb in front of the FWPD Central Division, his earpiece in his left ear, and waved Sanders into the Explorer. The morning was crisp but with a perfect blue sky and almost no hint of wind. For a November day in north Texas, it was as good as it gets.

Hunter continued his phone conversation as he pulled into traffic, barely acknowledging Sander existed in the seat next to him. "All right, good, so all the paperwork's done. When do you expect to get in front of Feldman?" Hunter listened, grunted a few monosyllable responses his eyes surveyed traffic. "Call me as soon as you've got a signature. We'll move on him this afternoon."

He signed off and finally looked at Sanders. "Good morning Sunshine."

Sanders nodded with a broad grin. "Was that Reyes?"

"Yeah, he's got the warrants ready and has an appointment with Judge Whacko at eleven. We should be just about finished with Gentry by that time. We'll regroup at the precinct, split up and serve the warrants at both his house and office at the same time." Hunter had made his way through the maze of one way streets in the downtown Fort Worth and maneuvered onto the highway. "By the way, did you check us out through Dispatch?"

"Yep. This Gentry guy's over off University, right?" Hunter nodded, retrieved his Starbuck's cup from the holder and sipped. Sanders continued. "So, who is this guy again and why are we chasing around on this if we think Bennett's our guy?"

Hunter smirked and in a very bad Chinese accent, said, "Ah, young Weedhopper, never wise to put all eggs in one basket." After grinning a moment at his own joke, Hunter continued. "So, Steve Gentry's name came out of the conversation with ADA Daris. Gentry's a defense attorney who seems to specialize in defending gangbangers and who might be able to add names to our list of potential vigilante suspects. He might also be able to confirm names already on our list."

"A defense attorney? This ought to be interesting. They're not normally all that anxious to help out the boys in blue. How much do you expect to get from him?"

"Well, if you think about it, we're not asking him to inform on his clients. In fact, we're actually trying to protect his clientele. He'll help to protect his future income. Besides, most of these guys are real crusaders. You know, protecting the downtrodden and all that crap. He's probably one of those who are all fired up to hang some middle class cracker for taking out ghetto brothers."

As the words left Hunter's mouth, discomfort flashed across his face. He quickly added, "Ah, no offense intended."

Sanders broke into laughter. "None taken. I'm betting that's not the worst thing you've ever called a..." Sanders smirked. "A man of color."

Hunter snorted, gave Sanders a sideways glance. "Yeah, that's it. A man of color. That's the term I was searching for." Hunter shook his head as he took the University exit off I-30, looped around under the overpass and went south for a short block. He pulled into the parking lot of a pair of brown, six story glass office buildings.

They entered the lobby, nodded to the security guard and walked over to the building's directory. Gentry and Associates in Suite 410 was a short ride up a lanky elevator.

They stepped off into a non-descript hallway leading off in two directions and lined with several doors, portals to an assortment of legal and other professional offices. Once they found Suite 410, they walked in and stiffened as the small, but full waiting area silenced. All heads turned their way as if they had 'cops' tattooed on their foreheads. Both detectives instinctively dropped their hands to brush their weapons, confirming they were still there.

Sanders kept an eye on the clientele as Hunter flashed his badge and told the receptionist they had an appointment with Gentry. She made a call, nodded and buzzed them in through a locked door.

She pointed down the short hallway and turned her attention

back to the computer on her desk leaving them to find their way. Hunter led, moving slowly, perusing the framed articles lining the hall. Most showed various versions of smiling people at obvious charity events, two men seemed to appear in almost all of the pictures. Hunter assumed one of them was Steve Gentry.

As Hunter paused to read a story about an innocent man having spent time in prison until he was released based on new DNA evidence, movement from down the hall caught his attention.

"Detective Hunter I presume?" Steve Gentry stood in the doorway of an office at the end of the hall. Fairly ordinary looking, in his early forties, Gentry was maybe six feet tall and two hundred pounds. He looked to be in decent shape but probably not a serious fitness freak. His dishwater blond hair was slightly longer than you might expect for an attorney but neatly groomed. His clothes, though not what a high end defense attorney might wear, were impeccably tailored and pressed. "My receptionist let me know you were here. Please come in."

Hunter and Sanders followed into the office and stood as Gentry sat at his desk. Hunter quickly surveyed the office absorbing his surroundings. The office faced west with a large window behind Gentry's desk, which looked out over the I-30 to the Fort Worth Botanical Gardens.

As he looked around, he noted the expected accoutrements of an attorney's office, the book shelves full of case reference books and legal journals, more framed photos of Gentry with local dignitaries, several diplomas from his college, his law school and the Texas Bar Association. He also noted something unexpected. The office was impeccably clean and almost obsessively organized. In Hunter's experience, most attorneys were overworked and understaffed, which their offices reflected.

"Please have a seat, Detective." Gentry's voice broke Hunter from his observations and he realized that Sanders was already seated. Gentry frowned and tapped his foot.

"Oh, sure." Hunter moved to the remaining chair and tried to deflect Gentry's tension. He pointed to the window. "Great view."

"Yes." Gentry continued to face forward, his face tense, his manicured hands gripping the arms of his high backed leather chair as if he were about to be ejected from a fighter jet. "It is lovely, but I'm sure that's not why you're here. As you probably noticed by the crowded waiting room, business is booming these days. I don't want to be rude but I'm paid by the hour, so exactly how can I help you gentlemen today?"

Hunter, seeing they hadn't exactly gotten off to a good start, put on his best WalMart Greeter smile. "We certainly appreciate your time Mr. Gentry and we'll get through this quickly. Detective Sanders and I are heading up the task force focused on the recent murders of several local gang members."

Gentry visibly stiffened, cleared his throat. "Well, I'm happy to help, but other than losing future potential clients, I can't imagine how that has anything to do with me."

Hunter smiled. "No, I'm sure you're right. But you may be able to help us out. According to the DA's office, you specialize in representing gang members and might be able to provide us insight into crime victims or relatives of crime victims who might have decided to take the law into their own hands."

Gentry stared at Hunter a moment and seemed to deflate slightly as he relaxed his grip on the chair. He leaned forward in his chair. "I'm more than happy to help where I can." He reached over to his phone and punched an intercom button. "Can I get you some coffee or soda?"

Both Hunter and Sanders nodded and indicated coffee as a female voice crackled in the speaker.

"Sharon, can you bring some coffee in for the detectives and me? Thanks."

Hunter spent the next ten minutes explaining his discussion with the DA and the input he hoped to get from Gentry. Gentry seemed reticent to speak at first and expressed concerns about client confidentiality. Once Hunter reminded him that he would likely lose more clients soon, he spoke for twenty minutes outlining several situations he'd encountered in the last year where there were threats made.

As he spoke, the three men fell into a relaxed conversation. Sanders took diligent notes and drilled down into the details of each incident. Meanwhile Hunter listened, asked questions and continued his casual perusal of Gentry's office. He smiled internally as he noticed the gray wool overcoat hanging on the coat rack and the family pictures displayed on the credenza. It was almost a carbon copy of Daris' office, and for that matter, almost every office in the city. He shook his head as he realized that every attorney, regardless of which side they represented, had family members who could have been victims and could easily have access to law enforcement records related to gangs. He wasn't sure if that took Daris off his list or if it merely added a few thousand others to the list.

The conversation was winding down and the cups were empty. They'd spent far more time than expected and had added to their list of suspects.

Hunter looked across the desk at Gentry. "I really appreciate your time today. As you can imagine, in my position, defense attorneys don't generally like to cooperate with me. Usually, we're on opposite sides of the table."

Gentry nodded.

Hunter continued. "Can I ask you a personal question, and by all means, if you don't want to answer, I'll understand."

Gentry's cooperative demeanor faded, replaced by the original tense look. He shrugged. "Sure, you can ask."

"Why do you do it? Why do you defend these guys? I mean, sure, there are a handful in the mix that might actually be innocent. I'll grant you that, but by in large, most of your clients would just as soon cut your throat and steal your car as look at you."

Gentry sat, contemplated for a moment. When it seemed that he wasn't going to answer, Hunter stood up. "Just curious." Sanders stood to follow him out.

Gentry motioned for them to sit back down. "Actually, Detective, I'll be happy to answer your question." He paused, let Hunter and Sanders settle back into their seats.

"When I was in my late teens, early twenties, I was a pretty typical numbskull like most boys at that age. My friends and I partied just a little too much, flirted with the tough side of town and danced right on the edge of the line." He stopped, seemed to be remembering misadventures. "We were having fun, rarely if ever, truly crossing the line. When we did, we got back on the good side quickly."

"Anyway, one of my friends, a black kid, got arrested and accused of aggravated assault." His face looked grim. "This was the seventies in Fort Worth, TX. He was a black guy. The victim was white. You can guess how long it took to convict him."

Hunter and Sanders listened intently, nodded.

He continued. "Now you might be thinking that maybe he did it. The problem was I knew he didn't. He was with me when the crime occurred and nowhere near the incident." He leaned back in his chair, clearly upset by the memory. "I tried to tell the Police but they wouldn't listen, no one would. You see, I had stepped across that line just enough to have a couple of minor arrests on my record and therefore, my credibility was shot."

"My friend went to prison and I vowed to fight the system and make sure the same thing didn't happen to others. I became an attorney and immediately began what I believed at the time to be a crusade to defend the wrongly accused."

"Unfortunately, what I've learned in the last two decades is that ninety percent of the people that walk through my door are, in fact, guilty. If they aren't guilty of the crime with which they've been charged, they're guilty of ten others. I spend my time getting criminals off on technicalities and nitpicking the work done by you and your colleagues. All the while, I'm eating Tums like candy trying to fight the nausea that comes with knowing I'm enabling people who break the law." He paused. "Not exactly the noble cause I pursued." He smiled. "And that probably wasn't the answer you expected."

There was an uncomfortable silence, all three men lost in thought. After a moment, Hunter broke the silence. "Why do you still do it?"

Gentry shrugged, a defeated grin came across his face. "What am I supposed to do? My chosen career path doesn't exactly lend itself to moving to the DA's office or becoming the next Johnny Cochran. I'm kind of stuck, the idealist who realized too late that the reality is fuzzier than I want it to be." He held up a finger and looked thoughtful. "And I actually do find an innocent one every now and then."

Chapter 25

"What? God damn it! You've got to be kidding me." Hunter's head was about to explode, eyes wide, veins bulging. "What the hell do you mean there's a problem with the warrants?"

Sanders snapped his head around and watched as Hunter listened intently, muttering sporadic obscenities. Finally, he barked, "I'll be there in ten minutes." He threw his earpiece onto the dashboard. "God damn it!"

Sanders' muscular frame shrank down in the passenger seat as he tried to disappear for the short ride back to the department.

Hunter burst into the task force room, Sanders trailing behind. Reyes, Parker and Lowe jerked up from their work. Hunter didn't wait to get seated. "Okay, Jimmy, run it down for me. What the hell is going on with the warrants?"

Reyes looked sheepish. "We met with Feldman at eleven, reviewed the documents and went through all of our reasons for the warrant. He barely looked at the requests and didn't read anything beyond what we had highlighted. He huffed and puffed for a few minutes and said we were just on a fishing expedition and we didn't have anything but speculation." Reyes looked earnestly at Hunter. "I continued the argument, I pushed him hard and he finally relented to signing off on a warrant specific only to collecting Bennett's guns for ballistic testing."

Everyone in the room was silent. Hunter seemed to be boiling under his skin.

Reyes continued. "I know it's not what we wanted but if we can get the guns…"

"It's bullshit is what it is!" Hunter's eyes flared. "If he's our guy, he'll have been smart enough not to use his registered weapons so whatever he turns over to us won't be a ballistics match and while we're off wasting time testing unused guns, he'll be trashing all the evidence we might have found during a real search."

Reyes nodded. Sanders and Parker just kept their heads down. Lowe had sunk so low in his chair, he seemed to have disappeared.

Hunter stood up and started pacing fiercely back and forth at the front of the room. His mind was racing, trying to think of any way to either convince Feldman to sign or to circumvent Feldman all together. No matter how hard he paced, nothing came to mind.

Finally, the futility of his mental anguish set in and he stopped pacing and sat at the table. He stared into the sun streaming in through the blinds. "All right, what are the specifics?"

Reyes sat up. "No physical search of the premises, either the office of home. We have a list of known, registered weapons including the two 9mm pistols, a shotgun and a deer rifle. He is required to relinquish those weapons. We can run ballistics tests on the pistols and hold the rifles as a precaution. We have up to two weeks to complete the tests and must return all weapons unless they can be linked to the crimes."

"Additionally, we can require that he provide any and all weapons in his possession." He stopped, smirked. "Of course, since we can't search, I can't imagine him just handing over something not on the list."

Hunter's head tilted with a thought. "That's assuming he knows our warrant is limited and lists those weapons."

Reyes smiled. The rest of the team seemed to relax. "Well, we can certainly run the bluff. Not sure how far it will get. He is an attorney after all."

Hunter nodded. "It's worth a try." He sat and drummed his fingers on the table for a moment. "Alright, since we're pretty limited on this thing, Sanders and I'll make the visit. We'll bluff as much as we can, ask as many questions as the good lawyer will answer and at a minimum, bring back the weapons on the list."

Hunter sat for a moment, his level of disgust slowly dropping. As he thought, his nose finally registered the stench in the room. "Boys, this place smells like a barn. You might consider taking a few minutes to dispose of some the toxic waste that's built up. You wait much longer and the damage might be permanent."

He looked over at Billy. "Let's grab some lunch, check out with dispatch and go pay our friend a visit. Well, assuming this smell hasn't completely ruined your appetite."

Billy smiled. "I think I can force something down. So, where does this guy live anyway?"

"Ah, we get to go see how the other half live. He's in a little posh town in northeast Tarrant County called Southlake."

Billy scrunched his nose. "Isn't that the country place that used to win all the A football titles?"

"Oh yeah. That's the place, only it's grown up a bit since then, and much more exclusive. I'll fill you in on the drive up."

Chapter 26

After a quick lunch at Mexican Inn Café in downtown, Hunter steered northeast on Hwy 121 moving through Riverside, Haltom City and Richland Hills. Full of Tex-Mex and enjoying the beautiful sunshine and crisp temperature, his tension over the search warrant hassle had subsided. He still wasn't happy, but had come to grips with the ruling and was now thinking about how to manipulate it to his advantage.

Sanders broke him out of his thoughts. "So, when I was growing up in Euless, Southlake wasn't much more than cow pastures and dirt roads. Some of my more redneck buddies used to go there to bird hunt. I remember they had a pretty good football team for a little country school."

Hunter nodded. "Well, let me catch you up on some history… Over the last couple of decades, there have been some major investments made along the Hwy 114 corridor between Grapevine and I-35. The first of those was Solana. That was a business campus built to house the likes of IBM and Fidelity Investments. It was supposed to be the Tarrant County version of Las Colinas but never quite got there. Nonetheless, it brought in some big name companies and all the executive management players that those companies employee."

"All those execs needed a place to live and they didn't want to drive all the way from Dallas so they started building neighborhoods in the little towns up and down 114. More recently, Alliance Airport and Texas Motor Speedway were built near the junction of 114 and I-35. This brought more jobs and more money to the area. As all of this was happening, that little country town of Southlake just happened to be sitting in the perfect location. It straddles 114 just north of where 114 and 121 meet and just northwest of the top of DFW Airport."

"With great access to DFW, downtown Dallas and downtown

Fort Worth, that little hick town transformed into the Beverly Hills of Tarrant County almost overnight. Southlake became known for gated neighborhoods, huge lots, local celebrities and McMansions. Guys like Pat Sommerall and Terry Bradshaw live in the area. Troy Aikman bought property there but later decided not to build."

Sanders grinned. "Those are big names for a little town."

"Yeah, that little town has become the place to be. It's where high school cheerleaders go when they grow up to become trophy wives."

Sanders snorted.

Hunter continued. "It's one of the wealthiest zip codes in America. 90210's got nothing on these guys. I read a couple of years ago that the median household income was over $200k." He raised an eyebrow for emphasis. "And that little football team… They now play in 5A and have won three state championships in the last decade. Hell, they even finished ranked number one in the country a few years ago."

"No kidding. Man, once I got permanently sidelined, my interest in the game just disappeared so I haven't kept up with the scene. I don't know. Maybe I'm just not cut out to be a spectator."

They exited the freeway and traversed the back country roads, winding among the hills and properties that grew larger with every mile. Hunter had contacted the Southlake PD in advance to let them know about serving the warrant but declined their offer for backup due to the narrow nature of the warrant.

The further northeast they traveled, the scenery changed from low rent industrial to semi-rural and then started shifting subtly to upper scale neighborhoods and gated communities. By the time they made the right hand turn off Davis onto FM1709, the number of Mercedes, Jaguars and BMW's had dramatically increased. As they moved east, the number and size of the McMansions just seemed to grow exponentially. When they passed the Southlake Town Square with its faux early nineteenth century architecture, open courtyard with fountain and gazebo and its impressive city hall building, both detectives gawked.

Looking around slowly, absorbing the sites, Sanders shook his head. "You weren't kidding about seeing how the other half lives." He whistled. "Damn."

"Yeah, well, don't get too enamored. They shit just like the rest of us and if Bennett's our guy, he's going down just like any other murderer."

Hunter referenced MapQuest on his phone, realized he'd gone one street too far. He found a break in the traffic that was flowing in and out of the town square shopping area like an ant hill, made a quick U-turn and then a left turn onto Carroll Avenue.

As they drove south on Carroll, both men turned their heads at the sound of a small airplane that seemed way too close to the ground. They quickly realized they were driving parallel to a private airstrip and that the plane landed in someone's massive backyard.

"Holy crap." Sanders had a look of disbelief on his face and turned to Hunter. "We're not in Fort Worth anymore Toto".

"Yeah." Hunter smiled. "Mercedes and Beamers and Planes, Oh My!"

They both laughed as they continued to weave through breathtaking neighborhoods. They drove past various versions of small mansions set back off the road on half acre plus lots, each with three car garages, manicured lawns and the feel that money might very well grow on trees.

After passing an elementary school and cutting back up into an even more impressive neighborhood, they found Rainbow Street and turned.

"All right, our boy Bennett should be coming up on the right. Look for 4235."

They pulled to the curb in front of one of the more impressive homes on the block. Behind immaculate landscaping, a sprawling rock home with an enormous stained wood front door sat on what had to be over an acre of land. The side entry garage sat behind a remote controlled ornamental iron gate. Behind the gate sat a Mercedes E550 sedan. It shined in the sunlight.

The detectives stepped up onto the expansive porch under the high rock archway and rang the bell. Both casually looked through the ornate windows on each side of the door.

Sanders eyed as much of the home's interior as possible and mumbled, "Damn, this place is amazing." He nodded quickly toward the door. "Here's our guy."

The door cracked open, Jim Bennett surveyed the two men suspiciously but didn't speak.

Hunter, seeing Jim Bennett for the first time, took a slight double take, hesitated and with a slightly deflated look, casually flashed his badge. "Mr. Bennett, we need a few minutes of your time. May we come in?"

Bennett stood for a moment, studying the two detectives, slowly stepped back and gestured for them to enter. He moved to the detective's right toward what appeared to be his home office.

Hunter followed Sanders across the threshold, looked around, absorbing the environment. To his left was a separate dining room with an ornate table large enough to seat twelve comfortably. Directly ahead was a cavernous living room with two story high vaulted ceilings and dark hardwood flooring. The walls matched the wood finish, the top of the room ringed with open railing from upstairs walkways. Floor to ceiling windows looked out over a lagoon swimming pool, backyard kitchen and entertainment area. It looked more like the lobby to a resort than a home.

As he turned to his right following Sanders and Bennett to the office, he shook his head at his surroundings. *What must it be like?*

Once in the office, Hunter looked around, noting the size of the office. It was L shaped with most of the open space to the left of the door. Bennett settled behind his desk, light streamed in the windows as they went through a quick round of introductions. After a moment, Bennett looked at Hunter with a strained smile. "So where are Crawford and Pokorski? Did they take them off the case and bring in the A Team now that that nut bag judge is on the verge of letting that thug off?"

Hunter leaned forward. "Mr. Bennett, we're not here about your daughter's case." *Not directly.*

As limited as the smile was, it faded quickly. "Well then, exactly why are you here?"

"Mr. Bennett, we need to ask you a few questions. Can you tell me…"

"Hold on Detective." Bennett leaned over the enormous mahogany desk. "You can stop right there. If you're here on something other than my daughter's case, I'm going to need to know what's going on before I answer any questions. I'm sure you guys did your homework before knocking on my door so you know I spent a couple of decades sitting on your side of the desk. I can assure you, I know the game. If you want my help, let's be straight with each other and I'll do the best I can. If you want to play cloak and dagger, I'll lawyer up faster than you can get the first question out of your mouth."

Hunter paused for a moment, sizing him up, then proceeded. "All right Mr. Bennett, let's open the kimono." He reached into his jacket pocket and laid the search warrant on the desk but didn't offer it to Bennett. "Here's the deal. Detective Sanders and I are investigating the recent string of gang member killings…"

Bennett interrupted again, this time with a snort of laughter. "Wait a minute. You're kidding me, right? You're investigating me for those killings? So… Let me get this straight… My daughter was killed by a gang member, I happen to own a gun so now I've gone on a rampage killing gangbangers." He leaned back in his chair and smiled broadly. "Fellas, I gotta tell ya, that's a hell of a stretch."

Hunter continued. "As I was saying Mr. Bennett, we are investigating those murders and are speaking with a number of people who may have been victimized by gangs and may have a reason to retaliate. You, as you so eloquently stated, fit that profile."

Bennett nodded toward the search warrant on the desk. "I must fit more than just the basic profile if you've cobbled together enough to get a search warrant." He paused, his eyes moving from the search warrant to Hunter. "I am curious though, if you've got a search warrant, why only two of you and why the pretense of just coming to chat? That's not exactly protocol."

"Well, continuing in the spirit of full disclosure, the warrant is only for the confiscation and ballistics testing of your weapons, it's not for a complete search of the premises."

Bennett pushed back from the desk and stood quickly. Both Hunter and Sanders jumped, reflexively reaching for their hips. He quickly put out both hands. "Whoa, fellas. I'm just getting you what you came for. No need to get jumpy." They all relaxed. "You know, if you'd really done your homework on me, you would have known that you didn't need the warrant. I'll be happy to cooperate... Now, what exactly do you need?"

Hunter explained the specific list of weapons and asked for any others not listed. He insisted on escorting Bennett to the gun cabinet in the garage to collect the weapons.

When they returned, they packaged up the weapons they'd expected to find along with a twenty-two caliber rifle not on the list and sat back down.

Bennett settled in. "So if I had an attorney here with me, this is where he'd tell me not to say anything. Since I am an attorney, and have nothing to do with these murders, I'll be happy to answer your questions." He laughed quietly. "I guess the old adage about an attorney representing himself having a fool for a client must be true." He put his palms out and shrugged his shoulders. "In this case, I think we're pretty safe since I know absolutely nothing about these cases."

"Thanks for your cooperation Mr. Bennett, we really only have a few questions." He referenced his notepad. "Can you tell me where you were last Thursday night?"

"Sure." Bennett leaned forward, tapped a few keys on his desktop. "I spent most of the evening driving home from Austin. I'd been down there all week meeting with clients."

"You drove?"

"Yeah, I often do these days. The security hassles at the airport really make it just about a wash from a timing standpoint. Besides, it gives me time to be alone with my thoughts." He seemed to drift for a moment, then shook his head as if to dismiss bad thoughts. "Ever since Nicki... Well, having time to think and remember is nice."

"What exactly happened with your daughter?"

The pain washed over his face like a flood. In an instant he seemed older, broken. "Well, all we really know is what that animal said in his confession and what we can put together based on the investigation."

Bennett stood and walked to the window. "She was a Junior at TCU living on campus in Clark Hall. She was studying to be a Special Needs Teacher." He looked back at Hunter and Sanders, smiled wistfully. "She had this over developed sense of wanting to help others.

She got that from her Mother."

His face tightened again. "Anyway, it was an uneventful Saturday night on campus. Her roommate said she'd finished studying and decided to walk down to Mojo's for a cup of coffee." He dropped his head. "Everything else we know came from either the crime scene or his confession. Nikki..." He paused. "Was found in an alley off University. She'd been raped and strangled."

The pain in Mr. Bennett's voice floated across the room, soaked into Hunter's posture. He was barely able to speak. "I'm sorry for your loss. I just have one last question for you. You said you had been in Austin all week. When did you go down?"

"Sunday afternoon. I can provide you with a copy of that week's expense report along with receipt copies. I've got them right here." He reached into a drawer, rummaged through a folder and handed a neatly stapled stack of papers to Hunter.

Hunter stood. "Thank you for your help today Mr. Bennett." He and Sanders collected the weapons and the documents and moved toward the front door.

The three men stopped in the open doorway. Bennett looked Hunter square in the eye. "Detective, I'm a hell of a good marksman and believe me, the thought of using those skills has crossed my mind more than a few times. I'm not your guy though." He paused. "When you find him, let me know. I'd like to shake his hand."

Hunter nodded. "It seems that about half the city feels that way." He motioned to the weapons. "I'll get these back to you within two weeks."

Hunter and Sanders stowed the evidence and climbed into the SUV. As they pulled away, Sanders gave Hunter a sideways look. "So what happened to all those hardnosed tactics?"

"Didn't need 'em. He's not our guy."

"Oh really? You know this because he told a sad story about his daughter and had a couple of pages of receipts."

"Nope."

"Well, then what exactly?"

Hunter smiled. "He doesn't look anything like Donald Trump."

Chapter 27

Sanders laughed as they turned off of Rainbow Street and wound their way through the posh suburb. "You're kidding me. You're still hung up on what that crazy old drunk from the alley said... Man, that dude probably gets visited by little green men in flying saucers."

Hunter just looked ahead. "Mark my words. Bennett's not our guy."

"So, if you're so sure, why'd you execute the warrant?"

"Well, I may be sure but I'm not stupid. If there's even the faintest possibility he's our guy, testing his weapons is the only prudent thing to do. Can you imagine the shit storm in the press if he was our guy and it came to light later, after he's knocked off a few more gangbangers, that we had a warrant and didn't execute it?"

"I don't know about the press, but the regular folks might declare us heroes."

They continued to banter. When they drove back past the elementary school, something flashed in Hunter's peripheral vision. He started to turn his head but his movement was interrupted when Sanders started talking. "So I've been meaning to ask you something ever since we met and this seems like as good a time as any."

Hunter's attention was now back in the conversation but his mind continued to work. "Go for it."

"Why is it that everyone calls you Cowboy? I mean, you don't exactly fit the stereotype. You don't wear boots, no hat, no big ugly belt buckle. You don't talk like a Cowboy. I don't think I've ever heard you say 'ya'll'. Hell, I've got a deeper Texas drawl than you do. So what gives?"

Hunter grinned. "It stems from a rather crazy situation during my days back on patrol. You see, this one day..." Hunter's face froze, his shoulders pushed back suddenly. He yelled, "Shit!" and slammed on his brakes. Sanders just about hit the windshield as smoke billowed off the tires. Hunter jerked the Explorer into a hard U turn.

Sanders hung on for dear life. "What the hell?"

"The Kings!" Hunter was now flying down the residential streets. "I just saw one of their cars pulling out of that school and heading toward Bennett's."

"What? No way. You had to be seeing things. Why would they be... Oh shit." Sanders reached for his cell phone and banged in 9-1-1.

Hunter was barely able to keep the SUV on the road as he flew back through the neighborhood, blew through the stop sign and fishtailed around the corner onto Rainbow. Sanders was screaming into his cell phone, requesting backup, rattling off his badge number, Bennett's address and a synopsis of what was happening.

The V8 roared and they moved down the street as if it was the quarter mile at a drag strip. As they crested the small rise in the street, Hunter's heart sank when he saw the car parked a few hundred feet in front of them, at Bennett's curb. Two gangbangers were casually standing in the yard leaning against the car.

Their head's spun at the sound but it was too late. Hunter kept his foot on the gas until the last possible moment, slammed on the brakes as the SUV crashed into the parked car sending it and the two gangbangers flying into Bennett's front yard.

Sanders was out almost before the impact, his gun leveled at the two dazed men lying on the ground. As he pounced on the closest one, driving his knee into the small of his back, he turned to see Hunter rounding the front of the car. He waived him toward the front of the house. "Go, go, go. I've got these guys!"

Hunter turned toward the house and the open front door in full stride. Two steps up the sidewalk, the sound of the gunshot pierced his ears but he never slowed down. He thought he heard himself yelling but his mind was racing so fast, he couldn't be sure.

His gun was out as he blew through the door, no cautious entry, no hesitation. "Police! Police!" In a split second, he surveyed the dining room and the huge living room, no longer thinking about their beauty, just seeing a blur of shapes and letting his instincts drive him forward.

He turned toward the office, running. He burst through the office door, remembering the layout and automatically sweeping to his left, his Glock leading the way. His breath caught. Bennett lay crumpled on the floor, leaning against the wall. His dead eyes stared upward, a single entry wound in the middle of his forehead.

As his brain processed the blood splatter on the wall, he instinctively began a sweeping right turn. He stopped instantly at the sound of the hammer being cocked behind his right ear.

"Uh uh, Cowboy, don't you move."

The air seemed to suck out of his lungs, his peripheral vision blurred. He knew that voice, terror ripped through his whole being. He stopped instantly, tried to speak but nothing came out.

Shadow shoved the barrel of the gun against the back of his head pushing him forward a couple of steps. Now he was standing directly in front of Bennett's body, looking into his dead eyes, with his back to Shadow and Shadow's gun just inches from the back of his head.

"Drop yo gun, Cowboy. Didn't know I was gonna get a two-fer today. Must be my lucky day. I get the bastard been poppin' my boys and my favorite cop all at the same time."

Hunter slowly leaned down, dropped his gun on the floor. *Stall him. Stall him.* His mind raced, his heart pounded, his brain was nothing but chaos. His voice sounded distant, like it wasn't coming from him. "You shot the wrong guy Shadow."

"What the hell you mean, I shot the wrong guy? This the guy you got a search warrant for. He the muthafucka been poppin' my boys. Turn around and look at me. Tell me what you mean."

Hunter turned slowly, like a glacier. *Stall him. Stall him.* Now he was staring down the barrel of an enormous pistol. As calmly as possible, Hunter said, "We were wrong. He wasn't the guy." Almost inaudibly, he added, "He wasn't even in town."

Shadow's face tensed, his nostrils flared. He glared at Hunter. "Guess that's too damn bad for the rich honky and too damn bad for you too." His arm started to rise.

Hunter stared straight into his eyes, no sign of humanity. *One last shot.* "Shadow, you kill a cop, you get the needle. It's automatic."

The expression on Shadow's face sent a chill down Hunter's

spine. It was the sickest smile he'd ever seen. "Like I give a fuck." Shadow's arm moved up quickly and his hand tensed.

The room exploded with the gunshot. Hunter stumbled backward, tripping over Bennett's feet, his back hit the wall. His vision blurred for a split second but he didn't fall. In that space between life and death, Hunter's mind processed a million thoughts. The most prevalent of those were – *Am I dead? If I'm dead, why can I still see? Where was the muzzle flash? Why is the room filled with pink mist?* Hunter blinked and Shadow's body crumpled to the floor.

Hunter gasped for air, only then realizing that he hadn't been breathing. His heart rate rocketed up, his vision started to tunnel and he reached out with his hand to find something, anything, to stabilize himself. He stared down at the carnage in front of him. The side of Shadow's head was just gone, a strange smirk still on his face.

For a moment there was nothing, just silence, dust and pink mist settling, highlighted by the sun streaming in the window.

Sanders called from the hall. "Hunter? You okay?"

Chapter 28

Hunter leaned against the wall, out of breath, still focusing as Sanders slowly moved to the door. "Cowboy?" Sanders had his gun raised, surveying the room for any remaining threats. "Cowboy? You okay?"

Hunter nodded his head as he heaved in deep breaths trying to keep upright. He was pale, his eyes wide, pupils dilated.

Sanders didn't look much better. He slowly lowered his weapon and looked down at Shadow on the floor. The realization that he'd not only just shot someone, but that he'd just shot the little brother of his boyhood friend seemed to hit him. Like Hunter, he reached out, found the door jam with his hand and steadied himself.

He looked over at Hunter, nodded toward the wall. "Ah, you might want to move your arm."

Hunter followed his eyes and saw that when he'd fallen against the wall, his arm had landed in the splatter of blood and brains that had exited the back of Bennett's skull and plastered to the wall. Hunter pulled his arm away, surveyed the mess on his jacket sleeve. "Shit."

Putting his hands on his knees, he slowly straightened up. "I think we should probably step outside. The Southlake guys will want to secure the room as a crime scene." He reached over, picked up his gun and carefully followed Sanders out through the door.

When they reached the front porch, they were met with the cool, crisp air and the sound of sirens and police cruisers barreling down the street. Hunter stepped to the side of the porch, leaned over into the front landscaping and puked up every ounce of his Tex-Mex lunch.

As Hunter gathered himself, Sanders directed the Southlake Patrol Officers into the house. With the first responders occupied for a moment but realizing that most of the rest of the Southlake PD would be descending on them within the next few minutes, Hunter signaled for Sanders to come over. He spoke quietly but looked Sanders straight in the eye to make sure he was paying attention. "Listen to me. That was a good shoot. He had your partner at gunpoint. You came in. You identified yourself and told him to drop his weapon and you fired only after he ignored you and made a threatening move toward me."

Sanders looked confused. "But Cowboy, I didn't identify my..." He stopped in midsentence, his eyes widened.

Hunter glared at him. "Do you understand me?"

Sanders nodded, spoke slowly. He seemed to struggle to get the words out. "Yeah, it was exactly how you said."

"Good because as soon as the Southlake Detectives get here, which based on the number of cars arriving, should be any minute, they'll separate us and get statements. What we say needs to be absolutely in sync."

"No problem. We're good."

They spent the next few minutes in silence. Hunter's mind drifted to Frank and how close he'd just come to meeting the same fate. *I'm still alive because my partner was here for me. Frank's partner wasn't.* The memories flowed back and the pain seared through his mind.

True to his prediction, within minutes two Southlake Detectives had arrived, separated them and spent the next two hours debriefing. Hunter and one of the detectives sat down in the dining room just to the left of the entry hall. Hunter sat where he could look into the hall. As they spoke, he relived each moment of the day, each decision, each missed opportunity, in meticulous detail. As Hunter's initial shock and confusion wore off, his anguish over the death of Jim Bennett overwhelmed him.

During the questioning, his mind continued to drift. *How did Shadow know about Bennett? Had he followed them? No, not possible. He would have noticed, especially with the unexpected U turn in the middle of FM1709. No way.*

The questions ate at him while he watched the controlled chaos of the crime scene. Throughout the session, the crime scene and medical examiner teams traipsed in and out of the house. Hunter watched as both bodies were eventually wheeled out.

The scene outside the window became more hectic with every minute. It seemed like most of the Southlake Police Department personnel were on the scene, all the major media outlets had arrived and the neighbors gathered at the tape line. His heart sank and he was almost physically ill again when Mrs. Bennett arrived, was told what had happened and collapsed in the front yard. She was carried away in an ambulance, most likely to spend a heavily sedated night at Baylor Grapevine Medical Center.

As the debriefing wound down, it became clear the Southlake PD had no desire to pursue heavy investigations of two Fort Worth Detectives in the death of a gangbanger, especially one who had just murdered a prominent local resident.

Hunter watched the mayhem realizing the real nightmare was waiting for them once they finish with the scene. He shook his head and felt his stomach churn. He pushed it out of his mind. The only way to stay sane was to force himself to think about how they had gotten into this mess.

It was late afternoon when they brought Sanders back into the room. Hunter knew he had to get back in front of the situation so he took control of the conversation. He spoke quietly but firmly. "Detectives, if we've satisfied your questions, can we talk about the bigger issue at hand?"

The two Southlake detectives looked questioningly at each other and the more senior of the pair responded. "And that is?"

"How exactly did Shadow end up here? How did he know about the warrant?"

Bowing up slightly, the detective cleared his throat. "Well, obviously we will conduct a thorough investigation into the circumstances of Mr. Bennett's death, but it seems pretty clear who did the shooting, ballistics will confirm that..." He paused for a moment, looked a little uncomfortable. "As for how he ended up here, well... With all due respect, I guess I assumed he knew you were investigating the gangbanger shooters, figured you would be talking to suspects and tailed you here."

Hunter stood, started pacing, slowly shaking his head. "You're right about him knowing. We had interviewed him so yeah, he knew...

But he didn't follow us here."

The Southlake detectives smirked.

Hunter noticed, stopped and turned toward them. "Guys, I'm not just being arrogant. I've been a detective for over a decade. I've pissed off some pretty mean people. Trust me. Looking for a tail is second nature. I do it when I'm driving to the grocery store. Besides, did you see that pimp mobile they were driving? It stands out like a sore thumb in the ghetto much less in the great white suburbs. Add to that the fact that we missed the street we were looking for and made a very conspicuous U-turn on 1709 right in front of Town Square. No. There's no way they followed us here."

Sanders chimed in. "If they didn't follow us, how the hell could they have known about Bennett? I mean, we just got the warrant this morning and the only people that knew we were looking at him were the judge and the taskforce." He looked at Hunter incredulously. "You can't seriously think…"

Hunter shook his head. "No. No way." He continued to pace, snapped his fingers and looked around at Sanders. "His phone! Where's his phone? Whoever tipped him off had to have called him between the time the search warrant was issued and the time he got here. There'll be a record of all his incoming calls."

The Southlake detectives, who had been watching the conversation like a tennis match, quickly refocused. "We pulled it and bagged it as part of his personal effects. I can get one of the techies to pull off a log of incoming calls ASAP." He reached for his phone and stepped toward the hall. "I'll call right now."

Hunter paced furiously, rubbed his forehead and shook his head. *How could I have let this happen?*

"Detective, so what's the story here?"

Hunter turned to the voice coming from the front door to see a short, round man with a bushy mustache wearing a charcoal gray suit. By the way the Southlake detective in the hall snapped to attention, Hunter surmised the suit was the boss.

The detective gave a quick synopsis of the situation but it was obvious from his comments and questions that the Chief had been well briefed before he'd walked in the door. Once he was satisfied he was up to speed, he turned and strutted into the dining room. Without introducing himself, he turned to Hunter and Sanders. "Gentlemen, we take great pride in the fact that Southlake is a haven from serious crime. Typically our biggest concern is making sure our football players maintain their eligibility." He snorted. "Hell, a busy Saturday night is when someone knocks down someone's mailbox."

He walked toward the front windows with his hands clasped behind his back as if imitating General Patton. "But today... Today I get to explain to the residents and to the media how one of our most prominent citizens got his head blown off in his own home by a Fort Worth gangbanger... And the best part is that it happened just moments after two Fort Worth detectives confiscated his legally held weapons."

Hunter sat stoically, didn't respond. It didn't seem that the Chief was looking for a response.

After an uncomfortable silence, the Chief moved to the door. He stopped as he went through but did not turn around. He just stared into the foyer. "I had a lengthy conversation with your Lieutenant. I believe he will be expecting a call from you on your way home... Now, if you would, please get the hell out of my city."

Chapter 29

Both the sun and temperature were rapidly dropping by the time Hunter and Sanders got back to the SUV, still sitting at a strange angle on the curb after crashing Shadow's car. The grill guard absorbed most of the impact. Hunter stopped, inspected the damage and made a mental note about getting it into the shop.

With Shadow's car already towed away, his two gangbanging buddies long since processed and the bodies removed from the house, the chaos level of the crime scene had dropped significantly. The on-scene reporters from the three local stations still hovered, waiting for interviews with the detectives but were too late. All they got were shots of Hunter's banged up Explorer pulling away.

Hunter looked in his rearview mirror at the reporters in the street, noticed Andre Kipton in the group reaching for his cell phone. Moments later Hunter's cell phone buzzed. He punched the ignore button, then looked at the call history to see multiple calls from Sprabary, Kipton and Stacy.

The initial silence only heightened the new rattles and creaks from the damaged frontend. Finding time to make those repairs was one more thing to add to the ever growing list.

Both men were drained, their thoughts seemed to weigh them down like anchors. They had made it all the way back to Davis Boulevard before Sanders quietly, almost inaudibly, broke the silence. "I've never shot anyone before... Hell, I've only drawn my weapon once and that was just procedural." He shook his head slowly, stared glassy eyed out the windshield. His voice grew even quieter, the words barely forming. "I just killed Jimmy's little brother."

Hunter shook his head, his voice equally thick. "No you didn't. You saved my life by killing a thug who was milliseconds away from killing your partner. You had no choice…." He paused, blinked a few times, cleared his throat. "Thank you."

Sanders nodded.

Hunter's phone buzzed. It was Kipton. He ignored it again.

Sanders glanced over at Hunter. "You ever shoot anyone?"

Hunter shrugged, exhaled heavily. "Just once."

Since he didn't elaborate, Sanders prodded him. "Come on now, you can't just leave me hanging. What happened?"

Hunter smiled slightly. "Well it was nothing as dramatic as today. It just kind of happened." He shifted in his seat. "On patrol, I responded to a liquor store robbery, pulled up just as the guy bolted from the store and headed down an alley. I followed him in my car, hit the brakes and jumped out behind the door when I realized the alley was a dead end. I figured that he'd just raise his hands and give up."

He shook his head, looked deeply out at the road in front of them. "It scared the crap out of me when that guy turned around and pointed his gun at me."

"Did you kill him?"

"Kill him? Hell, I was lucky to even hit him. All I managed to do was wing him in the right shoulder. I guess he won't be pitching in the majors when he gets out of prison."

Sanders looked surprised. "The guy's still in prison? I mean, no offense, but it's been a few years since you were on patrol."

"He's *back* in prison. He got out, did the same thing again, only that time he was stupid enough to kill a store clerk. He's doing life in Huntsville."

Hunter's phone buzzed again. This time he answered. "Hunter here… Yes… Okay. Just two? Are you sure? I need those numbers emailed to me immediately. In the meantime, how quickly can you get traces on those addresses? Alright, thanks for keeping me in the loop."

He hung up, looked over at Sanders. "Shadow only received two calls from when we got the warrant signed to when he got to the house. Southlake's sending them to us and tracing them right now."

They had now crossed over the Trinity River on the east side of downtown, about five minutes from the station.

The camaraderie born of shared distress faded a moment later.

Hunter's phone buzzed once again. He looked at the caller ID. *Shit, Sprabary.* Exhaling, he answered. "Yes sir... Yes sir... Yes sir... Well, we, uh, yes sir... Five Minutes... We'll..." He pulled his earpiece away and looked at it curiously, then looked at Sanders. "He hung up on me."

It was Sanders' turn to exhale heavily. "Great."

Chapter 30

The entrance to the police station was blocked by a makeshift barricade manned by several patrol officers. There was a crowd of people milling about chanting and holding signs, stopping Hunters and Sanders from pulling through.

Hunter rolled his window down to talk with one of the officers. He had to yell over the noise from the crowd. "What the hell is going on?"

The officer gestured over his shoulder. "Alton Grice and his Ebony Warriors are protesting our lack of progress on the gangbanger shootings. They've been here all afternoon."

Hunter sighed. "That's all we need."

"No shit. From what I hear, you've already had a pretty crappy day. We'll get the barricade out of your way so you can pull in. Glad to see you're in one piece."

"Me too."

Even though it was close to eight o'clock in the evening, the station was still active. When they walked into the squad room, conversations quieted, eyes turned. It seemed that people didn't know whether to pat them on the back or avoid them. Sanders leaned toward Hunter, mumbled under his breath, "Bad news travels fast."

"You have no idea." He continued to walk, ushering Sanders forward so that he wouldn't stop. "Look on the bright side, at least we're here to get stared at. After all, it's the bad guy that's dead, not us."

Sanders made one last survey of the faces as they made it to the stairs and started up to the task force conference room and Lieutenant Sprabary's office. "Yeah, well, I'm not sure Bennett would view it quite like that."

Sanders' face registered regret for his words instantly. Hunter waved him off, absorbed the pain. He stopped on the stairs, gripped the rail, his faced flushed slightly. He nodded softly. "No, he wouldn't." He stood still another moment, his eyes distant, glassy.

Hunter carried his laptop and before they went to see Sprabary, he directed Sanders to duck into the taskforce conference room, hoping that someone might be in there. Both Reyes and Parker glanced at him, tired and worried.

Sanders had carried in the box and bags containing Bennett's weapons. He set them on the table. Hunter immediately sat down without a word and started booting up. Parker and Reyes eyed each other and then watched him for a moment. Reyes leaned forward. "It's good to see you guys in one piece. It sounds like things got a little crazy out there today. Are you okay?"

Hunter looked up from his laptop, stopped tapping keys for a moment. "Yeah, thanks to Sanders, it looks like you're gonna have to deal with me for a little while longer."

Reyes and Parker both looked at Sanders. He shrugged.

Hunter spoke as he clicked on the keyboard. "Look, we'll give you the complete blow by blow when we can. Unfortunately, we have to face an ass chewing with Sprabary." Both Reyes and Parker cringed, Hunter continued. "While we're in there, I need you guys to take care of a couple of things for me."

Reyes grabbed a pen and his notebook. "Whatcha got?"

"First, we need to get these weapons over to ballistics for testing. Tell them it's hot and to expect a note from Sprabary expediting the tests. Second, as best we can figure, Shadow was tipped off by someone that we were serving a warrant on Bennett. There's no other way he could have even known who Bennett was."

Parker nodded. "Yeah, it's not like they moved in the same circles."

"Exactly. Southlake PD was able to pull his cell phone log for today and is running traces now. I don't want to wait on them. After all, it's not their asses on the line so they don't have the same sense of urgency. There were only two inbound calls during the three hours between us getting the warrant and Shadow showing up at Bennett's." Hunter turned his laptop to Reyes. "Here they are. I need exact locations for those phones and owner's names and addresses."

"You got it Cowboy. I've got a contact, shouldn't take more than a half hour."

Hunter looked at Sanders. "Well, if we're lucky, Sprabary will have finished screaming by then." He nodded toward the door.

Sprabary's office door was open. Hunter stopped Sanders in the hall. "I do the talking. You say nothing. Understand?"

Sanders nodded. Hunter stepped into the open doorway.

Sprabary was on the phone when Hunter knocked on the door, covered the phone, glared at the two detectives. "Get your asses in here and sit down." He took his hand off the phone. "Yes Chief... Yes sir... They've just arrived. I will debrief with them now. Yes sir... I'll have a response to the media shortly. Yes sir, before the evening news. Yes sir, I'll call you shortly."

Hunter could hear the dial tone coming through the ear piece before Sprabary managed to finish that last sentence.

Sprabary hung up with a deep sigh, leaned back in his chair and put a sarcastic smile on his face. "Well, gentlemen, did you have a nice field trip to the suburbs? How'd you like your welcoming committee in the parking lot?"

Neither man answered. His smile transformed to a glare. "Well, let me tell you about my afternoon. Let's start with my phone call from that obnoxious prick of a small town Chief telling me about how two of my detectives turned his quiet little suburb into Fallujah. He gave me a blow by blow."

Sprabary continued. "I've also heard from the Captain twice, the Chief once and I've gotten messages from a number of city officials I didn't even know existed." After a few more minutes and several more colorful expletives, Sprabary ran out of steam.

"So, I've got a couple of basic questions. First, what's your gut feel? Was Bennett our guy?"

Hunter shook his head. "Not likely. He was extremely cooperative and his alibi was strong."

Sprabary closed his eyes and rubbed his temples. "Great, just great. Based on my pleasant conversation with my friend from Southlake, I understand we had confiscated Bennett's weapons." He leaned back in his chair, opened both arms wide. "So, not only did we serve up a victim for the gangbangers, we served up an innocent one that we had just disarmed. Shit! Could it get any worse?" He closed his eyes, shook his head and leaned forward, elbows on his desk. He pointed at Hunter. "I want those weapons tested immediately."

Hunter nodded. "Yes sir. They're already on their way to the lab. If you send them a note, it will speed things up."

He made a quick note on his desk pad. "Okay, so my second question is, how the hell did that ghetto lizard happen to end up at your suspect's house moments after you left?"

Hunter leaned forward. "Southlake is taking lead on the Bennett murder investigation. They have asked us to assist and have been open with information. They attempted to question Shadow's two accomplices but they lawyered up immediately so that's a dead end. I doubt the DA will deal since they've already got the shooter and the accessory charges are slam dunks. Southlake is tracing phones to determine how Shadow knew Bennett was a suspect."

There was an uncomfortable silence, the obvious implications hung in the air. Sprabary looked intently at Hunter. "Only a limited number of people knew that information." Hunter didn't respond. "Most of them cops."

Hunter nodded. "Yes sir."

Sprabary leaned forward, poked his finger in the air. "I don't give a damn who owns this investigation. We're going to find out how that got leaked and we're going to do it immediately. I won't have some two-bit suburb department closing this case before us. Do you understand me?"

Hunter nodded again. "Yes sir. I've got Reyes and Parker working leads as we speak. We should know more before we leave tonight."

"All right... Speaking of tonight, the Chief's insisting that we talk to the media before the evening news cycle." He shuffled through some papers spread over his desk. "I put together some generic bullshit for a statement. I need you to read it over to make sure it's accurate and I'll have Legal review it to make sure I'm not stepping in shit anywhere."

Hunter reached out for the paper. "Do you want us to attend the press conference?"

"Absolutely not. If you're there, those vultures will want to question you on details. Without you there I can plausibly defer answers based on not having thoroughly debriefed you yet." His expression softened almost imperceptibly. Get out of here and try to get some rest tonight. If Bennett's not our guy, this has just jacked up the intensity on this investigation tenfold."

He motioned them to the door, then held up his hand. Sprabary looked at Sanders. "Billy, the only good part of my conversation with that ass from the suburbs was that he indicated everything pointed to this being a good shoot. Nonetheless, I've set up an eight A.M. meeting for you with Internal Affairs. I've briefed them and told them I expect this to be a formality. You're on desk duty until they clear you, but I'll make sure that's expedited. We'll try to get it done in a day or two. Just tell them what happened and you should be fine."

Sanders nodded. "Thank you sir. I'll be there."

They started to leave again. "Guys." They both stopped in the doorway. "Look, this whole thing didn't turn out the way we'd have liked, but it sounded like you guys did it by the book today and that if you hadn't been on your game, those thugs would have gotten away with it. I appreciate that... And I'm damn glad you made it back." He dismissed them with a wave of his hand.

Hunter and Sanders both nodded, turned and headed down the hall without speaking. Hunter led them straight back to the conference room, barely slowed down to open the door. "What have you got for us, Jimmy?"

Reyes looked up sheepishly, slowly shaking his head. "You're not gonna like what I have to say, Cowboy."

Cowboy glared impatiently. "Well, it's late, spit it out."

Reyes leaned forward, still hesitant. "We were able to trace the numbers. The first was a throw away cell phone. I've got a guy working to see if he can give me a location for where it was used, but... Now that we have the information on the second call, I don't think we're going to need it." He paused for a moment. "That second call... Came from this building."

Hunter stood still, stared at Reyes. Sanders slowly sank into a chair as if all the air had been sucked out of him. After a moment of silence, Hunter ran his hand through his hair and slowly started to pace. "Do you have an exact location?"

"Yeah, the pay phone in the lobby area outside booking."

Hunter nodded, continued to pace. "That area's open to the public, right?" His voice had a hopeful tone to it.

Reyes nodded and shrugged at the same time. "Yeah, it is. It's also under twenty-four/seven electronic surveillance. We've got cameras in all four corners."

Hunter looked up, a strange combination of hope and dread crossing his face at once. "Do we have the tapes yet?"

"Hadn't had time."

Hunter didn't hesitate, reached for the desk phone, punched in a number. "Harrison, Hunter here… Yeah, yeah, that was Sanders and me… Yeah, thanks. Look, who's in charge of our internal security, specifically who owns the surveillance cameras in the building?" He reached for a pen and paper as he mumbled "Uh huh" a couple of times. "Thanks."

He clicked off and was dialing another number before anyone could break his stride. "Sean Jackson? This is Detective Jake Hunter. You're in charge of our station security cameras, right?" He nodded, stared across the room as he heard the answer. "Good, then I need some immediate assistance. When can you get here?" He listened, exhaled loudly. "Yes it needs to be tonight. It's tied to a murder and police involved shooting. All right, see you then."

He hung up, looked at the team. "On his way, thirty minutes."

An hour later, the members of the task force along with Jackson stood, gathered around a flat screen monitor, jaws slack.

Hunter spoke, his eyes never leaving the monitor. "Run it back… Are you sure on the timestamp?"

"Positive." Jackson ran it back and hit play.

Reyes shook his head. "I can't believe it. That little bitch! Man, we got her red handed."

Chapter 31

After viewing the surveillance tape, Hunter and the team retreated back to their conference room, all still stunned at the betrayal they had witnessed. All except Hunter sat at the table looking distraught. As usual, he was up pacing.

Reyes cleared his throat. This got Hunter's attention who stopped and turned toward him. "So boss, shouldn't we tell Sprabary before the press conference?"

Hunter paused for a moment, slowly shook his head. "No... No I don't think so." He started his pacing again, held up a finger as if to make a point. "A couple of reasons... First, his not knowing gives him plausible deniability during the press conference. Think about it, he's already going to be talking about how our actions led to the death of an innocent civilian, if he has to divulge this detail at the same time, the PR black eye is going to be even worse. If he doesn't know, he'll honestly answer that it's being investigated. Second, before I walk into his office with this information, I want to be able to hand a case to the DA that is absolutely solid."

Blaine arched his eyebrows. "Um, you saw the same tape I did, didn't you? Looked pretty solid to me."

"Let me rephrase. I want it to be beyond bulletproof. I want to cover every angle." As he continued, he ticked off each item on his fingers. "I want to pull her employee records to confirm her picture. I want prints taken off that phone to see if we can prove she used it. I want her timecard from today proving she was at work. And I want her computer logs to determine if she was away from her desk at the time of the call." His voice built as he continued. "We are about to arrest a FWPD employee as an accomplice to the murder of a high profile attorney, a former prosecutor and most importantly, an innocent man. I don't want anything overlooked."

Everyone sat up straight now, heads nodded around the table. They talked for another few minutes, divvying up the assignments. Hunter sat, rubbed his temples. "All right, with the exception of the prints, all of this can wait until morning. After the press conference tonight, all hell will break loose. We need to be ready to hit it hard in the morning. I'd suggest we all get out of here and get some sleep."

Hunter drove home in a daze. His mind replayed what had happened, Bennett on the ground, the blood splatter, the sound of the hammer of Shadow's gun behind his head, staring at the barrel, the explosion... He shook his head as he pictured Shadow's face, the pink mist in the air. *How did I let this happen? I should have been more careful. Jim Bennett was innocent.*

This self-admonishment continued in his head until he got past Loop 820 and only stopped when it was replaced with thoughts of Gina and the accident. It was going to be a long, sleepless night.

When he pulled into his driveway, there was black Ford Escape parked at the curb in front of his house. He stopped before entering the garage, surveyed the Escape, saw someone sitting in the driver's seat. He instinctively reached for hip but paused when he saw the door open and Stacy Morgan step out.

He smiled as a hint of nervousness passed through him. He hit the garage door opener and drove forward into the garage. As he got out, she was walking up the driveway with something in her hand.

He nodded. They both stood for a moment in the driveway, neither seemed to know what to do. To this point, their flirtations hadn't gone beyond the occasional lingering glance or grabbing lunch.

Stacy looked at Hunter, her eyes washed with concern. She smiled meekly. "I wasn't sure when you'd get home but I thought you might need someone to talk to."

His eyes blinked, fought back the emotions of the day. He tried to smile to acknowledge her kindness. It came off looking more pained.

She held up two cups of Starbucks coffee. "So, an hour ago when I got here, these were hot. As it is, I hope you have a microwave."

He looked down, shuffled for a moment, still adjusting to the situation. He gestured toward the front door. "It may come as a shock, being a guy and all, but I have most of the modern conveniences." He reached out, took one of the cups and realized how cold it had gotten, and by extension, how long she'd really been waiting. He looked at the cup and smirked. "Not that I don't appreciate the thought, but considering the time and the day I've had, we might opt for something a little stronger."

Stacy hooked her hand in his arm as they moved toward the door. "Good idea."

Hunter nervously pointed to the couch. "Why don't you get comfortable while I get that bottle?" Stacy sat down as Hunter rummaged in the kitchen, apparently trying to find a rarely used cork screw. He continued to ramble, trying to fill time. "So this buddy of mine, a real wine guy, visited a little place in Napa called Parry Cellars last year. He brought me back a couple of bottles of their 2005 Cabernet. He gave me this long drawn out explanation of how good it was, rattled on about tannins, oak barrels and stressed grapes. I'm not sure what any of it means. All I know is that I shared the first bottle with my parents over the summer and everyone loved it."

As she turned to comment, she caught movement in her peripheral vision and jumped as the large black cat lazily leaped up onto the couch. Hunter had turned the corner, wine in hand, just in time to see her reaction. He smiled, more easily now. "Meet Panther."

She exhaled deeply. "Holy crap, he scared me... You weren't kidding when you said he was big, he's enormous. I guess maybe he does live up to his name."

Hunter handed her a glass and sat down next to her. "Yeah, when he decides he wants to sit somewhere, it's an effort to move him." He turned toward her, a more serious look on his face, held up his glass in a toast. "Thank you. It's been a really bad day. This helps."

She clanked his glass. "Well, in our world, trying to do the right thing can sometimes blow up." She paused, but reached out and lightly touched his hand, stopping him before he could raise his glass. "That shouldn't ever stop you from doing what you do, and what you know is right."

They sipped their wine. He turned away for a moment, leaned forward with his elbows on his knees. He shook his head slowly, struggling with his words. "This shouldn't have happened. We should have been better."

Stacy reached over, pulled his shoulder to get him to look at her. "You followed procedure. There were legitimate reasons to question Bennett. There was no way you could have known... I mean... How the hell did Shadow know?"

She may have asked the question rhetorically but when Hunter remained silent, she paused. "Wait a minute... How exactly did he know?"

Hunter sipped his wine and studied Stacey's face. They'd known each other a long time. He knew he could trust her. He leaned back on the couch and spent the next ten minutes spilling everything they'd learned earlier in the evening.

"Oh my God." Stacy sat stunned. "How could she? How could anyone? She might as well have pulled the trigger herself."

Hunter just nodded, sighed. "Yeah, well, it certainly explains how Shadow and the Kings have always seemed to be one step ahead of us. No telling how long she's been playing for the other side." He took a long drink. "Makes you wonder..." He didn't even finish his sentence, just shook his head and stared over at Panther. He was busy giving himself a bath, stopping just long enough to look at Hunter with complete disinterest.

Stacy moved closer to Hunter on the couch, reached out, closed her hand on his wrist. "You can't think like that. What you do... What we do... It makes a difference. It does." She said it a little too forceful, as if she was trying to convince herself as much as him.

They were both silent for a few moments, her hand on his wrist. After a moment, Hunter looked at the clock, set his wine down and picked up the TV remote off the table.

Stacy looked taken aback for a moment. "What are you doing?"

"It's ten o'clock. Sprabary's press conference will lead off the newscast."

"Oh Cowboy, don't do that. Don't torture yourself. You know it's just going to be a bunch of self-righteous assholes playing Monday morning quarterback."

She reached for the remote but Hunter gently took her hand

stopping her. "I need to see it. It'll only be a few minutes. I'll turn it off after the coverage." He looked at her. "I promise."

Her shoulders sank in resignation. Hunter pointed the remote at the TV and hit the button.

Chapter 32

Lieutenant Sprabary stood in a small conference room off the atrium of the Tarrant County Courthouse waiting to be called to the podium. The television news cycle turned these situations into entertainment and required him to take his queues, hit his marks and play his part as if he were an actor in a weekly police drama.

He wasn't a TV cop. His head hurt, his stomach was in knots and sweat already covered his forehead. This was real and it sucked. His team's investigation, however unintentional, had led directly to a man's death. The ballistics report he received moments ago only made it worse by confirming what he and Hunter had already surmised. Bennett was apparently not involved in the gangbanger shootings. He was innocent.

This was a black eye for the department, most likely a career limiting event for him and would certainly result in lawsuits costing millions. As awful as the situation was, he knew police work was messy. It might sound cold, but shit happens. The part that really gnawed at him was that there was only one way this could have happened. Someone in the department had leaked information to Shadow. They had broken their oath and betrayed the city and the department. More importantly, if it was someone on his team, they had betrayed him.

How could someone do that? Why would they cross that line?

He shook his head to clear his mind. He looked down at the paper in his hand, tried to read the words. His hands shook, his vision blurred. *God, just get me through the next twenty minutes.*

There was a sharp knock on the door as it opened quickly. A Public Relations Officer looked at him and the Southlake Chief grimly. "Chief, Lieutenant, the news programs are on air and they'll be ready for you in three minutes."

Sprabary nodded, took two deep breaths, straightened back his shoulders and set his jaw.

*   *   *   *

Hunter's TV came to life on channel five, the local NBC affiliate. Though it didn't matter which local channel he chose, all the stations would lead with the story.

He looked at his watch just as the intro graphics for the news flashed across the screen. The Ken and Barbie talking heads were casually straightening papers in pretense that they were caught hard at work. Without preamble, Ken, with his perfectly combed salt and pepper hair, his rugged chin and his thousand dollar suit stared into the camera and tried to project the stature he believed he carried. "A shootout rocks a quiet suburb leaving two dead and two in custody. Good evening. I'm Steve Crawford." He casually turned to Barbie.

Looking like a former USC cheerleader, the blonde flashed a hundred watt smile. "I'm Amy Johnson. The shootout took place this afternoon in the bedroom community of Southlake. Misty Covington is live on the scene with a detailed report. Misty, can you tell us about the tragic events?"

Hunter's eyes burned through the flat panel like lasers, his jaw clenched, shoulders tight. Stacy had moved closer to him and was holding his shoulders as if she might have to restrain him. He hadn't even noticed her touch.

*   *   *   *

The Victim had paced back and forth across his living room carpet for most of the evening waiting for the news to come on. One of his coworkers had mentioned something about a shooting, but he'd only heard bits and pieces of news earlier in the evening on the radio. He had been unable to get a clear understanding of exactly what had happened. He didn't make any calls to his network of contacts, concerned about looking too interested.

Now he sat in front of his TV, tuned into NBC and listened as that cute blonde Amy segued to Misty for an at the scene report.

A petite brunette with hot caramel eyes, a little over layered in a turtle neck sweater and a North Face jacket looked straight into the camera. "Thanks Amy. I'm standing in front of the Southlake residence of Jim and Rose Bennett where earlier this afternoon, Jim Bennett, local

171

attorney and victim's rights activist, was shot to death in his own home office. What's more bizarre and terrifying about this shootout is the second death at the scene of an unknown man, allegedly linked to gangs. NBC news has learned it is believed that there is a connection between this shootout and the recent killings of multiple Eastcide Kings gang members."

She went on to recap the gangbanger shootings that had taken place over the past week and a half, adding commentary about the ongoing debate of whether the police are reacting appropriately. The Victim now stood in front of the TV. "Oh come on, tell us something we didn't already know. What really happened in Southlake?"

The reporter continued. As she walked toward the Bennett's home, the camera panned to capture the visual of the yellow police tape. "Neither Southlake nor Fort Worth Police have discussed the specifics of what happened inside the house or the identity of the second fatality. However, we do know that two individuals were arrested at the scene and both are believed to be members of the Eastcide Kings. We'll know more once the police release further details. This is Misty Covington reporting from Southlake. Amy, back to you."

The Victim stood stunned. *What happened? Jim Bennett? Oh my God! They shot Jim Bennett? How the hell? Why would the Kings shoot him? What does he have to do with them? With any of this?*

He stumbled back to the couch and slumped down, ran his hands through his hair and closed his eyes. *Oh Jesus. They must have thought...* The anger started to build. This wasn't supposed to happen. *Those idiots! Fucking animals! What should I have expected? I should have known they'd do something like this. Typical. Random.*

The news had promised to go to a live press conference shortly but had gone to commercial. When they came back, the Victim calmed, settled onto the couch and turned up the volume.

* * * *

The scene of the house and the police tape hit Hunter like a baseball bat to the chest. Jim Bennett was dead. He leaned forward, put his elbows on his knees, brought his face down to his hands and began rubbing his temples.

Stacy leaned forward with him and rubbed his shoulder.

Hunter's eyes were closed. "Jesus, this is a disaster." His voice was barely more than a whisper.

The news came back from commercial and Hunter looked up to see Steve Crawford looking directly into the camera. "We continue with our coverage of the police involved shooting in Southlake. A joint press conference with police representatives from both Fort Worth and Southlake is scheduled momentarily. On scene is News Five's Carlos Mendez. Carlos, what have you got?"

The scene cut to the foyer of the Tarrant County Courthouse in downtown Fort Worth. A mid-twenties Hispanic in a charcoal blazer, held a microphone and fiddled with his earpiece as he looked off camera. Behind him was a temporary stage and podium with dozens of reporters crowded around.

Someone cued him and he snapped to life turning to the camera. "Steve, Amy, I'm here at the downtown courthouse where in a few moments, we expect to learn more details about this afternoon's shootout in Southlake."

He turned, allowed the camera to take in more of the chaotic scene just in time to see someone step up to the podium. He turned back. "Let's listen."

* * * *

Sprabary took a deep breath and followed the FWPD spokesperson through the door. The level of commotion and the number of reporters surprised him, his heart rate jumped momentarily and he had to purposely tell himself to calm down.

The Southlake Chief followed him and now stood beside him, both behind the spokesman at the podium. They had met for the first time a few minutes before as the public relations team prepped them. They had barely been cordial to each other. The Chief had spent most of his time arguing with the PR team about why he wasn't going on first.

Sprabary glanced in his direction and saw the complete look of panic on his face and almost broke into a smile. It was just enough to get him to relax as he heard the spokesman start his introduction.

"Good evening. As you know, there was a police involved shooting today in Southlake. We will attempt to answer your questions, but please keep in mind, there are multiple ongoing investigations that will limit the information we can provide."

"We have Lieutenant Jeff Sprabary of the Fort Worth Homicide Division and Southlake Police Chief Daniel Morton. Lieutenant Sprabary will speak first followed by Chief Morton and then both will be available for a few questions." He turned to Sprabary, gestured to the podium. "Lieutenant…"

The room vibrated, the glare of the lights intensified and several camera flashes popped. *So this is what it's like to be a celebrity. Might not be so bad if the reason I'm here didn't suck so much.* He walked to the podium, pulled out his note sheet and cleared his throat.

*   *   *   *

The Victim was watching the screen with such intensity, the rest of the room had fallen away. He was literally on the edge of his seat staring at the TV as Sprabary was introduced.

So that's Sprabary. Hmm, never met him before. Kind of young to be a Lieutenant in Homicide. Must be pretty good. Too bad this happened on his watch, can't help his career. Not that he matters. Hunter, or as everyone over there calls him, Cowboy, is the one I need to think about.

Sprabary stepped up to the podium, shuffled with a piece of paper. *Hmm, looks nervous. Don't blame him, I would be too if my team had just screwed the pooch and gotten somebody killed.*

Sprabary squared up, looked straight ahead. "In an act of misguided retaliation, members of the Eastcide Kings street gang gunned down a citizen at his home in Southlake. Mr. Jim Bennett, a resident of Southlake and former Arlington Prosecutor, was fatally wounded. Our heartfelt condolences go out to his family. Police officers shot and killed one suspect and arrested two others at the scene. We believe the shooting may be connected with the recent string of local gang member shootings. Detectives from the Fort Worth Police Department Gang Shooting Task Force had interviewed Mr. Bennett earlier in the day and were involved in the shooting and capture of the suspects. Because the shootings occurred in Southlake, Chief Morton and his team will lead the investigation and the FWPD will cooperate fully."

Jim Bennett? How did he end up in the middle of this? Why would the police be talking with him anyway?

*   *   *   *

Reporters shouted questions immediately, microphones and recorders jutted forward, but Sprabary waved them off as he turned the podium over to Morton. Hunter leaned back but showed no sign of relaxing.

Stacy started kneading his shoulders. "Sprabary seems to be handling himself all right, considering."

Hunter stretched his neck in response to her touch. "They haven't gotten to the questions yet." He continued to watch the press conference as Morton droned on about keeping the streets safe in his quiet suburb. Hunter snorted. "What a jerk."

"I take it you two were introduced today?"

Hunter rolled his shoulders as her massage began to take effect. "Oh, yeah, he let me know what a big mess we caused him."

When Morton stopped talking and the PR officer opened it up for questions, Hunter gently stopped Stacy's hands and leaned toward the TV, the momentary relief from tension gone.

*   *   *   *

"Finally!" The Victim waved his hands and spoke at the TV as Chief Morton finished his statement. "What a windbag. Could you just go back to writing parking tickets?"

The PR officer stepped up to the podium. "We have time for a few questions." The room erupted and he raised both hands to quiet them. "One at a time. One at a time." Pointing to the front row. "You."

"Was the other fatality a member of the Kings and do you have an identity?

Both the PR officer and Morton turned to Sprabary. He stepped up to the podium. "Based on what we know at this point, we believe he was a member of the Kings, however we're not at a point where we can confirm his identity."

Sprabary pointed to another reporter. "Next."

"Was Jim Bennett a suspect in the gangbanger shootings?"

Sprabary answered without hesitation. "He was a person of interest in the investigation and we believed he might have information that could help the case. We do not believe he had anything to do with the shootings."

The reporter continued. "But was he at one time a suspect?"

Sprabary now had complete control of the podium, having usurped both the PR officer and Morton. "As I said, he was one of many people we have interviewed as part of the ongoing investigation. He is not a suspect in those killings." He pointed to another reporter. "Next."

Bennett a suspect? You've got to be kidding me. What idiots.

"Were your officers on site when Bennett was shot?"

"Our detectives arrived moments after the suspects arrived and heard shots fired inside the house." Sprabary started to move to another reporter but the follow up question came too quickly.

"If you're detectives had been there earlier, why were they returning?"

Sprabary glared at the reporter. "They had reason to believe Mr. Bennett was in danger so they returned to his residence. Unfortunately, they were too late."

Reason to believe he was in danger. What the hell does that mean? What are they, psychic?

He quickly moved to another reporter to avoid the follow up only to have that reporter continue with the line of questioning. "What led them to believe he was in danger?"

"I can't answer that since this is an open investigation."

The Victim stood up and gestured at the TV. "What bullshit. There had to be a reason the cops returned."

*   *   *   *

Sprabary had hit his comfort zone and was working the crowd like a skilled politician. They had hit him with some tough questions but so far, he had successfully dodged the bullets. He pointed to another reporter. "Next."

Andre Kipton stepped forward. "If Jim Bennett was only a person of interest and not a publicly identified suspect, how did the Kings know to go after him?"

Sprabary paused as if the wind had been knocked out of him. His command of the room evaporated and his mouth carped for a moment before he could get words to come out. "That's still under investigation."

Kipton raised his pencil to follow up but before he could, the PR officer stepped in front of Sprabary, who was still clearly shaken by the last question. "That's all we have time for this evening. We will provide press briefings as further developments occur." He quickly turned his back on the reporters as they screamed follow up questions, and physically guided Sprabary and Morton through the door into the quiet of the conference room.

*   *   *   *

"Oh my God, you incompetent idiots!" The Victim was almost yelling at the TV. "How could you? You led them right to an innocent man."

He began to pace as the reporter on the scene recapped the press conference.

As he paced, thoughts raced through his head, random, chaotic. *The police have no idea who I am. No idea why I'm doing it. Jim Bennett's now dead because the cops are clueless. The gangbangers are still out there, doing what they do, ruining lives. He's just one more victim. They have to be stopped. The police aren't going to do anything. I'll have to.*

He calmed and his resolve hardened. As he did, new thoughts came into view. *I've got this city buzzing. I made the headlines today even without firing a shot.*

He stopped pacing, ran his hand through his hair and aimlessly looked around his obsessively clean apartment. His eyes landed on her picture. *I'm doing this for you. I won't let what happened to you go unpunished.*

*   *   *   *

Sprabary's heart was pounding as they pushed through the door into the conference room. He wasn't sure if he was scared, pissed off or excited. Whatever it was, the rush of the moment had his head spinning. His career may be in a death spiral but at least he was going down in style.

Morton didn't seem nearly as elated, his moment in the spotlight had been upstaged by his FWPD counterpart. He huffed over to the credenza, picked up a bottle of water and cracked the seal on it. He looked at Sprabary. "I hope you know I have no intention of whitewashing this investigation. If I can prove your boys screwed up, I'm going to take them down."

Sprabary's momentary high crashed to earth. He set his jaw,

glared back at Morton. "First, I can assure you that Hunter and Sanders went by the book. Second, you're not going to get the chance to do anything because my team will find out how this happened and take them down before your boys figure out the paperwork."

The PR officer stood by silently but looked ready to throw himself between the two men. After a short stare down, Morton took a long swig of water, nodded to the PR officer and turned to leave. His spoke as he walked toward the door. "You know where to find me." In the doorway he stopped and glared back at Sprabary. "And trust me, I know where to find you."

*   *   *   *

Hunter sat motionless. After a moment, he picked up his glass of wine and swallowed it like a shot of tequila. He abruptly stood up, startled Panther who shot off down the hall, and walked to the kitchen. He poured another glass of wine, let it sit for a moment as he leaned forward with both hands on the countertop.

Stacy remained on the couch. The silence between them was accentuated by a commercial for Lute Riley Honda playing on the TV. The incessant jingle seemed to linger even after the commercial was gone. In the momentary pause between commercials, the silence was stifling.

Hunter finally picked up the glass, took a long gulp and returned to the couch as the news cast returned. He had to step around Panther who had returned and was now staring at Stacy with a look of disdain.

Before the news anchor launched into his next story, Stacy reached over, picked up the remote and punched it off. The screen went blank and the silence rushed back to engulf them. This time Stacy didn't let it linger. She put down her wine glass, slid toward Hunter on the couch and gently took his face in both hands. She turned his face towards her and pulled him close.

Hunter started to say something. Stacy leaned forward, held up her finger and shushed him quietly. "No more talk tonight." His mind cleared as their lips touched.

Chapter 33

"A girl could get a complex waking up alone in a strange bed."

Hunter turned away from his laptop, looked over toward the family room to see Stacy standing there with her arms crossed, wearing only his long sleeve dress shirts, socks and a smirk with one eyebrow arched.

Hunter smiled. *Oh my.*

She started toward him. "Well, I guess technically speaking, I wasn't alone. There was an enormous black cat staring at me when I opened my eyes." She shuddered. "Kind of freaked me out."

"Sorry about that. He's a little territorial." He let his eyes drift over her. "You look lovely this morning, Miss Morgan." He stood, pulled her toward him and kissed her softly. He turned toward the kitchen, stopped, turned back to her and kissed her hard, pulling her into him.

"Oh, now that's more like it." She beamed.

"Yes it was." He kissed her again. "Sit. Let me get you some coffee." He moved into the kitchen. "I didn't want to wake you. You slept with that adorable smile on your face. My head was racing and I just needed to input all my notes."

She took the cup from his hand, inhaled deeply. "Mmm." She curled her feet up under her on the chair. "You do know it's six in the morning?"

"Yeah, got started a little late today." He smiled.

She rolled her eyes. "The scary part is that you're not kidding."

"Yeah, well, it's going to be a busy day. I've got to meet with Sprabary late this morning. I need to tie up all the loose ends before then. He's not going to like what I've got. We may not be any closer to finding our gangbanger killer, but at least we can shut down a department leak."

He hit save, closed his laptop and turned to see her smiling at him while she sipped her coffee. The rush of a new beginning washed over him. He fumbled with his coffee mug like a teenager on a first date. She giggled at his awkwardness, reached over and took his hand. They finished their coffee in silence, sharing smiles and stares.

When a ray of sun intruded through the blinds, Hunter broke the silence. "Well, if I'm going to beat the traffic downtown, I need to get showered." He got up, reached out his hand. "Don't suppose you care to join me?"

Stacy took his hand. "Thought you'd never ask."

Chapter 34

Hunter and Stacy avoided any deep conversation about relationships or commitments before they left the house. Whether to go public with their relationship was a quick and easy decision: not.

In spite of the day that he knew was ahead of him, Hunter smiled most of the way to work. It had been a long time. Too long. As he passed over Loop 820 heading south on I-35, he relived scenes from the night and the morning. As he exited the freeway, thoughts of Gina crowded into his head. A wave of guilt flooded over him and his smile faded. *It's been over five years, why do I feel guilty?* But deep down he still felt married, he still loved her.

There had been other women over the years but not many, and none that had any real possibility to become long term. Stacy was different. They had been friends for years. Hell, she and Gina knew each other, had always liked each other as casual acquaintances. What happened last night wasn't casual, it wasn't an accident. That realization only made the guilt grow deeper.

Hunter shook his head to chase away the thoughts, reached over, turned on the radio and scrolled through the satellite stations. A talk radio host rambled on about the latest evils the government inflicted on its citizens. Crossing over the Trinity River, he lost himself in the rant wondering if the commentator actually believed what he was saying or was just being provocative to stir the pot and drive ratings. *He's making some good points. He's just a little over the top in his delivery.*

He parked at the station and walked through the back entrance.

Hunter needed to meet with Sprabary to bring him up to speed on the department leak investigation. He swung by the Lieutenant's office. Paige McClaren stopped him in his tracks with a held up finger before he could knock on the door. She was on an obviously personal phone call, but showed no sense of urgency to finish up based on his presence.

She concluded her call with comments intended to express her annoyance at being interrupted. "He's not in his office at the moment." She spoke without preamble. "What do you need?"

"Ah, good morning to you as well." Hunter smiled.

Her mouth tightened. "Whatever Cowboy."

Realizing he wasn't scoring points, Hunter continued. "I need to meet with him this morning. There's been a critical break in a case and he'll want to be updated."

"What case?"

Hunter didn't answer the question, just continued. "When is he available?"

Paige glared at Hunter and for a moment they were locked in a standoff. She finally huffed, turned to her computer and pulled up his calendar. "He can see you at ten. Don't be late. The rest of his day is booked."

Hunter smirked, nodded and gave her a mock salute. "A pleasure as always."

Hunter bolted through the conference room door to find the entire team hard at work banging on keyboards and shuffling through reports. The stale odor of the room had lessened since yesterday.

"Good morning gentlemen. Let's gather for a quick update." He sat at the table, broke out his laptop and got organized as the team took seats and said their good mornings. "Why don't we start with our little internal issue? Jimmy, you were driving that bus. What have you got?"

"We've got her dead to rights. Everything's fallen into place." He referenced his notepad. "We pulled her fingerprints from her personnel file, did a manual comparison to the ones we pulled from the phone, solid visual match. I've put a rush on a computer confirmation, but... Of course, there were others on the phone as well, but hers were definitely there. We've validated that she was working that day and confirmed that she logged off her computer about ten minutes prior to making the call and logged back on five minutes after." He paused to look around the room, saw the looks of confirmation on the faces. "It looks bullet proof to me, Cowboy."

Hunter nodded, typed a few words into his laptop, stopped and contemplated all he'd heard.

Reyes added one last thought. "Oh, by the way, we also double checked. She's at her desk this morning."

"Good, I've got a meeting with Sprabary at ten. We'll move on her immediately after. Not a word to anyone until then." Hunter paused, still torn with the idea that someone could betray the department at this level.

"I don't know if there's a lot to discuss on the main investigation. Obviously yesterday was more than just a minor setback, but we need to keep moving forward so we don't lose momentum. We'll keep processing through the leads as before and see what pops out. He's still out there guys and he's not going to stop." He looked up and surveyed the team. They were tired and dejected but he sensed there was still resolve on their faces.

Blaine caught his eye and made a gesture indicating they needed to talk in the hall. Hunter nodded. "All right guys, get back to it. I'm going to go torture myself with some of the sludge that passes for coffee around here. We'll regroup after I have my meeting with Sprabary." He got up and headed for the door.

"I'll get some with you." Blaine followed him out.

They remained quiet as they made their way down the hall and into the break room. Blaine surveyed the room, made sure it was empty before speaking quietly. "You remember the other day you asked me to check out Daris." Blaine's eyes darted around the room once again, Hunter nodded. "Well, it took a little luck, but you're not going to believe what I found."

Hunter motioned to a table, grabbed his coffee, and sat down. Blaine continued. "So I did a pretty standard background check on him, dug in all the usual places, basically came up empty. I was about to give up until I had a conversation with a buddy of mine..."

Hunter's eyes widened. "You didn't te..."

"No, no, no. Nothing to worry about... Anyway, he and I were having a beer and got to talking about cases and the taskforce. One thing led to another and Daris' name came up. I mentioned something about how he's got an impressive track record of convicting gangbangers. So this buddy of mine says he's not surprised considering. And I say considering what. He just looked surprised and said, you don't know…"

Hunter's impatience showed on his face as he gestured to move it along.

Blaine nodded. "Yeah, sorry. Bottom line… Daris' fiancée was brutally attacked several years ago by a gangbanger. She lived but just barely. Apparently she's still pretty messed up. My buddy said that's why Daris joined the prosecutors' office. Said he was originally going to be a big firm lawyer, had a line into one of the biggest firms in the city. Gave it up. Now he's apparently just this side of being a crusader when it comes to locking up gangbangers."

Hunter absorbed all of this for a moment. "How come none of this was in the records?"

"Well, I'm sure it's all there. It's just that since they hadn't gotten married yet, her name wasn't Daris so there was no direct connection."

Hunter sat lost in thought. *Certainly fits the profile. Would know gangs. Would have access to intel.*

He looked across at Blaine. "We need to get everything we can on him. Go deeper, credit cards, telephone records, email if you can get it. We especially need to know where he was on the two nights in question." He stopped but snapped his finger. "Oh yeah, also check to see what kind of cars he owns."

"Already working it. Hadn't thought about the car angle. I'll add that to my list. Just started so don't have anything yet but should know more before the days over. Getting a full history on the case, doing a full work up on Daris. If there's anything to see, I'll find it."

Hunter's jaw clenched. "Parker, work this on your own. Be careful. No one can know we're looking at him. No one." He stared off into space for a moment, realized he hadn't even sipped his coffee yet, then realized it was already cold and pushed it away.

Blaine nodded. "No problem Cowboy. I'll keep you posted as I go." He shook his head. "Jesus, this case just gets weirder by the day."

Both men sat in silence, lost in their own thoughts.

"There you are Parker." Both men's heads snapped toward the door as a voice rang out across the room. Jimmy Reyes was standing there. He smiled at their reaction as if he'd caught them in something but didn't know what. "Hey, I need your help with a report I'm trying to finish."

Blaine stood up. "No problem man, on my way. This coffee tastes like crap anyway." He nodded to Hunter and followed Reyes out the door.

Hunter looked at his watch, nine-thirty. A half hour before he could get in to see Sprabary. He tapped his fingers on the table, then pulled out his earpiece from his jacket and made a call.

"I thought you'd never call." Stacy's voice giggled. Hunter smiled as his nervous energy dissipated.

Chapter 35

"If I've got to go see Sprabary," Hunter murmured as he and Sanders walked down the hallway. "I'm sure as hell dragging your sorry ass with me."

Sanders was back from his meeting with Internal Affairs. "Well at least this time, our news is good... Right?"

Hunter looked around to make sure no one was in earshot. "I'm not sure finding out one of your dispatchers has been leaking information to the Kings is exactly good news but I guess it's better than not knowing."

The two made their way through the maze of cubes to the Lieutenant's office. Sprabary's door was open when they got there and he waived them in before Paige had a chance to say anything. Hunter just nodded as they passed her desk. She rolled her eyes in response.

Sprabary looked at his watch as they entered, the sun streamed in through the vertical blinds. "I trust you boys have managed to keep from getting shot at today?" He smirked.

They both nodded. Hunter couldn't resist responding. "So far."

Sprabary smiled at his response and seemed to be in an unusually good mood. He motioned for them to sit. "Good... So, what did you think of the press conference last night?" He looked directly at Hunter as if Sanders wasn't even in the room.

Hunter squirmed in his chair not really sure what response was expected. "I thought you did well, sir."

Sprabary started to laugh. "Of course you do. I'm your boss. What the hell else are you going to say?" He leaned back in his chair. "Well, let's just hope the media attention gets redirected soon. I'd rather not have to do another one of those for a while unless it's good news." He waived his hand as if shooing it all away. "Give it a day or two and

God knows some idiot politician will get caught with his pants down and all of this will be forgotten." He paused, leaned forward, more serious now. "Speaking of idiots, I was cooped up in that conference room before and after the press conference with your buddy from Southlake. I assured him in no uncertain terms that my team would be the first to figure out how the Kings ended up at that house." He eyed Hunter and then Sanders. "Are you boys going to make me an honest man?"

Hunter leaned forward, set his notepad down on the edge of Sprabary's desk. "Good news is we know how the Kings knew Bennett was interviewed."

Sprabary motioned for him to continue after Hunter paused. "What's the bad news?"

"Hunter took a deep breath. "They were tipped off by one of our dispatchers."

Sprabary's face paled as he leaned forward and rubbed his forehead. "Jesus, are you sure?"

"Yes, sir. Desiree Johnson. We have…"

"Desiree? Hunter, are you sure? She's been here for over five years. She's one of our best dispatchers. Whatever you've got better be solid."

"Unfortunately, it is." Hunter spent the next ten minutes laying out the details of everything they had – the caller ID, the fingerprints, the video surveillance tape, her timecard, her computer login.

Sprabary sat in silence when Hunter finished, his jaw slack and shoulders slumped. After a moment, he sighed, got up and walked to his window. The sun beat into his eyes. He spoke, but didn't seem to be directing his comments at Hunter or Sanders. "She's a single mother." He shook his head. "An accomplice to murder, no way around it." He leaned on the window seal. "Poor kid."

He turned back from the window, walked back to his desk, his eyes moist. He reached into his desk, pulled out his Smith and Wesson 9mm, clipped it to his belt. "All right, if we have to do this, I'm going to do it with you two backing me up and we're going to be very discreet. Let's go."

Hunter, a little taken aback by Sprabary's uncharacteristic

human side, stood and stepped toward the door. The three of them strategized quietly as they made their way through the halls, down the stairs and into Dispatch.

Desiree Johnson sat at her workstation wearing her headset and typing on her keyboard when Lieutenant Sprabary's hand gripped the back of her chair. She started to swivel but he held firm not allowing her chair to move. She turned her head to the right looking down the row of dispatchers. Hunter caught her eye, nodded and made a slow but obvious move to put his hand on his weapon, never breaking eye contact. Her eyes widened and she turned to the left and was greeted by Sanders, his hand on his weapon as well.

Hunter could see her chest begin to rise and fall with her increased breathing rate. He saw Desiree slowly reach up and take her headphones off.

Sprabary leaned down and whispered in her ear. "Desiree, I need you to get up very quietly and step into the conference room with me." The nod of her head was barely noticeable. Hunter saw a single tear squeezed from her right eye as she stood slowly, turned and wobbled toward him. Sprabary walked closely behind her.

Sanders stepped in and secured her work area, retrieved her purse and followed them down the hall and into a nearby conference room. A uniformed female police officer was waiting inside.

Sprabary's human streak came to an abrupt end once they were behind closed doors. He gripped her shoulder and shoved her into a metal chair. "I'm placing you under arrest for the murder of Jim Bennett." He glared up at the uniformed officer. "Cuff this piece of shit, frisk her and read her her rights."

The officer quickly stepped through her tasks. The anger in Sprabary was clearly building. The instant the officer finished, he turned, slammed his fist down on the metal table making a sound like a shotgun blast. "Do you understand your rights?" He didn't wait for a response. "How the fuck could you do this? How the fuck could you betray this department?"

She was crying heavily now but Sprabary didn't slow down. "Do you understand what you did? You killed a man yesterday. You might as well have pulled the trigger yourself." She continued to sob.

"You know what else you did? You just made your kid an orphan." She wailed hysterically. "I hope it was worth it."

Sprabary started toward the door.

Almost incoherently through sobs, Desiree screamed, "You don't understand. You don't understand."

Sprabary turned on his heels, stepped back to the table, leaned on it with both hands. She looked up at him, tried to control her sobs. His voice was steady. "I'm going to give you one final piece of advice and you'd be wise to listen carefully. I'd strongly suggest you don't say another damn word until your attorney gets here. Maybe, just maybe, he can help you get out of prison in time to meet your grandchildren."

He turned to Hunter on his way out. "Book her as an accomplice to First Degree Murder. Make sure she has an attorney and call the DA. Cross every T and dot every I. No mistakes." He stopped in the doorway, turned back to Hunter, his face a strange mixture of anger and disappointment. "I guess you made an honest man out of me. Now I get to go call that prick from Southlake."

Chapter 36

"Well, look who's decided to grace us with his presence." Bernard had one hand on his hip. He was dressed in his usual black attire and looking paler than ever. "I was beginning to wonder if you had forgotten me. Based on what I hear in the news, you've been a busy Cowboy." Bernard nodded to Sanders but stayed focused on Hunter.

Hunter grinned, breathed in deeply, letting the coffee aroma waft through his senses. "You know I'd never stay away long. Let's just say that life's been a bit hectic over the last week."

After booking Desiree, Hunter had left messages for the whole team to meet in the conference room at three o'clock. Hunter suggested to Sanders that they stop at Starbucks first. He figured that they'd better show up with some kind of peace offering for the team since Sprabary had moved too quickly to get any of the other guys involved with the earlier arrest. A couple of boxes of real coffee and pastries just might pacify them.

As Bernard worked to complete the order, he looked around furtively, leaned over the counter and whisper to Hunter. "Was that really you involved with that situation out in hoity toity land?"

Hunter nodded. "Wasn't one of my better days." He motioned over his shoulder toward Sanders. "If it hadn't been for Billy here, you might have one less regular customer."

Bernard made an overly exaggerated surprised expression and spoke as he handed the packaged up order to Hunter. "Are you okay?"

"Nothing a few days on a tropical island wouldn't cure." Hunter took the goodies and nodded. "I'll make sure I check in more often."

"You do that. In the meantime, stay out of the suburbs. They're dangerous places." He waved and went back to tend to waiting customers.

THE VICTIM

By the time Hunter and Sanders made it to the conference room, it was a little after three and the whole team was already there and hovering. They came through the door and were greeted with an assortment of stares, glares and frowns.

Hunter held up the large Starbucks bag and set it down on the table. "All right guys, I know you're pissed about this morning. I don't blame you. All I can tell you is it was out of my control and I'm sorry. Once Sprabary understood the situation, he wanted to take care of it himself and as quickly and quietly as possible."

That seemed to sooth the ruffled feathers. To emphasize his point, he motioned to the goodies and continued. "I brought an apology."

As the group descended on the snacks, Hunter and Sanders stepped to the front of the room. In addition to the core taskforce members, Hunter had left messages asking his gang experts, Myers, Nguyen, Sanchez and Hogan to join.

"All right guys, let's get going." He stood up and started pacing. "While the last two days haven't exactly been boring and plugging the department leak this morning was certainly a good thing, all in all we really haven't made much progress on the actual case that brought us together in the first place." He continued to pace while talking. "In fact, the whole situation in Southlake has probably set us back. At least it has in the eyes of the media and the general public... So, we need to regroup a bit, do some brainstorming and see if it makes sense to take a different tack."

Hunter stopped, pinched the bridge of his nose. "Considering the distractions of the last two days, it probably makes sense to go around the room, get an update from each person and reset our baseline." He looked at Sanders. "Billy, can you capture the highlights on the white board?"

Sanders nodded, picked up a marker and turned to the board. He took notes as one by one the team members gave detailed readouts on the progress, or lack thereof, for their investigative tracks. He captured statistics on the number of cases they'd reviewed, the number of people of interest identified and how they were categorized. Additionally, they recapped the details around the two known shootings.

By five o'clock, they had made it around the room twice and the whiteboards had very little white left. Hunter leaned on a table in the back of the room. His brain was tired but this had been good. "Well boys, it looks like we've exhausted what we know so we can put a checkmark by step one. For step two, I think we're going to need some nutrition. Why don't we take a break, have someone order something and then start brainstorming?"

Reyes chuckled. "I'm all for food, but if you expect any creative thinking, we're gonna need some adult beverages to go with it." That brought a chorus of 'hell yeahs'.

Hunter smiled. "Well, we are all officially off shift and if we were to move this conversation to the food instead of having the food come to us, then we'd also be off city property." He sat back down at his laptop where he'd been taking notes throughout the session. "Let me capture the last of these notes while you guys pack up. How does Angelo's sound?" As they responded with happy sounds, the thought of Angelo's famous barbeque made his mouth water and his stomach growl. Another long, intense day had left him starving.

The guys disbanded and made their way to White Settlement Road on the western edge of downtown. As Hunter left the building, he grabbed his cell phone and called Stacy. She'd been on his mind all day, memories of last night creeping in at the most awkward moments.

"You again?" The smile in her voice beamed through the phone. "If you don't stop calling me, I'll claim Police harassment."

He laughed. "I've got news for you, if I'm going to harass you, it won't involve a phone." He paused a moment. "Well, now that you mention it, hmmm…"

"Oh geez, gross, I guess that's what I get for bringing it up. So, am I going to see you tonight?"

"Funny you should ask, that's why I'm calling. How would you like to meet me and the team at Angelo's. We were working through stuff at the station and decided we might be better with some barbeque and beer."

There was a slight pause on the other end of the phone. "I thought we weren't going public so soon."

THE VICTIM

"We're not. Uh, I mean, we don't have to. Look, you know the crime scene details better than anyone and I think you could add to the conversation. Getting to see you is just a private perk."

"You're sure this won't be too obvious?"

"Are you kidding? They won't suspect a thing. Who do you think these guys are, detectives or something?"

Chapter 37

There may be plenty of contenders for the best barbeque in Fort Worth, but there's no doubt about the most famous. Angelo's Barbeque has been around since the late 1950's and despite its unassuming exterior, it is considered 'the' place to go if you want real Fort Worth barbeque.

Hunter walked in, looked around at the mounted big game trophies, breathed in the tangy smell of dry rubbed brisket and immediately felt at home. He looked over and saw that the guys had commandeered a table in the back and were elbow deep in meat. He walked to the counter and looked up at the menu. He smiled at his own waste of time. He knew what he would order.

A familiar voice rang out. "Hey Cowboy, the usual for you today?" Jason George, a stout bearded man and grandson of Angelo, the founder, was working the pit, but took a quick break to serve one of his regulars.

Hunter smiled. "Ah, Jason, you know me too well. Need a cold Michelob Ultra to go with it, might be a long evening. Oh, and I also need a…" He reached into his pocket and pulled out a slip of paper. "A sliced turkey dinner with a dry baked potato and a side salad."

Jason cringed. "Who's the health food for?"

"A CSI who's on her way." Hunter watched at Jason sliced his brisket. "How's Skeet doing?"

Jason grinned. "You know Dad, just as ornery as ever. Hard to believe but he actually took the night off tonight."

The two continued with the small talk until Hunter had both dinners and headed over to the table.

Parker, Reyes, Sanders and Andy Lowe were sitting on one side of a table for eight. Carter Hogan and Pete Nguyen were on the other side. All had their food and drinks and seemed relaxed as they debated the upcoming Longhorns – Aggies game.

"What are you, pregnant?" Reyes grinned at Hunter as he set his tray down. "Looks like you're eating for two."

It took Hunter a moment to realize what he was talking about, nodded and grinned. "Yeah, now that'd be something, wouldn't it?" He pulled out a chair and sat down. "I asked Stacy Morgan if she'd join us tonight. She was the lead CSI at both crime scenes and knows the physical evidence better than anybody here. I figured if she had to put up with you guys for the evening, the least I could do was buy her dinner."

Blaine grinned. "So, if I was a hot, divorced CSI, would you buy me dinner too?" That brought laughter from everyone at the table.

"Guess we'll never know since you're not any of the above." Hunter tipped his beer to Parker, took a swig.

"Good evenin' boys, did you save me a seat?" Stacy's smile lit up the room, her lilting voice danced in Hunter's ears.

Hunter stood up to greet her just a little too fast, he smiled a little brightly and his eyes lingered too long. When he turned back to the table, Sanders eyed him with a smile that said, 'I saw that'. Hunter kept his look stoic and acted as if he hadn't seen Sanders' expression.

They settled into casual conversation as they ate. Eventually, the discussion rolled around to the protests outside the station. Parker leaned back in his chair. "Can you believe those idiots?"

The rest of the table fidgeted in their chairs, clearly uncomfortable with where the conversation was headed. Parker, who had had just enough beer to lose his self-awareness, continued. "I mean, they're protesting while we're busting our asses trying to break this case. What we ought to be doing is spending more time arresting gangbangers."

Carter Hogan shifted in his seat and glared at Parker. "Just exactly what should we be arresting them for? They are the ones getting shot here."

Parker leaned forward. "Give me a break. These guys are just a bunch of thug felons."

Hogan's voice went up a few decibels. "You have heard of that 'innocent until proven guilty' concept, haven't you?"

"Oh yeah, great concept." Parker's voice was drenched with sarcasm. "All I'm saying is that, with all due humility, we've got a lot of law enforcement talent sitting around this table. Every minute we spend trying to catch a guy who's doing the community a favor, that's a minute we can't spend somewhere else. That just means there're a lot of crimes going unsolved."

Hogan's eyes were about to pop out of his head. "I bet you wouldn't say that if we were talking about a bunch of Lacrosse players."

"Last time I checked, Lacrosse players don't kill people."

"Well, you might want to tell that to the parents of Yeardley Love. They might disagree."

Hunter cleared his throat, put his hands out to stop the conversation. "Hold on guys. Everybody just calm down for a minute. What goes on outside this team needs to stay outside this team. Regardless of what we think of the victims in this case, we need to focus on our task."

He looked around the table and waited until he got nods from everyone. "Now that we've had a few bites, some lively debate and maybe a few too many adult beverages, let's see if we can make some headway on this thing." He took a bite of brisket, chewed for a moment, gestured with his empty fork. "So, what do we know? We've got four dead Kings, killed in similar fashions and circumstances by the same shooter..." He paused for a moment. "Well, there's still the possibility of two shooters but I think we're pretty sure it's just one."

He looked around the table and saw heads nodding in agreement. He continued. "The shooter's apparently a white guy..."

Sanders snickered, tried to lighten the mood. "Yeah, who looks like Donald Trump... Assuming you believe the drunken ravings of Sir Elliot Winston." He said the last bit in his best haughty British accent. That brought smiles around the table.

"I'll grant you the source isn't impeccable, but..." Hunter turned his palms up and shrugged. "Anyway, whoever our shooter is, he's been able to get close to his victims without them feeling threatened. That tells us they either knew him or didn't see him as a threat. My guess, considering white businessmen and Kings don't exactly run in the same circles, it's the latter."

Blaine smiled. "That's a mistake they won't make again."

Hogan shot him a stare. Parker put his hands up in mock surrender.

"So that's a part of this thing I'm still trying to get my head around." Pete Nguyen, who specialized in Asian gangs and looked young enough to be in one, had been fairly quiet. "I mean, gangbangers may not be Einstein's but they aren't stupid. In fact, when it comes to the street, these guys are top of their class. So explain to me how a white businessman just walks up to Kings on their turf and shoots them before they even pull their weapons." He leaned back in his chair, shook his head. "Not gonna happen. Think about it. If this guy just strolled up to them, wouldn't they get suspicious? Maybe think he's a cop and scatter? Maybe think that any white guy crazy enough to confront them directly is a threat? At the very least, wouldn't they draw down on him before he got within ten feet?"

The table was quiet for a moment, most taking the time to continue nibbling on the remnants and dinner and sipping on their cold beers.

Stacy looked at Hunter. "Cowboy, you remember the first crime scene and how we thought it looked like a robbery gone bad?" Hunter nodded, she continued. "Based on the body positions, it looked almost as if our shooter was cornered and he had to shoot his way out."

She arched her eyebrows at him, his heart rate jumped. He wasn't sure if it was because he was lost in her eyes or because the team was on the verge of understanding something they hadn't before.

Reyes snapped his finger. "Hold on a second… You remember when we were talking about vigilantes and someone brought up Goetz? Well, you remember when the whole Goetz thing happened, there were some who accused Goetz of setting himself up as a target so that he'd have an excuse to shoot his attackers…" He stopped, surveyed the team and let the concept hang in the air.

Nguyen was nodding his head. "That would make sense. If this guy puts himself out there as a target, the Kings would think he's just another chump to thump."

Hunter picked up the thread. "And if they think they're moving on him, they'd have no reason to expect him to turn the tables on them. I mean, other than Goetz, how many crime victims just happen to be loaded for urban hunting?"

"Hmm... The victim becomes the killer." Stacy smiled.

The table went quiet, everyone seemed to need time to contemplate this new hypothesis. Muffled country music and clattering dishes filled the moment while the guys finished up their meals and drained their beers.

Hunter pushed his empty plate away. "Okay, this is progress." He looked around the table. "Looks like we could use another round. I'll grab that and then let's see if we can take this to the next step."

He was back a few minutes later with two handfuls of bottles. As he distributed them around the table, he framed up the next part of the conversation. "So, he gets close to the bad guys and reels them in for a sort of revenge thing. So that's some headway on the Why and the How, but what about the Who? I mean, what do we know about this guy?"

"One thing's for sure, he's got balls of steel." Parker raised his beer in mock salute. "I mean, seriously, a lone white guy strolling into Kings territory like John Wayne... Popping them in their own back yard? This guy's certifiable!"

Hunter smiled as the rest of the team laughed.

Carter Hogan shifted in his seat. "So... This comment may not be all that popular, but... Have we considered this might be someone associated with law enforcement?" That brought the laughter and smiles to screeching halt. Uncomfortable looks bounced around the group.

Hunter cleared his throat. "That concept's been kicked around a bit."

"Well, it's mostly circumstantial, but... I get the sense this guy knows gangs, their habits, their hangouts. His planning is meticulous, not a shred of evidence. He's obviously not intimidated by gangbangers and he's pretty good with a gun."

"Maybe he just watches a lot of CSI." Reyes grinned and gave a nod and a wink to Stacy. She smiled back.

Hogan continued. "Sure, guess that's possible. But... These weren't just random go-find-a-tough-lookin'-black-guy-to-shoot murders. Both shootings were Kings *and* were carried out at known King selling locations." He looked around the table, stretched his palms out. "Now the guys sitting at this table might be able to tell the difference between a King and a local thug but..." He pointed out toward the rest of the restaurant. "How many folks in this restaurant could? Look around. Hell, to these rednecks, every black guy under thirty is a gangbanger. Now, take that one step further, even within law enforcement, how many folks could tell you the locations where the Kings sell? Most of you guys don't even know that."

Blaine looked over at Hunter, their eyes met. Hunter's head shake was almost imperceptible.

"Playing devil's advocate, who says he knows?" Hunter leaned forward, put his elbows on the table. "Maybe he just got lucky."

Hogan shrugged. "Possible, but I don't buy it. Everything this guy's done has been planned to perfection. He seems to have known exactly who to go after and where they'd be. Besides, think about how lucky he'd have to be to just stumble on both of those locations. He would have been aimlessly driving the back roads forever."

Hunter thought for a moment. "You may have something. I'll be honest. I really had no idea that the first scene was a known selling location." He paused, let a thought process. "Carter, how many locations do the Kings use?"

"Well, it shifts and varies, but on any given night, maybe fifteen to twenty locations. Of those, probably ten are almost always manned."

Hunter looked disappointed, shook his head. "Damn, that's more than I expected, but..." He tapped his finger on the table while his thoughts caught up. "If all we have to go on is the first two shootings, both of which were targeted at Kings and both were at known King regular selling locations, specifically one of those ten... Is that enough to predict that the next shooting will also be Kings and will also be at a known selling location?" He leaned back in his chair, shrugged. "If so, does that mean we can predict it will happen at one of those remaining eight known locations?"

There were thoughtful looks and head nods around the table before Sanders spoke up. "Sure, maybe, but even so, if you're thinking about staking them out, it's still eight locations *and* we have no idea when he'll strike again." He looked around the table. "We've got enough manpower to stake out what, maybe two locations on any given night?"

"Two out of eight locations gives us a twenty-five percent chance of being right... Not odds I'd want in Vegas but better than we've got sitting in the office." Hunter grinned.

"You mean sleeping in our beds, don't you?" Reyes exhaled. "Considering the first two shootings happened between midnight and two am, I don't think its office time we're giving up."

Parker drained his beer. "Sucks being us."

Chapter 38

The Victim drove slowly past Gordon Boswell Florist and pulled his BMW to the curb on South Lake Street. He stared through the windshield at the industrial glow of the Dannon Yogurt plant. *Looks like they're running three shifts these days. The health food craze must be recession proof.*

He surveyed the area and saw no one, just as expected. Even though he was in the heart of the hospital district, this little side street was usually quiet at ten o'clock on a Wednesday night. That was one thing he liked about this street. He got out, stepped to the curb, absentmindedly reached into his pocket for change, then remembered the other thing he liked about it. No parking meters.

He walked down the sidewalk toward the corner and perused the historic old houses that had been converted to professional offices. This part of town used to be the home for many of Fort Worth's high society. A few mansions had been preserved as historic landmarks.

He turned onto Pennsylvania Avenue and headed quickly toward the Progressive Parking Garage. Typically the parking garage for visitors to Cooks Children's Hospital, the facility also accommodated long term parking for staff.

He was scrunched into his jacket to fend on the night chill. It wasn't terribly cold but even nice nights in late November tended to make you shiver. He wasn't wearing his long coat, tonight was merely surveillance. Tomorrow night would be perfect weather for his long coat.

Normally he wouldn't have gone to the trouble of using the Impala to reconnoiter but after the last episode by the school, he thought it might make sense to drive something that blended a little better. Besides, he liked the feel of his ghetto bomb, that rumbling V8 and all that metal.

He went in the entrance connected to the hospital to avoid the security guard at the front entrance. He walked to the second level and surveyed his surroundings before leaving the stairwell. *Can't be too careful.*

He looked toward the southeast corner of the garage, a relaxed smile in his eyes as they landed on the Impala. He hit the remote starter when he was twenty feet away, heard the engine come to life, relieved to find everything was in working order.

Sitting behind the wheel, he let the rumble of the engine filter through his spine into his chest. Closing his eyes, he inhaled deeply, a musty smell wafting up from the seats. Like most of the car, they were original equipment. Even being a clean freak, there's only so much you can do with twenty-five year old fabric.

"Ah, the smell of the eighties in the evening. Heaven." He chuckled when he realized he'd actually said that out loud. Maybe the papers were right. Maybe he was a little nuts.

He looked at his eyes in the mirror as he adjusted it. The clarity of purpose made him smile. *They should all be as sane as me. The world would be a better place.* He slipped the shifter in drive and rumbled down the ramp to the exit, turned right onto Pennsylvania Avenue.

The night was crisp, clean, the air was just cold enough to chase away the humidity. With no clouds in the sky, he could actually see stars. On this night at least, they were holding their own in the constant battle with the city's light pollution.

Much of his day, in between meetings and phone calls, was spent mapping out his route for the evening. It was going to take a while as he had identified eight locations to cruise. Having already scouted the I.M. Terrell location, he wouldn't revisit it tonight. While it seemed like a prime target, he had a concern about the limited number of access points. The last thing he needed was to get trapped in that part of town.

Tonight would be dedicated to drive-by's of several other potential target locations. He needed to determine which locations were still active, how many Kings were on site and to identify his entrance and exit options. *No room for error.*

As he moved east along Pennsylvania, an eerie calm washed over him and he slipped into an easy cruising pace. He'd struggled to focus at work over the past week and a half. After years of thought and months of planning, he'd finally kicked off his mission and job responsibilities seemed even less important than ever.

He punched on the radio, smiled at the thought of satellite technology pumping his favorite tunes into an old beater that had an eight track player as original equipment. His mind drifted back to the night before, the press conference. *Jim Bennett didn't deserve that. No one did.*

The anger built again and he shook his head to clear his thoughts. *Stay focused.* He scanned through the stations. The Seventies station was playing Dr. Hook's 'Sharing the Night Together'. *The seventies were so cheesy. Fun tune, though.* He punched once to the Eighties station. It was something truly awful by Rick Astley. *MTV, what a plague.* One more punch to the Nineties on Nine. He heard a rhythmic drum beat and a driving acoustic guitar. His ears perked up. *Now we're talking. A little 3 Doors Down.*

He drummed on the steering wheel as the song Citizen Soldier got through its intro. As the lyrics kicked in, he nodded his head and sang along thinking of himself. *Yeah, that's me. The guardian of the weak.* The music got him pumped up and he drove on.

Pennsylvania Avenue had an odd mix of light commercial, former residential, healthcare related storefronts and a series of small community churches. Even with the gleaming downtown skyline just to the north, it was not a pretty part of town.

As he came up on the intersection with South Main, the landscape changed dramatically. The old historic mansions were well behind him now. At this point it was just empty lots, boarded up buildings and run down warehouses with more broken windows than not.

He found driving in tough parts of town interesting. Unlike high end neighborhoods where everything was homogeneous, up to code, controlled by HOA's and somewhat boring, in the low end areas, time, neglect and lack of concern created the strangest bedfellows. As he moved past South Main, he slowed. The first target site.

Up ahead a half block on his right was a dingy bar named Tommy's Place, a brick building not much larger than a two car garage.

It was painted neon blue, had no windows and a steel door and looked like a standalone prison cell. On his left was Lois', an almost identical building painted gray. There were only a handful of worn out cars in either parking lot. He shook his head. *A white guy wouldn't last sixty seconds in either place.*

He smiled as he turned left onto Crawford Street. He'd driven here before and knew that sitting in the midst of all this squalor at the corner of Crawford and Annie was a small outdoor church that ministered to the homeless on weekends. It sat on a tiny lot and consisted of an outdoor alter, several wooden crosses, a handful of signs and banners and about twenty long white wooden benches, ten on each side of a grass path. It was immaculately maintained and for reasons he didn't understand, seemed to be considered off limits to the local thugs and vandals.

A couple of turns later, he passed two houses, shacks really, on his left and came to S. Calhoun and E. Tucker. On the northeast corner sat an abandoned, two story building. Painted several shades of gray, a metal awning ran the length of the building's front with a rusted, unusable fire escape on the south side. Back behind the fire escape, near where E. Tucker dead ended in the high power lines and railroad tracks, was a loading dock.

When he passed, he found what he expected, three Kings hovering in the shadows, their car backed into the barricade. They looked up and stared at him, apparently determining if he was a potential customer or future mugging victim.

He didn't speed up or slow down, just kept moving down one more block where the road forced a ninety degree turn and headed him back toward E. Hattie.

At Hattie, he looked around in all directions, making sure he was alone and thought about what he'd seen. He made mental notes about how to maneuver the streets, where cars, houses and buildings were and how formidable the players looked. He liked what he saw, nodded to himself, pulled away and continued on Hattie toward I-35.

Based on his research, his past explorations and his hands on experience with the Eastcide Kings, he knew that the real heart of their territory was roughly twenty square blocks southeast of the I-30 and I-35 intersection. His first two targets were picked because they were either on the edge or slightly outside that box. They were warm ups.

As he crossed the bridge over I-35, he moved into the heart of their territory, an area known as the Historic Southside. He also drove right past Van Zandt Guinn Park. He looked over, thought about the last shooting. He didn't exactly smile. He'd certainly succeeded in his objective that night, but he'd barely made it out alive and he'd left witnesses. He knew that would make future events more dangerous. After all, while the gangbangers wouldn't talk to the cops, he was sure they'd briefed their colleagues.

He crossed S. Kentucky Street. From that point forward, he'd be in some of the toughest, poorest neighborhoods in all of Fort Worth. What was once nice, working class neighborhoods had degraded over the years into a residential ghetto that could rival anything Detroit or Los Angeles offered.

Blocks with more boarded up houses than legally occupied homes were surrounded by vacant lots where the city had taken the initiative to bulldoze condemned shells. Scattered here and there were defiant homeowners still relentlessly maintaining their homes. He passed one. *Give it up man. It's a losing fight.*

Passing the Star Two Food Store on the corner Tennessee and Hattie, he noted the two Kings sitting in the shadows on the hood of their ride at the edge of the parking lot toward the back of the building. *Hmm, a little too public for now, but if I have to change my method, it could be an easy drive by target.*

He continued to Riverside and turned south. He pulled into the entrance for Glenwood Park. He looked across the creek to the playground and saw four Kings. They had entered from the other side of the park with their ghetto mobile parked behind them. *A little too open, might be tough to get set up without them seeing me. Can't approach or exit from this side because of the creek.*

He pulled through to Rosedale, getting another view through the trees. The sights, sounds and smells from the night already had him slightly depressed, but as he cut back on Freeman Street, he knew it was only going to get worse. He weaved around until he could turn left on Leuda and marveled as he drove. It was probably the most desolate, poorest single street in the city. He went through several blocks with almost no legal, functioning homes. Even the few he saw looked like they should have been condemned long ago.

He passed two more target locations, both in boarded up houses, both with at least four Kings hovering nearby. He made his mental notes, determined where he could park, how he could approach, whether or not even with proper planning and execution, he could get out alive.

When he got back to New York Avenue, he stopped. He'd seen too much, his head was spinning. *How do these people live like this? How do the innocent ones tolerate the parasites?*

His stomach churned but he resisted leaving his dinner on the pavement. He pulled away from the stop sign, his eyes moist from sadness. *I guess that's why I'm here. Someone has to help them.*

Chapter 39

Thursday morning found Hunter standing at the front of the conference room staring at a city map where he had plotted all the known selling locations for the Eastcide Kings. His mind processed the conversation from the night before. He'd gotten the addresses and some additional intelligence from the gang guys before they left Angelo's. He was still trying to figure out how to cover eight locations with only enough men for two.

In the back of his mind, he continued to think about what Hogan had said, that the shooter could be someone in law enforcement. His mind drifted back to Tim Daris' office, the pictures and the coat. Combine that with what Blaine had found out and Hunter's blood was pumping faster than normal this morning.

The rest of the team filtered in while he contemplated locations and entered more notes into his laptop. By nine A.M., the core team of Reyes, Sanders, Parker and Lowe had congregated around the tables with their various forms of morning caffeine in front of them.

Hunter had been so engrossed in thought, he had neither noticed nor acknowledged them. Sanders finally overtly cleared his throat. At the sound, Hunter broke from his self-induced trance and turned toward the room. A look of mild surprise crossed his face followed by a self-conscious grin. "Good morning boys."

Reyes pointed toward the map. "So what's got you wrapped around the axle this morning?"

Hunter smiled and raised his index finger. "I think I might have something." He turned back toward the map. "After you lightweights gave up and called it a night, Hogan educated me a bit on the Eastcide Kings."

Standing in front of the map, he outlined a lopsided square on the map by running his finger east along I-30, south on Riverside Drive, west on Rosedale and north on I-35 back to his starting point on I-30. "This box is the Eastcide Kings turf. Sure, their reach goes outside this area, but they are the undisputed owners of what happens inside this box."

He pointed to an X on the map. "This is their headquarters." He pointed to several circles drawn in black inside the square. "These are their primary selling locations. Here is another house they use as kind of a satellite crib. Notice that all of these are well inside the boundary of their turf."

He now took a red marker and made two circles on the map. "Here are the locations of the first two shootings." He turned and pointed to Sanders. "What do you notice about them?"

Sanders cocked his head slightly. "They're both on the west side of the area and one's not even in the box."

Hunter was animated now. "Exactly." He started pacing. "What does that mean? Is it significant?" He didn't wait for an answer. "I'm not really sure but I think it is. I think there's a reason he hasn't hit deep in their territory."

Parker laughed. "Could it be that he's only a little nuts instead of completely insane?"

Hunter nodded. "Something along those lines. Maybe not exactly." Still pacing, almost talking to himself now. "I don't think this guy's crazy at all. At least not in the certifiable sense. I think everything he's done to this point has been planned. He hit these targets specifically because they weren't in the heart of the territory. Call it practice, warm ups, whatever."

He turned toward the group. "Gentlemen, this guy's just getting started. If we don't stop him, he will systematically step across this map and hit every one of these locations. I may be taking a bit of a leap, but this guy has something personal with the Kings, he's done his homework and now he's hitting the targets in a logical fashion, starting with the easiest one's first."

Sanders pointed to the map. "If that's the case, why didn't he hit that location just west of I-35 or the one at Terrell High School before the location at the park? I mean, they're actually outside the box while the park is inside."

"Good question." Hunter rubbed his temples, slid his hands down in front of his face and steepled his fingers together. "I've been thinking about that very question all morning and I don't have a good answer. I did come up with one theory." He pointed back to the board. "Take a close look at those two locations on the map. Both are boxed in geographically with limited entry and exit points. Logistically, if something goes wrong, he gets trapped with no way out."

Everyone in the room nodded at the picture Hunter had painted. Their body language indicated they thought he was onto something.

Reyes spoke up. "So, how does this help us predict his next hit? We don't know if he's ready to make his move deeper into their territory or if he's still warming up."

Hunter started pacing again. "You're absolutely right. There are a couple of factors to consider. First, he's got a difficult choice. Either he hits targets which are outside the box but risky due to limited access or he hits targets inside the box. Those, as Parker indicated, require a whole new level of crazy. Neither option is good. The second thing we have to consider is just our practical ability to stake out a location inside the box without scaring off the targets. Inside that box, we stand out like turds in a punchbowl."

That brought a few smiles. "The reality is, I'm not sure we have much choice. I think we have to stay outside the box. There are two bits of good news... First, if he hits one of the locations we're at, it will be relatively easy to trap him. Second, we'll be both north and west of the box so if he hits inside we may get lucky and run into him as we respond."

There were nods around the room and the team was leaning forward in their chairs. Hunter spent the next hour going over the details and logistics of the two stakeout locations.

It was almost 10:30am by the time he finished. "Okay boys, you guys need to take the rest of the day off and get some sleep. We're going on the night shift for the next few days. We'll see if we get lucky." He nodded. "See you tonight."

He turned toward Billy. "Sanders, I need you to stick around. We've got an errand to run."

Chapter 40

The predicted cold front had moved in by late morning so Hunter and Sanders decided to drive instead of walk the short distance across town. Sanders got into the unmarked Chrysler Police Cruiser, looked around the car, made a face and shook his head. "Nice Ride... What's that smell?"

"Had to get my Explorer in the shop. Best I could get on short notice. Not sure on the smell. I've been trying to figure it out all morning. It's kind of a cross between a sweaty pig and a beer fart."

Sanders cracked his window. "Yeah, with a dash of puke thrown in just for flavor." He waved his hand across his face. "Damn, tell them to put a rush on your ride."

As they weaved through the downtown Fort Worth one way streets, Hunter filled Sanders in on the last conversation he'd had with ADA Tim Daris.

Sanders nodded but scrunched up his face. "You can't really think Daris could be our guy based on the fact that he had family pictures on his credenza and a long wool coat hanging behind his door."

"At that point, it was more of a gut thing, based on his body language." Hunter explained as they pulled into the parking garage. "Since then I've had Parker check him out more thoroughly." He raised an eyebrow and glanced over at Sanders. "Seems our Mr. Daris was a little less than forthcoming on his motivation to nail gangbangers."

"Okay?"

As they walked through the parking structure and into the building, Hunter quietly filled him in on the background check that Parker had done. "So when you add my gut reaction to the fact that his fiancée was brutally attacked, giving him the ultimate motive for becoming a prosecutor... Well, you know... It's worth checking."

Sanders shook his head slowly. "I don't know. The thought of someone on our side, especially a prosecutor, doing something like this? Man, it just seems crazy."

"Doesn't that go without saying? Whoever's doing this is obviously twisted." When they reached the elevator, Hunter exhaled loudly and looked over at Sanders. "We've got to go where the trail leads even if we don't like the direction."

The door opened and they stepped into the elevator lobby just a beat before the opposite elevator doors opened. Tim Daris stepped out followed by Edmond Curtis, both looked pissed. They both turned toward the receptionist and took a couple of steps before Daris stopped and turned toward Hunter. He nodded, his scowl not lightening. "Detective."

Hunter stepped forward. "How fortunate Prosecutor, you were just the guy I was hoping to see. Do you have a few minutes?"

Daris paused, frowned. "Sure... Why not? I can't imagine you doing anything to make my day worse." He turned, started walking toward his office. "We'll get some coffee on the way."

As the group passed, the receptionist looked up. "Good morning, Mr. Daris."

"There's nothing good about it, Susan."

Daris hung his gray, wool overcoat behind the door, stepped over and settled in behind his desk. Hunter was once again perusing his office, especially the pictures.

Daris blew across the top of his coffee cup, took a sip and put the cup down on his desk. "Well Detective, it seems we've had equally difficult weeks. Of course, neither of ours have sucked quite as bad as Mrs. Bennett's, have they?"

Hunter shifted in his seat, met Daris' glare, cocked his head as if to question the statement.

Daris leaned forward. "Oh, I guess you don't know." His face morphed into a sarcastic smile. "The reason for my foul mood is that the gangbanger who raped and murdered Nicole Bennett was just found not guilty and walked out of the courtroom laughing while Rose Bennett collapsed in the row behind me."

Hunter felt the air evaporate from his lungs, his face drained and it was hard to catch his breath. The realization of what had just been said hit him like a baseball bat. *Oh my God. That poor woman.*

Daris let out a short laugh, more of a snort. "I guess we really did a number on her this week. Hell, maybe I should feel good. All I did was let her daughter's killer walk free to go do it to someone else. At least I didn't get her husband killed." He leaned back, looked away for a moment. "I'm sorry Detective. I shouldn't have said that. As you can see, I don't handle losing well."

"What kind of..." Sanders leaned forward but Hunter cut him off.

Hunter calmed himself before he spoke. "No need to apologize Prosecutor. We all have to live with the consequences of our jobs. Sometimes that results in a lot of sleepless nights." He paused for a moment before he continued. "I guess these situations hit especially close to home for you."

Daris looked at Hunter with no expression. "I'm not sure what you mean, Detective."

"Well, you've been in her shoes before, right? Getting to watch as the gangbanger who assaulted someone close to you walked out the door."

Daris didn't react, just held his stare at Hunter.

"She was your fiancée, wasn't she?"

"Well, I'm not sure if I should feel flattered or insulted. Any way it goes, I'll tell you this... You're on thin fucking ice Detective. I may be impressed that you do your homework but investigating an ADA is a dangerous path and one I'd suggest you not go down." He leaned forward and glared at Hunter. "I think our time is done." He started to get up but stopped when Hunter spoke.

"I just find it interesting that you didn't mention it in our last meeting. Considering the situation, seems like it might have been relevant. Certainly gives me some insight into your motivation, your drive to convict gangbangers."

Daris started to say something, stopped, shook his head and stood up. He turned away and looked out the window for a minute. "Just to show that I have nothing to hide here... Yes, I was once engaged to woman who was brutally assaulted by a gangbanger. Yes, the attack changed her life and ultimately derailed our wedding plans. Yes, I use that situation as motivation every day of my life as I do all I can to prosecute criminals."

He turned back toward the desk and Hunter, put his hands on the back of his chair. "Now, I've been more than cooperative. There's nothing else to know about that situation." He set his jaw. "Understand this, my personal life is none of your goddamned business, Detective, and if I find out you're continuing down this path, I'll stomp you like a rodeo bull... Cowboy. Now, before this conversation escalates any further, I'd suggest you leave."

Hunter and Sanders stood, all three postured for a moment before Hunter shrugged. "Just doing my job."

"Maybe if you'd have done your job a little better on Tuesday, Jim Bennett would still be alive."

The words stung in Hunter's ears. "You son of a..." Hunter lunged forward but Sanders had him by the shoulders and was shuffling him out the door before he could do anything. As they turned to leave. Hunter stopped in the doorway and turned back toward Daris. "Let's not forget who served Jim Bennett up to me on a silver platter." They both glared at each other.

Daris pushed his chin out. "Just do your job and stay the hell out of my life."

Hunter's eyes narrowed. "Oh, I'll do my job. Count on it. I'll get this guy... Whoever it is."

Chapter 41

The Victim sat alone in his home office staring at the wall. He could feel the nighttime cold from outside seeping through the window. A shadow was cast from his desk lamp, the only light on in the house. Her picture lay flat on his desk right next to one of the Berettas.

He had done his reconnaissance the night before, continued to contemplate throughout the day. Now it was just a matter of watching the time tick away to ensure his prey would be out. His eyes shifted to the clock on the bookshelf. *Eleven twenty-three. Just a little longer. I'll get to the garage by midnight. That should be just about right. The cockroaches always come out around the midnight hour.*

He smiled as the classic Wilson Picket song, 'In The Midnight Hour' started playing in his head. He hummed along as he reached over, picked up the semi-automatic pistol with a gloved hand and began wiping it down with the white hand towel.

His mind drifted back in time. She was there, smiling, laughing, teasing him about something silly. The sun was out, the sky was blue, life was good. *So long ago. Another lifetime. One stolen by that animal.* He sneered at the next thought. *More payback tonight.*

*   *   *   *

Sanders looked toward the parking lot as they walked out the back doors of the station, held his hand out to slow Hunter down. "Oh no. Do we really have to use that car again? Dealing with that smell all night will kill me."

"Not to worry. I had it cleaned after I dropped you back at the station. Now there's a hint of vanilla layered on top of all that other nasty shit." He laughed and kept walking to the car. "Good thing you wore a jacket. At least we'll be able to crack the windows."

Sanders shook his head. "Great."

It was just before midnight as they pulled out of the parking lot with all four windows at half-mast. Since this was Sanders' first official stakeout, as they made their way through the downtown streets to get to their stakeout position, they discussed tactics and possible scenarios.

Turning east onto Hattie Street, Hunter smiled. "The most critical part of a stakeout is to avoid driving your partner crazy. Keep in mind, we might be here all night since there really haven't been enough shootings to establish a timing pattern. We're kind of shooting in the dark to see if he even strikes tonight."

Sanders nodded. "I'll keep that in mind."

*   *   *   *

The Victim pulled out of the parking garage at about a quarter after twelve and headed east on Pennsylvania. He wore black dress slacks, a white dress shirt and his Nike running shoes. The holstered Berettas and his charcoal gray wool overcoat were concealed in the trunk. He didn't want to have those items in plain sight in case he got pulled over for something silly like rolling a red light.

He'd get rigged up properly once he'd made a first pass on his planned target. Unlike the previous excursions, his pulse was only slightly elevated, more excitement than fear. What lie ahead of him was planned. He was ready. He knew his mission and knew it was right.

His mind went over the plan as he drove east on Hattie into the heart of the beast. *It'll be dark. The third house on the right. I'll come up from the corner.* The only variables were the targets. Would they be there? Could he lure them out? Had they figured out his game? No way to know but to go forward.

*   *   *   *

"Crack Daddy calling Chicken Picker. You out there Chicken Picker?"

Sanders looked at the radio, then turned to Hunter with a question on his face. Hunter just shook his head. "Welcome to a stakeout with Reyes."

Hunter rolled his eyes, picked up the two-way hand held radio. They had decided in their earlier planning session to have cars equipped with the standard police band radios in order to monitor normal dispatch traffic but to additionally use a set of hand held radios set to a specific radio band to communicate directly with each other. This would help to avoid someone stumbling on their transmissions. "Really Reyes? Must we?"

Howling laughter came through the speakers. "You know me boss, just trying to have a little fun, keep this night from killing us with boredom."

Hunter didn't acknowledge the humor. "We'll assume you're in position?"

"Roger that Chicken Picker."

"Sanchez. How about you and Myers?"

"Roger that Chicken Picker" More laughter in the background.

Hunter looked over to Sanders. "It's going to be a long night." He clicked the mic again. "Hogan? You and Nguyen?"

"Roger that Chicken Picker."

"All right boys. Let's stay off the radio unless we need it. Use cell phones for idle chatter. Check in with Sanders once an hour and stay awake."

The four units had split the assignment with Reyes/Parker and Sanchez/Myers staking out the school and Hunter/Sanders and Hogan/Nguyen taking the abandon building near the outdoor chapel west of the Hattie Street I-35 Bridge.

Hunter and Sanders had positioned themselves a block northwest of the abandoned warehouse where they had a line of sight on the small group of Kings as they serviced their clientele at the corner loading dock. Meanwhile Carter Hogan and Pete Nguyen had parked in the almost full parking lot of Tommy's Place where they watched the Kings' customers come in and out of area.

Similarly, Reyes and Parker parked between a couple of dumpsters on the dark side of a housing unit and watched their batch of gangbangers from across the football field, while Sanchez and Myers positioned themselves up on I.M. Terrell Way, the main entry point to the high school area. Like Hogan and Nguyen, their role was to watch anyone entering the area and be ready for anyone leaving hot.

By half past midnight, they were all positioned and settled in for a long night.

Chapter 42

The Victim sat in the Impala. Using a pair of high powered binoculars, he surveyed the scene through the windshield and nervously tapped his finger on the steering wheel. It wasn't exactly the scenario he'd expected. The house was crowded and lit up. *Bunch of people. Wonder what they're celebrating? Maybe the welfare checks arrived today.* He smiled at the joke.

He looked at his watch. It was a few minutes after one o'clock. He continued to watch, thought about the mission, possible tactics. *This many people changes everything. Too many people. Too much risk. Maybe I should abort? Go to one of the other locations.*

He was parked about a block and a half east of his target location on E. Leuda Street, in front of one of four empty lots where the city had bulldozed abandoned houses. The condemned structures had been replaced over time by a collection of junk and trash. Trading one blight for another. Over his shoulder was another dilapidated house that looked ready to implode into itself and a set of unkempt railroad tracks.

The car idled and he continuously checked the mirrors making sure no one surprised him from behind. He wasn't worried about being seen from the impromptu party. He was a good distance away and the darkness where he parked was complete. Most of the street lights had either been shot out or just neglected by the city.

As he continued to watch the festivities, he slowly realized the golden opportunity presenting itself. *What a strike. I'm in the heart of the beast with a dozen possible targets all in one spot. Sure, it's risky but what's life without some chances? I'll get more than just one tonight.*

He mapped out his final plan, got out and went to the trunk. The night air was cold, the darkness and the neighborhood intimidating. He did a slow three sixty, then popped the trunk. He slipped the custom holster on and checked the weapons. *Locked and loaded.* He wrapped himself into the long wool coat, felt its warmth, reached into the pockets making sure his access to the weapons was clear. He closed the trunk, stood for a moment listening to odd mix of sounds in this sparsely populated part of the city. So much of the neighborhood had been abandoned, it had almost become rural again. Crickets, frogs, the highway hum and distant music. One last survey of the area. He was ready.

He pulled away from the curb, went west toward Virginia Street only slowing to pull through the intersection. He eased along the street as his eyes scanned the scene locking momentarily on each parked car, front porch and dark space they found, always coming back to the target.

The Impala rolled to a stop at the corner of Tennessee and Leuda and he paused, eyes locked forward. The party was across Tennessee, two houses down on his right. His heart rate was building, a bead of sweat had appeared on his forehead despite the cold outside.

Now he could see the target clearly without binoculars. He could even hear the thumping music coming from the house. There were cars parked in front of the three houses closest to the corner with some up in yards and broken up drive ways. *Lot of cars but not as many people as I'd thought.* He looked around, made mental notes. *Two on front porch. Couple making out against that car.* He looked at two more gangbangers standing in the front yard near the sidewalk and smiled. *You ready to play boys?*

He scanned in all four directions. Everyone else appeared to be enjoying the warmth and music of the house. He pulled through the intersection and slowly toward the house. The two in the yard stared him down as he approached. He knew they couldn't see through his window tint but his stomach still flip flopped with nerves.

Just before he passed, his hand reached under the dash and flipped a switch disabling the brake lights so that when he stopped a few houses down, nothing would catch their attention. It was critical to his plan that they not notice him park the car. He kept his eyes focused as he passed noting that the two in the yard went back to their cigarettes and beers as soon as he passed. *Checkpoint one cleared.*

He pulled to the side of the road two houses down in front of another empty lot, checked the mirrors and waited before shutting off the engine. *No reaction. Alright, good to go.*

He rolled down the window and then killed the engine. He listened but heard nothing but the thump of the music. Some idiot chanting something about ho's and bitches. It seemed that every other word was an f-bomb. He shook his head in reaction to the de-evolution of music and society.

Now was the moment of truth, the trickiest part of his plan. As in the past, the plan was simple. He would present himself as a target and see if they bite. If they do, then he's justified to defend himself with deadly force. If not, he'd just continue on and drive away. After all, he wasn't a murderer. The issue he faced now was getting back down the street so that he could approach from the other side of the house. His car would be in sight in the perfect direction for a quick departure when he passed the house.

He had surveyed the area several times, looked at maps and even perused Google Earth. He knew a utility right of way ran behind all four of the houses. The empty lot gave him perfect access. He'd be able to walk behind the houses back to Tennessee, west to the sidewalk in front of the houses and toward his parked car. The one concern was that he'd never actually been behind the houses.

He started to open the door, realized his heart was pounding like a freight train. He stopped, took two deep, slow breathes and got his pulse under control. *Now or never.* He opened the door quietly, stayed low as he got out and moved to the front of the car in a crouch.

Without standing up, he moved to where he could look back down the road using the car for cover. *No signs of movement. They're clueless just like the last ones.*

He took off in a trot staying as low as possible until he was deep enough into the empty lot that the fourth house provided him cover. He wasn't too concerned about someone from that house noticing him. Like many on the street, it was boarded up and showed no signs of life.

He made it to the back of the house and to the utility easement in a few quick steps. *So far, so good.* He once again crouched down, stopped and listened for signs of life. The music continued thumping. A different rapper raging on about killing cops.

For the first time, he was behind the houses and could make a real assessment. No concerns about anyone from the houses fronting Cannon Street seeing him, plenty of trees and thick overgrowth along the back fence line. His two challenges now stared him in the face. The first was that the easement hadn't been kept up very well so the undergrowth was thick. He'd have to trash through it pretty hard. Although he did feel a little odd traipsing through the underbrush in slacks and a dress shirt, the bigger challenge was that, unlike the front yard of the party house which wasn't overly crowded, the backyard had at least a dozen partiers in various states of intoxication.

There was a fence and some overgrowth. In some neighborhoods, that might have been bushes or even real landscaping. Here it was just overgrown weeds and grass. He took a deep breath and started making his way low and slow along the fence line of the first two houses.

As he moved, his heart pounded. The trashing and crunching of every step sounded like the fourth of July. *Thank God, they're drunk and the music's blasting.* He moved steadily until he got close to the fence of the party house. He stopped but only briefly. No need to linger.

Just as he began to move and trash through the underbrush, the music stopped. He dropped to his knees, the blood rushed through his ears, his breathe caught in his throat. *Did they hear me? Oh shit.* He waited.

"Hey muthafucka!" The voice sounded like it was right on top of him. "Hey, turn the music back on nigga!"

With that, the tunes cranked back up. The Victim's head was spinning now. He was on the verge of hyperventilating. He stayed on his knees for several minutes trying to regain his composure. Finally, he moved on, made it past the party house and the corner house and stopped at the edge of the sidewalk on Tennessee.

He looked up and down the street to make sure it was clear enough for him to make it to the street corner. *Looks good.* He stood, slid his hands into his coat pockets, gripped the two Berettas and walked quickly to the corner. *No turning back now. They're between you and the car. Only way to get home is to walk past them.*

He stood up straight, turned west on Leuda and started walking at a brisk pace toward the party and his car. He scanned as he went.

Same set of characters in the front yard. Won't have to worry about the love birds. She had now moved down and was on her knees in facing him. *Right in the front yard? Really? Damn.* He shook his head, continued his scan. *The guys on the porch look stoned. They'll be slow to react. Keep focused on the two in the yard.*

Neither of the gangbangers noticed him until he was almost on their sidewalk. When they heard him, they both spun around quickly toward him, both seemed confused, as if they couldn't believe what they were seeing. He kept his head straight and kept walking in spite of feeling like he was going to puke or pass out at any second.

They recovered from their surprise quickly and moved toward him, one stepped directly in his path, the second moved to his right between him and the house.

The one directly in front of him smiled a stoner smile, snickered and held up his hand. "Yo, whoa now, hold on my brutha. Where you think you goin' tonight?"

The Victim tried to step around him moving left toward a parked car. "Leave me alone, please."

The banger stepped in front of him and the Victim repositioned himself with his back to the parked car, now facing both gangbangers and looking toward the house. He knew this wasn't going to be a long conversation.

"I like the way you say 'please' but you picked the wrong fuckin' street to stroll down tonight, Cracker. Me and Thumpa gonna mess you up." He nodded to his buddy and grinned. He looked back at the Victim, his eyes narrowed with recognition. "Hey wait a minute. I know... Holy shit!" The stoner stepped toward him and made a move for something in his waistband.

His arm never made it that far. The blast of the first Beretta sounded like a cannon, the bullet ripped through his chest and exploded out the back leaving a massive hole. The second Beretta was up and aimed at the second gangbanger. His eyes flew wide with the realization that his life was about to end. He too, didn't get the chance to pull his weapon before the bullet blew through the front of his throat, nearly decapitating him.

The two quick blasts were perfectly executed and the bodies fell in neat piles on the sidewalk. There was a moment of silence, a fog of smoke and blood mist and the smell of cordite.

"What the hell?" Mr. Blowjob was heading his direction, stumbling, trying to get his pants pulled up and get to his weapon at the same time. The Victim, feeling in charge and bulletproof, raised the Berettas and popped two quick rounds into him from ten feet away. He smiled. *Shooting fish in a barrel.*

The feeling of invincibility evaporated in the next second as all hell broke loose. The gangbangers on the porch must not have been as stoned as he'd thought because the windows in the car behind him exploded spraying glass all over him as he stood in his daze. In an instant, bullets flew all around him.

He bolted to his left and started firing randomly in the direction of the house. Somehow, his brain registered that the music had stopped. In the next moment it seemed as if there was an army chasing him. The eruption of gunfire sounded like a thousand soldiers all firing at once.

Bullets seemed to be coming and going from all directions. Car windows continued to explode, tires blew up, doors pinged and ricochets bounced off the sidewalk. *Holy shit!*

He had somehow made it to the abandoned house with twenty more feet to go. He continued shooting with his right hand, ducked behind a parked car, stopped only long enough to holster one pistol and hit the remote starter on his car. He heard the car start. In that few seconds, the beat up Honda he was behind nearly disintegrated from bullets.

He rose up, firing as fast as his finger could move in the direction of the crowd and ran for the car. He stumbled, or was he knocked down, but didn't fall completely, grabbed the door handle and fell into the car. He yanked the gearshift into drive, hit the lights and the gas pedal without sitting up and the car shot off down the street.

The back window exploded and it sounded like he'd been caught in a hail storm with bullets riddling through the car. He peaked up over the dash just long enough to get his bearings, realized the hailstorm had stopped even though he could still hear the guns blasting away a half block behind him.

The next thing he knew he was at Illinois Street. He took a hard right and gunned the car again realizing as he moved the steering wheel that his left arm hurt like hell. *No time to worry about that now. Got to get out of here.*

He floored it as he blasted north on Illinois. He blew through the Hattie Street intersection without looking, heard a horn blare, and made the next six blocks to Vickery in a blink of an eye. He checked his rearview mirror, saw nothing, took a fast left on Vickery and headed for the Freeway.

Chapter 43

"Only one thirty? It seems like we've been here all damn night." Sanders took another drink of coffee, scrunched his face. "Coffee's already cold. Shit." They'd only been there a little over an hour and his butt was already sore. He was cold, bored and trying not to yawn.

"Welcome to being a Detective. Pretty exciting stuff, isn't it?" Hunter reached around behind his seat and came back with an old fashioned thermos. "This ought to at least resolve your hot coffee issue. Pour that cold stuff out the window."

Sanders fidgeted around in the passenger seat, leaned forward to get a better line of sight and looked out at the three Kings milling about on the corner. "I'd suggest we bust these guys for distribution except based on the lack of traffic tonight, there wouldn't be much of a case."

"Yeah, whoever took over for Shadow won't be too pleased with tonight's sales numbers." Hunter paused for a moment, reached into the back floorboard and brought out his laptop. "That reminds me, we need to find out who the new boss is over in Kingland." He keyed in some notes.

Sanders looked at Hunter like he'd lost his mind. "I don't know about you, but I'm guessing we probably won't be able to just stroll in there like we did last time."

Hunter shrugged. "I don't know. I'm sure they're pissed, but you might be surprised. This is a business to those guys and people getting shot is just one of the costs." He smirked. "Besides, it wasn't me that shot him." He busted out laughing.

"Nice." Sanders shook his head and smiled like he couldn't believe what Hunter had just said.

"Least I can do considering you saved my life. Guess I owe you something."

THE VICTIM

Sanders snapped his finger as he remembered. "Speaking of owing me something, you never did get a chance to tell me how you got the nickname 'Cowboy'."

Hunter sighed. "It's really not that interesting, but what the hell... It all stems from an incident that happened when I was in uniform. We got this call..."

"All units in the area..." The radio crackled to life. "Multiple shots fired near the corner of Tennessee and Leuda. Possible gang involvement. Please respond."

Hunter hit the ignition. "Answer the call. Tell 'em we're on the way and rolling the whole task force." He closed his laptop, tossed it in the back floorboard and grabbed the stakeout team radio while Sanders worked the Police Band. They talked over each other in urgent staccato bursts. "Reyes, Hogan, Sanchez, looks like our guy may be in play." He shifted in to drive and gunned the cruiser. "Let's move! Corner of Tennessee and Leuda. See you there."

"Already rolling, Cowboy." Excitement echoed in Reyes' voice.

More information came in as they raced down Hattie Street with lights and sirens blasting. First responders arriving on the scene described it as a warzone and immediately requested backup. Hunter took a hard right on Tennessee and could already see other units arriving. He slid to a stop at the curb when he got to the Leuda intersection.

He and Sanders exited the vehicle with badges visible and weapons drawn. Hogan and Nguyen had already arrived and taken charge of the scene. Patrol units were setting up a perimeter covering both sides of the street stretching from the intersection west to the vacant lot four houses down.

Hunter paused at the front of his car and scanned the scene. There were several vehicles parked along the north side of the street with blown out windows, flat tires and visible bullet holes. He could see that at least one leaked fluid onto the street. Even from where he stood two houses down, he could see at least two bodies on the ground. No one was near them. *Obvious fatalities.*

His head swiveled when he heard a guttural scream as a woman burst from a house on the south side of the street. She fell to the ground gesturing toward her house, screaming incoherently. Hunter was too far away to understand her. All he caught was the word baby. Hogan and Nguyen were at her side in an instant and Nguyen just as quickly was up the stairs and in the house. Hogan stayed with the woman, consoling her while continuing to direct the scene.

Tires screeched and car doors slammed behind him. Hunter turned and saw Reyes and Parker running toward him. He pointed to them. "You guys direct the uniforms and seal the area. The perimeter needs to expand. No one goes in or out unless they're law enforcement."

Reyes never slowed down as he passed. "On it, Cowboy."

Hunter turned toward Billy. "Sanders, as soon as Sanchez and Myers arrive, I want the three of you going door to door. We need to search every room of every one of the four houses on this side and probably the first five houses on that side... Be alert!"

Hunter started walking toward the heart of the crime scene, popped in his Bluetooth and told the phone to call. Stacy answered in a sleepy voice. "If you're calling to tell me good-night and you miss me..." There was a long yawn. "You're about two hours too late, but I'm glad you called."

In spite of the war scene in front of him, he smiled. "I wish this was a pleasure call. Unfortunately, I may be ruining your night." He gingerly stepped down the sidewalk avoiding all the spent shell casings.

"Our boy again?"

Now in front of the party house, he could see all three dead gangbangers and surmised based on the interaction with the woman and Hogan that there was another victim in the house across the street. "Don't know for sure yet, but we've got at least three dead Kings, possibly an innocent down and a crime scene that looks like something out of Beirut."

"Guess it wasn't at one of the stakeout locations?"

"Nope. It's in the heart of jungle." An ambulance had arrived and the Paramedics rushed into the house across the street as Nguyen directed them. He looked back at the position of the gangbangers on the ground, the two close together, the one ten feet away with his pants down. "I know I'm bypassing the process, but if this is our guy, I want you here. You led the other scenes and know the patterns." He paused for a second. "Besides, I haven't seen you since this afternoon."

"Well..." A smile in her voice. "When you put it that way, how can I refuse? See you soon."

Hunter went back to his car, found some latex gloves and walked to the party house. He stopped in his tracks as the Paramedics rushed past him working frantically and pushing a gurney. His heart sank when he saw the tiny, limp shape. After they had pulled away, he realized he hadn't moved, he was still just staring at the spot where the ambulance had been. *Jesus, we've got to find this guy.*

He noticed that Sanchez and Myers had arrived and teamed up with Sanders and were already knocking at the first house on the south side of the street. He paused, slowed his thoughts and made a full circle trying to absorb as much of the scene as possible. He turned his attention to the party house and the dead gangbangers, made observations about the position of the bodies, the massive number of spent shells, broken glass and car fragments scattered on the ground.

"Hey Cowboy."

Hunter turned to see Carter Hogan walking toward looking as pale as possible. "What've you got?"

"Looks like the third, fourth and fifth houses from the corner were all hit in the crossfire. Blown out windows, bullet holes all over. So far, only the one casualty. The little boy you saw being transported." He paused, his voice cracking. He cleared his throat and continued. "Didn't look good. Took at least two rounds while lying asleep in his bed."

Hunter blinked, looked down at the ground for a moment. The silence between them hung like a cloud. "Jesus." Hunter's voice was barely more than a whisper. "What else you know so far?"

"Not much. The usual. No one saw anything."

"Okay. I've got Sanders, Sanchez and Myers working the door to door on that side of the street. Why don't you grab Reyes and Nguyen and work this side. I'm going to look around and direct traffic." He surveyed the area again, noticed the mounting number of response vehicles on both ends of the perimeter. "It's going to be a long night."

Hogan turned and headed in the direction of Reyes. Hunter went back to his observations, noted that the trail of empty shell casings started at the front porch of the second house and flowed west down the sidewalk like a shiny river. That matched up with Hogan's comment about the houses across the street. *Whoever they were shooting at was moving east to west either down the sidewalk or in the street.*

"Hey Cowboy." This time it was Sanders yelling from across the street. "You need to hear this." He motioned him over to the second house.

Sanders had waited for Hunter on the bare concrete front porch at the top of the steps and held the front screen door open. "Got an eye witness who's actually willing to talk." Hunter made an overly surprised facial expression, stepped directly into a tiny living room area. He paused and looked around the room, his gaze stopping when they landed on an elderly black man sitting on an old, faded couch. The couch like the rest of the house Hunter could see may have been aged, but it was well kept.

The man nodded to Hunter and he returned the gesture.

Billy closed the door and stepped into the room behind Hunter. "This is Mr. Frank Jackson." He looked around quickly, realized that with Sanchez and Myers already seated, there weren't enough chairs. He resigned himself to stand and continued. "Mr. Jackson is the man who called 911."

Now Sanders looked to Mr. Jackson. "Sir, can you tell Detective Hunter what you saw."

The man twisted in his seat to face Hunter, leaned forward putting his weight on a rough honed pine wood cane. "Sure, sure." He paused as if recalling the evening. "I looked out my winda there and seen that white man walkin' down the sidewalk." He shook his head. "Can't imagine what on earth he was doing on this street."

Hunter took advantage of the man's slow speech and jumped in. "Mr. Jackson, where was the man when you first saw him?"

Mr. Jackson nodded, stretched out his arm and with a crooked index finger pointed toward the intersection. "Oh, he was way down at the corner of the street... Just walkin' along like he was strollin' in the park on a Sunday afternoon. Must be crazy."

Hunter cocked his head. "So this was before the shooting?"

"Yes sir."

"So it wasn't the gunfire that woke you up?"

"No... No, I was up already up, walkin' 'round the house."

Just like Sanders, Hunter had remained standing and had been taking notes. Now he stopped and looked down at the man. "Pretty late to be up walking around your house. Was there some reason you were up?"

Mr. Jackson's eyes met Hunters but then looked away and down to the floor. "I've got a condition... Causes me pain... Sometimes makes it hard to sleep."

Hunter let the silence linger and just looked at the man. Mr. Jackson sat for a moment, clearly uncomfortable with the topic. "Doctor call it Levator Syndrome or some such." He looked away. The four detectives traded glances indicating they had no idea. "Anyway, I was up walkin', heard that damn music and looked out the curtains. That's when I saw him."

"Where was the music coming from?"

"Same as always, right across the street where those hoodlums hang out. Thump, thump, thumpin'. Guess they was havin' some kind of party or somethin'. Hell, looked like one of 'em was havin' sex leanin' against the damn car..."

All four detectives were writing furiously. Hunter kept the lead. "What happened with the man walking down the sidewalk?"

The man shook his head. "It was the damndest thing. Never seen anything like it. He just come walkin' down the sidewalk right into the middle of 'em. Like he wanted to get thumped." He was getting more animated and talking with his hands. "Sure 'nough. There were two of 'em standin' out front by the sidewalk and when he got to 'em, they stopped him like they's gonna take him down. Next thing you know, all hell broke loose."

"Did the walking man have a gun?"

"Oh yeah, he had a gun. Mighta had two. He dropped 'em two by the sidewalk and the sex boy 'fore I even knowed what was happenin'. I ducked down and grabbed the phone. By the time I look up again, there musta been twenty folk standin' in the front yard just blastin' away. Sounded like a war goin' on out there." He pointed toward the front window and waved his hand in the direction of where the car had been parked. "The walkin' man..." He grinned. "Well, he weren't walkin' no more. He was runnin' and then jumped in his car." He smiled like he was remembering a great moment from an action movie. "That car was gettin' hammered when he took off."

"Did you see what kind of car it was or get a license plate number?"

"Naw, didn't see no plate. Was an older model big sedan. Think it was a Chevy."

"What color?"

"Hard to say. Coulda been gray or light blue or maybe light green. Street lights ain't so great 'round here."

They reviewed his story for close to an hour. Hunter thanked him and returned to the crime scene. From the porch, he saw that Stacy and her team were in full force and combing the entire scene inch by inch. Doc and the ME team were working the bodies and Carter Hogan was orchestrating what seemed to be an army of uniforms.

Hunter found Stacy as she was busy bagging some shattered pieces of a car taillight. She looked and smiled. "Well, good morning. Fancy meeting you here."

"Are you kidding? This is one of my favorite hangouts." He gently touched her on the arm and guided her away from what she was doing. "So what are you seeing?"

"Well, it's definitely our guy. While we've found almost every kind of shell casing out there, there are definitely several 9mm's with similar markings to the other scenes." She handed him an evidence baggie with several shell casings. While Hunter looked at them, she turned and pointed to the area where she had been standing. "I'll tell you one thing. I don't know how he or his car made it out of here in one piece. There was an amazing amount of fire power focused at him."

"Yeah, we've got an eye witness who said the same thing." He spent several minutes going over what Mr. Jackson had told them. He finished up by bringing the conversation back to the car. "He said it was an older model Chevy sedan."

She nodded. "Well, you can add to the description that it's full of bullet holes, probably has no windows left and all the taillights are broken out." She held up the baggie of taillight pieces. "We should be able to get an exact model and year based on these. In the meantime, if he's driving, he should be very noticeable."

Hunter nodded. "I'll find Hogan and get a BOLO out on the car. We'll also get with the tech center and see if we can get someone checking the traffic cams to see if we got him on any."

Hunter and Carter compared notes. Hunter left him with instructions regarding the 'be on the lookout' and the traffic cameras. He assumed the car would be ditched and untraceable, but needed to check all the boxes.

Back at the party house, Hunter smiled when he saw Doc supervising his crew as they loaded up the three corpses. "Doc, how is it that even at four in the morning, you can still manage to look like an English Professor on his way to class?"

"Fine breeding my friend." Doc reached out his gloved hand to Hunter. "And how are you this lovely morning?"

"A whole lot better than those three."

"Yes. It seems our three lads have enjoyed their last soiree. Such a pity too. They appear to have been model citizens."

Hunter smirked. "Yeah. If we don't stop this guy soon, we'll all be out of work." He looked over as one of the body bags was loaded into the van. "Did you learn anything from your first look?"

"Just the obvious... Cause of death for each, contingent of course on the autopsy, was quite precise gunshots." Doc looked over the rim of his glasses at Hunter. "One thing I'll say for our perpetrator. He's a damn fine marksman. These boys were dead before they saw the muzzle flash."

Hunter nodded. "Any ID on the bodies?"

Doc sighed. "It seems the one with his pants down around his ankles was named Damien Jones. The other two didn't have wallets, but I feel quite confident they'll be in the system. We'll have ID's for you by the time you get back to the station."

"Thanks Doc. Look forward to hearing the details when you've got them." Hunter moved back to the middle of the scene and spent a few moments taking it all in. The chaos had started to subside. He watched as the ME team loaded the last body in the van and pulled away. It appeared that Stacy and her team were wrapping up and his detectives had formed a group off to one side and were comparing notes.

It wasn't quite sunrise but it would be soon. About all that was left was to figure out a way to dodge the gathering media wanting information or an on camera statement. He looked over at the yellow police tape and saw Andre Kipton trying to get his attention.

As he headed over to the group of detectives, his mind processed everything he'd seen or heard. Just before he got to the group, he stopped. *Damien Jones? Where have I heard that name before?* He stood for a moment. It didn't come to him. He shook his head and headed over to wrap things up with the team.

Chapter 44

The sound of the train cars clacking by jarred his senses, and goose bumps ran up his arms. *Damn, it's cold.* He rubbed his arms with his hands as he looked over toward the train. *Oww. What the hell?* He looked at his right hand and saw blood. There was a jagged hole through his wool coat on his left shoulder, and an even darker stain. He touched it again, realized it was soaked through. *Crap.*

The feel of the blood started to clear his head. He surveyed his surroundings. *How long have I been sitting here?* Looking at his watch made him shake his head. It was 3:30 in the morning. He took a deep breath, thought for a moment and replayed the events of the night... The party, the shooting, speeding away toward the freeway, diverting to the storage lot, parking between the beat up storage trailers. The rest was fuzzy. He had to have been sitting there for almost an hour. He must have just passed out.

His focus was coming back now. He took a deep breath. *Okay, that was a close one. Now what? Guess I should take an inventory of the damage.* He quickly looked over the rest of his body, made sure his shoulder was his only injury. Other than knowing it was bleeding, he didn't know how serious it was. It hurt but it didn't seem to be life threatening.

Now the car. He looked around and realized the only glass left was the front windshield and it had a hole in it. The floorboards and seats were covered with shattered glass. There were a couple of obvious bullet holes in the back of the passenger seat headrest. He chuckled. *Well, old girl. You took a hell of a beating tonight.*

He reached to open the door but the pain in his shoulder shot through his torso and exploded in his head. *Holy crap. Maybe it's worse than I thought.* He reached across his body with his right hand and opened the door. Getting to his feet took a moment and he had to steady himself, but once he was standing, he felt better.

He stepped to the back of the car and laughed out loud when he saw the near total destruction. The back of the car looked like a particularly twisted exhibit of junkyard art. All the lights were blown out and holes riddled the bumper and back of the trunk. *All right, got to get my shit together and get rid of this car.* He popped the trunk and pulled out his duffle bag emergency kit. Tonight he'd need everything in it.

He shed the wool coat and carefully took off the holsters. *First things first, just in case...* He found his spare magazines, popped out the empties and got both Berettas back to full ready condition. He slid one behind his back into his waistband.

Paging Dr. Pepper, Dr. Pepper to the emergency trunk please. He smiled at his lame humor as he pulled out a pair of scissors from his first aid kit and cut away the blood soaked sleeve of his shirt to examine his arm. *That doesn't look too bad.* From what he could see, the bullet had just creased the outside of his shoulder. *Damn, hurts like hell for just a crease. Can't imagine what it'd be like if I'd really gotten hit.* The bleeding had stopped. All that was needed was basic first aid.

Twenty minutes later, his arm was cleaned up and bandaged, and he fought to put on the spare shirt and jacket from his duffle bag, He felt like a new man. He stuffed the holster and second pistol into the duffle bag along with the first aid kit and set the bag on the ground. He left the trunk open with the blood soaked shirt and jacket laying on the spare tire.

Over the next several minutes he used a towel to wipe down every surface inside and out on the car to eliminate prints. *There's no way they can trace this car to me but my prints will lead them right to my door.*

After finishing, he rested for a moment. *Now what?* It was past four in the morning. He leaned against the front of the car, looked forward at the skyline of downtown Fort Worth. He surveyed south back toward Vickery and north toward the railroad tracks and came up with a plan. A few minutes later, he was under the car using the sharp end of the tire iron to puncture a hole in the gas tank. He watched as almost twenty gallons of gasoline pooled under the car. He laughed. *They don't make cars like they used to. Gotta love a huge gas tank.* He soaked the towel, his bloody shirt and his wool coat in the gas as it poured out. Careful not to get gasoline on him, he laid the soaked items in a line creating a long fuse stretching several feet away from the car and terminating in the pool of gasoline under the car. He took one last look around, pulled out a cigarette lighter and casually lit the fuse.

As it burned and led the flame toward its destination, the Victim picked up his duffle bag, slung it over his right shoulder and walked north toward the railroad tracks. He never looked back but could hear the swoosh as the fire caught. The smoke wafted behind him as he stepped across the tracks and disappeared into the maze of warehouses in between the tracks and Lancaster Boulevard.

He'd pushed tonight to the absolute edge, but survived. He smiled. *Man, getting shot at is a hell of an adrenaline rush... Kind of cool. That is, of course, if you don't end up dead in the process.*

Chapter 45

"Rectal cramping!"

The room went quiet as the members of the taskforce stopped what they were doing and turned toward the door. Hunter had been keying notes into his laptop and now saw Sanders walking into the conference room with a wide grin on his face. He looked unnaturally fresh considering how little the team had slept the night before. Hunter looked at him with a blank expression. "Good morning to you too. Uh, is that a special way to say hello?"

Sanders laughed. "No, I just thought you'd want to know what Levator Syndrome was."

"Levator Syndrome?" Hunter cocked his head. "Okay, I give up, what the hell are you talking about?"

"Our witness last night..." Sanders gave Hunter a look like he expected him to remember but Hunter's face remained blank. "The old guy last night. He said he was up walking around because of a medical condition. He said it was Levator Syndrome. I looked it up this morning. It's rectal cramping."

Hunter furrowed his brow. "Oww. That sounds painful."

Reyes punched Parker in the shoulder and snickered. "Yeah, talk about a whole new meaning to 'pain in the ass'."

The rest of the team laughed. Hunter shook his head and tried not to grin, looked back to Sanders. "So, now that you've proven you know how to waste time, I don't suppose you actually did anything productive this morning?"

Sanders grabbed a chair and sat down at the conference room table, still smiling. "As a matter of fact..." He reached into his bag and pulled out a manila folder. "While the rest of you have been sleeping, I've been working."

Before Sanders could start his debrief, Hunter held up his hand, smirked. "All right, it's clear you've had your extra shot of caffeine this morning, but before you take off, let's make sure we're covering all the bases." He stood, went to the whiteboard, started to write but stopped when his phone vibrated on the table. He reached over, looked at the number, punched it off and set it back down.

Hunter went back to the board. "Okay, Jimmy, you were collecting and summarizing eye witness accounts, right?"

"Yep."

"Blaine, you were gathering information on our dead gangbangers, correct?"

"More than you'll ever want to know."

"All right, we'll connect with Hogan later to see if he's been able to track anything down from his King sources."

He stopped for a moment, stared at the board. "I've been working to gather data on the crime scene evidence."

There were several snickers from behind and Reyes mumbled. "I bet you have."

"Now, now, gentlemen, envy does not become you." He smiled as the room laughed harder.

Taking it all in stride, Hunter turned, tossed the marker to Sanders and sat down. "I guess that leaves you Mr. Coffee. You were tracking down all things related to the car, right?"

He opened the folder and, pulled out a stack of papers. "Okay, so tracking our shooter's car has been interesting, lots of angles but mostly brick walls including the ultimate dead end, but I'll save that for a minute just to keep your attention." Hunter shook his head and rolled his hand to prod Sanders along.

"Based on our eye witness description of the car, we reached out to the traffic techies to see what the local cameras caught. We hit pay dirt pretty quickly. We caught an older model light green Chevy sedan blowing through the intersection at Illinois and Hattie just about the time of the 911 call. Pictures were clear enough to see that most of the glass in the car was nonexistent. The angles didn't catch a plate or the driver's face. A few minutes later, we caught the same car headed west on Vickery. This time we got a clear shot of the plates."

Hunter sat up. "Really?" Hunter's phone buzzed again. He once again looked at the number, punched it off and nodded to Sanders to continue.

"Don't get too excited. We ran them. Get this. They don't exist."

Hunter raised an eyebrow and cocked his head.

"Yeah, that's right. The plates don't show as stolen. They literally don't exist in the system at all."

Hunter scratched some notes on his pad. "That's one you don't hear every day."

"Well, I'm not sure it matters much now. We checked the next logical camera where Vickery connects with I-35 and we got nothing. That was pretty confusing until we got a call from Crime Scene about an hour ago. They found a burned out car in a storage lot just west of I-35 off Vickery. No detailed report yet but it's most definitely the car on the tape. The prelims indicate it was completely fried."

Hunter perked up. "We need to get a full work up on that car immediately."

"Already requested. In the meantime, I was able to confirm that the back of the car had multiple bullet holes." Sanders shuffled through his notes. "I've let them know the car's connected with our case so they've secured the scene and have a team working it now. I requested they tow what's left of the car in and take it apart. Based on the condition though, they don't expect to find much."

The room was quiet for a moment. Hunter stood and paced, the wheels clearly turning. "Do they have a time on the fire?"

"Estimate it around three-thirty in the morning. FWFD got the call a little before four. By the time they got there, it had pretty much burned itself out. The lot is just dirt and rocks with a handful of old trailers. Nothing for the fire to burn except the car."

"Where did our guy go? He couldn't have just disappeared. Did you check the cameras for someone walking?"

Sanders made a quick note. "Didn't, but will."

"Okay. Check cameras in all directions. Don't assume he left via Vickery."

Sanders nodded. "Will do. That's it on the car."

"Thanks." Hunter stopped pacing, looked to Reyes. "Jimmy, how about you?"

Reyes spent the next thirty minutes recapping the eye witness notes that had been taken by all of the detectives. Hunter spent most of the time pacing at the front of the room stopping occasionally to scribble notes, asked questions and ignore his phone which buzzed a half dozen more times. Nothing new jumped out. Hunter's morning Starbucks fix had worn off and the long night was taking its toll. He rubbed his temples, squeezed his eyes shut.

When Reyes finished, Hunter got up, walked to the window and adjusted the blinds. It was now late morning and although still cold outside, it was sunny. The strands of light streamed in, bouncing off the dust particles suspended in the air. Hunter was lost in thought until the buzz of his cell phone on the table caught his attention.

He reached over, picked it up. This time he sighed heavily and answered. "Hunter here... Uh huh... Sure... Two o'clock." He hung up without further comment and sat back down with a determined look on his face.

He looked up to see several questioning faces staring back at him. He tapped his pen on the table, arched an eyebrow. "Seems the boss man wants an update on our progress so we'd best get back to it." He looked down at his notepad. "Parker, you're up. Tell us all we need to know about the three fine specimens that left our planet last night."

A pained look came across Parker's face. "Um, I guess you didn't know. The number's actually four Cowboy. We got confirmation this morning that the little boy didn't make it." The room went silent, the color drained from several faces.

Hunter's eyes didn't lift from his notepad, his voice was raspy and barely audible when he spoke. "No I hadn't heard. Guess that puts a new light on what we're doing." He looked up at Blaine, blinked several times and cleared his throat. "I realize it may not be relevant to the case, but... Can you give us his information?"

Parker nodded. "Yeah." Everyone in the room became instantly fixated on their notepads and he cleared his throat. "Jonathan Montrel Tolbert. Ten years old. Fourth grader at Van Zandt-Guinn Elementary School. Shot twice. Both 45 caliber. Most likely from one of the several Kings who were randomly blasting away at our shooter."

Parker stopped, let the moment sink in. Hunter looked up to still see most heads down and hands aimlessly scratching notes. "Guys, I don't need to tell you this ups the ante. This is now the second innocent to get caught up in this mess. If you think the media has been going crazy over the death of a suburban attorney and father of a murder victim, get ready because the frenzy just skyrocketed. I'm sure that's what prompted Sprabary's call." He leaned back, ran his hand through his hair. "I hope no one had plans for the weekend."

He slapped his pen down on the table and abruptly stood and walked to the whiteboard. He stared blankly at it for a moment, took a few deep breaths. "Okay Parker. Tell me about the three Kings."

Parker sat up, face determined. "The King who looks like he got it first was Marlin Cooper. Nineteen. Rap sheet already a mile long. Took a 9mm through the heart at almost point blank range. Killed instantly. Our man Marlin had a 9mm still in his waistband. Didn't have a chance to use it."

Hunter jotted notes on the board as Parker continued. "King number two, Devon Tucker, at least saw it coming. His hand was on his thirty-eight when a 9mm ripped through his throat and blew out his spinal cord. He was Twenty and based on his rap sheet, looked to be a role model for his buddy Marlin."

"Our third guy, better known as Mr. Pants Around The Ankles, was Damien Jones..."

Hunter stopped and turned around, held up his hand to stop Parker. "Yeah, so why does that name sound familiar?"

Parker shrugged. "Hmm, don't know." He opened a folder, started scanning. "Similar story to our other guys. A little older, twenty-two. Took two 9mm slugs from about ten feet away." He stopped, looked over at Hunter. "Very nice placement by the way. Our shooter appears to be damn good with a gun... But I digress... Back to Mr. Jones... Long rap sheet... Oh, hold on... Holy shit. Now that's interesting."

Parker creased the folder so it would stay open and tossed it across the table to Hunter. "Check out his last arrest. He was the suspect in Nicole Bennett's rape and murder! He's the guy that got off because of that crazy judge."

Hunter's eyes widened as he took a quick step forward and pick up the folder. "Holy shit is right. I don't know about you boys but I'm not a big believer in coincidence." He went quiet and scoured the folder, nodding his head every few seconds. The energy in the air had amped up. Everyone sat on the edge of their seats and leaned forward, elbows on the conference table.

After a few moments, Hunter put the folder down and began pacing and rubbing the bridge of his nose. He turned to the team. "Okay, this changes things. I know we kicked the concept of our shooter being in law enforcement around some but now we need to look at that a bit harder."

"A bit harder?" Parker looked incredulous. "Let's nail this bastard. He's making us all look bad."

Hunter held up a cautious finger. "He is, assuming he's our guy. I don't want to jump to any conclusions. Let's not forget Jim Bennett." He turned to Reyes. "Jimmy, here's what we need. It's going to take some digging so leverage whoever you need."

Reyes took out his notepad and nodded.

Hunter spoke as he resumed his pacing. "We need to take a look at each King taken out by this guy. Cross reference every arrest. I want to know everyone associated with every arrest... Arresting Officer, Booking Officer, ADA, Judge, Defense Attorney... Hell, I want to know the Bailiff and the Court Reporter... Everyone."

Reyes shook his head and exhaled. "You weren't kidding. That's going to take a while."

"Understand. But I don't want to jack Daris up again until we have a hardcore link."

Reyes raised his eyebrows. "Again?"

Hunter stopped pacing, remembered that he hadn't shared his suspicions of Daris with the whole team. "Uh, yeah. Call it a hunch but I've had Parker doing some low key data gathering about our old buddy Daris and I had a rather tense conversation with the Prosecutor on this topic a couple of days ago." He shrugged, grinned and turned to Parker. "Speaking of which, did you happen to check out what kind of car he drives?"

Parker nodded. "BMW... Just like every other lawyer I know."

Hunter nodded, slight disappointment on his face. "Oh well."

Reyes smirked, looked at Parker and back at Hunter, shook his head. "We'll get on it Cowboy."

Chapter 46

"No. No need. I'll be fine. I'm sure it's just a bug. I'll get some rest and be back at it tomorrow. Thank you." The Victim hung up the phone with his office and gingerly rubbed his shoulder. *Damn. How could something so minor hurt so freaking bad. You'd think I'd been hit by a cannon ball.*

He looked across his living room to the large windows. The morning sun was streaming through the sheer curtains. He yawned, squinted. His whole body ached. It had been a long night. After crossing the railroad tracks, he'd had to walk well over a mile just to get to a part of town where a taxi would pick him up. Just to be safe, he'd had the cab drop him several blocks from his condo. With all that maneuvering, he hadn't made it home until well after six am.

With no sleep, he was running on pure adrenalin and caffeine. He stepped into the kitchen to get his third cup of coffee knowing it wouldn't have much effect. *God I need a nap.* He shook his head to clear his mind. *No time. Lots to do. It's going to be a long day.*

He sat for a moment, stared into space and thought. He had to analyze the night before, step by step, to make sure he hadn't left any kind of trail. He also had to consider how to move forward with his car, his coat and his bloody shirt now reduced to ash.

First step was to see what had made the news. Since it all happened too late to make the papers, he switched on the TV and started surfing. His timing was off to catch the local news. He continued to flip channels without success. *Hmm, doubt I've made enough of a splash to get mentioned on Oprah.*

He landed on CNN Headline News and caught just enough of a report to hear them say that sources close to the investigation indicated there were no suspects at this time. Most of the coverage was on the protests and the racial unrest. That was all he needed at this point.

He punched the TV off, stepped across the room, stretched out his sore muscles along the way. He dug into his duffle bag and pulled out a cell phone, tapped in a number and hit send.

"Who is this?" The voice was gruff, more from lifestyle than age.

"I'm a repeat customer who'd rather not use names over the phone."

There was a pause. "Uh huh. Well alright, Mr. Repeat Customer, I'm game. What did I supposedly provide you in the past?"

"A car."

"A car? Who do I sound like to you, Clay Cooley?"

The Victim laughed at the reference to one of the local over the top used car salesmen seen on late night TV commercials. "Well, not just any car. A well-worn green '85 Chevy Impala with an impeccable engine, a remote starter and absolutely no history."

The line was silent for a moment. "Hmm. That sounds like a very special car. One that didn't exactly come with a warranty."

A wry smile broke across his face. He loved the cat and mouse games of the underworld. "Unfortunately, it's well beyond help from a warranty. I'm more interested in a replacement. Something similar, not exact. Preferably different make, model and color, but with the same special features."

"Okay, let's assume I can help you with this request. If you are a repeat customer, then you know how this works."

"I do."

They spent the next several minutes carefully discussing details without saying anything specific enough to be used as evidence if recorded. By the time they were finished, a replacement car was ordered, a price negotiated and a pick up time and location was set for later that evening.

One thing the Victim had learned from his line of work and especially since he'd decided to embark on his mission was that absolutely anything could be bought on the open market if you had enough cash and the right phone numbers.

Of course, having the right phone numbers was the hard part for most people. It required that you have access to really bad people.

Fortunately, or unfortunately, for him, he had more than enough access to the scum of the earth. The best part was that with the leverage he had to apply, most of the scum he encountered were more than happy to provide him anything he wanted.

After he hung up the phone and got another cup of coffee, he went into his home office, sat at his desk and began to doodle on a note pad as his mind drifted back to the night before.

While it had clearly been a successful excursion, the results were obviously less than perfect. He'd lost his car, been shot and though he was very careful, he felt sure he'd probably left some trace evidence behind. The biggest issue though, was that his mode would have to change. *As stupid and arrogant as those animals are, even they won't fall for the same scam again. I've gone to that well one too many times and there were way too many of them who saw what happened.*

He continued to ponder that thought as his eyes drifted to her picture. He absent mindedly rubbed his sore shoulder. "I'm making them pay for what they did." He nodded to her and held up his coffee cup in mock toast. "I'm not done yet."

He put down his cup, his face growing solemn. *I'm definitely not done yet but I don't see this ending well.*

Chapter 47

"I don't give a damn what it takes. Do you have any idea how many times my phone has rang this morning?" Sprabary's face was red and his voice hoarse. He'd been ranting for almost thirty full minutes while Hunter absorbed his wrath.

As if on cue, his desk phone rang and Hunter fought the urge to make a smart ass remark. Instead, he just shifted in his seat and looked down at the floor.

"You see? You see what I'm talking about? I'm getting hourly calls from the brass upstairs and I've gotten so many calls from the media that I've told Paige not to even bother putting them through to my voicemail. Not only do we have Alton Grice and his Ebony Warriors out there, now they've been joined by the New Black Panthers and some of Louis Farrakhan's people. This is getting out of hand."

Hunter tried once again to slow him down. "Well, sir, I know last night wasn't great, but..."

"Wasn't great? It was a goddamned train wreck. Not only did three more Kings get blown away while we were staking out the wrong locations, but an innocent kid got shot while sleeping in his bed." Sprabary pushed back from his desk and threw his pen down. "I'm damn sure not losing any sleep over three more gangbangers cashing in... But Jesus, a kid..."

He paused, calmed a bit, then continued in a quiet voice. "Hunter, we've got to stop this prick. The body count is out of control and now with Jim Bennett and this innocent little boy..." He let his thought hang in the air.

Once Sprabary had relaxed enough to have a conversation, Hunter spent the next thirty minutes bringing him up to date on the evidence found at the scene, the car, the traffic video and the fact that they had been close to getting the guy.

"It was luck of the draw on which location we chose to stake out. We just never thought he was crazy enough to strike right in the heart of their territory." As he spoke those words, Hunter had a thought. *Reduce his strike options.*

He stood up abruptly drawing a curious look from Sprabary. "Sir, if we're done here, I need to get back with the team. We've got several things we're still chasing down from last night and I need follow up with them."

Not used to being cut short, Sprabary seemed a little surprised, but nodded. "Let me know what you need. More resources. Whatever. We've got to nail this bastard soon."

"You got it Lieutenant." He was up and out the door before the conversation could get started again. He didn't even give Paige an opportunity for a passing snide remark.

As he weaved through the cubicles and down the halls, he scrolled through the call log on his phone noting the number of missed calls and waiting voicemails. Almost all were from various reporters. Half of those were from Andre Kipton. Hunter shook his head. *Damn, he's relentless.*

Almost lost in the long list of calls was one number that made him smile. He punched it to return the call as he trotted down the stairs.

"Well, nice to know your phone works." The words were harsh but there was a smile in her voice.

He smiled but didn't take the bait. "Got time for a quick lunch. I need a break. It's going to be a busy afternoon."

"Give me ten minutes and I'll meet you out front."

"See you there." He punched off his phone, made a quick stop by the conference room to grab his laptop and tell the guys to be ready to do some planning after lunch, then headed out.

Hunter and Stacy spent an hour smiling, flirting and talking about everything except work. She had made him drive all the way out to Central Market so they could eat something semi healthy. Apparently no healthy options existed in the downtown area. He just shook his head and smiled. Things were going well between them considering how little time they'd actually spent together and the level of pressure both were feeling because of the case. A non-working lunch seemed to help both as Hunter kissed her goodbye and headed back to work with the guys.

Rejuvenated, he blew into the conference room like a man on a mission. "Hey boys. How's it going?"

A group of weary faces looked up from their various laptops, notepads and telephones. Reyes cocked an eyebrow. "I thought you were going to meet with Sprabary when you left. You don't exactly look like you've gotten your ass chewed."

"Ah, that was this morning." He smiled. "I've had time to put it all in perspective and come up with a plan."

Blaine chuckled. "Sounds like Cowboy's been riding over to the crime lab." That brought laughter from the rest of the team.

Hunter didn't acknowledge Parker's comment but never stopped smiling either. "Catch me up on what we've got and then we can talk about where we go from here." He surveyed the room. "Anything new?"

Sanders leaned forward and pulled out his folder. "Well, not much. We did get a preliminary report on the car." Hunter had already opened his laptop and nodded indicating he was ready to take notes. "As we suspected, the car was officially off the grid. Based on the VIN it was a Katrina car. It had been caught in the flood and totaled. Someone recovered it, cleaned it up, tricked it out and created new plates for it. No way to trace it. No identifying items found in the car. The one break we got was that they did find some blood on the driver's side door."

Hunter stopped keying. "Really?"

"Don't get too excited. The water and fire damage was such that we couldn't get any useable DNA, but the lab boys indicated there had to have been a significant amount for any of it to have survived the fire. Also, there was some bits of clothing found that also had blood on them." He put down the folder and looked over at Hunter. "Sounds like our boy got hit during his attack last night."

"Excellent. We need to contact all the local hospitals to see..."

"Already done." Sanders interrupted. "We're still waiting for responses from some of the smaller, outlying ones. But we've heard back from all of the majors. No gunshot victims treated." He shrugged. "Sounds like he either crawled into a hole and died or he was able to patch himself up." He leaned back in his chair. "We have all the local hospitals and urgent care centers on the lookout for anything resembling a gunshot wound."

Hunter stood up and started pacing as he contemplated this information. "Still, we can use this. If nothing else, between losing his car and getting hurt, you've got to figure this slows him down. Maybe buys us a day or two before he strikes again."

Reyes looked up. "Maybe it scares him enough that he just stops and we can all get back to our normal boring lives."

Hunter's head was shaking before he even finished the sentence. "Don't think we'll be that lucky. No. Our guy's playing this hand to the end. Whatever his game is, he's stepped over that 'don't look back' line." He stopped pacing and looked over at Reyes. "The only way this guy stops is when we stop him."

Parker looked grim. "I hope you have a plan because I'm not sure we've got much else. We're still running through the victim's arrest and trial records. No clear patterns. Seems like these guys have crossed paths with everybody involved with Tarrant County law enforcement. I mean we've got some names showing up more often than others but most would be expected."

Hunter looked up. "What about Daris?"

Parker pulled out a paper. "Our buddy Tim has prosecuted more than his fair share, but then we kind of suspected that already. No pattern that stood out." He scanned down further. "That crazy nutbag of a judge, Feldman, seems to have gone out of his way to set way too many of them free. Most of the arrests were made by the gang guys. There was one patrolman, Colin Freeman, who seems to have made an interestingly high number of arrests. We're checking him out now. Since Bailiffs and Court Reporters work closely with specific judges, Feldman's team is on a bunch of these. We're checking them out as well. There are two defense attorneys, Steve Gentry and Trent Howard, who seem to dominate the numbers. Based on what we can tell, gang defense is their specialty."

Sanders looked over at Hunter. "Gentry's the guy we visited the other day. Seemed fairly straight up. Maybe we should visit Howard too."

Hunter nodded. "I also want to visit our overzealous patrolman.

What was his name? Colin Freeman?"

Parker nodded.

Hunter looked at Sanders. "Sounds like you and I have a late afternoon field trip."

Parker put down the paper, lean back and exhaled loudly. "We've still got some more to work through but that's where we're at now. Not exactly earth shattering."

Hunter shrugged. "Keep working it. In the meantime, let's talk about how we can keep the pressure on him." He walked over to the whiteboard, started to write something but stopped and turned toward the team. "Why did we miss him last night?"

Reyes smirked. "Bad luck?"

Sanders chimed in. "More like being in the wrong place at the wrong time."

Hunter pointed to Sanders. "Yes but why were we in the wrong place at the wrong time?"

Sanders shrugged. "Not enough manpower?"

Hunter nodded. "Or conversely, too many possible targets to cover at once." He walked over to a city map on the wall they had used to mark the known King locations. He pointed as he continued. "There are way too many potential target locations to cover at one time. Even if we had the manpower to cover all of them, trying to coordinate that kind of stakeout would be impossible. Last night, we were hoping to get lucky and didn't. My suggestion is that we make our own luck by reducing the number of target locations. In fact, we should reduce the number to one."

Parker raised his hand. "Can't argue with your logic Cowboy but there're a couple of fairly major hurdles. Say for instance, how do we get the Kings to only man one location?"

Hunter smiled. "We ask them nicely." That brought a round of laughter from the team. "If that doesn't work, I'll have to be a little more persuasive."

Sanders shook his head in disbelief. "They didn't like us much the first time we paid them a visit. I'm guessing their attitude towards us hasn't exactly improved. I mean, considering..."

"I'm sure you're right about that." Hunter looked back at Parker. "What other hurdles?"

Parker continued. "Won't our suspect get a little suspicious if all of a sudden, there're no Kings to be found."

Hunter nodded and contemplated the thought. "At some point isn't it natural for the Kings to react to his attacks? Especially since the last one was so blatant?"

"Sure, but shutting down isn't exactly their style. Their bravado usually outweighs their intelligence."

"Good point." Hunter sat down at the table. "Let's figure out how to work this without being too obvious..."

Chapter 48

Hunter signaled for Sanders. "Found our targets for the afternoon. Did you get a chance to do some background on them?"

Sanders raised his eyebrows. "Yeah. I got the basics and an interesting tidbit."

Hunter looked curious but wanted to get moving. "Good. Pack up and let's roll. We're going to have to catch both of these guys in between stuff."

Sanders finished up and walked with Hunter to the parking lot. Hunter let him know the game plan for the afternoon. He'd made arrangements to catch Colin Freeman at the end of his shift and Trent Howard was in court today so they were going to catch him in between sessions.

Sanders got into the passenger seat of the Police cruiser, waived his hand in front of his nose. "Dude, when are you getting your ride back? This car still reeks."

Hunter smiled as he turned the key. "I've just started getting used to it. Nothing quite like this aroma to get you going." He backed out of the parking spot, laughed. "But since you asked, hopefully on Monday. The city has a contract with the body shop so they're expediting it."

They had to maneuver past the protesters. It was obvious to both that the number, volume and anger of the crowd had intensified. The mood in the car became serious and both men got quiet.

As they cleared the lot and moved down the street, Hunter awkwardly broke the silence. "So, Wednesday night at Angelo's, Parker was out of line. I should have cut Parker off before he got going. He's a good guy but his political correctness gene is missing."

Sanders looked out the passenger window and shook his head.

"Thanks, but it's really not your issue. If I have a problem with Parker, I'll settle it with him."

Hunter nodded. "Good enough. I just thought he was being an ass."

Sanders seemed to contemplate that for a moment. "Oh, I don't know. He's got a right to his opinion. I may not agree with it but I can understand it."

Hunter cocked his eyebrow. "I don't think Carter felt nearly as tolerant."

Sanders smiled. "Yeah, Parker was about one comment away from a whole bunch of trouble." He shrugged. "My personal view is a little complicated because of my background. Keep in mind that I've seen the race thing from both sides. I spent my early years growing up with future gang members and my teenage years in a mostly white middle class world."

As Hunter drove, Sanders continued. "By the time I got to college I was too white to hang out with the black players and too black to hang out with the white players."

Hunter turned into the parking lot for the Tim Curry Justice Center. "I thought college football teams were kind of past all the race stuff."

Sanders smiled. "You've watched too many Hallmark Afterschool Specials. Most teams are just one notch better than a prison when it comes to race relations."

Hunter laughed and parked the car. "Ouch."

As they stopped, Sanders turned to finish his thought. "The reality is that gangs aren't a race problem. They're an economic problem. You've got kids growing up where they don't see any hope. Most don't have fathers at home. The male influences they do see are either unemployed or severely underemployed. They don't have any real opportunity ahead of them. Why wouldn't they see the gangs as their only alternative?"

Hunter turned off the engine. "Sounds pretty bleak."

"It is." Sanders opened the door to get out. "One more reason we need to get this guy."

They walked down the sidewalk and into the building. Hunter

checked the directory in the lobby, then his watch. "County Court Number Three is on the fourth floor. Howard has a hearing in front of Judge Mills which should be finishing up any time."

They took the elevator up, found the courtroom, looked in and saw Howard sitting at the defense table. Hunter nodded to a bench across the hall. "Looks like he's about to finish up. We'll wait in the hall for him."

After a couple of minutes, the courtroom door opened and people streamed out. Hunter and Sanders stood, stepped across the hall and met Howard as he came through the doors.

Hunter stepped in front of him, flashed his badge. "Mr. Howard. Can we speak a moment? We need to ask you a few questions."

With an exasperated expression, he looked at his watch. "We'll have to walk and talk. I've only got about ten minutes before I need to be in my next session. What's this regarding?"

Hunter followed his lead and walked beside him. "We're investigating the recent string of gang member shootings and we wanted to get your input. Seems like several of the victims were your clients."

Howard stopped, looked at Hunter. "I haven't followed closely enough to know. Who are the victims?"

Hunter pulled out his notepad. "Let's see... Darrel Johnson, Jarvis Wright, Marcus Stevens, Terrance Washington, Damian Jones, Marlin Cooper and Devon Tucker."

Howard nodded. "Damn. Sounds like someone's trying to put me out of business. How can I help you?"

"Can you think of anyone who'd want to target these guys?"

"You're kidding, right? Pull out the phone book."

Hunter smirked. "Well, we were hoping you could narrow that down a bit for us."

Howard turned down the hall and started walking again but didn't seem to be quite as rushed. "Look Detective, thirty percent of my clients are truly scum and probably ought to be shot in the street. Another sixty percent get basically what they deserve through the courts. That last ten percent are the only reason I do this job. They are the ones who are either innocent or victims of circumstance."

He slowed again seemingly in thought. "Based on that list of names, it sounds like whoever's doing this is batting about seven fifty when it comes to taking out some of the real bad guys."

Hunter nodded and stopped when Howard did. "How much do you know about the Kings operation?"

Howard stood with his hand on the door to another courtroom. "Due to attorney client privilege and clients who like to brag, I know more about how they operate than the Police ever will. If they could make me a state witness, the Kings would be out business tomorrow."

"One last question. Ever known anyone personally whose been victimized by the Kings?"

Howard gave him a suspicious half smile, nodded. "Yeah... Me. One of my disgruntled clients tried to kill me. Still have the scars. Needless to say, I didn't represent him in that trial." He pushed the door open. "Sorry, gotta go."

"Thank you." Hunter's voice was met with a swinging door. He looked at Sanders, shrugged and nodded toward the elevator.

Sanders crawled into the passenger seat. Hunter cranked the engine and backed out. As they pulled onto the street, Hunter glanced over to Sanders. "Any thoughts?"

"Yeah. Is it just my imagination or is there some rule that says all attorneys in this city have to be six-foot-one with flowing blonde hair and big white teeth?"

Hunter snorted. "It's genetic."

Sanders shook his head. "I don't know. Seemed pretty straight but not too surprised or too upset about the loss of clients. Maybe a bit of an angry undercurrent. I mean, how many defense attorneys would say that 30% of their clients deserved to be shot in the street?"

"Good point."

Ten minutes later they had made their way across town, through the protesters and back into the Central Division station. They were just in time to catch Colin Freeman at the end of his shift.

Hunter had arranged to have him come to the conference room. It was Friday after five and the conference room should be empty. It had been a very long week for the team and knowing they would work over the weekend, Hunter had sent the guys home.

When Hunter and Sanders walked in, Freeman was standing,

surveying the conference room. There were white boards full of notes, maps with locations marked and various pictures and documents taped to the wall, the products of almost two weeks of investigating. If he was embarrassed by his obvious curiosity, he didn't show it.

He was a big guy, taller than either Hunter or Sanders and beefy with broad shoulders. With his red hair and ruddy complexion, he'd look right at home in a Boston Irish pub.

With a sense of excitement, he extended his hand to Hunter and then Sanders. "Colin Freeman, how are you?"

"Fine. Finishing up a long week. Thanks for coming." Hunter motioned toward a chair. "Have a seat. We'll keep this brief. It's Friday night and like us, I'm sure you want to get out of here."

Freeman sat. "No problem. Happy to help."

Hunter sat across the table. "We're part of the team investigating the shootings of gang members and as part of doing background work on the victims, your name came up. Seems you've been pretty active when it comes to arresting gang members."

Freeman stiffened, his initial excitement shifted to suspicion. "Just doing my job, Detective."

Hunter smiled, tried to lighten the mood. "Yeah, you're doing great actually and that's why we wanted to talk. We were hoping to get your insight."

Freeman relaxed. "Okay, sure. How can I help?"

"Well, to start, how have you managed to make so many gang related arrests?"

Freeman leaned forward. "I focus on gangs whenever I can. If you ask me, I think gangs are one of the core crime problems in America. Anytime I can schedule my patrols in gang infested areas I do. Then I just pay attention. Finding them breaking the law isn't exactly hard."

Hunter nodded. "That's commendable, but if you have that much interest, why haven't you looked into joining one of our gang units?"

Freeman sat back, waved his hand dismissively. "What a waste. Our 'gang units' do nothing but coddle a bunch of felons. It's a waste of time and money. Trying to rehabilitate these guys is ridiculous. We should be focused on getting them off the streets."

Hunter looked up with a stare and met his eyes. "So you've decided to take it upon yourself to take them off the streets wherever possible."

The room was silent for a moment. Freeman pushed his chair back from the table and glared at Hunter. "My insight, huh? What a load of crap. You're looking at me as a suspect." His face was beet red now. He poked the air with his finger. "I've got news for you. I don't need to shoot these animals. Why would I? As you said yourself, I'm making a pretty good dent by arresting them."

"Yeah, well, here's my concern with that." Hunter opened his hands. "It's got to be really frustrating for you since very few of your arrests have actually resulted in convictions."

Freeman stood up abruptly, leaned forward, towering over Hunter. "I'm done here. If you need to talk to me again, you can contact my union rep." He pushed back his chair, stepped around the table and pushed through the door.

Sanders, smirked. "I'm guessing you're no longer on his Christmas card list."

"No doubt." He looked at his watch. "I don't know about you, but I've got better places to be right now."

Chapter 49

Hunter woke Saturday morning with a smile on his face and the delicate scent of perfume floating on the air. He and Stacy shared the morning paper, a relaxing breakfast and the alternating attention of Panther, who seemed to be warming to this occasional new visitor.

In spite of having to work on a Saturday morning and another cold front moving in, Hunter was still quite content late that morning as he walked into his favorite Starbucks to meet up with Sanders.

"Long time no see, Cowboy. From what the papers are saying, you must be working night and day." Bernard looked even more gothic than usual.

"Did you go up a notch on your gauged earrings, Bernard?" Hunter nodded toward his ear. "The usual, by the way. In fact, make it two, my partner will be here momentarily."

Bernard framed his ears with his hands. "My, aren't we observant? You should think about becoming a detective or something."

"You should think about the long term ramifications of doing that to your ears. Like, for instance, future employment outside of coffee service."

"Now you sound like my mother." Bernard called out his order, rang it up and turned when he heard the door open. He nodded toward Sanders. "Perfect timing. Looks like you're training him well, Cowboy."

Hunter smiled, turned toward Sanders. "Grab a seat. I'll bring the coffee to the table." He waited at the counter a moment for their order. When he got it, he turned back to Bernard. "Think about what I said about those ears."

Bernard rolled his eyes and turned to help the next customer while Hunter made his way to sit at the table Sanders had found.

Sanders smiled as he took the cup of coffee Hunter offered.

"Thanks. You look awfully chipper this morning."

"I'm just reveling in the fact that I'm not a King and therefore my life expectancy should be slightly longer than the average fruit fly."

Sanders eyed him warily. "Yeah well, based on our plans for the day, let's just hope the Kings don't decide to impact that prediction for either of us."

"Not to worry my friend. I have taken appropriate precautions that hopefully will improve our odds a bit." Hunter took a deep breath of steam rising from his cup, listened for a moment to the sounds of a jazz saxophone playing over the harried sounds of the coffee shop. "Ah, nectar of the gods." He took a sip. "Besides, if those guys have any brains at all, they'll understand that for once, we're actually on their side."

"Why does that not make me feel any better?"

As they finished up their coffee, they reviewed the case and kicked around different theories. There wasn't much new to be discussed but you never knew when reviewing something might pop loose a new line of thought.

Hunter drained the last of his coffee, nodded toward the door and stood up. "So, what was your take on our conversations yesterday afternoon?"

They rehashed what had been said by both Howard and Freeman as they made their way from downtown to the Kings headquarters off Vickery. No new revelations came.

As they'd done before, when they pulled in and parked, they both took off their weapons and locked them in the console.

Before they got out, Hunter made a quick call on his cell and then waited for about two minutes. He watched in the rearview mirror until he saw two Police patrol units pull up to the curb, blocking the entrance to the parking lot.

Hunter nodded to the mirror. "Looks like our backup is in place. Time to go have a chat with our favorite group of crime victims."

They both subconsciously took deep breathes, got out of the car and headed up to front door. As before, they went through a similar process of getting past the welcoming committee, getting frisked, walking into the bar and letting their eyes adjust to the darkness. As before, the eyes of the Kings loitering around the room seemed to burn through them. This time, everyone seemed a little twitchier.

The main sentry had them wait just inside the front door as he walked over to the lounge area, leaned down to someone dressed in a suit with his back turned to them. The man listened for a moment, stood, turned toward them and glared.

"Well, well, well." Hunter's voice was a whisper and his lips barely moved.

The sentry motioned them over and they weaved through the chairs and tables until they were standing in front of the apparent new leader of the Kings. He motioned for them to sit. They did.

They were silent for a moment. The man glared at them as if contemplating whether to let them live. Finally, he cleared his throat and leaned forward. "Well, one thing's fo sho. I give you credit for having balls. So, should I call you Cowboy or are we bein' formal?"

"Spike, you can call me whatever you want." Hunter leaned back, crossed his legs trying to look as relaxed as he could. "I'm just here to help you out."

"Help me out?" Spike snorted. "You helped Shadow out, didn't you? Now, look where he at. Muthafucka's dead, ain't he?"

Hunter didn't take the bait, just opened his hands gave a slight shrug.

Spike looked over at Sanders. "You the muthafucka who shot Shadow, ain't you?"

Sanders' entire body stiffened. He glanced at Hunter for direction and received an almost imperceptible nod. He turned toward Spike and nodded slowly to answer his question.

Spike stared for another moment, leaned back in his chair and preened at his new wardrobe and accessories. "Well, you ask me, was only a matter of time. Shadow'd got too big for his britches anyway. Boy had gone all Hollywood, got soft. Probably best thing for everyone. Got a real man drivin' the bus now."

It was all Hunter could do to contain himself. Spike's words made him want to laugh out loud. The cycle never ended. Cut the head off the snake and it grew another just as stupid and vain as the one before. *How long would Spike last? A year? A month? Hell, maybe a week.*

Spike rambled on for a few more minutes about how things were going to change with the new boss. Hunter let him go on, figuring he'd eventually run out of steam and want to know why they were there.

Finally, Spike ran out of bravado to spew, looked at Hunter. "Don't 'spose you're here to tell me you caught the cracker been shootin' my boys?"

"Nope. But I am here to talk to you about how we can work together to do just that."

"Work together? You kiddin' me? Why would I do that?"

"Well, I'd think as the new leader, stopping this guy would be your top priority. After all, it's going to be awfully difficult to recruit new members if the current ones keep dropping like flies."

Spike leaned forward, pointed at Hunter. "That ain't no problem. Got people beggin' to be Kings. Besides, now we know how this honky operates, we gonna be ready for him next time."

Hunter smiled. "Don't you think he's smart enough to change his approach after three hits?"

That seemed to confuse Spike. He clearly hadn't considered that possibility.

Hunter seized on the opportunity. "Look Spike, we want to catch this guy as bad as you do but he's good. He hasn't left any evidence behind and he continues to be one step ahead of us. We've come up with a plan but will need your cooperation to make it work."

Spike, having had his ego appropriately stroked, motioned for Hunter to continue. "What you got in mind?"

Hunter spent the next ten minutes laying out the details. As he spoke Spike's face grew darker and his body language closed up. He was obviously not buying in.

Finally, Hunter finished, leaned back in his chair and put his hands out. "Well?"

Spike's head was shaking before he even started talking. "Let me get this straight. You want me and my boys to stay off the streets, stop doin' business, pretty much go into hidin'? Are you kiddin' me? Kings don't hide from nobody. Ain't gonna happen."

"We're only talking about a few days Spike. It's our only way to nail this guy. Otherwise, he's just going to keep picking you guys off until there's no one left." Hunter paused for a moment, then added.

"Besides, you really don't have any choice."

Spike bowed up. "What the hell's that 'sposed to mean?"

"It means that if you don't work with me on this, I'm going to go all 'Patriot Act' on your ass. I'm going to call my buddy with the FBI, tell him I have reason to believe that you and your boys have converted to Islam, have been radicalized and are in the process of planning a major terrorist act."

"What the hell you talkin' about? We ain't no towel heads and you know it."

"Doesn't matter. Under the Patriot Act, the FBI can bust in here, round all of you up and lock you away in a black hole for as long as they need while they take their sweet ass time interrogating you and investigating my claims. You have heard of the term 'enhanced interrogation' haven't you? Let me give you hint, it's no fun. All my buddy needs is probable cause and let's just say I can create all that I need. By the time they get through with you, you'll have wished that the shooter had found you instead of them."

"You can't do that." He looked over at Sanders for some kind of confirmation.

Sanders just raised his eyebrows, nodded and shrugged as if to say, 'it's out of my hands'.

Spike leaned back in his chair, stunned. He might have even been a bit pale. He sat and stared into space. After a moment, he gathered himself, bowed up a little although not very convincingly. "All right, I get where you comin' from. I'll work with you. I'll need some time to work it with my boys."

Hunter leaned forward. "No problem."

They spent the next few minutes working through details and how Hunter wanted it to work. Spike continued to try to look somewhat defiant but Hunter could tell he was resigned to the inevitable.

As Hunter and Sanders left the building and walked to their car, Hunter waived to the two patrol units and they pulled away. Once they sat down and Hunter turned the engine, Sanders looked over at him incredulously. "Patriot Act! Are you serious?"

Hunter gunned the car out of the parking lot and smiled. "Hey, whatever it takes."

Chapter 50

"I was beginning to think you had been abducted by aliens and they'd confiscated your cell phone." There was a definite edge in the voice on the other line.

"Ah, come on Andre, you know it's been a busy couple of weeks." Hunter put on his best 'we're all friends' voice.

"Uh huh. I've heard that before." He paused. "I don't suppose you've cracked the case and are now calling to give me an exclusive in depth interview."

"Not exactly. If anything, it's more the opposite at least as far as the case goes."

There was silence on the other end of the line. Hunter could almost feel Kipton's skepticism. Kipton finally spoke. "So let me guess. It's Saturday afternoon, you're bored and you missed my voice. No wait. I think I've got it. You're stumped in the investigation and it's use the media time."

"Well, no offense to your voice, but it's more the latter than the former." Hunter wanted to cut to the chase so he just kept rolling. "Look Andre, other than working too many hours, the main reason I haven't returned your calls is that we just don't have anything. You've gotten all the daily press releases so you know the basic details. There are a couple of tidbits that, if they were known by the public, might elicit some leads. Unfortunately, I can't officially comment on them."

Interest seemed to be brewing in Kipton's voice. "Okay, so you're going to be my 'source close to the investigation', right."

"Exactly. You agree not to use my name and I'll answer whatever questions I can."

"Cowboy, your timing is perfect. My editor was pushing me for a story for the Sunday edition. I've got just enough time to get something done."

Hunter smiled like the cat that ate the canary. "Well, don't get too excited. Like I said, we aren't exactly close to breaking the case."

For the next thirty minutes Kipton pummeled him with questions. Hunter proceeded to tell him about how little progress they've made, how few leads they had and how the Kings weren't being cooperative.

He did tell him that they'd found a burned out car that they thought might be connected to the case but that it was so completely destroyed, no usable evidence was found.

As he hung up, Panther head butted his hand. He responded by giving the cat a thorough petting. Panther's purring almost drowned out the sound of a beer bottle being opened. He turned and smiled as Stacy handed him a cold bottle of Corona. She'd even included a lime.

He took the bottle, pushed the lime in, made a mock toast and drank a quick gulp tasting the sourness of the lime mixing with the bitterness of the beer. He pulled out the chair next to him and gestured for her to sit down.

She sat, took a sip from her glass of wine and smiled a mischievous smile. "So, what was all that bull you were spreading?"

Hunter leaned back, raised his bottle. "Oh, just planting some seeds."

She arched her eyebrows.

Hunter smiled. "All right, here's the deal. There's only a limited window for catching him in our net. Either the Kings will stop cooperating or we'll run out of manpower for the stakeout. The last thing I want is for our shooter to think we're getting close to him. He needs to think he's in the clear so he won't hesitate to make a move."

She leaned over and kissed him. "Well, aren't you sneaky."

He reached over and pulled her closer. "Yes I am, and the best part is that until otherwise notified, I believe we both have the night off."

"Mmm..."

Chapter 51

The Victim gritted his teeth, reached across with his right hand and with one swift, painful yank, pulled the bandage off his wounded shoulder. He made a loud, guttural sound and sucked in three quick breathes to offset the pain.

Considering it had been less than three full days, the wound seemed to be healing up nicely. He moved his arm around and could tell the overall soreness had dropped as well. *Give it another day or two and I'll be as good as new. Just a battle scar to show for my troubles.* He grinned at the thought. *I'll need to come up with a good story for the ladies.*

He spent the next few minutes tending to the scab and applying a new bandage. He slid on a t-shirt and jeans, moved into the kitchen to grab a cup of coffee and sat down to read the Sunday paper.

The last few days in the local media had mostly been articles rehashing old information, talking about the growing protests and commentary lamenting the death of the little boy. The Victim had lamented that as well but blamed it on the reckless actions of the gangbangers, shooting every which way, completely out of control. Unlike his carefully planned attacks.

The national media didn't seem to really care about the shootings. They were mostly focused on the growing number of protesters, getting sound bites from the protest leaders and waiting to see if the city was going to explode. Even with that, their interest was starting to wane as they were now all chasing after the latest 'blonde American girl kidnapped in foreign country' story. That certainly outranked gangbangers getting whacked.

He settled in with his coffee, unconsciously rotating his shoulder every once in a while to keep it loose as he scanned the paper. He checked the editorials first and rolled his eyes as he perused John Ray

Phillips's column. According to him, this was nothing short of an undeclared race war against blacks. *More like an undeclared war against animals. What an idiot.*

There was a lengthy article about the little boy, Jonathan Montrel Tolbert. In spite of extreme life-saving efforts, he had died early on Friday morning. The Victim began to read through the article, his shoulders slumped, his eyes blinked back tears. The article talked about a ten year old boy who went to Van Zandt-Guinn Elementary, made good grades and dreamed about being a fighter pilot.

The Victim put the paper down, got up and walked across the room to the large family room windows. He stared out at the Sunday morning sky lost in thought, his eyes glistening with tears. *This shouldn't have happened.* He contemplated the randomness of a bullet being fired from a gun going through a window and hitting someone while they slept. He replayed the scene in his mind. *If they were actually aiming at me, they shouldn't have been firing in that direction anyway. They were just firing at shadows.*

He bowed his head for a moment, turned and shuffled back to his paper. Finishing up the article, he noted that the funeral was scheduled for Tuesday at noon at Mount Olivet. They were letting school out early and providing buses for students wishing to attend. They expected a large crowd.

He pictured Mount Olivet in his mind. It had been several days since he'd been over there. He made a mental note that he needed to go visit her again soon. He thought about his schedule. *Maybe next weekend.*

He continued to scan through the paper and landed on an article by Andre Kipton, the local Police writer. As he began to read, he noted there were quotes from 'a source close to the investigation' and realized there might be some new information. He sat up and leaned forward as he read.

He got through the initial recap of events and the discussion of the outrage of the citizenry. His focus was drawn to a series of quotes indicating there had been little progress made in the investigation, few real leads and almost no physical evidence that would help identify a suspect. *Am I really that good or are these guys just that bad? Maybe all my years of training are paying off.*

There were a couple of paragraphs about his car and how it might be connected to the case but because of the near complete destruction in the fire, nothing concrete had been learned from analyzing it. *How fortunate. I thought I'd really blown it on that one. Guess I dodged a bullet there.* He laughed. *Figuratively and literally.*

The last part that got his attention was when the quoted source was lamenting about how much harder the investigation had been because the targets of the crimes, the Kings, weren't cooperating. Seems their lack of trust of the Police was still overriding their need for protection. *I knew these guys weren't exactly Mensa material but not working with the Police when your buddies are dropping like flies is just plain stupid.*

He finished the article, set down the paper and contemplated the implications. It basically meant that although Thursday was a close call on several levels, at the end of it all, there had been very little negative impact to his mission. The Cops were no closer to catching him and the animals he was hunting were still sitting ducks.

All of a sudden, his shoulder didn't feel so bad after all and there was a bit of a bounce in his step as he moved around his apartment cleaning.

He stopped for a moment as he thought about his next steps. *Even if the article is completely accurate, I still need to be careful. The Kings may not be cooperating but they won't fall for the same tactics as before. I'll have to change my approach.*

As he went to his cubby hole to retrieve the Berettas to clean them, he smiled slyly. *I think that calls for a recon mission tonight. It'll be a good chance to check out my new ride. If all looks right, I can be back in the saddle as early as tomorrow night.*

Chapter 52

"Yo, brutha, you need ta get ya some shades or somethin'." The gangbanger named D-Funk shook his head as he perused Sanders, a look of annoyed disgust on his face.

It was shortly before midnight on Monday night and Billy Sanders was decked out in his best gangbanger rags. He and Hunter had spent a good chunk of the afternoon at the Kings headquarters working out the details of the sting operation. They were now back finalizing details and getting ready to deploy to their positions.

Part of the time was spent piecing together a set of clothes that would take Sanders from his normal clean cut, All American look to something resembling King scum. It was a challenge on several levels, not the least of which was finding clothes that would fit his college running back physique.

"Why do I need sunglasses? It's the middle of the night."

"You gotta hide those bright eyes. Ain't nobody gonna believe you a banger lookin' all happy an' shit."

Sanders gave a little nervous laugh, not really knowing how to respond. He did step out to the parking lot for a few minutes and came back in wearing a pair of wraparound shades he typically wore when working out.

D-Funk just looked at him and shrugged. "Better."

* * * *

As the Victim walked across the open space in the parking garage, he hit the remote starter for his new ride and heard it roar to life. *Mmm. Nice. Even has a better rumble than the Impala.* He slid into the driver's seat of the 1976 Camaro, closed the door and paused to get his bearings.

Not only was this a different car, he'd also changed parking garages on the off chance someone connected the burned out Impala to the old parking garage. This new location was downtown and at nearly one am, was completely deserted.

His new ride was anything but new. While he had made sure that the engine, transmission, steering and brakes were pristine, the rest of the car looked like a junker. The interior seemed to be falling apart and the exterior looked like a botched experiment in bondo and primer. The most prevalent color was a cloudy brown.

He pulled out of the parking structure and weaved his way through the empty streets of downtown while he thought about tonight's mission. He wasn't wearing his slacks and white dress shirt this time. He hadn't replaced the wool dress coat lost in last week's fire. Instead, he was sporting the Bill Belichick look, blue jeans, tennis shoes and an old gray hoodie sweatshirt.

Instead of wearing his fancy two gun shoulder holster, he merely had one of his Beretta's sitting on the passenger seat and one in the driver's side door.

Tonight was a different approach.

*   *   *   *

Hunter tapped his fingers on the steering wheel and looked at his watch. Fiddling with the heater controls, he wanted to get warm before he killed the engine for what might be a long night.

It was a few minutes after one in the morning and the team was in place. Like last time, he'd set up the team with offline radios so they could communicate without being picked on a Police scanner. The mobile units also had the standard Police radios to keep track of events going on in the area. Billy was equipped with a concealed microphone and earpiece which provided two way communications with the rest of the team.

After much discussion earlier in the day, the team had decided that the best location to stakeout was the parking lot of the Star Two Food Store at the corner of Hattie and Tennessee.

All of the other locations had limited surveillance points or were in hard to secure residential areas. Of course, the ample sightlines for this location were the result of a lot of open space and the fact that the store was located at a busy intersection with easy access and at least four possible escape directions. *Guess you take the good with the bad.*

Hunter was parked, in his newly repaired Explorer, facing north on Illinois, just south of Hattie. While it was a fairly long block from the store, he had a clear sightline across Hattie and could cover any west bound escapes. He had Jimmy Reyes parked on Annie in front of a business that butted up to the back of the store. Reyes wouldn't be able to see the action but was the closest vehicle and could cut off any northbound exits.

Blaine Parker could at least see the front of the store from his location covering the corner of Cannon and Tennessee and Carter Hogan was about half a block east on Hattie. Sanchez, Nguyen and Lowe were positioned out of view in the back of the store. Sanders, because of his obvious ability to blend in with the Kings, was undercover and milling about the edge of the store parking lot with three actual gang members.

Everything was in place. The trap was set. The only question now was whether the mouse would go for the cheese.

* * * *

Where oh where are you tonight? The Victim laughed as he remembered the old song from Hee Haw. Considering he was nowhere near old enough to have watched the show, he pondered for a moment how he even knew the song.

It was now close to two o'clock. He had made an initial drive past several of the known King locations. Just like last night, his prey was hard to find. *They may not be smart enough to cooperate with the Police but apparently they're smart enough to reduce their profile.*

He had seen a few driving in cars and walking the streets, but the only place they seemed to be conducting business was at the local convenience store. *Makes some sense. It's a pretty public place with lots of space. Assuming I was using my usual approach, they'd see me coming a mile away. Maybe they aren't as dumb as I thought.* He smiled. *Good thing I'm not using my same approach.*

He finished up his loop of locations and turned back toward Hattie Street to do some final reconnaissance before making his move. He could feel it now.

* * * *

"Yo, word is you used to hang with Shadow's brother." D-Funk was leaning against the trunk of a car as Sanders walked back toward him after talking with a potential client.

The rules Hunter had worked out with Spike were simple. The real Kings were to do nothing but hang around in the background and look tough. Sanders was the only one to engage with potential customers as they either drove up or walked up to the group. Once Sanders determined their intentions, he'd subtly show them his badge and ask them to move on.

Sanders eyed him suspiciously, hesitated but answered anyway. "We grew up in the same neighborhood until we were teenagers. Jimmy was a good kid."

"You friends with Shadow's brother and you still capped him. Dude, that's cold blooded." D-Funk looked to his fellow gangbangers as if to say, 'yeah, I went there.'

Sanders adjusted his jacket trying to stay warm and looked at him with a blank expression for a moment. He shook his head, answered quietly. "I didn't have a choice."

The four men stood for a moment in silence, just looking at each other, each clearly wondering where the conversation would go next. Fortunately, the mood was broken by a car pulling up and waving to them. Sanders turned, put on his best gangbanger attitude and sauntered over to the car.

*   *   *   *

"Heads up guys, I've got something." Hunter leaned forward as he watched a middle aged white male walking east on Hattie. He wasn't dressed in business clothes, but instead jeans, tennis shoes and a sweat shirt. Nonetheless, he was heading straight for the Kings on the corner and clearly, any white guy walking alone in this neighborhood in the middle of the night had to be viewed as a suspect or at least, mentally questionable.

"Got a guy on foot heading east from my location. He's probably a hundred feet from you, Billy."

"Got a visual." Billy had sent the last very surprised customer on his way and positioned himself where he appeared to be talking to his gang brothers but was really looking down the street.

"Anybody else see him?"

"Not in my sightline yet, Cowboy." Blaine's voice crackled over the radio.

"I won't be able to see him until he gets into the parking lot." Carter added.

"Stay alert everyone." Hunter hit the ignition, pulled out his binoculars and watched as the man moved closer to the Kings position. "Sanders, make sure the Kings stay back. Move toward him but if he makes a move, signal us, get down and find cover. Remember, this guy is lethal." He paused. "He's twenty feet out, about to come around the dumpster."

"Got him." Sanders was up and moving toward the street. His heart was pounding, his hands were in his pockets, the right one clutching a thirty-eight caliber pistol.

As the man came around the dumpster, Sanders was in position just a few feet away waiting for him. The man was looking down and didn't immediately see Sanders standing there.

Sanders cleared his throat. "Yo cracker, what you doin'?"

The man startled and jumped back, arms flailing, voice cracking to life. "Leave me alone! Leave me alone!"

Sanders reacted with a quick step backward, catching his foot on a rock and almost falling down. He started to draw his weapon but held.

Hunter's Explorer was already moving down Hattie. "Report! Report!"

The man stumbled forward, heading in an arch toward the store, his wide eyes locked on Sanders. "Don't you touch me! Don't you touch me. I'll call the Cops." Now he was almost in a full run heading toward the store.

Sanders stabilized. "Not him! Not him." He took a couple of deep breathes to calm himself. "Just some crazy white guy. Everyone stand down." He leaned over and put his hands on his knees trying to slow his heart rate. "We're all good here." He shook his head as he heard snickering from the Kings leaning on the cars.

Hunter slowed down as he came to the four way stop in front of the store and looked over at Sanders standing in the parking lot. They exchanged looks of relief and frustration. "Reyes, the guy's coming your way. I don't think he's our guy but I want you to have a chat with him to confirm."

"Yep, see him now. Will do Cowboy." Reyes got out of his car, flashed his badge and waved the man over.

*   *   *   *

You animal. Let's see how you deal with me instead of some poor retarded schmuck walking down the street. The Victim was pulling through the four way stop on Hattie going west as he watched the gangbanger accost and intimidate the man walking down the street. He scared him so bad the man almost fell down before he ran away.

He drove on past the store noting the other three gangbangers standing there laughing. *I may not be able to get you all but I'll damn sure get a couple of you.* He was so focused on them, he didn't notice Hunter at the intersection.

*   *   *   *

Hunter took a couple of right hand turns and resumed his position. "All right boys, let's all take a deep breath." He looked at his watch. It was now well past two in the morning. "That's probably our excitement for the evening but let's stay alert. We've got another hour or so before we call it a night."

He sat back, killed his engine and looked at his watch again. *He's usually hit earlier than this. Probably not our night.* He was still settling back in when he saw the beat up Camaro take a left into the parking lot and stop close to the dumpster just like a dozen other cars had done throughout the night.

He yawned and took a quick glance through the binoculars to see Sanders slinking across the parking lot toward the car. He put the glasses down, stretched his neck out and picked up his cold coffee.

*   *   *   *

Jesus, don't these people ever stop. Sanders sighed as he saw the Camaro pull in and stop. *No wonder these gangs sell drugs. The line of customers is endless.*

The driver was slumped down and didn't look directly at him but sat there with the car idling. He looked back over his shoulder as he walked across the parking lot. The three Kings were still having fun at his expense, laughing and pushing on each other. He almost grinned himself as he thought about how silly he must've looked stumbling and bumbling.

He stepped up to the driver's window, arms crossed across his chest striking his best King pose. "Yo buddy, what you looking for tonight?"

Wearing the sunglasses at almost three in the morning made it hard to see much beyond the driver's face, partially hidden by the hoodie.

The driver's voice was calm and slightly familiar. "I'm looking for you." The face turned up toward him wearing a strange grin. A second later the driver's grin disappeared and Sanders couldn't breathe as each man recognized the other.

Sanders broke out of his gang pose and reached for his pocket but was too late. The Beretta was up. His body jerked as his mind registered two quick muzzle flashes. Before the explosions reached his ears, he felt himself flying backward, the ground slamming into his back. For just a moment, all movement in the world stopped.

The sound of tires squealing and a searing pain shooting through his entire body ripped him back to consciousness. He tried to speak, to move, to breathe, but nothing seemed to work. Choking on dust and gunpowder, Sanders couldn't mistake the smell of copper in the air.

"What the hell? Sanders! Sanders!" Hunters voice sounded funny, kind of echoey in his ears.

*   *   *   *

"Move! Move! Sanders is down! Go!" Hunter hit the gas, his tires smoked as the SUV turned onto Hattie. He saw the Camaro turn left onto Tennessee out of the parking lot. "Reyes, he's coming your way. Brown Camaro." He steered across the road and lurched into the parking lot. "Reyes!! Where are you?"

"Shit! He's past me! He's past me! I was out of my car questioning the walker."

"I'm on him." Parker's voice was tense as his car flew through the intersection heading north on Tennessee. "He's a few blocks up. I got his taillights."

Hunter was out before his truck fully stopped. He had his earpiece in and was calling 9-1-1 as he slid down beside Sanders. "Billy, talk to me." He looked down to see complete terror in Billy's eyes. He was trying to speak but nothing came out.

He screamed into his earpiece. "Officer down. Officer down. This is Detective Jake Hunter. I need an ambulance at the corner of Hattie and Tennessee NOW!" He reached down and propped up Billy's head. "Breathe man, just breathe."

Billy's entire left shoulder and upper chest were soaked in blood. He pulled back his jacket and shirt to see where at least one bullet had ripped up through his left pectoral muscle and had completely blown up his collar bone. There was too much blood to see if that was the only wound.

He looked around for something to use as a compress on the wound as he heard the sirens wailing in the distance. He settled for taking off his jacket and using it to stop the bleeding. "They're on their way. Just hang in there man."

Sanders reached out with his right hand and grabbed Hunter, their eyes locked as he tried to move his lips. Still nothing but air and a gurgle came out.

*   *   *   *

Blaine tromped on the gas pedal as he flew through the quiet, dark neighborhood, his eyes fixed on the taillights that were three blocks ahead of him. He blew past Annie, then Tucker and was coming up on Stella as he watched the taillights swing left onto Vickery.

He caught a split second flash of headlights to his left and heard tires squealing on the pavement. His instincts jerked his hand to the right just a couple of inches but it was enough. The car lurched as it hit the dip in the road at the intersection. His eyes registered something in front of him, he felt the impact, the airbag deployed and chaos exploded in the sounds of metal tearing and glass shattering.

*   *   *   *

It's not like in the movies. When people get shot, they don't get up and run down the bad guy. The pain is excruciating, even from a minor wound. Most people pass out immediately. Someone who is very strong may remain conscious but will usually go into shock.

Sanders was still conscious but struggling. He was gripped at Hunter and moved his mouth as the ambulance screeched to a halt.

"Over here. Hurry!" Hunter waved his free hand as the paramedics, arms loaded with supplies, ran toward him. One paramedic took over for Hunter, deftly pushing him aside as he ripped open a large gauze pad and applied it to the wound. His partner rapidly hooked a saline IV in Sanders' arm and started checking his vitals and transmitting the details to John Peter Smith Hospital.

Hunter focused on calming Sanders down as he gasped for air. "It's all right man. Parker's in pursuit. We'll get him."

"Gen..." Sanders gripped Hunter's arm, gritted his teeth, let out a groan.

"What? What is it man?"

"I... I saw... Him..." Sanders sucked in a deep breath, crunched his eyes closed.

"The shooter? You recognized the shooter?"

Sanders nodded, but was interrupted by the lead paramedic. "We've got to transfer him."

Hunter shoved the paramedic back. "Give me a second!" He turned to Sanders who was fading, close to passing out. "Billy, give me a name. Billy, talk to me."

Sanders' eyelids opened, showing more white than pupil. He sucked in a deep breath. "Gen... Tree..."

Hunter looked confused. "Gen Tree?" He thought for a moment, played the investigation back through his mind. "Gen Tree? Who the..." His eyes lit up. "Gentry! Steve Gentry? The Attorney?"

Sanders nodded and passed out as the paramedics moved Hunter out of the way. In a matter of seconds, they had Sanders on the gurney and into the back of the ambulance.

They were pulling away as another ambulance screamed past on Hattie and turned north on Tennessee. Hunter watched as the two ambulances went in different directions.

All the energy seemed to drain from his body as he reached down to pick up his bloody jacket.

"Hunter! They need you." Sanchez was standing by Hunter's Explorer holding the handheld radio out to him. "It's Reyes. Parker crashed. They lost the guy."

Chapter 53

Oh my God, oh my God. What happened? That was a cop! Ah, sweet Jesus, I shot a Cop. His hands were shaking as he drove, sweat was pouring off his forehead, he felt sick and couldn't catch his breath. *What the hell am I going to do now?*

He weaved around aimlessly, on autopilot, almost catatonic, just staying off the main roads until he ended up on Riverside Drive. He went north until he got to Airport Freeway and east on the access road to Beach Street. It was an area he knew well.

He finally circled under the freeway and pulled over into a Wal-Mart parking lot. He couldn't believe it. Even after three in the morning, there were a number of cars. He found an empty spot in between two vans, pulled in, shut down the engine and leaned his head on the steering wheel.

His heart was racing and he was breathing like he just finished running a fast mile. He took a few deep breaths to slow his heart rate and try to calm down. It worked, but only a little.

He reached over and picked up his Beretta. It was still warm to the touch from being fire. His hands were still shaking so badly he set it back down.

He reached for the glove compartment, took out his Police scanner and turned it on. He took a deep gulp of air and scrunched his eyes tight. He had to think. *What's going on?*

*   *   *   *

Hunter stared at the mangled car, bowed his head and was quiet for a long moment. Finally he looked at Parker sitting on the back of the ambulance getting some attention from the paramedic. He shook his head. "How the hell did you walk away from that? You must have a seriously ballsy guardian angel."

"Daddy always said, 'better to be lucky than good'."

The paramedic smiled. "Not only did he walk away, once they get a few stitches in him at JPS, he won't even miss role call in the morning."

Hunter nodded at the paramedic. "Well, he'll miss role call today but only because he'll be with me nailing this bastard to the wall." He turned to Parker. "Go and get your head stitched up. I'll meet you there in an hour or so and you can ride with me back to the station."

"You got it, Cowboy."

Hunter patted him on the shoulder and headed over to where the rest of the team members were standing, most gawking at the wrecked vehicle and shaking their heads. He had borrowed a FWPD wind breaker from one of the patrol units. His blood soaked jacket was still lying in the dirt at the other scene. "Okay boys, gather around. We've got some work to do."

The team closed into a tight circle, expectant faces focused on Hunter.

"Alright, we've got good and bad news. The bad news is we're down two men for a while..."

Reyes raised his hand. "Any word on Billy?"

He paused, his mind replaying Sanders' face, all that blood. "Nothing yet. All I can tell you is that he was awake and coherent. He took at least one round in his upper chest and shoulder area. I'm no doctor but... Let's just say it wasn't a nick." He paused for a second. "I will say this, the good news on several fronts is that he was clear headed enough to identify the shooter." Everyone reacted in unison, bodies leaning forward, their attention laser focused.

"The guy in the car was Steve Gentry. He's a defense attorney who specializes in defending gangbangers." This statement was met with confused looks. He nodded in response. "Yeah, I know. Doesn't make much sense to me either. That's why we've got some work to do."

"Sanchez, I want you and Lowe to stay and work the two scenes. We need every ounce of information you can get from witnesses and the crime scene teams. Oh, and get some patrols to find our three Kings who were at the store. They seem to have disappeared in all the chaos."

"Reyes, I want you focused on getting warrants. I don't care how many judges you have to wake up. We need an arrest warrant for Gentry and search warrants for both his home and office."

Reyes nodded and smiled. "Do I get to pick the judge?"

"As long as they sign." He turned to Hogan. "Carter, we need a coordinated search for Gentry. Notify all transportation hubs, airports, train stations, bus stations. Get a BOLO out for Gentry. Coordinate with the uniforms and get someone on his house ASAP. Chances are slim he'd go back there, but just in case... I don't want him to know we're looking so use the car computers and text messages. No radio calls. This guy's smart enough to be monitoring a scanner."

"Pete, I want to know everything there is to know about Steve Gentry. Family, friends, church, school, everything. If Sanders recognized him, there's a good chance he recognized Sanders and knows he shot a cop. We're going to have to find him, so we need to know where he might go."

He looked at his watch. "Alright, it's half past four now. I want everyone to meet back in the conference room at seven. I expect to be moving on search warrants shortly after that." He looked around and saw determined faces. "Any questions?"

He was met by head shakes and silence. "Let's go find this bastard."

*   *   *   *

He'd been sitting in the same parking spot for over an hour, his mind still jumbled. Steve Gentry looked toward the eastern skyline. It was five o'clock and he could already see the darkness beginning to fade. The Police scanner was active with chatter but none of it seemed to be focused on him.

He'd heard the dispatcher broadcast a ten double zero, officer down, to the location of the shooting. *I shot a cop. They set me up. Those bastards. That story in the paper was just bullshit. They were working with the Kings all along.*

They had a BOLO out on his car but the description was pretty vague, no license plate number. Still, there was no question he needed to get out of it. They hadn't said anything about him by name or even provided a description of the driver beyond 'white male'. *Maybe he's dead. I know I hit him point blank in the chest. Even if he's not dead, he probably won't be in any condition to talk for a while. I probably have some time.*

He plotted out an inconspicuous route to get back to downtown. He needed to swap cars and get back to his apartment. *I'm not going to make a run for it unless I have to. I don't want to look guilty unless they know something. I do need to be prepared and I need to be invisible.*

He started his car and sat for another few minutes making a mental checklist. *Get passport, laptop. Pack clothes. Get rid of anything associated with attacks. Empty my cubbyhole. Got to stay one step ahead of them.* He backed out of the parking space, turned and headed for the exit. *If I'm lucky, the cop will die and I won't have to run at all.*

*   *   *   *

Hunter's mind seemed to be almost twitching, synapses firing in a thousand directions at once as he drove south on Main Street toward John Peter Smith Hospital. It wasn't quite six o'clock yet so the sun hadn't officially risen, but the sky was light enough to feel the day coming. It was going to be sunny but cold.

He turned left into the Emergency Room entrance and pulled around to the rear parking area. Every space was filled with an official vehicle, most of which were FWPD patrol cars. The sight brought home the realization that an officer, his partner, had been shot and was right now in this building fighting for his life. His stomach knotted up, thoughts of Frank popped in his head. He finally found an open spot, parked and began the walk to the door.

Maybe it was just his imagination but the chaos and volume of the crowded waiting room seemed to quiet as he entered. He looked around to see a sea of blue uniforms and concerned faces. Nothing fills an emergency room waiting area faster than a fallen officer. A waving hand caught his attention and he saw Lieutenant Sprabary signaling for him to come over. He quickly moved across the room acknowledging guys he knew as he went.

When they finally found a private spot, Hunter blew past the formalities. "What's his status?"

"He's was alive when they got here. Still waiting on the doctor." Sprabary's voice sounded tired. He nodded down the hall.

A surgeon walked toward them, his face exhausted, pale.

280

When he stopped, their eyes asked the question. The surgeon blinked and nodded. "Your officer is stable for now. He was hit once. No vital organs impacted."

"Just once?" Hunter seemed confused, looked at Sprabary. "Everyone on site said there were two shots."

Sprabary shrugged. "Maybe the second one was a near miss."

They both looked back to the surgeon. "That one did plenty of damage, fortunately none of it life threatening." He looked at his watch. "They're closing him up now. He'll be in recovery within the hour, but won't be in any condition to talk for quite some time."

"Thank you Doctor." Sprabary shook his hand, looked at Hunter. "Your turn."

Hunter spent the next ten minutes briefing him on what had happened, on the potential suspect and on all the actions that were in motion now to make an arrest.

Sprabary nodded. "I want hourly reports until this asshole's in custody. I don't plan to leave here until Sanders is awake." He blinked a few times, cleared his throat, his face displaying a rare moment of emotion.

Hunter looked away for a moment, was surprised to see Stacy across the room. "Will do Lieutenant." He turned and once again made his way through the crowd.

When he got to Stacy, he took her by the elbow and guided her to corner where they could talk. "How did you hear?"

"I've got my sources." She seemed a little miffed that he hadn't called. "I thought about helping to work the scene but it sounded like they had half the force over there. Figured I bump into you here eventually."

"Sorry for not calling. It was the middle of the night. I didn't want to wake you. Things were a bit crazy." He hoped the litany of excuses didn't sound as hollow to her as they did to him.

She pushed past her irritation. "Sounds like he's going to pull through. Is everyone else okay?"

Hunter shrugged. "Parker wrapped his car around a tree. He's getting stitched up. I'm here to pick him up and get moving. We think we know the shooter."

As he had with Sprabary, he gave her a complete rundown. "I need to get Parker and get over to the station by seven." He looked down at his watch, realized how fast the time was moving. "Thanks for being here."

Stacy's eyes glistened and she gently put her hand on his chest, obviously wanting to hold him but aware of the packed room staring at them. "Stay safe. Keep in touch today."

Hunter reached up and took her hand for a long moment and squeezed it. Their eyes connected and said what he needed to say before he turned and headed down the hall looking for Parker.

* * * *

Hunter bounced his SUV into the back parking lot of the FWPD's Central Division station, eliciting a slight groan from Parker. The sun was now fully up and even though he was only ten minutes late for the team meeting, he felt like the day was slipping away from him.

"Sorry about that." Hunter looked over, grinned and pointed to Parker's bandaged up head. "That's a good look for you."

"Just another battle scar." Parker rolled his eyes. "The wife's gonna love it."

The two made their way through the oddly quiet station, up the stairs and into the conference room. Every team member was actively engaged either on the phone or banging on a computer. Several looked up and smiled when they saw Parker with his new look.

Hunter was all business. "Sorry we're late guys. Let's get moving."

For the third time today, he found himself giving a long winded update on status, this time it was about Billy's condition. Everyone seemed relieved to know Sanders was going to make it and to see Parker back in the saddle.

"All right, Reyes, where do we stand on the warrants?"

"Everything's written up. The documents are being couriered over as we speak. I've been on the phone several times with Judge Spicer this morning. He's on board, says he'll review immediately. I expect to have signatures within the hour."

Hunter nodded his approval. "Sanchez. Anything from the scene?"

"Really wasn't anything to get from Parker's wreck. Just made sure we kept security on the vehicle." He flipped through his notes. "Minimal physical evidence at the shooting scene. No cartridges. Assume they landed in the car. Didn't find the second bullet. Assume it flew off into space. We were able to round up our three stray bangers. They couldn't tell us much more than we already knew. Confirmed it was a white male wearing a gray hoodie in the car. None of them could pick Gentry out of a picture line up." He grinned. "One did say, 'hey, that guy looks a lot like my lawyer'."

That brought some laughter to the room. Hunter turned to Hogan. "Carter, where do we stand on the search?"

"No sightings at this time. We've got pictures and descriptions out to all local departments, both airports as well as every train and bus station. As you suggested, nothing was transmitted over the radio. We dispatched patrol cars to sit on Gentry's apartment and office in case we see him coming or going. Got them in place about thirty minutes ago. Nothing yet."

"Good move." Hunter turned to Nguyen. "Pete, what did you find out about our boy?"

Nguyen leaned forward. "Still turning over stones but here's what we've got so far. Single, forty two years old. Local guy, grew up in Haltom City, went to UTA, got his law degree from Baylor. Record is spotless. Other than making a living defending scum, he looks like a choir boy."

"What about his family?"

"Well, that's where it gets a little interesting. Both parents are deceased, both natural causes. Nothing remarkable there. But... He had a twin sister who is also deceased. She was a victim of a gang related rape and murder, five years ago. In fact, the anniversary just happened to coincide with the first attack. I'm still reviewing the case file for more details."

"Interesting." Hunter was now in his familiar pacing mode. "Sounds like we have our motive and our trigger. Have I ever mentioned I'm not much of a believer in coincidence?" He saw several sarcastic nods as he continued to pace quietly for a moment. His mind wandered back to the conversation he'd had with his Dad. He smiled at how accurate his father had been.

"Pete, I want you to keep digging. We need to know everything there is to know about the sister from cradle to grave. If she's the key to him doing this then she'll likely be the key to us finding him."

He looked at his watch. *Damn, half past eight.*

His thoughts were interrupted when Reyes' phone rang. Reyes answered, mumbled a few answers, hung up and looked at Hunter. "We've got our signatures. They're faxing them over now."

"All right boys, hit the head and grab some coffee. Looks like it's gonna be a busy morning."

* * * *

"Good morning. Gentry, Cohen and Sparks. How may I help you?"

"Hey Sharon, this is Steve." Gentry tried hard to sound like it was just another day. It was obviously anything but. "How are you this morning?"

"Doing fine. Typical Monday morning. Phones are going crazy. It seems our clients were busy over the weekend. Oh, you're eight-thirty is here. Are you on your way?"

"That's why I called. I'm running late this morning. I'm going to have to cancel most of my meetings. Please apologize for me. I think I should be there by lunch."

"Okay." The cheeriness had left her voice. "I'll take care of it. You'll have some unhappy people to deal with when you get here."

If she only knew. He thought for a minute. *She doesn't sound like anything out of the ordinary is happening, but...*

"Have there been any calls for me or any unscheduled visitors?"

"Nope." She sounded a bit harried now. "Nothing but the typical Monday stuff. Anything else? The phones are ringing off the wall."

"No. We're good." He hung up. *Hmm... It's almost nine o'clock and they haven't hit the office yet. Maybe I'm good. Maybe they don't know yet. I need to know if that cop's alive.*

He set his cell phone down on the table at the Starbucks across the street from the front entrance to his office building. He sat back and stared blankly out the window watching his colleagues and clients come and go.

THE VICTIM

*   *   *   *

Hunter, his team of detectives and a supporting group of SWAT officers moved quickly and quietly down the hall in the upscale apartment building. They had stopped by the management office on their way in and gotten a passkey to let themselves in assuming Gentry wasn't there.

They positioned themselves on either side of the door in proper assault formation. Hunter was the only detective near the door and even he was happy to let the SWAT guys take the lead.

Hunter reached out and banged on the door. "Fort Worth Police! We have a search warrant! We're coming in!"

The SWAT officer on the other side of the door slid the passkey in, had the door open in less than a second and was barreling into the room before Hunter could pull his hand back. The team followed in a loud, chaotic rush. Moments later, the SWAT leader indicated the 'all clear' and allowed Hunter and the detectives to move in and begin the search.

The first thing Hunter noticed was that the place was immaculate, almost to the point of being sterile. *Cleanliness is a sure sign of a sick mind.* "Reyes, take the kitchen. Parker, Hogan, take the bedroom. I'll take the office."

Each detective donned their latex gloves and headed for their respective assignments. The SWAT team filed out leaving one officer at the door to ensure there'd be no surprise appearances by the suspect. The team leader caught Hunter before he disappeared into the office. "We're set to meet you at the office in an hour."

"Perfect. I'll call you on the way over. Doubt we'll need you there but want you available just in case."

Hunter moved into the office and looked around. Like the rest of the apartment, it was immaculate. He took his time, surveyed the room. Noted the lack of personal items, except for the two framed pictures on the desk. An old picture that appeared to be him as a young man with his parents and twin sister. The other picture he assumed was the same twin sister as a grown woman. Hunter picked up that picture, held it in his gloved hand as he continued his initial search.

He eventually began working his way through drawers, shelves and cabinets. After several minutes, the only thing of note weren't things that he found, but things that seemed to be missing. There didn't seem to be anything of a personal nature. No bills, letters, cards or personal papers. No passport, credit cards or ID's of any kind. Nothing that would indicate he even lived here.

As he continued to poke around the desk, something gnawed at him, something about the desk. He kept staring at it as he walked around the room. After a moment, he stopped, snapped his finger and smiled. He moved the chair out of the way, crawled under the desk and started knocking on panels with his palm. After a few pokes, one of the panels came loose and revealed a hidden compartment.

He pulled the door open and looked in only to be more confused than before. The compartment was completely empty. *Who has a secret compartment built into their desk but doesn't put anything in it?*

"Hunter!" Parker's voice came in from the bedroom.

Hunter took one last look at the hidden compartment, shook his head and left to find Parker.

"What's up?" Hunter poked his head in the door of the bedroom.

Parker stood back staring at the closet, looking confused. "Well, I'm not sure. We haven't exactly found anything. It's more that some things appear to be missing." He pointed to the clothes hanging in the closet. "Notice how neat everything is, except... Except it looks like there are number of random gaps ." He pointed to an empty space in the back of the closet. "See that spot. Doesn't that look about the size of a suit case? You put those two things together and I think our boy beat us here and packed his bags this morning."

Hunter nodded. "That would match the fact that there is a secret compartment in his desk that is empty and there's no sign of a passport or credit cards." They stared at the closet for another minute before Hunter broke the silence. "Let's pack it up and head over to his office."

As the team packed up, Hunter took one last look around the office. He picked up the picture of Gentry's sister, thought about what it would be like to lose a twin, especially in a sudden, violent fashion. He continued to pace for a moment, stopped. *If I'm about to leave town, potentially forever...*

He quickly reached into his pocket, popped in his earpiece and made a call. "Pete, I need you to find out something for me."

*   *   *   *

Steve Gentry still sat in the Starbucks at almost eleven o'clock. He was on his fourth cup of coffee and had seen nothing out of the ordinary at his office. The caffeine had taken his already heightened anxiety and put it through the roof. If someone had been watching as he nervously fidgeted in his seat and repeatedly looked at his watch, they might have called the Police just as a precaution.

He thought about another cup of coffee and then thought better of it. He'd continued to monitor the police scanner discreetly through an earbud. Things had calmed down with almost no chatter about the search for him. That in itself seemed a little odd but he wasn't exactly experienced at being a fugitive. Hell, for all he knew, he wasn't a fugitive at all.

As the morning had passed and he'd run it over in his mind, he'd decided that if nothing happened by noon, he'd just go into work. If he didn't, all he was doing was bringing undue suspicion on himself. After all, this was the second time he was late or missed work the day after one of the shootings.

He looked at his watch one more time. *Jesus, is this thing going in reverse?* It was straight up eleven o'clock. He decided he needed to get out but needed to hit the head first. His bladder was about to pop.

He felt better as he left the men's room. He nodded as he walked past the barista, but stopped in his tracks as he opened the door. His breath caught in his throat as he looked across the street just in time to see three patrol cars and a FWPD SWAT truck roar up to the front of his building and spill out their passengers.

For a moment, he just stood in the doorway. When another customer brushed past him, his head cleared long enough to stumble out the door and down the sidewalk to his parked BMW.

He got in and sat. *They know. Oh my God, they know.* He continued to sit for what seemed like a long time but when he compulsively looked at his watch again, it had only been three minutes.

He shook his head to clear his thoughts and started to drive. *It's over. I've got to get out of here.* He had made precautions but had no real plan. He knew only that he had to do one thing before he left.

*   *   *   *

The search of the office hadn't taken long and was quickly winding down. The Receptionist squawked about their rights and the Partners were fuming and glaring. It didn't matter, they were done. Nothing new was found. Hunter hadn't really expected anything. He was staring out Gentry's office window at the Starbucks across the street when his phone rang.

He answered. "Hunter here... Hey Pete, were you able to find what I asked about?" He nodded. "Okay, great." He hung up, turned and headed for the door.

Chapter 54

Hunter blew north on Sylvania through a part of town that hadn't changed much in the last twenty years and likely wouldn't in the next. He was leading a procession of FWPD vehicles based on a hunch he hoped was right. He had his grill lights flashing, but ran without sirens and had the other cars in the same mode. The last thing he wanted was to announce their arrival.

Pete had done a good job and confirmed the specific location down to the street and the plot. Hunter knew exactly where he was going.

When they got to the intersection of Watauga Road and Sylvania, Hunter and Parker continued north while Reyes and Hogan took a left and headed west down Watauga. Each set of detectives had a SWAT team and two patrol cars in tow.

A few hundred feet north of the intersection, Hunter took a hard left into the main entrance of Mount Olivet Cemetery. He killed the lights and slowed in order to be slightly less conspicuous and maintain as much respect for others as possible.

He veered left on the main road toward a section on the south side of the cemetery and looked to his left and to see Reyes and team coming in the south entrance behind the maintenance building. Reyes followed Hunter's lead, killed the lights and slowed down. Once the two sets of detectives and the SWAT teams were through the gates, the patrol cars sealed the two entrances. If Hunter was right and Gentry was here saying his last goodbye to his sister, he now had no place to go.

Hunter knew the cemetery well and had coordinated with Reyes to converge on a plot on the northern edge of the Catholic section. As he approached from the east and Reyes approached from the south, he could see a lone figure standing in the sun, facing north with his head bowed.

Hunter clicked his radio. "I think we've got him. I've got a visual. Gray sweatshirt, blue jeans. Doesn't look like he's seen us yet. Follow the plan. We'll come at him from both his rear flanks. If we're lucky, he won't notice us until we're on him."

"We're locked and loaded Cowboy."

Trying to balance speed and stealth, Hunter approached from the southeast and Reyes approached from the southwest, both teams curving around the large bend surrounding the giant crucifix in the center of the section. Their target had remained standing still outside the circle on the northern edge.

The cars came to a stop fifty feet away from the target in each direction. The teams moved quickly and quietly out of their vehicles with guns drawn, the SWAT team members fanned out behind the detectives making a wide arch. Gentry remained still, facing north, head bowed.

The four detectives were now off the road and on the grass, less than twenty feet from Gentry, four guns sighted on his back. "Gentry! This is Fort Worth Detective Jake Hunter! Turn around slowly with your hands in the air!"

The silence of the cemetery seemed to suck the oxygen out of the air. Hunter's heart pounded in his ears. Gentry didn't move, just stood there. Hunter and team held their ground but Hunter's attention was momentarily diverted to what he saw in the background. Across the cemetery maybe a hundred yards, beyond where Gentry stood and directly in the line of fire, Hunter saw three yellow school buses, dozens of cars and what must've been a couple of hundred people.

He signaled Parker over, pointed out the issue and sent him to alert and reposition the SWAT teams in order to avoid firing lines that could endanger the crowd.

"Gentry! I won't ask again!"

Gentry's head lifted slowly and he began to turn. His left hand was out to his side but the right hand wasn't visible.

"Let me see both hands!" Hunter steadied himself in a shooting stance, his finger sliding from the trigger guard to the trigger. The rest of the team followed his lead. The sweat glistened off the faces of the officers in spite of how cold it was outside.

As Gentry finished turning toward them, Hunter was able to see his right hand clutching a pistol pointed up underneath his chin. Hunter signaled to the team to hold their position.

"Gentry. Put the gun down. No need to go there."

The anguish on his face was visible, tears streaked his cheeks. "It was self-defense. You know that. You saw the crime scenes. In each case, they attacked me. I was just walking down the street. I have a right to do that you know." He pled his case but with little conviction.

Hunter fought the urge to argue with him, to point out that he shot Sanders without provocation and that Jim Bennett and the little boy were dead because of his actions. "You've got a point... But we can't resolve that here. That's for the courts to figure out. You're an attorney. You know the drill."

The man was visibly shaking now. "They won't understand. I can't take that chance. I can't go to jail... I won't go to jail."

"That doesn't have to happen." Hunter was now just talking to talk, diffuse the situation anyway possible. More Police were arriving by the minute. He caught Parker in his peripheral vision directing the troops. With the bandaged head, he looked a little crazed. Hunter stared for a moment but composed himself, refocused on Gentry. "Just put the gun down and we can talk this out."

Gentry's shoulders drooped. He shook his head. "Don't bullshit me. I know the deal. That last guy was a Cop." His body shook with sobs. His voice was quieter but still carried across the manicured grounds. "I didn't intend for that to happen... I'm sorry."

This tack wasn't getting them anywhere. Hunter relaxed out of his shooting position, pulled his gun back and made a show of putting it on the ground. He knew he was covered with a ridiculous level of force. "Gentry, I'm unarmed. I'm going to come over and cuff you. We've got to take you in." Hunter began moving forward very slowly. The rest of the team fanned out to maintain their firing lines. He was now just a few feet away and closing. Gentry hadn't moved.

Hunter's voice was low and calm now. "Steve. The only way to make this thing right is to put down the gun and face up to what you've done. We're not here to hurt you. We just want this all to end."

The look in Gentry's eyes showed complete resignation. He looked up at Hunter, gave a slight shrug. "I can't."

Time seemed to almost stop as Hunter saw Gentry's hand twitch. He reached out through what seemed like molasses but his hand had barely moved. He saw Gentry's face contort and his eyes roll back. Hunter was so close he felt the explosion of the round as it left the gun. The top of Gentry's head simply disappeared into a cloud of pink mist. Hunter's mind flashed back to Shadow.

In an instant, Gentry's body lay in a heap at his feet. For just a few seconds, the world stopped and there was complete stillness. The only sound registering in Hunter's ears was the echo from the gun hanging in the air.

Time rushed back and everything happened at once. Someone grabbed Hunter and pulled him back as bodies flew past him toward what remained of Steve Gentry. Voices came from all directions. Everyone moved in a dance. It was as if the whole scene were choreographed. Everyone knew their parts. Except Hunter. He didn't remember the steps. He just stood there, his mind locked in place, remembering Gentry's eyes.

"Cowboy. You okay?" Reyes was standing to his left. He'd picked up Hunter's gun. "Here, holster this thing. Doesn't look like you're going to need it today."

"Hey boss. You might want to clean yourself up a bit." Hunter looked to his right to see Parker holding out a towel. It was only then that he realized he was wet. *How did I get wet?* He took the towel, swiped it across his face and watched the towel go from white to red.

"Thanks." He nodded to Parker, continued to wipe off the residue.

He slowly walked over to his Explorer as he watched the team continue to secure the area and begin to process the scene. He leaned against the SUV for a moment, then walked around to the back and opened the lift gate.

Hunter sat on the edge of the cargo bed of the SUV lost in numbness, while the controlled chaos continued around him. They didn't need him for this part. Parker had it under control. There'd be paperwork to fill out and people to debrief but for now, the job was done.

He looked out across the grounds, noticed again the line of buses in the distance. After a moment, the realization of why they were there hit him and the emotion swelled inside his chest. He fought it back but couldn't shake the thoughts in his mind. Two lives intersected and ended up here, each clearly the result of gang violence but both ending up here for very different reasons.

His thoughts were interrupted as he saw the hordes of media who had attended Jonathan Tolbert's funeral, heading toward the scene. They were led by Alton Grice and Calvin Jackson, both trying to upstage the other.

Hunter stood and began to walk away from the scene. It had been a while since he'd been here and there was someone he needed to visit.

Chapter 55

The constant beeping of the heart monitor provided an ominous backdrop for what was actually a fairly festive conversation in room 207 of the critical care unit at John Peter Smith.

Billy Sanders sat propped up on his bed, the entire upper left portion of his torso, shoulder and arm were immobilized. Multiple tubes, IV's and monitor cables ran from his right arm and under the sheets. By any standard, he looked to be in terrible shape.

The only giveaway was the weak smile on his face as he entertained his first extended visitors since he'd come out of surgery the day before.

It was an unusually warm Wednesday afternoon in November and the sun streamed in through the blinds. Hunter stood at the foot of his bed as he finished providing a blow by blow description of what had happened at the cemetery. Stacy sat in the lone chair and only occasionally rolled her eyes when he got a little too carried away with embellishment.

Sanders shifted in his bed. "So, it's over."

Hunter nodded. "Yeah, we stopped him. The impact of his destruction will be felt for quite some time. Rose Bennett is a widow. There's a family who now only has memories of their little boy. And Desiree's little girl will likely spend her formative years visiting her mother in prison."

He pointed to Billy. "We're just lucky you have the reflexes of a cat. Had he been able to hit you where he was aiming, not only would we have visited Mount Olivet for a very different reason, but we'd still be spinning our wheels. Without you're ID, we still really had nothing on him."

Billy's voice was barely over a whisper. "Glad I could be of service."

"You know, if you really think about it, up until Monday night, the only two people who had ever even seen this guy who were still alive, were a street drunk and a guy with a cramping asshole. That's not exactly what you want to take with you into court." Hunter smiled. "Speaking of which, that wino wasn't quite as crazy as we'd thought. Steve Gentry did have the Donald Trump toupee thing going." That brought laughter from both Stacy and Billy, Billy's ended with another grimace.

"Anyway." Hunter continued. "Hindsight twenty-twenty, we've been able to piece together some history. Turns out that the guy who was accused of raping and murdering his sister had been a former client of his and he'd gotten him off on a technicality. The guy should've been serving time when the crime happened."

"Guess it would be rude to make a comment about karma." Billy laughed, then regretted it as he winced in pain.

Hunter continued. "Interesting note on timing. Had you not been able to croak out his name while you were lying in the dirt, we would have completely missed him. When we checked his car, not only did he have his suitcase packed, he had close to twenty grand in cash and two complete sets of fake ID's. Looks like after he said goodbye to sis, he planned to be gone. We'd have probably never found him."

The conversation lulled for a moment until Sanders spoke up. "So I guess now that I'm officially past my first case, the lieutenant will pair me up with someone as a permanent partner." It was a statement, but the question hung in the air.

Hunter avoided Sanders' eyes. "Yeah, well, about that... I've already had a conversation with him and made a recommendation." He paused for a moment, clear his throat

Sanders tried to hide his reaction but the disappointment on his face was clear. Stacy looked down to hide her face.

"I told him that considering during this probationary period, you not only shot someone but you managed to get shot as well, it might make some sense for you to remain under my tutelage just a little longer." Hunter smiled. "So if you're okay with this, once you get off your lazy ass, we'll be a permanent team."

Sanders grinned. "As long as you don't come up with any more hair brained ideas about me going under cover as a gangbanger, I'm good with it."

Hunter's facial expression got serious. "You did good kid. We would've never gotten this guy without you and there's a good chance, I wouldn't be standing here. So thanks. Enjoy your rehabilitation and your time off. We've got lots of work to do when you get back."

Hunter gave Stacy a look and she stood to leave with him but before they made it out the door, Sanders stopped them. "Hey, before you go..."

Hunter stopped. "What's up?"

"Well, considering that we are partners now and considering that I did save your life and all, the least you could do is tell me the story about how you got the Cowboy nickname."

Hunter grinned. "I guess we never got around to that, did we?" He stepped back in the door and let it shut. "It all stems from this little incident way back when I was on patrol. You see, there was this..."

Hunter's phone rang. "Hang on just a minute." He pulled his earpiece from his pocket and punched the button. "Hey Lieutenant... Yes... Uh huh... Right... Okay."

Hunter punched his earpiece off, slid it back in his jacket and looked at Stacy. "We need to go." He turned back to Sanders and grinned. "Hate to do this to you buddy but the story's going to have to wait. Feel better, okay."

"What? Wait... No..." Sanders could hear Hunter laughing all the way down the hall.

The End

Afterword

While I believe that people can overcome almost anything, especially in this country, not all of us start with the same advantages. I feel very fortunate to have been born in the United States, the greatest country on earth, and in the great state of Texas. I'm also fortunate to have been born physically and mentally healthy. Maybe most importantly, I was born to two parents who loved me, educated me, disciplined me and cared for me. These advantages afforded me the opportunity, through hard work, to chase the American Dream.

For those who were born without these advantages, the American Dream is still there but their mountain is harder to climb.

According the FBI, there are approximately 33,000 violent gangs in the United States with over 1.4 million members. These gangs range from small, local gangs to international, well structured, criminal organizations. Gangs use violence to support illegal activities such as robbery, drug and gun trafficking, fraud, extortion, and prostitution. According to the 2011 National Gang Threat Assessment, 48 percent of all violent crime in most jurisdictions is related to gangs.

What is missed in the statistics is the 'why' behind gangs. Sure, there are some people in this world that are naturally violent and no matter what advantages they have in life, they will choose to be pariahs. Let's all pray those are the small minority. Most who end up involved with gangs do so because they find themselves in a social and economic situation where there seems to be no alternative, where their futures have already been decided.

Education, family stability and economic opportunity are the keys to reducing gang membership levels and correspondingly, the level of violence and crime associated with gangs.

In The Victim, Fort Worth seems to be a seething pool of gang crime. That's mostly literary license. In fact, the Fort Worth Police Department has done an amazingly good job of combating gang violence and promoting alternatives.

Nationally, most major city police departments have programs targeted at gang prevention. Additionally, there are numerous private organizations such as Panzou Project, My Life My Power and Gang Prevention Inc. that are focused on helping youth avoid the trap of gang life.

I'd urge you to get educated on this major social issue. It may be someone you know who is the next victim.